'One of those contemporary masterpieces that seems like it came out of the author's head, fait accompli... Any time you put the book down to, say, drive a car or get a sandwich, it's a shock. It pulls no punches, so be prepared to be knocked sideways.'
Dave Eggers, *Guardian*

'It reads like Faulkner in another skin. It is a brave book. And like the best, and most dangerous of stories, it seems as if it was just waiting to be told.'
Colum McCann, author of *Zoli* and *Dancer*

'James has conducted an experiment in how to write the unspeakable – even the unthinkable. And the results of that experiment are an undeniable success.'   *New York Times*

'An epic novel of late-18th-century West Indian slavery, complete with all its carnage and brutishness, but one that, like a Toni Morrison novel, whispers rather than shouts its horrors.'
Time Out

'An exquisite, haunting and beautiful novel, impossible to resist. Like the best of literature, *The Book of Night Women* deserves to be passed down hand to hand, generation to generation.'
Dinaw Mengestu, author of *The Beautiful Things That Heaven Bears*

'Lilith's narration is one of the novel's strongest features, written in the vernacular and carrying its own drum-like rhythm which is as lyrical as it is hypnotic.'   *Independent*

'Darkly powerful.'

The BOOK *of* NIGHT WOMEN

MARLON JAMES

ONEWORLD

A Oneworld Book

First published in Great Britain and Australia by
Oneworld Publications, 2009
First published in paperback by Oneworld Publications, 2010
This paperback edition first published by Oneworld Publications, 2014
Reprinted, 2015

ISBN 978-1-78074-652-4
eBook ISBN 978-1-78074-713-2

Oneworld Publications
10 Bloomsbury Street
London WC1B 3SR
England

To the railroad of bones

Contents

Niggerkin *1*

Joseph Andrews *173*

Nightwomen *243*

Oriki *325*

Gehenna *371*

I
am the
woman they give
dead women's
clothes to.

—Christine Gelineau,
"Inheritance"

Sugbon kini a le fi be eni ti ikooko pa iya re je?

Niggerkin

PEOPLE THINK BLOOD RED, BUT BLOOD DON'T GOT NO COLOUR.
Not when blood wash the floor she lying on as she scream for that son
of a bitch to come, the lone baby of 1785. Not when the baby wash
in crimson and squealing like it just depart heaven to come to hell,
another place of red. Not when the midwife know that the mother shed
too much blood, and she who don't reach fourteen birthday yet speak
curse 'pon the chile and the papa, and then she drop down dead like old
horse. Not when blood spurt from the skin, or spring from the axe, the
cat-o'-nine, the whip, the cane and the blackjack and every day in slave
life is a day that colour red. It soon come to pass when red no different
from white or blue or black or nothing. Two black legs spread wide and
a mother mouth screaming. A weak womb done kill one life to birth
another. A black baby wiggling in blood on the floor with skin darker
than midnight but the greenest eyes anybody ever done see. I goin' call
her Lilith. You can call her what they call her.

Two thing you should know if you want to know her. As soon as
Lilith born the womens regard her with fear and trembling because of
them green eyes that light up the room, but not like sunlight. Nobody

did want the young'un and the overseer Jack Wilkins had to make special arrangement for a niggerwoman to take care of the child, for the mens and womens did content to just leave her in the bush and make the land take her back. Another thing. Girl like Lilith don't born with green eye because God feel to be extra kind to nigger girl. This much was for sure, Lilith be the only girl to grow up in a hut calling a woman mother and a man father but she didn't look like neither.

That woman. That girl. People recall when she was still a little pickney on the Montpelier Estate, them few years when a nigger not black, playing rounders with boys. She swing the club, clap the ball clear 'cross the field and make one run to all four base and beat the boys but couldn't understand when the wet nurse slap her and say that a good girl was supposed to make manchild win. Lilith cuss and ask if manchild can't win if girl don't lose and she get another slap. Some take as sign when at seven Lilith tell them same boys that is 'cause they have worm between them legs why they can't run fast like she and the girl get a swift kick from a passing niggerwoman who tell her that there be a grave already dug for the uppity. Lilith cuss under her tongue and say, Is you must go to grave since you already stink like dead puppy. Then there was the time when she get a well-deserved thumping for telling a white playmate from Coulibre Estate that she be a damn fool for saying that sky wet when everybody know it dry 'cept for when rain fall. White pickney and black pickney play all the time when they little, as if they be combolo, one and the same. But Lilith too spirited. Too spirited for a nigger girl black like pitch with legs too smooth for a slave and hair too woolly and lips too thick like fruit and eyes that seem robbed from white lady. A slave woman fate write before she born, but Lilith didn't grow up regarding them things for she live with Circe, the only nigger at Montpelier Estate who didn't work.

People say that Montpelier Estate was so huge that you could tell you're there as soon as the wind start blowing to the east. In 1785, the year of many death but one birth, the overseer judge Circe too weak to do field labour. He give her a new hut that make from wood, not mud like what common nigger live in. He give her a man to live with in the Bible way. He also give her Lilith, which was just as well since plenty people knew that there was nothing Tantalus could do for a woman, much less breed niggerkin. Circe sleep in a bed while Tantalus and Lilith make do with the floor. Tantalus go near that bed only once and he have a scar below him left eye to show for it.

The hut door was to the north, the kitchen to the south, the red armchair that come from the overseer Jack Wilkins' house to the east and the bed to the west. Circe shoulder thick and broad like man, her legs bow a little and her breasts strong and wide. But she short. All over her head, grey hair pop up like little flowers. A straw hat with a pink ribbon be on her head that she never take off, and when she go to sleep the hat cover her face. Circe didn't take too kindly to mothering. Some say that this was on account of who Lilith papa be, but word loose like wind on Montpelier Estate.

By the time Lilith commence her fourteenth year, Circe grow tired of Tantalus the mad nigger. She come from church one Sunday afternoon and sit down in the armchair only to feel wetness soak through her dress. Piss, to be sure, for Tantalus didn't got no cum. Circe go for her cast-iron pot and beat him out of the house. Since that time, nobody put clothes on that nigger and the overseer tie him to a breadfruit tree like an old dog. Lilith, after washing Circe good blue frock down by the river near the ratoon fields, come home to see Tantalus tie up under the tree and bawling and grunting and hissing and whinnying and grabbing him cocky in a indecent way and it make her feel like she was the most meanest thing in the world to have such a pappy.

Niggers already done make a song 'bout Tantalus the mad nigger. Lilith scared that soon the song was goin' pick up a new verse 'bout her. Already she too tall and too loud and the other pickneys says she too big to play even though Lilith still feel like little girl. Lilith look around the dusty patch and it small now. You titty big like yam, a niggerboy tell her when they playing. And you balls little like cherry, she say to him. The little boy punch her and she jump 'pon him like wild dog and nobody could pull her off until they beat her hand to let go of him balls.

Commencing also be this—the white pickneys reach the age when they become white and nigger become black and they don't play together no more. Lilith know one in particular, the girl from Coulibre who use to grab her hair and call her black sheep and always want to go on quest past the ratoon fields, which was forbidden. The same girl Lilith call donkey cause she laugh like a hee-haw. Plenty time Lilith say, Let we be the wickedest pirates! And the girl would say, Aye! and she lead the white girl astray to plunder the booty, cherry or plum or banana. They would tie cloth over one eye and be Henry Morgan and Blackbeard. And they talk secret-like so the boys wouldn't know. The white girl call her lank chicken and Lilith call her rank goat and they scream and laugh, and the girl take Lilith hand and neither think it uncanny. Then one day the girl come to the plantation dress up in bonnet like her mama and bawl out, Mama, pray tell why is that nigger addressing me? Lilith get a slap for that from a thin house niggerwoman who smell of mint and lemongrass. Lilith don't go near the great house after that and the white girl stop coming to Montpelier altogether.

Lilith think she is still girl but even Circe tell her otherwise. This was an evening not long after she throw Tantalus out of the hut.

—Look 'pon you, Circe say as she lean back in her red armchair and fan 'way mosquito.—Worthless and good for nothing. Sake o' you, man start hitch up round here like pee-pee cluck-cluck.

Outside cricket was chirping like they agree and inside the hotness wouldn't leave the room.

—Word be that is you they come to, Mama.

—Wha' you just say in me earshole? Word from who?

Lilith don't answer.

—You soon start takin' man, Circe say.

—Me not takin' nothing but the word of God, Mama.

Two thing happen in Lilith fourteenth year. One day she was out in the yard romping when all of a sudden she feel wet, wet, wet. Blood slip from her like whisper and run down her leg. She scream and two boy laugh. Lilith run to the hut where Circe was dismissing a coloured gentleman who wasn't from Montpelier Estate. As soon as she see Circe her mouth shut up and she couldn't do nothing but mumble.

—Speak up! Damn girl, Circe say.

Lilith start cry. She couldn't say her cho-cho be bleeding. Circe would think she done some nastiness for sure. Some nastiness with boy that Circe always saying that she born to do. Circe grab the girl.

—After nothing no do you. Why you trying me patience, pickney? Circe go to push her off but then see new blood running down Lilith leg.—Shithouse. You turn woman now, she say.

From then Lilith couldn't go nowhere, nor talk to nobody, most of all boy.

—And don't make me see you near any of them Johnny-jumper or I goin' kill you for sure, Circe say.

Lilith look in the old silver tray that the great house throw away. Lilith look down the well and the dead part of the river. Lilith watching Lilith and trying to see which part of her turn woman. She watch her lips and bite down so that they look smaller. She look at her eyes and try to see them with nigger colour. She see her legs that too long, and hear her voice that cracky-cracky like old witch. Lilith did think that turning woman was going to make her smile but instead things was pushing out of her skin without permission. Things growing and won't stop and pussy blood come and go when it feel like. Some woman did get possess by the Bosi, the spirit that take over people shape and have her do things that the Bible don't like. The Bosi plump up a woman titty and arse and burn down her voice and tear her in two. Lilith grab herself. Lilith seeing how pickney is the only thing that not be a slave and start to wrap osnaburg cloth tight round her titty so they won't grow. But her body turn enemy 'pon her. By evening the toughest cloth would ease into the shape of her breast like two clay pot. Not long after that one of the house womens say she should be breeding, just like her mama.

Lilith perplex, for she don't know what breeding have to do with she. Lilith want to run and skip and jump and whinny like horse. She still want to do them things until she pass by the only nigger who was skipping and jumping and whinnying too. Tantalus the mad nigger. Lilith think that maybe the first thing a woman must learn to do is to stop smile.

One more thing happen in Lilith fourteenth year.

Circe tell the chile to stop call her mama. Lilith did flabbergast but then all of a sudden what Circe say make sense and that flabbergast her more. For Lilith remember the whispers from the womens who wash by the river. They talk 'bout how certain nigger lucky that she don't work and how she never take to mothering but love the rutting, and about how certain woman barren and certain man nature cut. Lilith come to know the silence that happen when them same big people see that she was listening. Is not like Circe was one to hide anything though. Plenty time Lilith arriving when a man of colour leaving and one time she come home to see a mulatto from Kingston climb off Circe as her bow legs flap up in the air and she yell, Get out of the house you little bitch so big people can be private.

—What they mean when they say Tantalus nature cut? Lilith ask the same evening, as if sunset was going give her the answer.

—Who say that?

—Three womens. They was washing by the river.

—Three bitches they be. But that mad nigger business is everybody business.

—What be him business?

—Next time you pass that naked bastard take a good look for yourself. You not too fool, so you must know what man supposed to have.

Jack Wilkins slice it off himself long years ago. That mad son of a bitch used to play with himself and watch the old mistress when she take bath. Wilkins catch the nigger himself.

—No, Mama—

—Me warn you not to call me—

—No, Circe. Me don't know them things.

—Eehi.

Circe resume to eating sweet potato and goat milk.

—So you not goin' ask?

—Ask?

—You not goin' inquire after her? Who you mama be?

—No.

—Humph. She was a stupid gal just like you.

—She dead?

—Of course she dead, girl like that born fi dead. You take after her, that is for sure. Couldn't beat it out of you.

—And Tantalus not me papa?

—You better ask Tantalus. Couldn't beat no decency into you, that for sure.

—Me goin' be decent just like you, Mama.

—Circe.

—Me goin' be like you. Me goin' have plenty man come a-callin' for tuppence.

Circe jump at her quick but Lilith dash through the door.—You better find someplace for you skinny backside, you hear me! Circe shout and slam the door. Lilith frighten and her heart beating but she also feel good. Wonderful good. One time Lilith try to clean the old armchair and Circe scream to not touch nothing and Lilith get frighten and run. Another time Lilith pick grape for Circe, and she eat a bunch, then throw 'way the rest and say, They spoil, you little wretch. Circe cook for herself and most time forget to cook for Lilith. She wait till the woman fall asleep to thief the last potato sticking in the pot. Lilith hear that white people get governess to hold they pickney and tell them story, but only Tantalus ever do that and he did mad one time, then get back sense and gone mad again. Lilith stomp her foot and sniff hard for her tears to behave.

—Time you go find man and come out of me house, Circe say.

Montpelier, like other estate on the east coast, have one white man for every thirty-three negro. White man couldn't abide by they numbers alone, so they pick out a bunch of niggermens to put them in charge of other slaves. Johnny-jumpers they call them, five to ten in number and they work with whip and on some estate, knife and gun. When a field nigger not keeping up the quota of ground to plough or cane to cut they whip him in the back or punch him in the face or kick him in the balls and tell him work harder 'cause he not no prince regent here. The Johnny-jumpers raid the slave settlement at night like they be pirate, taking the supper that just cook, or if they hungering for a something else, grabbing the daughter or the mother even if her titty lanky and her pussy no good. They do as they please at night for Jack Wilkins the overseer didn't care.

Is on a raid that a Johnny-jumper first set eye on Lilith. They shouting and gallivanting but stay wide of Circe hut as they run pass. People know to keep 'way from Circe ever since she tell a niggerman who thief her potato that the potato goin' know what to do and the very next day a big chunk stick in him throat and choke him to death. But from far off the Johnny-jumpers see Circe house and her open fire and her little girl who was only getting bigger. This was the week before the field niggers was to start reaping the provision grounds while the sugarcane still grow.

—Soon and very soon you goin' be taking man, Circe say as she look out the window as they pass, one of them sticking out he tongue at the hut.

—Taking man where? Lilith say, hearing they footsteps getting weaker and weaker.

—You go on playin' fool to catch wise, Circe say.

But Lilith plenty scared of the Johnny-jumpers. Even as a little pickney she hear of what they do in the field and more than once when she was little they sack the playground and kick the little boys. Some nights, Lilith hear the screaming and crashing and cussing goin' on in the slave settlement and wonder if one day they was goin' get bold and come into Circe hut to slap her and squeeze her breast. One day, when she coming from washing by the river, a Johnny-jumper that she see before, who not even taller than her, shout from across the path that Europa pussy too loose after the young'un so he coming for her. Fear seize Lilith and she run back to the hut, where Circe was getting visit from the overseer Jack Wilkins himself.

Lilith stop. The man regard her but she couldn't see him face since he didn't take off him hat. He swallow some more lime and sugar-water and give Circe the glass. Him shirt open and him chest hair white and bushy. Him breeches cream and dirty and loose and he swing a little when he walk right past her, that old man swing. Lilith jump out of the way but the tobacco air reach her. That night Circe laughing when she recalling what he say.

—What a thing! Seem you free paper burn. And to think of all people, he be the one that burn it. You to report to the field tomorrow morning. Don't make cock crow and you still in you bed.

Fear jump up and snatch the words out of Lilith mouth the whole night. Everybody know 'bout the life of a field nigger. Before sunrise she hear them—one, two, three hundred foot hitting the ground and rumbling like slow thunder. They used to wake her and scare her so much that she thought they was a militia marching to hell. The slave coffle. The field niggers. Before sunrise they in the field and by moon-rise they still working. And when crop time, no nigger leave. Sun burn they black bodies blacker. Ants, mosquito, rat, snake and scorpion bite them in the bush. Womens screaming, No, massa, no whip me no more, and mens screaming as backra chop they two little toe off. She see the slaves when they come back in the evening, tired, crying, limping and bleeding and some that come back in a sack.

And she hear other things too. Of the time in 1785 when they burn a nigger girl alive right in the middle of the cane field and how every year, right before crop time, she scream. And when the overseer chop off another nigger head and stick it on a pole until it rot off. And when they send five slave to the treadmill where them niggers run themself to death. The word was that Jack Wilkins wield the whip and do as he please. He instruct him slave-drivers to do the same and since then a month don't pass where they don't kill a nigger and gone to Spanish Town to buy a fresh one. Montpelier have deep pockets and a new nigger always better than a lazy one, Jack Wilkins was known to say.

The field was where Jack Wilkins was sending her.

Lilith 'fraid of sleep 'cause tomorrow was goin' come right after. She think that if she try her hardest to stay awake, then night would be force to stay and tomorrow would never come again. Lilith don't care if that was little girl thinking and she supposed to be woman now. She hold on to the awakeness for a long time before sleep beat her. The next morning she sick.

Circe frown, tapping her foot. The girl lying flat on the mat.

—Me say what sick you?

—Me, me don't know.

—You no know. Then how you know you sick? You belly hurtin' you?

—Yes.

—And you head woozy-woozy?

—Yes.

—You feel fat like you goin' burst?

—Yes.

—Then you either with child or you dead. Mayhaps you breeding. Me know you was taking man, you know, you at the time now.

—No! Is sick me sick. Me can't feel nothing, and, and, me just weak. Weak bad.

Circe look at her hard.

—Well. Make me ask one fool-fool question. You think overseer care if you sick or you well? Answer me direct. You think he care a raas? Unless you sick until you deading, you still have to get you—

—Then me deading.

Circe not one for backtalk.

—That you goin' be for sure once the overseer come here.

Circe step outside. The girl wait a while, then listen if she nearby. She move slow to the door. Circe gone. The fire still going, so she lean over it until her neck and chin well hot and some sweat start to rise out her skin. She raise her arm and let some of the heat work her armpit. But then she drop her left hand too low and near burn herself. Fire catch her skin hair and the room smell like burnin' goat. She cuss and dip her hand in the bucket and rub it hard, trying to get the smell off. She hear people talking and run back to her mat. Then the abeng shell blow.

Circe come back. Right behind her was the thin woman who slap her once, the woman called Homer.

—See it deh she say she sick. Me no want no problem with slave-driver, you know, me no want no problem. You know how backra go on when nigger say she sick and is lazy she lazy. Me no—

—Quiet, Homer say.

Circe hiss and go outside.

Homer stoop down. The girl try to not look too 'fraid. Homer eyes thin and sharp and her cheekbone high. Her lip thin like white woman but dry and chappy. Homer have the longest neck she ever see and smell like mint one moment, lemongrass the next. None of the pick-neys ever go near the big great house, not because they forbidden to play near the massa or mistress, but because they all scared of Homer. The girl feeling the same scaredness and shame and she angry that part of her still be little girl who easy to frighten. She want to be tough and hard like Circe or move slow and sure like nothing can bother her. Homer regarding her for long. The girl can't hold her gazing so she look 'way. Then Homer touch her forehead and feel her neck. The girl hide her left hand but Homer still frown like she smell something foul. Homer touch Lilith neck again and mutter, then get up and go to the doorway.

—She have the marsh fever. Give her plenty cerasee, but don't put no molasses in it, she say.

Circe make a big pot of cerasee tea and give Lilith to drink. Cerasee is the bitterest tea ever make and the girl cough and hack and cry but she didn't dare spit. Circe regard her again, then say she going to town. She put on her green calico frock and shoes, one of the only negro anywhere with a pair and gone. As soon as she think Circe far away, Lilith go outside and blink at the high sun. She out there a good while, looking if she can see the negroes working from where she be. She step out further and see pickaxe and hoe swinging up in the sky, then down in the ground. Just then a cart come from round back and she jump out of the way. A niggerwoman was cursing and driving and whipping the horse hard.

Lilith go back inside to find a Johnny-jumper waiting for her.

—Word 'pon de field say you sick.

She couldn't move. The man whip on the floor beside him cutlass. Every time the flame flicker the cutlass blink.

—Me come over, me meself fi give you de bettering.

—Me, me mother, she soon come back.

—You mama who me jus' pass goin' to town?

Lilith quiet. She think to run through the door but the thought of other Johnny-jumpers coming still her. She try to think like a woman.

—W... what you want from little girl? she say.

—Who tell you say you little? Penelope have two young'un and she look younger than you. Anyway, since you make me come all the way over yah fi de cho-cho me nah run round no more.

The Johnny-jumper take off him shirt and pull down him pantaloons. She remember him now, the same boy who say the day before that he was coming for her. She try not to look at how he ready. Plenty man come to Circe hut with it already sticking through they breeches, but they keep them on when Circe tell her to get out. And though that madman Tantalus show him cocky all the time it swing low like lame dog. Lilith thinking 'bout her bush, and how nobody tell her that is man who must decide what happen to it.

—What you name? she say.

—Dem call me Paris. You know who Paris be?

She don't answer.

—Big, big hero. Massa Jack say dat Paris stop the Trojan War.

—Circe say—

—Circe already get what she lookin' for. Me no care 'bout she. Anyway, hear what. Pussy not doin' me no favour all de way over deh, so get you black arse over yah.

She don't know what to do. The Johnny-jumper on the floor with him hand waking up him cocky. She try to think that she is Circe who choose who she rut. She try to think she is Circe who don't care when Lilith walk in on her and a free coloured from in town. If she just think 'bout that or anything else. The bat in the ackee tree, the pretty great house that just whitewash, mayhaps when she done think, he done rut. She make one step.

—Make haste, cow, he say.

He regarding her like he done fuck her already. He already grinning like man do when he leave Circe hut. The whip and cutlass on the floor. He was one of them man who didn't even have to beat and thump and slap, him voice was enough. She feel the voice on top of her, grabbing her neck and scratching her breast. Better he jump at her like a wild beast than frighten her to come over and make her feel that she be the reason why he doin' what he do. Better to get rip to pieces by the bush dog or wild boar in the hills than feel that she walk up to a man by herself and let him ravage her. By going to him, she rapin' herself. The whip and cutlass on the floor. The girl move over to the man. He getting himself excited. Her heart punching a hole through her chest. The whip and the cutlass on the floor. She walk right up to him and as he hold him hand out to grab her, she dash past him and run to the fire. She grab the pot of cerasee tea and don't care that it burnin' her finger.

—Wha de—the man say but before him could even shift, she turn over the pot of tea on him face. The girl once hear pig scream with knife halfway 'cross it neck and she hear woman scream 'cause slave-driver take 'way her newborn young'un, but she never hear scream like that. The man bellow loud and shake the room. And didn't stop. She scream too. He roll all over the ground and grab him face and scream more when skin and flesh coming off. The girl watching him face bubbling up and popping and the naked man spinning and bawling and jerking in the dirt. He screaming too loud. She cover her ear hard and shut her eye tight but she still hearing he scream and seeing him face. She screaming too, bawling for the noise to stop stop stop. Somebody was goin' hear. Stop stop stop. And when they hear they would come. And then they would kill her because nobody that young must have so much wicked-ness. Stop stop stop. That was the first time she feel the darkness. True darkness and true womanness that make man scream. She shudder and she feel 'fraid and proud and wicked and she feel good. So good so that she get more 'fraid. The man jerking like he have fits and he still scream-ing. Stop stop stop stop. Somebody was goin' hear.

Then the boy grab her foot and pull her down. The girl bawling and the boy bawling too. She turn 'way from him face. The pain too much for the boy and him fall over again and writhing and yelling. She go to run and he grab her foot again, him nails digging into her heel and she bawling like her heel just catch fire. The girl try to kick him off but him hand too strong, as if the screaming and the madness was making him stronger. Him bellowing now, like old dog or the darkest, evillest animal. The boy pull her ankle and the girl drop hard on her face. He pulling the girl towards him. She screaming. He pulling. She grab the cutlass.

Circe come right after dusk to see the floor 'wash in red. She follow the blood quick and stop at the naked Johnny-jumper foot. From foot up to thigh the black skin all chopped up with pink flesh peeking. From neck up be nothing but red. The blood didn't stop there. The trail leave him body then turn left as if goin' to the window. Under the window be the girl, crouching and hiding from the light. Her dress and her arms cover up in red. The cutlass at her foot, her eye wide open like dead owl and her breathing short and quick. Then she shoot a look at Circe and her two green eye make the big woman jump. Circe run out of the hut.

By nightfall she come back with Homer and two other womens. Homer walk right in but the other two womens stop when they see the body and look at the girl. Shit, one of the woman say. Lilith look straight at the three, her green eye flashing like wild animal.

—She is a mad raas, the other woman say.

Homer shush her. The woman frown. That woman short almost like a midget and her eye uncanny looking. She drive the carryall carriage that come to take the body. Homer walk over to the Johnny-jumper. Then she look at the girl. The womens, except Circe, wrap the body in black cloth. Homer shove the boy head in a sack. They put the body in the back of the carriage and the short woman ride off.

—Stupid bitch. The whole o' we dead now, Circe say.

The girl start to cry.

—Save you bawling, pussyhole. Time soon come when you goin' bawl till you bleed.

—Shut up, Circe, Homer say.

—You shut up, dry-up cow. Me look like you pickney?

Homer look at Circe and Circe hiss.

—Come chile, we have to make haste, Homer say to the girl. Homer hold out her hand. The girl don't look Homer in the face.

—Too spirited. She too spirited, that damn girl, Circe say. He was just goin' cut her down a notch. Get rid of that damn pride. She just a nigger girl.

Homer stop.

—What you just say?

—She too spirited. Think she be some nigger queen. She too spirited! She did need a man to fix her, damn girl.

The girl sob. Homer walk right over to Circe and slap her right cheek so hard that Circe stagger. Then she slap the left and Circe yell.

—You dead, you hear me? The two of you dead, Circe say. She bawling now. Homer grab Circe face by the cheek and squeeze hard.

—No nigger dead on this estate unless me say so, you hear me? And no nigger live either, Homer say and push Circe away.

Homer take the girl out of the hut. Circe still cussing. The girl can't bear to look up in the sky or at Homer beside her so she stare at the ground as she walk. Even then she didn't see the ground change from dirt to cut stone to wood floor until she feel the change under her foot. Homer open a door and they step into a dark kitchen that smell of ginger and pimento. Homer light a lamp in the dark. Orange light wash over the room but the girl still couldn't make out anything other than a big counter in the center. Homer take her hand and lead her to another door.

Steps lead down to a cellar. The girl couldn't see much more than the step in front of her, but smell something like that one stick of cinnamon that Circe have that she forbidden to touch. Homer lift up the candle and throw light all over the room.

—Over there, she say, pointing to a carpet on the floor.

—Over there you goin' stay.

Homer go back up the stairs and each step she make leave the room darker and darker. When Homer reach the top of the stairs the room turn into pitch.

—Don't come out until me tell you to, Homer say and shut the door.

· 2 ·

JACK WILKINS STRUT SO FAR AND WIDE OVER MONTPELIER that some nigger forget that Montpelier done have a massa. But most never even seen Massa Patrick Wilson in the flesh. The law start and end with Jack Wilkins, that is what all nigger who born there or get stole from the Africa come to see. But as Wilkins start to get on in years him grip on the estate slip and plenty slave-driver and even Johnny-jumper start to do as they please. Montpelier was going to the dogs and every man with a whip or a gun mark out five hogshead for himself and every woman as he own wench. Johnny-jumper takin' liberty too and one try to take Lilith. That error he wasn't goin' make twice.

Lilith wake up in a darkness that grip her throat. She try to scream, but the dark steal her voice. She trembling and the air smell old. Lilith can't see her hand. This was not night darkness that show things once the eye get used to it. Lilith blink plenty time and swing out her hand thinking the air goin' be thick like mud. She try to run, but trip over something and fall. The wood floor creak with old age. She fling around her hand like a madwoman and strike a shelf that let loose the smell of pimento. Lilith forget the pain in her knuckle and feel along the shelf, her hand touching bottle and bowl and sack until she come to the wall. She move along slow, her back to the wall until she reach a corner where the smell change to salt meat and the no-smell of flour and sugar. She move against the wall and trip again, over a sack. Lilith cuss and try to pretend that she not frighten. At first she think the scurrying was her mind gone aflutter in the dark. But then she hear scurrying again, on the floor and above. Rats. Lilith clutch herself 'cause she can't see nothing. She run away from the sound and trip again. As she land on the floor, something jump on her back and jump off.

A light open up and flood the stairs and banister.

—Quit with you screaming, fool! she say. Lilith don't know is who. The woman is only a shadow and not thin like Homer. She go to close the door and Lilith wish to scream out no, but then the woman leave the door ajar a little, enough for one thin blade of light to cut all the way down to the floor. That light show Lilith where she be, near the steps and surrounded by barrels, some upright and some flat. She set herself on a barrel and wait.

A long time, she reckon. Long enough that what she know happen, what she think happen and what she feel goin' happen bend and stretch and break and mix back into each other so that she could no longer tell for sure which was which. The shadow on the floor dark and sharp but it then start to creep across the wood like blood. Lilith pull up her feet and squeeze herself in tight. In the dark she smell him, the field stink of the Johnny-jumper, the frowsy arm and raw crotch that bring back sweat and wood and blood. She hear him scream. She hear him skin crack and pop and think she goin' vomit until she realise that something was frying upstairs in the kitchen.

The door open wide again and a figure come down, that she know for sure. The figure walk down the steps careful-like but with her back straight and her head high. She carrying a tray that she set down on a barrel next to Lilith.

—Don't waste me food, Homer say. She turn to go back upstairs.

—Me...

—Yes?

—Me...Lilith say.

—Bucket in the corner. Piss and shit in that if you have to, Homer say and leave her.

Homer leave the door open a little wider and from there Lilith hear the kitchen come to life. Man voice and woman voice talking and laughing and cussing. And pot frying and hot water hissing and things chopping, and one smell after another floating down in the cellar to keep her company. White people food. Lilith think she was goin' glut on just the smell alone, so much was coming. Then she smell the tray next to her and grab a johnnycake. She don't swallow the first before she stuff another in. Her mouth can barely handle it, to chew down something that don't taste like potato. She put something in her mouth that feel like meat but Lilith eat meat only once, so she not sure. This meat full of salt and have plenty little sharp bones that she have to spit out. Lilith rub her fingers in the oil and lick the bowl clean. Then she hear more laughing and more cussing and silence when Homer talk. Something about going into Kingston to get some herring and other fish to settle the Massa Patrick head.

—Like he got no head to settle, a woman say and everybody laugh again. Lilith did think the massa was Jack Wilkins and can't remember seeing this other massa.

—Gorgon say only last week he open war 'pon de rose bush, a woman say. More laughing.

—Shithouse. First Tantalus, then the massa, and even Massa Jack not too righted in him old days. Damn estate cursed.

—You hush you mouth before mad backra hush it for good, another woman say.

—Nothing wrong with Massa Jack head, 'cept that is whiskey own it, a man say.

—And even that don't tame him breeches none, a woman say.

More laughing again. Laughing was a strange sound to Lilith. Something that strike her as a house nigger thing 'cause no laughter happen in Circe hut. Lilith listen for the day to change. The noise of the kitchen as they make breakfast. The quiet when they gone to the dining room to serve the massa and mistress. The noise when they come back and the smell of lunch cooking. The quiet when they gone to serve and the mumbling, laughing and quiet cussing that come with them eating they own lunch upstairs. A man belch loud and a woman say thank merciful Jesus that is not you other hole, to which he fart loud. More laughing. Maybe house-slave life was everything Lilith think.

By Lilith own reckoning two day pass. She have only the talking and joking upstairs, the smell of breakfast, different from lunch and supper and the blade of light from the door that go from bright to weak to gone, to tell her how time pass. Sometimes she wish she could hear all of what they say so that she could laugh too. Lilith sit in the dark and think about how a real laugh would sound. She chuckle under her breath and cover her lips as if somebody was watching. Even with the little light she could feel the dark moving in close. And the rats. Most time Homer bring the food. Other time is one of the two other womens who help get rid of the Johnny-jumper body. Neither woman talk to her much other than to remind her to not go upstairs. Sometimes she hear whispering and wonder if is about her.

A morning come as laughter rise and bounce and then vanish all of a sudden. She hear big boots step hard through the quiet. Somebody get throw against a door. Move out of the way, sodomite, a voice say. A loud man voice that have the sound of the field. Not one house nigger saying nothing.

—Wheh de fookin' gal deh?

—Hello? Is which wicked nigger curse they chile with a name like Fookingal? Homer say.

—Don't cross youself wid me, woman. Me'd beat the piss out o' you.

—Nobody beating nobody in this kitchen. Say you piece, then get out.

Lilith hearing Homer.

—Paris. Where him be? Four day gone and nobody no see him.

—Anybody here look like Paris keeper?

—Don't smart you mouth wid me, dry-up pussyhole.

—Then make me stupid up me mouth, then. Johnny-jumper gone missing four day and you come to the great house for him whereabouts? You reckon he tired of the Johnny-jumpering and turn chambermaid?

—You think you mouth pretty, bitch? Me didn't come to the great house just so, me go to Circe hut first.

—Now that even curiouser. And why you go to Circe hut, if you please? Circe no too old for the boy?

—Is not Circe, is—you go on. Circe tell me plenty thing.

—What Circe say?

—She say ask that bitch Homer.

—Oh. Me still want to know why when your boy gone missing you think to go to Circe, of all people. What is the meaning of that affair?

—If only you did as pretty as you talk.

—And if only you was as smart as you big. No boy name Paris in here.

—You can't keep her forever, cow. Just watch when we get her. First we goin' beat her face off. Then we goin' fuck out her cunt. Then we goin' kill her. Then we goin' fuck her again. Or we just goin' deal wid her the way massa and Maroon did deal with you. Me papa tell me 'bout you.

Homer don't say nothing for a while.

—Devil take to talking to him young'uns nowadays? For me certain you ain't got no pappy. Now get out before me tell the massa how you dare come in this house with you stink self. Get out!

A door slam. Lilith jump.

—Food can't cook itself, Homer say.

Lilith soon lose track of night and day. She hear shadow whispers in what seem like daylight, but shouting in what feel like night. Sometimes she hear a voice, a tongue that roll like a white woman. She don't know what be what when she hear them sounds coming down from the kitchen. The door did ajar, but just a little bit. Lilith expecting Homer mouth, with all the creaking her footsteps make, but the woman didn't say nothing. Lilith see her through the door crack and gasp so hard that she sure Homer hear. But Homer keep on washing. Her dress was pull down from her shoulder and rest low on her hip. She washing herself by the drum of water and looking out the window. Homer back look like a washboard with big thick scars running across, from her neck and shoulder right down to the middle of her arse. Lilith think she seeing an animal. Homer carry herself so tall and proud that one would think she be the only unblemished nigger in Montpelier. Lilith can't think of what a woman of Homer cunning could have do to make somebody whip her so bad. Homer wiping her shoulder with a rag. She lift up her shoulder and grab some leaves from off the counter and rub in her armpit. Mayhaps that be the mint and lemongrass people always smell on her. Then she turn round.

Lilith nearly stagger back and lose her balance. She figure Homer must hear her now for sure. Lilith look again and as stunned as when she look first. The scars continue from her back to her front, so much that she don't have titty no more, just two stump that mark off in scar marks. Her belly have marks too but they be smaller. Mayhaps she was pregnant when they whip her. Lilith be thinking that she don't ever want to be like Homer. She think of Homer and her own back itch. She wondering what kind of wickedness or uppityness Homer could have do to make them beat her so. So bad that she be the most obedient nigger ever since. Homer whiter than plenty white man, it seem. But nothing make a nigger more black than whip scars. Lilith don't want none of it. She sad for Homer and she shame and she angry that this woman act like nothing above her. Lilith touch her breast and feel how they smooth. Homer washing. Then both woman hear another woman singing and the voice getting louder. Homer jump. She pull up her blouse but it stubborn. She pull and pull and cuss and look out and cuss again. Lilith think to help her but stay. The frock stubborn over her wet skin. The singing getting louder. Homer manage to pull up the frock halfway and Lilith see a look that she would never expect from Homer face. She wasn't doing no hissing, she was sniffing and huffing like she frighten. She manage to slip in her sleeve and was pulling up the bosom when another woman, one of them who did help clean up the Johnny-jumper mess enter.

—Woman you too old to be playing with you titty.

—Older than even that, Pallas, older than even that, Homer say.

—Tell that green-eyed gal to come upstairs.

Lilith step back. She try to step back quick but don't want nobody to hear the step creak. But Pallas didn't open the door, she only shout, Come upstairs, green-eyed gal.

—Lilith, this one name Pallas, Homer say when Lilith step into the kitchen. The other woman nod.

—What we goin' do 'bout her? Pallas say. She tall as Homer but round, and not so far gone in age. Her hair plait in two at the side and run all they way past her breast. Her white apron hide her purple dress that look washed out.

—Devil if I know. Johnny-jumper out there and you know how them be. Them just starting they foolishness.

—Maybe we should turn her over and make God do the rest.

Lilith look up. Pallas' eyes was waiting on her.

—No.

—What goin' happen when Massa Jack hear?

—I don't know.

—You supposed to know, Homer.

—I don't know! Lilith, sit down and eat, Homer say.—She can work here.

—What you goin' tell the others?

—Others? Since when me answer to no nigger round here? Me bring in new gal to do the work. That's all any soul need to know.

—She not new. Everybody know you not sending down food to feed rat. Most reckon is she the jumper after. You goin' have to tell him. He alone can sort this out. You have to tell him, Homer, Pallas say.

—He goin' know soon enough, Homer say.

—But if he is the last to know, you goin' be the one that feel it. Is not everybody 'fraid to touch you, Pallas say.

Lilith eating dasheen and pork. She look at the two womens talking and feel like is some other Lilith they speaking about. Neither talking to her. Circe used to do the same thing. Lilith wonder where the other slaves be. Mayhaps is Sunday, she think, and everybody gone to Sunday market.

—Anyway, things me have to say can wait till tonight, Pallas say and leave. Lilith and Homer in the kitchen, one eating and one drinking soup, neither saying nothing.

Most night as Lilith fall asleep, she fly up awake in fear that the Johnny-jumpers already in the cellar and ready to kill her. Is a week since and right in that instant between dreaming and waking she hear a whisper calling her the wickedest woman. A voice that trail off into the quiet. Paris didn't beat her or try to kill her and he not even try to have him way with her, according to how the womens describe it. Maybe she could have run 'way. Maybe she be the one that evil. Something in the darkness smell new but known. Lilith looking for him in the dark, coming for her with no head on him shoulder. The door seem so far away at night. Lilith begin to wonder if field labour was so bad or if she did just make the Johnny-jumper do as he please then a new day would come after the old one and she would forget. Now she goin' pay 'cause her life gone down a new trail and she can never get back to the old one. Lilith start to wonder if this new trail any worse than the old one. If a empty room better than a room with a woman who hate her, a man who mad.

The next afternoon, Homer give her a lamp and the task to swab the floor and sort out the shelves. They leave the door ajar and Lilith hear quick footsteps.

—Massa Jack coming! Massa Jack coming! The voice say. Lilith know the voice but couldn't recollect the face.

—Gorgon, what you talking 'bout? Homer say.

—Me riding past de field and hear 'im shouting 'bout how two missin'.

—Damn. He did always have a sense 'bout them things. That backra could just look at a crowd of nigger and know one gone. Not even old age—

—Homer, he lef di field and go straight to Circe hut.

—Shithouse.

—Shit for true. Me no want dat man see me here, Gorgon say.

The first footstep didn't stop the kitchen goings-on, but the second footstep stop everything cold. Lilith hear the footstep circle the kitchen one, two and three time.

—Homer, Homer, Homer, have you been losing step of late? Have you been slipping, you old cow?

—Me know me can still do a good day's work, sah, Homer say.

—Bloody hell, ask Homer a question and God be damned, a Homer answer you shall receive. Are you getting forgetful in your old age, perhaps even a little mad, is what I ask.

—Not yet, sah, by the grace of God.

—Good for you. Because for some reason, unbeknownst to me, of course, everybody on this bloody estate seems to think I am.

—Oh no, massa—

—Oh, don't oh-no-massa me. I knew you from when you still shat yourself. And so my newest Johnny-jumper and my newest field slave have both gone missing and yet not a soul has news on either. Uncanny, eh? Eloped, have they, Homer?

—No, sah. Me don't know—

—Damn, Homer, don't add tiresome to your list of flaws. Not now. You know of everything, I daresay even God gets his news from you. Are you saying you have no knowledge of their whereabouts?

—Me don't have no knowledge of the boy, sir.

—And what of the girl? You know how I feel about being taken for a fool, Homer.

—She, she downstairs, sah.

Lilith jump. She hear strong footsteps stomp across the kitchen then stop. Then two hard slap and a yelp.

—Crossing me now, are you? Is that how you'll have it? I give an order to send the girl to the field and you take it upon yourself to change it? Who for the sake of a fuck is the master here? Who?

—You, massa.

—Been far too long since you've met the cowskin, that's what I think. Far too long.

—No, massa! Me never mean to cross you, massa!

Another slap.

—No, please, massa. Is the mistress! Is the mistress demand more things to be done and we did need another slave and me didn't want to trouble you to go town to buy a new one so me just look at who be the newest and weakest, who if she leave won't trouble the field much. That is all, massa, God truth. God truth.

—Really? And you know nothing of this Paris boy?

—No, please, massa.

—That's not what I heard from Circe.

The room pause. Silent.

—Circe living with Tantalus a long time, massa, Homer say.

—Aye, indeed. Indeed. Maybe he did run away as the jumpers say. I shall send word to the constable today. Let him mount a search party and then we shall see what's what. And to what use have you put the girl? I will see her now, Jack Wilkins say.

—Yes, Massa Jack.

The door swing open, wider than before and the whole cellar wash in dim daylight. Jack Wilkins march down the steps with Homer right behind him. Lilith think first to hide but then decide to stand still and take what coming to her.

—And what have you been doing here all in the dark?

—She make the place clean and pretty, massa. Clean and pretty can't done. She—

—For fuck's sake, Homer shut up. I'm sure God blessed her with a tongue.

Homer shut up and bow. Lilith don't know who disturbing her more.

—Me working, massa, Lilith say and bow.

—You working. Working on what?

—Whatever need working in the cellar, massa.

—Whatever need working. Doesn't seem like you're very busy down here, Lilith.

—Oh, she plenty busy, massa. Is like she have three hand and—

Right then Massa Jack swing round and strike Homer hard in the face. She stagger back and fall against the step.—That's enough out of you, he say. He turn back to Lilith.

—And tell me, Lilith, by chance have you heard of a boy called Paris? Tall boy, thin, your height almost, maybe a smidgen taller. A new Johnny-jumper.

—Me mama tell me to stay away from boy, massa.

—Clever. Clever. I'm surrounded by clever niggers.

Lilith look at the man. Tall with a slight hunch. Hair near white but eye green and bright. Massa Jack shirt open right to the waist, as be him custom. But he thin and muscular, mayhaps even strong, from all those years acting as the headman of Montpelier. Lilith can't believe that this same man was driven to distraction sometimes as Homer say. He regard Lilith so long that she start to fidget.

—Can't have any nigger thinking they're too special, you know. That's why you were sent to the field. But this is as good a place as any, I wager. You find the cellar agreeable?

—Is hard work, massa.

—Well, niggers aren't here to have things easy, are they, he say and laugh. He turn around and go back upstairs, leaving Homer to rub her face. Homer sit on the step while Lilith rub her fingers. Lilith don't dare look at her. Not long after Pallas run down and stop on the step above Homer.

—He run away? Why the Johnny-jumpers saying Paris run away when they know what happen? Homer? Homer, this don't seem mighty peculiar to you? Why the Johnny-jumpers didn't just say she kill him? Why they lie when we and them is not friend?

—You ever see what happen when puss catch bird, Pallas?

—Yes, but...

—When puss catch bird. Think 'bout that for a while, Homer say and go upstairs.

· 3 ·

EVERY NEGRO WALK IN A CIRCLE. TAKE THAT AND MAKE OF it what you will. A circle like the sun, a circle like the moon, a circle like bad tidings that seem gone but always, always come back. Woman work round the sun and sleep round the moon and sometimes work round both, especially if it be crop time. Other times woman wait on the moon, especially if it fat with blood and rise low over the Blue Mountain. That be the season of the Sasa, the Asaase Yaa or the Ogun and the other forgotten gods.

Truth be told, slaves in Jamaica have more ranking among themself than massa. In this place two thing matter more than most, how dark a nigger you be and where the white man choose to put you. One have all to do with the other. From highest to lowest, this be how things go. The number one prime nigger who would never get sell is the head of the house slaves. That position so hoity-toity that in some house is a white woman who be that nigger. The head house nigger get charge with so much that she downright run the house, and everybody including the massa do what she say. Homer careful not to cross the line, though. Position can make a negro girl forget herself and there is always the cowhide, the cat-o'-nine and the buckshot to remind her of her place. After she, there be the house slaves who work the rooms and the grounds and the gardens. Sometimes is the prime pretty niggers or the mulatto, quadroon or mustee that work there. Then you have the cooks who the backra trust the most, because the cook know that if the mistress get sick after a meal there goin' be a whipping or a hanging before the cock even crow. Other house slaves be cleaning and dusting and shining and manservanting and womanservanting and taking care of backra pickneys.

After the house slaves come the artisan niggermens, like the blacksmith, the bricklayer, the tanner, the silversmith, niggers who skilled with they hands, followed by the stable boys, coachmen and carters. Next is the field niggers, headed by the Johnny-jumpers who be the right hand and left hand of the slave-drivers. They do most of the whipping and kicking but when the estate running right they have nothing to do, so they whip and kick harder. After Johnny-jumper come the Great Slave Gang, the most expensive slaves, the one who they buy for the long years of hard work. The mens and the womens strapping and handsome like a prime horse. Most be Ashanti, what the white man call Coromantee, but they not easy to control so they get punish plenty for they spiritedness. But a dead Coromantee man can set an estate back up to three hundred pounds so they careful not to kill too much. After that is the Petit Gang, the makeup of plain common nigger. Some cost less than one hundred pounds and they work the other fields, like the ratoon or the tobacco that some planters grown on the side. Other nigger look down 'pon them mens as worthless and them womens as good for rutting, not breeding. On some estate even the pickneys work, mostly in the trash gang to pick up rubbish on the estate or to carry water for the field slaves to drink, or to get firewood. That be the negroes.

Now while the overseer Jack Wilkins plough through so much nigger bush that some start to wonder what exactly the estate sowing, the old massa Patrick Wilson forgo woman flesh from the day he come back from the war, when less than a fortnight after, house nigger make two breakfast tray for two different room. All people know is that in 1779, a year after he marry and come to Jamaica, old massa was still young and he get all caught up in rule Britannia! Because it seem the whole world was trying to take what England got. The day he hear that even Spain join France to help the rebellious thirteen colonies fight war 'gainst England he get into quite the conniption, as the mistress say, and declare that a gentleman must answer the clarion call to serve king and country. So he leave him wife at the estate that he just inherit and set out for glory all the way in Gibraltar. By the end of 1779, the mistress belly did big with a coming young'un. Massa Patrick Edward St. Michael Wilson go all the way 'cross the sea to fight war when Jamaica itself did needed defending when the French try to take the colony in early 1782 and the negroes try to rebel in St. Mary, not far from Montpelier Estate.

The massa didn't return until June 1782 and all Jamaica was celebrating but he. Some of him planter friend joke that Massa Wilson go all the way to Gibraltar to fight the enemy when the enemy was tiptoeing to him own doorstep. But as the massa step through him own door and look around like he never see the estate before, people know that not all of him come back. Something happen, something that show in him limping, that trade part of him for a part of the war and that is the part he bring back to Montpelier. In 1782 he still young but him hair gallop down in age quick and was near full white. Massa Patrick was a tall man, but him body slump and turn him into question sign. There be no scar in him face but the few who see, say he have a long scar that go from him shoulder all the way to him navel and another one that run all the way down the back of him left thigh. Him eye circle with dark even in the day for the enemy shoot the daylights out of him. More night than less, Homer need two strong negro to catch the massa when he have night terrors and run naked right through the front door and down by the bird bath and screaming and bayoneting with him finger at the Frenchies and the Iberians and whoever running him down with four feather. Not even Homer tea could fix whatever wrong with the massa. The mistress have to make do with her own quarters after one night when the massa wake up, find him sword and start chop up the whole room to pieces, telling the chair, A cowpox on you, you goddamned Gallic bastard! The mistress get very melancholy and have nobody to tell her story to. From that time on nobody could speak anything 'bout the French or the Spanish in her house. For Montpelier become her house. The mistress take over with the estate running and the head butting with Jack Wilkins 'cause the massa did all but useless. As soon as the young son Massa Humphrey could read Mother Goose, the mistress ship him off to school in England.

Three year shy of a score, the night come when Massa Wilson put on him military fatigue and mount him white horse and charge down the cane piece. But the horse see the big cotton tree ahead even though the massa was charging same way and whipping for speed. Before he ram into the tree, the horse halt and fling the massa off. The old massa land headfirst in a branch and him neck snap like a twig. The branch hold him there while he swing like a nigger. The young son Massa Humphrey who was getting learning in England receive order to come back to the plantation directly to take up him station in life. When Humphrey Wilson reach Jamaica, the year was 1800 and he be twenty-one years of age.

The Montpelier Estate be the biggest in east Jamaica so niggers was expecting a big gathering of white people to pay them respects, but plenty didn't come. So things go on a Tuesday afternoon that a swarm of slave and the backra gather at the family plot on a hill with no tree about a mile from the great house and watch as the fat preacherman talk. He say some word and the mistress, who standing regal in black dress and black veil, start to cry and shout until she keening. The overseer Jack Wilkins nod to a white slave-driver and the man take the mistress hand and hold her up. Homer in a black dress and veil that look near exact like the mistress except her dress wash out till it grey. Homer take Lilith with her even though she didn't have no dress except the white one she always wear and her feet bare. Lilith stay close and look around for Johnny-jumpers. She didn't see any, but she see Circe, scowling in a newer dress than Homer.

Some negroes wonder how come a man of the old massa's standing and breeding and moneying have a funeral so empty of backra. They come to understand that this was nobody fault but the mistress, who didn't want nobody see her making a spectacle of herself. Others mumble more than once that they can't remember what the massa look like. When nigger think of the law on the estate they think of Jack Wilkins.

Jack Wilkins use the old massa death to push himself into the great house. The lanky man act like he be the massa from before the old massa come back from war, but now he and him wife start to invite themself to the table for supper like they be massa and mistress, even though the real mistress didn't eat in the dining room no more. Soon the two have breakfast and supper sent to they quarters and they didn't once ask if the mistress get fed.

Now, the time from when the old massa Wilson die till the young massa Humphrey come back to Jamaica was no quick thing. It be 1800 and they say the fastest ships, as soon as they done fight the Spanish and the French in West Indies, had to set sail to the Gold Coast to get more negro. So be that as it was, near four month pass between the old massa death and the new massa arrival.

The mistress prepare for her son arrival so often and get disappoint that she soon stop. She didn't take to the old massa death well at all. Many time she be found talking to him like he still there, about him giving her problems and forcing her to ask questions that nobody can answer. Sometimes she walk up and down the house and talk 'bout snow which cold, cold, cold and colder than that. Or she would talk 'bout Bond Street and Regent Street and spring and summer and the season that is neither spring nor summer but the time when gentlemens and ladies go courting. The mistress bawl out, Why oh why did she forsake Mayfair for this penal colony, and what sort of gentleman takes his wife and moves her to a place with no foxes! She and the other wives was never friend. She cuss that they talk like negro folk and have poor breeding and smell bad. House niggers in the kitchen laugh 'cause they used to think only negro woman could smell bad.

Friday, February 7, 1800, at around the one o'clock hour a big black carriage with two door on each side, four big wheel and four black horse come to a halt at the great house step. Two house negro was outside and the four black horse frighten them something dreadful. Nobody ever see carriage like this before and even a few slave-driver and slave come up to look. A negro with a white wig and red blouson and white breeches sit up front with a long whip in hand. The road from Montpelier gate to the great house was over eight mile long and the house was on a hill, so Jack Wilkins had time to see the carriage coming. But he didn't see no call to act all proper-like, so he sit there on the terrace getting drunk from lime and sugar-water and rum. By now more slave gather, including house slave who hear the commotion. Homer, coming from the great house, pass the kitchen and see Lilith watching from the window. Homer don't say nothing but stare at Lilith long and hard. Lilith stay by the window and watch.

A slave-driver go up to the terrace and ask Jack Wilkins 'bout the carriage but he just nod and take another draw of the pipe. Another nigger with a white wig on jump down from the back of the carriage and open the door. The first to step out was a man. Him skin dark like a quadroon but him hair black and straight and so long that it flow right down him shoulder. He look 'bout five foot nine or ten and build strong, even though him belly was sticking out a little. Nobody know who this man be. He wearing white breeches and brown boots and him blue jacket have tails and tassels on the shoulder like an infantryman.

A thick cravat wrap round him neck and he don't waste no time to pull it off. He sigh like a thirsty man who get a drink of water, which he then ask for. Homer send one of the women back for a pitcher. As he step down and look around, Homer start to approach but then right behind him another man step out.

At first the man seem like him head on fire. But that be him hair, light and red and with curls flying all over in the breeze. The fire hair burn all over the top of him head that have a little bald spot and run down him sideburn and stop, leaving him chin and face clean-shaven.

This man tall like a tree. He have to bow him head low just to get out of the carriage. People so used to lazy colonial dress that the moment this man step out everybody know that he be foreigner traveling from far. The man in a long grey coat that look like wool, a white shirt and cravat, black breeches that hem below the knee and shiny black boots. The man was sweating so bad that he near melt. He wipe him face and neck with a kerchief. Then he look all over the estate and scowl. He turn to the other man who was wrapping up the cravat in him hand and the man smile. The tall man frown even more. Homer push past both slave-driver and negro until she right before him. Then she bow two time and curtsy.

—Nobody send word that you be coming today, nobody at all, Massa Humphrey, she say.

—I had grown rather fond of surprises, but it seems that the surprise is on me. And how are you...Homer? You haven't aged a day.

—As good as the lord allow, massa.

—Then God help you then, he say.

When Jack Wilkins see the man who dress most uncommon coming up the steps he jump up and nearly topple the pitcher and glass beside him. The slave-driver beside him jump up too.

—Good heavens! Master Humphrey! Good lord. This *is* a surprise. But a wonderful...yes...surprise....Lookit you, young master.

—I'm hardly young, sir, whoever you are.

—Of course. 'Tis Jack Wilkins, my boy. I daresay you used to call me Uncle Jack when you were a wee lad. But you're quite the gentleman now, anybody can see that.

—Can they, sir, can they indeed?

—Milord?

—Nobody seems to have seen a gentleman among you but Homer. I had sent word on Monday that we had docked in Kingston. Four days ago! Good heavens, man, I've had to charter that carriage myself.

—My apologies, good, good sir. Things have been a wee bit busy, lordship, what with crop time.

—Don't take me for a fool, Wilkins. Crop time is not for another eight months.

The slave-driver grin but then Massa Humphrey scowl and he shut up real quick. Wilkins watch him step in the house and then regard the black-hair man following him.

—This gentleman, by the way, is Robert Quinn, Massa Humphrey say.—He'll be replacing you.

—Don't believe I've had the pleasure, gentlemen, Robert Quinn say as he step inside.

Homer watch Jack Wilkins cuss two word and stagger off to him house, to tell the wife. She run back to the kitchen as Robert Quinn and Massa Humphrey inspect the house. He don't like much, not the paintings, furniture or drapery and the heat reach right into him England coat and make him outright cuss.

—Goddamn if I haven't been banished to a penal colony, the massa say.

But Massa Humphrey heart break when he see he mother. She frail like ghost and mistake Massa Humphrey for he dead father three time before she see is her son. When she see is Massa Humphrey, the mistress fall in him arms and him eye open wide when he see how light she be, like feather and how she look skinny down to the bone. He step back and near push her 'way since the whole room did smell mouldy and sour and the smell was coming from her. Massa Humphrey face red and he huff and puff and race into the kitchen and slap Homer straight 'cross she face and push her chest in so hard that Homer stagger back on the stove and burn she hand. You bastards trying to starve my good mother to death? he say, him face red and him eye dark and he huffing and puffing. Homer take it on herself to be brave and say she try to feed the mistress every day with the food she always like, but she won't take no food, only a little biscuit and tea and so Jack Wilkins say to stop feeding her.

Massa Humphrey storm round the back and soon we hear words that the Bible don't like. Then we hear a crash and the overseer wife Missus Wilkins beg for her poor invalid husband. Massa Humphrey come back in huffing and puffing and go toward Homer, who jump, but then decide to stay still and take whatever he give. He go right up to Homer face and him blue eye lock with her brown eye and he say, Feed her. He walk away 'bout ten pace and stop, turn round to Homer and say, Please.

· 4 ·

Somewhere 'cross the sea but still in the West Indies, in a land called Saint-Domingue, the negroes revolt. They take over the whole territory and kill the governor and burn down the main city. That was 1791. Now in 1800 a niggerman name L'Ouverture set to control the whole island. The British try to take the island for themself but this black republic drive them, the Spanish and the French, back! There be not a single white man in Jamaica who wasn't fretting, 'cause Jamaica negro numbers here be huge indeed.

Sake of Saint-Domingue, more redcoats come to the country. Every now and then a bunch march past the estate fence, moving stiff like rigor mortis soon set in, burnin' like meat and acting like they don't notice. The white people seem to feel safer every time they see one, with they red coats bright like fresh blood. They wearing black hat that point out in the front and wide at the side, and have long hair that mix with flour and fat and tie back tight. Them neck get lost in a stiff collar and them hair blooming out from the side of the temples. They all sweat like pig and smell something horrid. One entire regiment get put twenty mile from Montpelier.

The Montpelier Great House build long before Britain seize Jamaica from them Spanish people in 1655. A Jew tobacco farmer was the first British owner. The Wilsons buy the property in 1721 and king sugar take over. Though many years pass since the Wilson ownership, Massa Humphrey be only the second of him kin to live here. Massa Humphrey talk 'bout how plenty friend think him take leave of him senses, but he be a gentleman after all and must make him own road in life. Massa Humphrey tell this story to the negroes who gather to receive him the next day but he don't look at nobody, as if he don't expect nigger to understand. Robert Quinn, who we come to know was an Irishman, take over as overseer, and live in the great house. Sake of Jack Wilkins getting on in years Massa Humphrey make he stay.

Montpelier Great House have a ground floor that make out of cut stone and two more on top that make out of wood and plaster. The first thing Massa Humphrey and Robert Quinn do was pull down all the blue and purple curtains and ask for white or yellow or no curtain at all. Sunlight run through the house along with the sound of big boys singing shanty that scandalous even to common folk. Massa Humphrey room as big as three bedroom put together and only he sleep in there. Sometimes when Homer come to wake him, he sprawl out on the floor and still asleep. Robert Quinn no better. The two sport together like arse and seat, always making joke, playing prank or going off, once Quinn tell the massa of it, to Spanish Town where the women prettier and safer than Kingston women. Sometimes they take the hussy back to Montpelier and the whole household can hear the goings-on. Especially from Robert Quinn room. Between the two it was enough to make a nigger wonder if white man didn't know they born with cocky until they come to the colony.

Now Massa Humphrey different from him father who lose himself in war, or him mother who have to make do. Massa Humphrey learn to love Montpelier and that was no easy thing. For it take some time to get season by this weather. And some of the white people too hoity-toity, thinking that they can beat the West Indian sun and still wear wool when they feel like. But sooner or later this place burn the England out of an England man. Some people, like the redcoat soldiers, fight and fight and not even see that they lose from the day they dock in Montego Bay. That is England a man scratching out when him balls itch, that is England he spitting out whenever tobacco juice leave him mouth. Plenty week pass before Massa Humphrey even talk to anybody besides Robert Quinn, who then talk to everybody else. The slave-drivers didn't like that at all. Sooner take Jesus for a sodomite than take me orders from a potato eater, one of the slave-driver say as he and a few put distance between themself and Montpelier.

But two and a half months of Homer cooking lead Massa Humphrey to start ask what feast she preparing tomorrow. Massa Humphrey don't have to cross him leg when he sit out on the terrace. He light him pipe at any hour. The man break wind whenever he ready, scratch whichever part he choose and love how the heat always give him excuse to take off him clothes. Negro girls learn to blush like white woman and turn away, but truth be telling he never did too hard to look at. Him wild and curly hair get wilder and curlier. He taller than him father and him shoulders strapping and jaw strong. This massa eye did hide all sorts of mischief in sea blue and as said before, when he drop he breeches the sight never did too hard to look at.

The colony can change a man if he willing and there be things he can do here that he can't do nowhere else. Regard this, coming to a land where a man can seduce, rape or sodomise any niggerwoman or boy or girl he wish and there be nothing that nobody goin' do, for every other white man be doing the same. Picture the one place in the world where God don't judge the quick and the dead and they free to do as they please. Some white man jaw drop with outrage but sooner or later a black apple pass by and they can't resist. Negro get to understand that white man body in bondage in the mother country and when they come to the West Indies, the cocky be the first thing they set free.

Negro take heed of the case of William Clarke, who rape and strangle five negro girl but nobody arrest until he kill Worthy Park Estate most expensive slave and get lock up for destroying property, not murder. But that don't stop the white man. As for the white woman, she can only turn her eye and sip tea.

—I haven't borne witness to so much sin since Venice, Massa Humphrey say to Robert Quinn one morning at the dining-room table when only he and Quinn taking breakfast and Homer serving tea.

—And you were raised in this Gomorrah, Robby?

—Aye. As ye were, stop with yer lying now.

—Robert, I left the colony at age eight, you left at what, seventeen? So I beg to differ. And what sort of mischief does a randy lad of seventeen get into?

Robert Quinn laugh, but see Homer looking at him and quiet down. As she leave the room, both man burst into a loud dirty laugh.

—I swear, the old hag thinks she runs this estate, Massa Humphrey say.

—She probably does, I'll wager.

—You'd wager your poor mum's arse if you could. I tell you this, though. Even back when I was a young pup, she was already old.

Soon June heat was 'pon Montpelier and Massa Humphrey mother ask 'bout the season and if he not going back to England to commence courting for a wife. He say no lady of good breeding would want a rogue like him, who been living far from the motherland nigh on half a year. Him mother make he swear to not even think about marrying a Creole woman. I'd see you with a Jewess first, she say.

Massa Humphrey soon displeased with how the negrowomens skinny. He don't want nobody to think that Montpelier can't afford to feed they slaves so he give instructions to fatten them up. That be the first time plenty negro ever taste meat. Robert Quinn say to him that everybody seem to think that it was nothing for Montpelier to replace a dead slave with a fresh one so nobody bothered much with keeping slaves healthy. Quinn take out two book and show Massa Humphrey how much money waste because Wilkins and the slave-drivers was just plain wicked to nigger. So Massa Humphrey order new kind of food to fatten the niggers up.

A few months after Homer put her there Lilith forget how she get to the great house and say, I be different from them nigger bitches. Me smarter and prettier and me tired of the damn cellar.

—What a mouth 'pon you, you think it goin' save you from the Johnny-jumpers? Homer say.

After that Lilith shut her mouth and she still. She stop puff her chest out and turn her eye away. Lilith quiet herself and don't give no trouble when Homer tell her to sort out the cellar and not come up unless told to. Homer remind her that thanks to her no negro safe when they leave the house for the Johnny-jumper taking set on anybody. Lilith know the other niggers don't like her. They know she have something to do with the missing Paris and that the Johnny-jumpers lay waiting any of them. War broke out between Johnny-jumper and house slave unawares to everybody but them. Whenever a house slave have to go further than the flower house, they always travel in two or three and one of the three was either Homer or Pallas. The Johnny-jumper when they see them would raise alarm but they wasn't goin' cross Homer or Pallas, since rumour be that Pallas was allow to carry musket and Homer was capable of any mischief. Johnny-jumper wasn't safe neither. One day a young one not much older than Paris grab Homer by the hair when she walk past. She point two finger at him eye and by nightfall he got the consumption. Robert Quinn find him so useless that he put him in the boiling house. The Johnny-jumpers wasn't going stop until Homer hand Lilith over and Homer was not one for people telling her what to do. Lilith suspect that this was not because of her but because of who Homer be. But she know the other house slaves hate her. They have to. For she was thinking that if she wasn't Lilith she would hate Lilith too.

Lilith was not allow in the other part of the great house so is a long time pass before she even see the mistress. Lilith come upstairs only when Homer need one more hand in the kitchen and had to go back down before supper. Nobody talk to Lilith. She didn't mind much since nobody used to talk to her when she live at Circe either. But sometimes when it get pitch dark the cellar wall start to close in on her and the kitchen wall and all other wall, but then she would look outside and think of seven man in the dark hunting her like wild pig and then raping her seven time and shooting her seven time and leaving her to rot. She scared till she sick and stay awake all night and only fall asleep at dawn. But with dawn Lilith come up from the cellar, her head held high like she studying Homer.

—Pussy-eye gal git you arse back down for de flour, a woman say.

—You foot sick? Go get it youself, Lilith say. The woman hiss. This woman they call Andromeda and she huff and puff and snort like bull. She always smell of the stinkin' toe fruit and nobody like her.

—No baba, down deh too dawk. Need you pussy eye to light de way.

—Not when you block the light with you stinkin' black arse.

Even woman who never care much for Lilith throw down they knife to burst out laughing. Pallas lose her spoon in the pot of soup and clutch her sides. Even Homer turn away and cover her mouth. The two mens whoop and holler and rub they backside to see if it big like Andromeda. Andromeda mood get dark. Her arse broad like two woman but she move fast and slap Lilith so hard that she nearly fall back down the cellar steps. Homer shout to Andromeda to step away from the girl. The house niggers still laughing. Andromeda turn to go back to her counter when the girl snarl and leap on to the woman like wild puss. She grab

Andromeda hair and pull out clump after clump after clump. Andromeda scream and try to shake her off but the girl hold on, scratching her face and clawing into her nose and biting into her shoulder until her teeth come away with blood. They falling to the ground and the girl push Andromeda hard enough that she land face first and break a tooth. Andromeda screaming and trying to rock the girl off but the girl clutch on tight and claw Andromeda face. Two mens it take to pull her off and then only by clubbing her in the back of the head with a rolling pin. The girl roll off the woman, look at the two mens with her green eye and pass out.

· 5 ·

WHITE MAN IS WHITE MAN IS WHITE MAN, BUT NOT EVERY nigger be the same nigger. And if she just come from the ship, more so be the difference. If the negro is a Igbo or she born to a Igbo, sooner or later she goin' kill herself. If she come from or born to an Angolan, then she goin' be lazy till her dying day. If she come from or born to a Popo or Ibibio, then she goin' work hard and laugh and merry and thank God for the massa. If she be Akan, her hand working as hard as her mind plotting. But lord help you if you get an Ashanti, what the white people call Coromantee. Not even massa whip can tame she. Coromantee blood that never know slavery mix with white blood that always know freedom and race through Lilith body like brush fire. Her titty turn into young pumpkin, her hip start get broad, her leg thick and tight and she look ready to drop plenty niggerkin. She turn fifteen, unbeknownst to her, but known to Homer and a few others.

One day later the most hellish noise wake Lilith up. One of the house slaves, an old niggerwoman who couldn't do much sake of her lumbago, start screaming and pointing at Lilith, only her voice did old and almost gone so the scream sound like a dying man breath. Lilith jump when she see the old woman and clutch herself, looking all over her person for blood or something worse. Beside her mat was a bunch of twig wrap tight and bind with straw. Lilith go to touch it but the woman scream again and flee. Not long after that, Homer come, with the woman hiding behind her frock tail.

—*Sasabonsam*, she whisper.—*Sasabonsam!*

—Shush you mouth, worthless nigger. And carry up the flour me send you down here for.

—*Sasabonsam!*

—Shush you mouth before me give you something to talk 'bout!

Homer look at Lilith and at the bundle like it be something accursed that just come out of her. She circle it quiet-like, like a puss, and Lilith get to thinking that the bundle was goin' run or strike. She frighten. She whisper Homer name so weak that it vanish in the air. Like plenty colony-born nigger, Lilith didn't know 'bout the Sasabonsam, but Homer know.

Sasabonsam come straight from the Africa, not in chains but by it own free will, and make him home wherever there be the most misery. Sasabonsam live in the cotton tree and give any man him time if he have a guinea. People go to this spirit at night and tie twig together in a bundle or fish a smooth stone out of the river for the Sasabonsam to enter it with all him malcontent. The shuman, they call it. A shuman at your bed mean somebody setting evil on you, mayhaps death. Sasabonsam be the wickedest Obeah, worse than poison. Only one thing can fight it and nothing that the white man brew.

—Sasabonsam take her spirit!

—Quiet you damn mouth, old woman.

—Homer? Lilith whimper.

—Silence! The two of you. And you, woman, don't make me talk to you again. Homer take off her apron and circle the bundle. Then she throw the apron on the bundle and grab it up like is an animal that going claw it way out.

—Homer? Homer?

—The Sasabonsam 'pon you, me chile. 'Pon you it surely be.

There be a girl name Clytemnestra who the master-at-arms, a slave-driver, fuck as be him regular custom. Homer send her to the man lodging to rob a spoonful of gunpowder. Then Homer send Gorgon up to the hill with no tree and she come back with a cup of dirt from Massa Patrick Wilson grave. Homer mix the two in a glass and fill the glass with rum. All this she do in front of Lilith, her back to the girl. When she turn round, Homer holding a knife. Homer hold out for Lilith hand but the girl flinch. She step back but Homer grab her. Come chile, me don't have no time to waste, she say. Lilith struggling but Homer grab her left thumb and squeeze.

—No Homer, no.

—Better this than to be dead by Tuesday.

Lilith try to push this out of her head as soon as she hear it. She used to think that she be a young'un from the colonies who born near white people with good breeding and not no stinking Africa woman who only know the bush. But even white people whisper when they say Obeah. The blackest black magic for which there be only one cure. For if Obeah be the black, Myal be the white even though the two still black. Lilith try to pull 'way her hand and Homer slap her.

—Behave! she say.

Her hand stay on Lilith face and Lilith think to ask her right there if she be a Myal woman. Homer prick Lilith thumb and she wince. Homer stick Lilith thumb in the glass until the potion start to turn red. She pull open Lilith dress and her two titty plop out. Lilith quick to cover herself but Homer slap away the hands and mark an X on her chest with the potion. Homer turn her around and Lilith jump when the cold potion drip down her back. Homer hand Lilith the glass.

—Make haste, chile, if you ever want to get it back.

—You want me to drink this? To get back what, Homer? Get back wh…, Lilith couldn't finish, didn't want to know.

—You soul, girl pickney.

Nothing more could be done until late night. Homer bring Gorgon and Callisto down to the cellar. Gorgon scowl when she see Lilith and hiss when Homer hand her the bundle.

—Bury it by the cotton tree four miles yonder. Turn east once you pass the ratoon fields, Homer say. Gorgon and Callisto turn to go.

That same night a niggerwoman go to sleep and didn't wake up. Her entire lifeblood bleed out of her pussyhole, arsehole, earhole and nosehole. They didn't find out who till four day later, when the stink lead Massa Humphrey hounds to her door. Lilith did think the woman would be one of them house slave who don't mean her no good, but she fall down on her mat and wail when the news reach her. Homer go to shush her.

—Hush up now, me chile. Don't make backra find reason to make you cry more.

—But she was me mama. She raise me like me mama.

—Mama who send Johnny-jumper over to rape you. No, chile, you and she was never flesh, not even combolo, you know that. All the same. That bitch never take to you from the day she hold you as a baby. One big mistake to make her take you, from that very day me say it, but nobody listen to old Homer.

—Me know, me kn . . . me know she never like me but she was me mama.

—Circe couldn't mama nothing, chile. Inside that womb deader than doorpost. How she to raise life?

Lilith curl up on the mat. Homer move to go over to her, then stop, then move again. She sit on the floor and Lilith push her head in her lap while she bawl again. Homer move to touch her hair but stop. Lilith face squeeze up with bawling and she grab Homer knee.

—Hush now, me chile, hush now, Homer say.

—She say me was just a stupid nigger girl, who couldn't do nothing right. She never say a nice thing to me ever. What me do to her?

—Circe be the only nigger me know who ever try to breed. She try real hard. Hard, hard, hard, but she barren like wilderness. Mayhaps 'cause you not her blood, she sow bitterness for you. Anyhow, since you leave her hut Jack Wilkins send her back to the field. Can you imagine? After fourteen year living like free coloured and showing off 'pon nigger she end up right back among they number. She blame you for that too. Who know? But the trap she set catch her back.

—I hope she did bawl. I hope she did bawl blood.

—All right, shush now. You taking things too hard, me chile.

—She try to kill me! How the raas me must take it?

—Just shush, chile.

—Me don't need shushing! Me . . . Lilith start bawling again. After a good while of sniffling and weeping and bawling, Lilith fall asleep in Homer lap. By the time Homer leave her in the cellar, word already spread through the house and the field that Circe set Obeah on Lilith but Homer attack with Myal and make Circe own lifeblood kill her. Homer go to the door and say this to the kitchen:

—No way that Circe woman could have come all by her lonesome to this great house and go down the cellar, so somebody in this kitchen was in league with her. Same grave Circe dig she fall into and worse goin' happen if that other nigger don't set herself right. Me done talk.

Homer go back her table in the kitchen and count off banana for supper.

Nobody think to mess with Lilith after that, but that was correspondence among house nigger and didn't reach the ear of any soul outside, not even the Johnny-jumpers. A doctor come up from Spanish Town and say that Circe be the worst case of the bloody flux he ever encounter, like the devil possess her body and was trying any hole possible to burst out. Quinn didn't want her disease to spread and Homer didn't want white man to know of war between the spirits so they both get what they want, unbeknownst to Quinn. The overseer order the jumpers, who order three field negro to bury Circe under a cotton tree four mile from the estate.

After that Lilith don't trust nobody. But when night come she feel a heaviness 'pon her and she wonder if the dark was making her blacker. She find herself forgetting the Johnny-jumper face. She wonder how Homer make do with all that lonesomeness, 'cause her lonesomeness make her want to scream. Sometime she think to run outside where Johnny-jumpers may be waiting and let them do what they want, just to feel somebody wanting her for something. She wish she was a field negro for they too busy to feel lonesomeness. She come to realise that Homer be her only protector and sometimes that make her want to call her name, just to make sure she upstairs, but other time she wish she could call and nobody answer. Time come when the name Homer please and sick her. Every time she steal a glance at the skinny woman, she see Homer already looking at her. Even when Homer back turn to her Lilith still feel her looking.

Lilith hiss.

Lilith get tired of coming through the back door. She grab the mop and bucket to swab the cellar floor and fling them in a corner. Lilith throw down the petticoat that the mistress always tearing and Homer always giving her to fix. She hate sewing. She hate that Homer keep telling her to clean the cellar and the shelves that never get dust. Lilith ask Homer when she goin' be a proper house negro and clean upstairs and how come she can't serve food like the other negrowomens in the house, since none pretty or have clean fingernail like she. Homer say, Pretty gal go a river and see herself in water. Pretty gal drown when she go down to kiss herself. Lilith hiss at what Homer say, but she mark that Homer say it.

October come. This be crop time on the estate, when no field nigger sleep. Even in the cellar, Lilith hear the marching of two hundred feet in the morning and in the evening. The songs they be singing so far off that all she hear is the *uh-huh!* when they all chop at once. The crackle and crunch of the mill that run day and night and keep every light sleeper awake. Lilith was glad for the first time that she was a house slave.

One day when Homer gone to Kingston with the massa, one of the cooks say that when Homer ready, she used to go out to the goat pen and cover herself with nanny goat piss so that a ram goat would back her into a corner and rut her. Other nigger say that Homer pussy no got no hole and she buy all her pickneys. Other nigger say that Homer cho-cho tougher than wood chip. Homer used to say that the man no born yet that could handle her, so the only answer was to have no man, except when Jack Wilkins set niggermens 'pon her before she pass child breeding age and she beget a boy and a girl. The boy get sell to salt farm in Bermuda and the girl get sell to a estate in the Cockpit Country to the west.

Homer go down the cellar one night and wake Lilith up. Homer by her close and Lilith don't like it. Homer pull out something from her apron.

—You know what this be, chile?

—Me didn't born behind cow. Is book, they call it.

—You don't say. Is when since you lay eye 'pon book?

—Tantalus did…but not to touch.

—Touch it, then.

Homer hand the book to Lilith and she take it in her fingers. Lilith expecting something like a dress or a jewel box that easy to break like any other backra thing. The book hard and soft at once, the cover when she run her fingers over it feel like linen or osnaburg, but the book also hard like wood and thick. The book red like wine or blood. She never feel or smell anything like that ever. A scent like oil, or mayhaps white man armpit, or dust and something else, all of them smelling something awful apart but together make the most wonderfullest thing. Lilith close her eye and breathe in the smell like tobacco.

—Even better when you open it, Homer say.

Lilith open the book. The leaves white in the center but get browner to the edge. She shut it back quick.

—Why you bring this down here? Me not fool, you know. Me know that Robert Quinn would kill we if he see we.

—You have more sense than me did think. Why you think that be so, me chile?

—Because is white people things. Nigger not to care 'bout them things.

Homer laugh.

—Then you is a real nigger for sure. Make me tell you something and you listen good. You see this? This book? As long as you can't read this white man will have all sort of power over you.

—So when me can read chain goin' break? You is one perplexing nigger, Homer, anybody ever tell you?

—Me not nobody nigger. Learn this, when you can make out word, nothing the massa can do will surprise you. A nigger, he no got nothing. He got nothing. But when you can make out a word, that is something indeed. You know how long me know that Massa Humphrey was coming? You think 'bout that. When a nigger can read, she can plan, if is even for just a minute. Make me tell you something else 'bout reading. You see this? Every time you open this you get free. Freeness up in here and nobody even have to know you get free but you.

—If the massa find out, you dead.

—If the massa supper spoil, you dead, what be the difference?

—Me suppose to answer that?

—It name question, me chile. White man is beast either way. Nothing you can change 'bout him. But you can change plenty 'bout you. Regard that a while. You not no fool and you not common. You remember that. One of these days you goin' know what me talking 'bout.

Lilith quiet for a while. The darkness telling her nothing.

—What that book name?

—*Joseph Andrews*. Henry Fielding write it. British man.

—That don't sound like nothing.

—You just wait.

So Homer commence teaching Lilith how to read. Lilith don't know why her, but glad to have the new feeling rise in her when she see a letter shape into something when they in front of her. A cup was something that she could hold and pour tea into, but a cup was also a c-u-p and when she hold her hand steady she could write it plain for Homer to see. Homer nod her head and then show her s-a-u-c-e-r. Lilith begin to see how reading and writing work and how you can write a thing and give it to a nigger and nobody can hear what she say even if she could only write that t-h-e b-l-a-c-k c-a-t s-i-t o-n t-h-e m-a-t. Writing be silent talking and Lilith like to have something that nosy nigger can't overhear. But more so every time Lilith learn a word the cellar seem not so dark. Or mayhaps it was she who didn't seem so dark. Lilith don't know, but she feel like she enter something or she goin' somewhere that most other nigger couldn't follow.

And that Joseph Andrews. That rascal. Seems all that white man have to do is bide him time and keep him place and everywhere he trip he goin' land right between white woman legs. Black woman hard to laugh, for she must keep it secret and quiet-like for all white man suspicious of negro mirth. Homer read the book and Lilith clutch her side and try to laugh quiet and get a pain that would make her cry if she still wasn't laughing.

'I am afraid,' said Lady *Booby*, 'he is a wild young Fellow.' 'That he is,' said *Slipslop*, 'and a wicked one too. To my knowledge he games, drinks, swears and fights eternally: besides, he is horribly *indicted* to Wenching.' 'Ay!' said the Lady, 'I never heard that of him.' 'O Madam!' answered the other, 'he is so lewd a Rascal, that if your Ladyship keeps him much longer, you will not have one Virgin in your House except myself. And yet I can't conceive what the Wenches see in him, to be so foolishly fond as they are; in my Eyes, he is as ugly a Scarecrow as I ever *upheld*.'

—That wild fellow sound like Robert Quinn, Lilith say.

—Eehi? What news you have 'bout Robert Quinn?

—My ears as good at night as yours, Homer.

They both laugh.

—How you come by book learning? You is just common nigger.

—Nothing common 'bout me, chile. Or you neither.

—How you come by book learning?

—Jack Wilkins' sister, she teach me. Lord God, that be a long time ago. Every time her governess teach her two word, she find me working the house and drag me away to teach me. She even beat me like how governess beat her. But she show me how word read and how word write and me soon start teach meself.

—And the massa never know?

—No massa live here them time. Only the overseer, Jack Wilkins' papa. Him never care 'bout what him daughter do. You could have call him a good man, even. Good for a white man anyway. That girl was a wicked little bitch. But she teach me how perfume read, then how it write. P-e-r-f-u-m-e. And how one letter put next to another letter change how they sound like.

—What happen to she?

—Dead from consumption at her fifteen year. She always did sickly. Massa Jack take the death hard. He wicked like the devil after that.

Lilith still wondering why is it that Homer helping her so. Maybe she feel sorry over that matter with Circe but that was a long time ago. Homer come in the dark to teach her to read but she look at her too long. And she keep wiping things off Lilith face, even sweat. And touching her face and giving her extra osnaburg cloth for monthly blood and tea for when them days get heavy. And talking to her 'bout how she must take care of herself because she busting out of her dress. And talking to her like she be a young'un. Lilith start to wonder what Homer desire.

One day right before evening start creep up, Lilith in the open kitchen stirring the pumpkin soup. Every house negro in the kitchen, 'cause the mother still have little sense about her and she begin to send out invitation to the Montpelier Estate New Year's Eve ball. The mother head not so bad when she have something to do. Is when she idle that the devil fly up in her. Two day before, she and Homer gone to Kingston to buy pretty things to string up in the ballroom. Plenty green ribbon and bow string up on the ceiling and hang down so low that they brush the head. On the walls more candle alight and plenty angel that make out of paper hang up in between the paintings of dead people. The mother excited.

So everybody in the kitchen wondering what they goin' be called to do when Homer rush in.

—Lilith, go downstairs, she say.

—To go do what? Everybody else up here cooking.

—Me say to go downstairs. We need more potato.

—One whole sack full right there in the corner.

—Don't backtalk me, negro girl.

—Me will backtalk and front talk you, negro. Every minute you send me go downstairs, what me look like, house rat?

—With them eye, more like a house puss, say one of the man.

—Must be combolo you be looking, pussyhole, Lilith said.

—Lilith! Go downstairs! Now!

—No.

—Me say—

—And me say no. What part of no you not be understanding, the n or the o?

—Jesus Christ, negro girl!

—Is what you talking 'bout, pussy-eye, what is En and what is Oh?

—Everybody shut up you goddamn mouth! say Homer.—Lilith, don't make me tell you again.

Homer push Lilith and she nearly stumble down the stairs. Lilith stay on the third step and look out. The mistress come in the kitchen before anybody could say anything. Her wig didn't fix right.

—Homer, I'm sure you're aware what season it is. Why have I not seen your sorry lot? There are fittings to be done, surely, the way I've been fattening the lot of you.

Homer look at the niggers in the kitchen and shout, Stand up, stand up, make the mistress see you! Everybody stand up and line up in front of the mistress, who walk from first to last and back again. The scowl never leave her face.

—I don't like the look of any, I'll tell you that much. The women in particular get lankier by the year. Good-bye to good china, I'll be saying after this. Homer, I could have sworn you had a new girl in the cellar these past months.

—A new girl, mistress?

—Yes, Homer. Contrary to popular belief, I do know all that goes on in my own house, I daresay this entire plantation. You've made this mistake before, Homer, do you recall?

—Me recall it plenty fine, ma'am.

—Wonderful. I'm sure your back recalls it quite vividly. Now, where is this new girl?

Lilith leap in front of the two womens with no help from Homer.
—Why, yes. Yes. She'll have to do, the mistress say without looking at her.

—She clumsy, mistress. She goin' break the china.

—Me not clumsy. Me young.

—And spirited. Perhaps too spirited. Homer, make sure she is cleaned up. I'll have none of those horrid niggerwoman stenches. I want her hair combed, her back scrubbed, her fingernails cleaned and her uniform fitted. Any hint of lice and I'll have both of you flogged within inches of your lives.

—Yes, mistress. I be doing it, mistress.

—That settles that, the mistress say and leave.

—Yes, mistress, I be doing it, mistress, Lilith say and curtsy and laugh at Homer. Homer go over and slap her cheek so hard that the little girl stagger and nearly drop. The girl get up to jump her but Homer look at her dead straight and say, Try it, you little bitch, just you try it. Lilith run downstairs crying. Everybody watching Homer as her straighten her frock, raise her chin high and go to her room.

· 6 ·

LILITH HATING THE DARKNESS BECAUSE IT NOT DARK NO more. In the dark she seeing things, like a swinging noose or a head exploding like a drop pumpkin. Lilith down in the cellar half asleep. But she can't remember the Johnny-jumper face. She can't remember if a black pot had green tea boiling or a green pot had black tea boiling. She can't remember if he scream once or plenty or if that scream different from any other scream she hear on a sugar plantation. But she seeing things.

She running wild in the ratoon fields. She can feel every footstep and her titty not so big that they jerk and hurt her. She running too far. Ratoon field be nothing but last year chopped cane that leave to grow back by it lonesome. Lilith run to the end and pull two stalk apart to see the new fields. A niggerwoman on her knees, shaking and blubbering. Her face swell and cut up and wash with so much blood that she drip red. She begging with a cry for the woman got no words. One of her eye shut. The white man standing with him legs apart, hip thrust forward, shoulder hunch and neck stuck out. He put the bottle to him head and drink again, him long yellow hair blocking him eyes. He rub the bottle 'gainst the nigger cheek and nudge her hard. The nigger put the white man cocky back in her mouth. The white man swig the bottle again as the nigger suck him. Lilith watchin' the white man thrust himself in the nigger mouth as the nigger suck in her cheeks. Then the white man start groan and make a big fuss and grab the nigger by the head before she can spit him out. Lilith can smell the struggle. The white man make one last groan and release the nigger, who grab her throat and spit and spit and spit. The overseer clobber that nigger and she fall back flat in the dirt. Then he whip out a musket. Lilith jump when he fire and the sudden gunpowder make her cough. The white man look around sudden, but the liquor almost make him drop. Lilith push back quick into the bush but look at the white man drunkenness and feel the sun on her skin and wonder about a man that can drink or carry on as he please. The man shove him cocky back in him breeches.

—What the blazes are ye up to, McClusky? a white voice say some distance away.

—Found meself a runaway, yes I did, the man say.

—Oh, for fook's sake, ye didn't shoot 'er, did ye? the voice say.

—Well, the bitch shouldn' 'ave tried ta run again, innit? the man say.

Lilith look at the dead nigger once and shudder, but beyond that nothing. She don't have green eye. She not no sister and she not no mother. Lilith say that over and over until her mouth whisper it. She watch the woman turn into nigger, then animal, then dirt, then nothing. Crow food. She look up and follow the sway of the white man, him hair flowing and him loose shirt lapping and her head swinging as him body swinging until he disappear in the field. She cock her finger and aim at the dirt.

—Pow. Pow, she say.

—Is nigger you shooting or whitey? Homer say and Lilith jump.

—Me didn't see you coming.

—Not much anybody can see in the dark. Other than what they either fearin' or wanting. Which be you?

—What you want?

—Follow me directly, Homer say.

Lilith not listening to her, and answer with a loud hiss.

—Come chile, make haste. We don't have much time, Homer say.

—Time for what? the girl bawl out, knowing where Homer is in the dark and looking elsewhere.

Homer say time to make the difference between smart and fool, strong or weak, living or dead. Lilith not understanding.

—Which one you want to be, girl chile? Dead or living? Homer ask.

Lilith say she not ready to dead yet 'cause she don't know where dead people go. Same place they was goin' when them living, Homer say. Homer climb up the stairs. Lilith wait like she pondering and decide to follow.

The sky wearing black.

—Stop the dilly-dallying, negro girl, Homer say and Lilith have to run to catch up to Homer as she disappear in the cane field. Homer didn't have no lamp but move through the cane field like is daylight. Lilith 'fraid that she will step on a rat or yellow snake.

Homer gone ahead of her. Lilith running soft like a goat thief, she barely seeing Homer ahead and could swear that Homer legs not stepping, but she gliding over the ground like a duppy. This would be just what she was expecting from a Myal woman and Homer did scowl when Lilith ask if she be one. She wondering if the black witch cooking up a new trick. Lilith walking and walking faster and faster until she realise that she running to keep up. Homer and the night is friend, Lilith know. She near out of breath now, but Homer still moving quick through the cane field. Lilith wondering how the hell a old woman can run so fast. The cane stalks lookin' like they bend out of the way before she pass. Lilith 'fraid. She run harder.

Then Homer disappear. Lilith think to scream, but know that if a white man hear a negro this time of night is a full day's whipping coming for sure, if they don't shoot her first. And even that not as awful as the Johnny-jumpers. Lilith shudder and cuss and shudder and cuss and cuss some more. Johnny-jumpers. Homer leave her loose in the field for a Johnny to jump her. She cuss herself that she didn't see this coming. If she was Homer she would turn her over too. This wild girl who take to attacking house nigger, this bad nigger who kill Johnny-jumper who did just want what all man want and will get one way or the other. Because of her there be war between Johnny-jumper and house nigger. Now it look like Homer turn her over and maybe that is best for everybody. But not she. Damn that bitch. Damn that lemongrass-smelling cunt all the way to hell. She wish she could remember what that Johnny-jumper boy look like.

Lilith crouch down in the cane piece, thinking that if she can bide her time till the morning hour at least she will know where to run. Then she look around. Just about every nigger know that sometimes the most wretched thing about being a field slave is the field itself. In the field a rat would bite you toe and in a fortnight the whole leg have to go. In the night a leaf is a blade, a stalk will whip you in the face and who knows what kind of man hide in the bush. And that was only the half. There was other things nigger fear in the field that have nothing to do with flesh. Rolling calf that come up from hellfire to take people back and Imilozi bush spirits that run ten pace behind a nigger, waiting for he to err and look back. Duppy, especially of that girl they burn in 1785. Lilith hear a creak and think of snakes crawling all over her body and strangling her like a rat. She would have to bear till morning. Lilith run back where she think she come from. She run back to the left and the bush swallow her up. Lilith see nothing but dark, not a darkness like sky or like the cellar, but a dark with prickly thing to scratch her. She run further, not knowing where she going but running until that be the only thing she could think of. Then she see a light. A little twinkle far off lead her to the cave.

The cave was just a hole in a hill that she barely climb through, but once inside it wide like a white woman closet. Lilith think maybe she under the same hill where they bury the old massa, but couldn't tell for sure. Plus there was no way she did run so far, that would be near seven mile. There be nothing to see, so she go by hearing and touching. The cold rock inside, the soft bush underfoot, the branch sticking out, then the sticky mud, then the sharp stones. She follow a smell that unlike the others, not musty or old or sour. Mint and lemongrass.

—Lookee here now. Girly sniff out the house for sheself. What more proof you need, the lot o' you? somebody say. Lilith hear the voice coming from further and it frighten her a little, but that was where the light be. Lilith foot start scratch her and she brush away the ants and cuss.

—You think you on excursion, chile? Get you backside in here, say a voice coming from the light. Homer.

—Why yuh bring 'er yah me want to know, say another voice, hoarse and scratchy like is an old tree whispering. The voice belong to a woman that Lilith hear before. Up in the kitchen warning Homer about Jack Wilkins, but before that in Circe hut. She almost a midget but without the big head. In the night her skin blacker but her eyes almost glow in the dark. Green like her own. Gorgon, the woman with the cart who ride off with the dead Johnny-jumper who face Lilith couldn't remember. Lilith step in to where the womens be.

—Nobody bring her here. Girly find the way herself, don't it? Pallas say.

Lilith see Pallas smile but look away quick when she see one of the women back away into the shadow of the cave, a tall, skinny one who swing like willow tree. She plait her long stiff hair in five and they stick out like branch from her head.

—Ah, de devil bring her 'ere, dat me know, Pallas.

—Devil is white man business, Gorgon. The girl would never find this place if she didn't have special eye to look. Don't it, Homer?

Homer come of a dark corner.

—Almost. Nothing special in the eye, but in the woman herself.

Nothing but good common sense. Something lost to most nigger, Homer say.

As soon as she see Homer she see all the womens. The cave they treat like a room, with a table in the middle and a candle on top. Three chairs be round the table, all different, including the red armchair she remember from Circe hut. The other womens sit on a rock or stand. Lilith couldn't make out the light, that brighten what it want to brighten and darken what it want to darken and she wonder if that too be Homer doing. When Lilith look up she see six womens all looking at her. Bantam-size Gorgon, who scratch her hair and frown; Hippolyta with the tree-branch hair, the tallest and skinniest, who remain standing in a dark corner; Iphigenia, who Lilith remember cursing Circe for taking her man once. Lilith smile but Iphigenia didn't smile back. Iphigenia face wide like crocodile and lips thick like molasses and she wearing a neck scarf and red dress long in the sleeve, like she expectin' cold air. Pallas in the cave without her headwrap and her hair straight and red like white woman. Beside her be Callisto, whose hair pull back and tie in one and who have a patch over her right eye like a pirate. Moving in and out of the dark but not sitting down was Homer.

—The chile find the way with her own inside map. That settle the matter, Homer say and press her two thin lip together like that is the final thing to say.

—Unu bloodcloth! Dat don't settle nothing! Gorgon say.—Me surer 'bout de devil dan me sure 'bout she.

Homer stop moving and look straight at Gorgon. Gorgon look straight back but then turn away. Homer look at Lilith. She seem to smile but Lilith couldn't tell for sure.

—Not even massa dog can find this place, but she find it, Homer say.

—Fuckery. You lead her half de way, knowing you, say Gorgon.

Homer look at Lilith.—Olokun give her new sight, she say.

In the candlelight Homer pick up a darkness that make her look different from before. Lilith think right there that if she cut Homer, black oil would pour out, not blood.

—Johnny-jumper, they after me.

—Johnny-jumper too busy right now taking woman without permission. They don't know these parts, chile, Homer say.

—Me know what me hear.

—Den go back out dere and look see, Gorgon say.

—Lord God, Gorgon, shut up, Callisto say. Callisto more interested in the knife in her hand. She put the point on her finger and it stay up straight.

—She find the place herself. That fine enough for me. Now stop wasting me time, Callisto say. Callisto have the kind of face that look like it chop out of wood, sharp with plenty corner. Gorgon gulp every time Callisto say anything to her.

Nobody look like no slave. Nobody slouch, nobody looking down at the ground, nobody wrapping her arms up to make themself smaller, and nobody hiding save for Hippolyta. Lilith feel herself straightening up. She try to look at the woman in front of her but that was Callisto so she look away.

—The opening not suffering from lonesomeness, Lilith, you can leave it be, Homer say.

Lilith step inside some more. Is then she see something that she didn't see before, something the light was hiding, not showing. All the womens, everybody from short, fat Gorgon to tall, meager Hippolyta have something in common but not quite. One or two have hair that not kinky, and one or two have hair like wool. Two or three have light mulatto skin, but one or two have the same wide lip. One or two tall like a tree but all sit and walk the same way. And the one called Hippolyta, when she finally step out of the dark, have green eye, just like Lilith and Gorgon. Lilith feel trembling come over her like they just dip her in a night stream.

—These womens be your sister, chile, Homer say.

Lilith regard them for a long time. Then she burst out a laugh.

—You all mad, she say.

Iphigenia and Gorgon laugh.—Circe? She think that dead cunt woman is her mammy? Iphigenia say, laughing so hard that she grab her scarf quick and push it up on her neck. Her voice and her laugh seem to come out of some dark hole, Lilith think. Iphigenia smile so wide that is like a sword slice her face halfway. It frighten her little bit, like Callisto eye patch and Hippolyta face in the shadow.

—She already know 'bout Circe, Homer say.

—And she still think Tantalus be her pappy? Eh-eh! That mad nigger can't even fuck off, much less fuck pussy, Iphigenia say.

—You and you mouth! But is true, Lilith. There be no field that Tantalus can water, Homer say. Lilith squeeze her knuckles tight. Gorgon laugh harder.

—Me give you joke, midget?

—Who de bloodcloth yuh a-call midget! No make me—

—Gorgon! Callisto say.—And you, shut you ass before me shut it good and proper. Go on, Homer, Callisto say. Homer still in the back with lightness and darkness flowing over her face. Lilith look around for the candle just to make sure.

—Tantalus balls cut off ever since they catch him playing with himself while peeping at the mistress. Long before you born. No way that nigger be your daddy.

—Lying witch, you out to cross me from me did born.

—But coo yah! Look 'pon you too. What little mouse have that big rat want? If you want, we can go out to where they tie him up and spread him legs apart, right now we can go. He old and nothing goin' wake him. Well? Come make we go, chile. You say you don't believe me. Uh-huh. You must listen when me talking to you. You didn't think it queer-like that you eye green? You who love look in silver tray at youself—oh yes, you think me never see you loving how you think you look. Where you think them green eye come from?

—Tell me.

—What you seeing should have tell you by now. Jack Wilkins, chile. He be you father. Jack Wilkins the overseer.

—You stink like shit.

—Me say Jack Wilkins be you papa. Don't go on like you never think so yourself. Jack Wilkins take you mama, as be the custom, just like he do the mama of every woman here. Every woman you see in this room come from Jack Wilkins seed. Every woman and you.

—You don't have green eye.

—Me from before that time. Plus no man can handle me, not even white man.

—Is not that people say.

—And how you would know? Who talk to you?

Lilith silent. Homer go to say something but stop.

—You want me to believe—

—Chile, you don't have nothing that me want.

—But Homer, don't we ... Pallas whisper.

—We don't want nothing from you. We be here to give you something. The first be the truth. Tantalus not your daddy, 'cause Tantalus can't be nobody daddy. That be Jack Wilkins. And that woman who suckle you was not your mama neither.

—Why you hate me so? Me never do nothing to you.

—Is so negro life easy that me have time to hate gal like you? Cut the damn foolishness, chile, we don't have much time left.

—Time for what?

—Me already tell you. Time to know what true and what lie, time to decide if you want to be slave or—

—Free? Oh. Me see now.

Lilith start to walk among the women. Looking at some, but not

Callisto.—First me did think unu was just some Myal woman fighting 'gainst Obeah. But the whole of you is some madwoman looking for young girl. All of you mad.

—Make she galang, Homer. Even if dat bitch Circe didn't breed her, she be more like her now, say Gorgon.

—Me not nothing like she, Lilith say.

—Eehi, Gorgon say and hiss.

Gorgon waiting for Homer to send her away. Lilith thinking now that she want to stay just to spite Gorgon, who too short to be 'fraid of, unlike Callisto. But she don't like how Homer talking and how she looking dark one blink, light the next.

—Freedom comin' before next Easter, Homer say.

—What?

—You hear what me say.

—Obeah woman tell you that?

—True is a true be.

—You either lie or you fool. Massa not 'bout to give no nigger free paper.

—Who say nothing 'bout the massa, chile? We not getting free, we taking free, Homer say.

Pallas, looking at Lilith, say, Homer, you sure 'bout telli—

—What she goin' do? Tell her new friendy the mistress? Mistress know you kill Johnny-jumper too? If it was up to she, that mistress would make all of them rape you and sell the young'un.

—You, you jus' wicked 'cause me be sixteen and the mistress favourite.

—Oh. Is that you making arrangement for, Homer say and Pallas and Callisto laugh while Gorgon hiss.—You the only one who don't know say the mistress head take her all the time? You think 'cause she throwing party the devil don't gone with her good sense?

—She look plenty sensible to me.

—Girly if you don't know that not everything be how it look, then you not ready, Pallas say.

—Homer, is long time Circe be poisonin' de bitch mind, you can't trust—

—Me have as much sense as you, nigger. Me find you cave and me can show the mistress where all of you plotting.

All of a sudden, the only sound in the room was the candle flicking. Every woman in the room look 'pon Lilith. Gorgon get up. Callisto hold up her knife by the blade and look at Lilith. Even Hippolyta come out of the shadow. Lilith gasp.

—Me can fling this knife between a wild boar eye at seventy pace, Callisto say.

—I, I, I can run.

—You, you, you can try.

Lilith smart mouth run out of smart.

—Ju-just 'cause all of we come from Massa Jack don't mean me and you be combolo.

—Listen to youself, you stupid chile, Homer say.—You think you and white woman goin' be friend? You think she goin' make tea and cucumber sandwich and invite you to sit? Don't tell me say me make big mistake and think you have sense. And you is fifteen, not sixteen.

Homer move towards Lilith. Lilith step back. Callisto get up too, still holding her knife by the blade. Lilith grab her neck and step backways slow.

—We goin' have to deal with her like Circe, Callisto say.

—Everybody quiet! Homer say.

—Callisto, the girly don't know no better. Leave her be, Pallas say.

—Me, me don't need nobody lookin' after me, Lilith say, stepping backways still.

—Not you I was looking after, Pallas say.

—Enough! Homer say.—We losing the night. Now listen to me, chile, listen to me good now. Things not be as they be, not as you see. And soon things goin' be hellfire worse, 'specially for the backra. There be things you must know, things that will put you over other negro and even the backra themself. You can feel it already. That thing in here. Homer point to her chest and almost touch Lilith nipple. Lilith step back.

—That thing make you spirited, even the mistress call you that. But spirit can't work when you no have no sense—

—Me have plenty sen—

—Quiet when me talking! Is this same spirit you not checking that make you backtalk you betters. Me be here long, chile, and trust me, you not the first nigger who couldn't control her mouth. Some gal think that whatever mouth throw, pussy was goin' catch. Then they get shoot like old horse. Watch youself.

—Why bother watch meself? You watch me plenty already. Morning, noon and night you in me business. Now you all coming down to the cellar, 'bout you teaching me to read. You must really be a sodomite.

Homer look at her hard. The other womens look at Homer.

—You hate me, you hate me just 'cause me soon be mistress favourite, Lilith say.—She pick me, even when you try to frig it up, she pick me. The mistress think me better to show off than you, so me no want to turn into you is if that you offering. Me hear you piss through you ears now that way down there shrivel up.

Callisto hold up the knife, but Homer wave her down.

—Yeah, yeah, calm down the dog, say Lilith.

—What you think this is, stupid negro chile, play-play? say Homer.—You think you is the mistress favourite new dolly? Me see prettier than you get kill 'cause the tea too hot, one more dumb bitch who think she and mistress be combolo.

—Y'all hate me because she think me pretty. You is just like Circe and me done with nigger like you. Me step me way out of Circe hut and me no done step.

—Step you way? Don't you mean chop you way? Pallas say.

—Go suck you mama, Lilith say.

Pallas dress fly up quick like a big black sun. When the dress fall back down there be the woman with a musket pointing straight at Lilith face. She nearly scream.

—Girly, certain talk I don't take from nigger, Pallas say and the musket click.

—Pallas, Homer say.

Pallas stick the gun on Lilith forehead. Lilith push herself straight into the rock.

—We only need six, Homer. That is what you same one tell me. Six tell six tell six. Seven just goin' curse we.

—Bloodcloth true. You same one say so, Homer, Iphigenia say.—Six nigger tell six nigger tell six nigger. Seven nigger? That is like six finger, or three nipple or two cocky. One alone bad enough.

Everybody laugh but Pallas, who eye and musket still on Lilith.

—Massa Jack give me this. Believe it? Then the sum'bitch only give me one bullet, Pallas say. She right in front of Lilith face. Lilith turn away.

—Pallas.

—But methinks that only mean that whoever me shoot, me better don't miss.

—Pallas!

—What! What, Homer? We did deal with that last bitch for less than what this one just say.

—She young and she fool.

—Me not—

—Me'd watch it before this musket fuck up me mouth if me was you. See it there now, she have me talking like Iphigenia.

The womens laugh. Callisto say, Pallas, you know if you fire you goin' have to tell why.

Pallas shove the gun back in her stocking. Lilith hope they think is sweat running down her cheek.

—Me gone, Lilith say.

Iphigenia laugh and say, Then Pallas right. You too fool. You better go practise you pussy with some plantain tonight for Johnny-jumper goin' fuck you till you fool.

—The mistress pick me, so me not going back to the field.

—The mistress do what me tell her, Homer say.

—She be the nigger and you be the backra. Me gone.

—And where you going? Homer ask.

—Me no have to tell you nothing, say Lilith. So keep you woman secret and you woman loving to youself. Me no forget how you slap me, she say to Homer.

—God strike me down dead if worse don't happen to you sake of that mouth. Now get out. Get out!

The cave tremble. The womens all stand and they don't look like womens no more. Lilith back away through the cave and stumble. Then she run.

· 7 ·

TANTALUS THE MAD NIGGER RUN AWAY. NOBODY KNOW HOW that sore foot, bad back, mad-as-hell bastard free himself from the rope, considering Robert Quinn retie it himself with a knot he learn while sailing for His Majesty. Tantalus' hair near totally white and years of bad living throw a hump in him back that stay there. Everybody think he was goin' mad again but he did have this thing that Robert Quinn call method to it.

Lilith say out loud that she hope they catch him 'cause she don't understand why anybody would want to run away from people as nice as the mistress. But as soon as she go down to the cellar, she be a different story. Truth be told, only Tantalus ever pay her any mind. He used to show her him most precious thing, a page tear out from a white girl storybook with picture and word. The page had a girl who mayhaps be a queen or princess sleeping in a big bed and a white boy standing over her who mayhaps be a king or prince or duke or any hoity-toity white man. The white boy look at the white girl like she be the beautifullest, preciousest thing. Almost every night, Tantalus would take out the picture and make up a fresh story about it, a new one every night. And when Lilith finally thief the picture so that she can make up story in the daytime, Tantalus never say nothing. Lilith tell herself these days that word is wind that passeth by, and he get what he deserve. That mad nigger was not her father. Not at all. Jack Wilkins be her daddy now.

—Ah goin' ask Massa Wilkins if you talking true, Lilith say couple morning later in the kitchen when only she and Homer up.

—Suit yourself. If you feel you must ask the sky why she blue, me not goin' stop you.

—Talk straight, woman.

—You seem to be thinking lately that me and you is same size. You don't think it uncanny that in slave life you be the only nigger who live in house with mama and papa? Even man and woman who soft for each other can't live together, for they know how things go.

—How you mean?

—Look beyond you mirror, chile. This be Montpelier. It no matter who you be, nigger is nigger and any day you could get whip, kill or sell. Just like that. Only thing sure in nigger life is that nothing sure. Nothing but you. Which other pickney you know did have mama and papa in they house? When you ever see Circe or Tantalus work?

—Why that be?

—Now you be the one who want to chat with you papa? Go ask him.

Massa Humphrey did bring him hunting ways to Jamaica but couldn't find nothing smelling of that mad nigger since Circe did done burn all of him clothes and him was naked most of the time. The hounds runs all over the estate and attack anybody who stink with cane work—plenty nigger and even a driver who say he couldn't remember when last he take a bath. Robert Quinn say Tantalus be an old worthless nigger so let him go, but Massa Humphrey say an example must be made in Montpelier. He go to send for the militia but nobody need militia when you got the Maroons.

Every nigger done know of the Maroons. Before they sign treaty with the king to end all the warring 'gainst white man, they was the greatest scourge backra ever face. The first Maroons was slaves let loose by the Spanish back when the British invade and take the island over. Them niggers run all the way up into the mountains and deep in the bush and no white man could reach them, but they could reach any backra they choose. Word was that they was four Maroon town in the colony, including one run by a niggerwoman ugly as Ol' Hige herself. At night they raid any estate, even Montpelier back in them early days before Homer born. They take pig, goat, corn and woman, but many womens leave by they own free will and plenty mens too. Soon it be the wisdom that any nigger who want to be free should wait for the night and set for the hills.

White man couldn't beat no Maroon. They fight and they war but Maroon could become ground, air or bush if he wish. Green as leaf or black like midnight. One hundred militia go into the hills, less than thirty was coming back. The Maroon trick be to get the infantry to pass through a passage so narrow that they can only go one by one. Then they pick them off. Who know why then in 1738, Cudjoe, the big leader, who did really small and hunchback, sign treaty with the king. Word was that some Maroon village was starving after white man burn down they provision grounds but nobody know for sure. What every nigger done know was that after the treaty, the Maroon, the slave sworn friend, become him sworn enemy. The backra pay two pounds for every captured nigger but most time Maroon done hunt and send back niggers even for free. A nigger who choose to run 'way to freedom now face a new enemy who breathe like he breathe and look like he look. One slave who run from Montpelier back in the days of Jack Wilkins talk 'bout how they fly through the bush and crawl 'pon the ground and lock him neck in chains before he make it to the river. They talk like they still in the Africa, like nigger who come from ship, and they knock him out when he beg and plead and bawl for them to not send him back. Maroon even side with whitey when estate explode in rebellion, taking they guns to catch and shoot nigger.

Tantalus get as far as the coconut fields seven mile from Montpelier when three Maroon catch him. Everybody in fear and trembling at the sight of them three strapping nigger from the bush, two with gun, one with machete, as they drag Tantalus with a rope tie round him hands and neck. One Maroon with hair down him shoulder was wearing breeches, the other pantaloon that tear off at the knee and the third one didn't wear no clothes at all. He have machete in one hand and spear in the other. Is like the whole estate stop when them Maroons come back with Tantalus and wouldn't leave until a slave-driver tell Quinn that they waiting for they two pounds. Quinn cuss when he see the other two hold out they hands for two pounds each.

Tantalus old and at first we think they was goin' show mercy. Three Johnny-jumper tie up Tantalus good and Tantalus start whimper and ask for Jesus to intervene. Everybody expecting Robert Quinn to come with a new whip, but the whole estate shudder when they see he come with an axe. Robert Quinn wave he hand and the niggers pull out Tantalus right foot and use plaster to draw a white line across all the toe. Two hold Tantalus foot while he scream and fight and one grip the axe with two hand and swing.

Homer see Lilith in the kitchen. She say, Worse thing him could ever do was run away. Better he kill another nigger than run away. You feel sorry for the man who raise you?

—No, me don't feel sorry, and he weren't no man, Lilith say.

But then something mighty peculiar happen.

As soon as they chop off Tantalus' toe him madness leave. He still huff and puff and bawl in a fever, but people understand him this time and some chuckle while others tremble at what he say. But the mistress' madness come back. Or maybe it was just old womanness, people start to reckon. Nobody live too long in the colonies and mayhaps that was not a bad thing. But nobody know what to do because is twelve weeks to the ball and the mistress take to talking to her husband in her bed-room. Mark this word: When the mistress head take her, she be some-thing else. Most of the niggers in spite of the madness come to like that something else. When she mad she don't have no sense but she also don't have no care and do what she want. She do her business in a bon-net that a man she didn't like give to her. And her mouth! When she mad she say what her unthinking mind think and plenty time it funny, like negro love.

—Why would I ever be caught dead at Coulibre with Mr. Roget and that slattern second wife of his? She's a Frenchwoman in every base sense of the word, the mistress say one day when she get another invitation to a ball.—I swear the cur carries ahead and behind her a fishy fetor! The mistress say this about the father priest who come pray for her—Pray for your own damn soul, you eunuch! Face's fatter than a pig's arse.

Other times, the mistress say that good-for-nothing son of hers bet-ter get married soon or even she is goin' to start pronouncing him a sodomite. White woman madness sound like black woman sense and the house slaves find her more agreeable to live with, even though the trouble was more than a handful. But the ball was goin' to hell and Massa Humphrey huff and puff 'cause he didn't want to take part in arranging nothing.

—And what in blazes are we supposed to do? Massa Humphrey say in the kitchen, couple days after the mistress' head take her again. Is morn-ing and he in the kitchen talking to Homer while Robert Quinn drink-ing tea. Homer dismiss the other negroes for a spell, for she don't want nobody hearing white people affairs. But Lilith, who was down in the cellar, didn't get the warning. She climb up the steps but stop when she hear a voice that she never hear up close. Massa Humphrey. She see him plenty time from far but never look at him before. She look at him hair blaze. She lick her bottom lip until it soft, and touch her hair. Lilith look at him as he pace from one end of the kitchen to the next and she rip the breeches off him legs and watch him pacing again. Lilith regarding the massa like she never regard a man before. She don't know what be the different, if he suddenly get new looks or she suddenly get new eye. She looking at a man who might be a prince or a king, not just a massa. She watch him turn again and stomp up the kitchen like bull. She listen how he voice rise and fall and laugh at Robert Quinn and cuss at Homer. She watch him and try to match them words with them pink lips.

There be two things that a white man can do at once. A white man can save her from the Johnny-jumpers and put her above other negro-womens. A white man like Massa Humphrey can also take her and hold her with the gentle hand that niggerman don't got and bury him head in her bosom and make him man sound and it wouldn't be like what she hear coming from Circe hut. Whatever Circe do for tuppence she would be doing something as different as dawn be from dusk. A white man can be a prince or a lord, and whether in the bed or by the pen can free a niggerwoman. This she know because she be a woman now. But there be what she don't know and would never say, why she need him to look at her but feel to run when he do, why she need him to say something but not to her, and why when Robert Quinn interrupting him, that bastard don't know him place. Why when breeze blow through him hair she feel hot and why when he smile at a good working nigger she feel hate for that one so bad she could scratch her eyes out. She don't understand why big woman sense also mix with folly and can't ask Homer. She watch the massa shiny boots and him breeches and the green waistcoat with flower trim. After that Lilith make every effort to see him, and that was not difficult.

Lilith catch glimpse of Massa Humphrey in the evening as he ride out to see the sunset. Sometimes he and Robert Quinn would come home at dawn, before even Homer wake up, and both mens reeking of rum and whiskey and tobacco and man-stink. Lilith would run between the two as they ignore her and put a kettle on the stove and make tea.

—Toss it all, my memory is as bad as my mum's, lately. Have I fucked this one? Massa Humphrey say one morning.

—Nay, I can't say ye have, Quinn say, and both think it so funny that they laugh till they cough. Massa Humphrey push back the chair and lose him balance and fall back to a crash on the floor and both mens laugh even harder. But that same day he back to him surly self, cussing Homer over the ball plans and wondering why he making a nigger plan his ball and not even once looking in Lilith direction. She bite her bottom lip and swing her hip and walk but when Lilith look up he not looking. That make her want to cease but it also make her want to go on. If only she could say something un-niggerlike. Uncommon. Like a lady of good breeding and learning. A woman who have quality that a dirty hussy like Circe never have. Something Homer would know if her bosom was of any use to a man.

Lilith tell herself that she not no foolish nigger. She know what being the massa favourite mean in real speak. She know that a nigger who not uncommon should think and plot. But she also see him hair blaze afire and she remember a white boy on a page tear from a book and everything come together and make her mind burn. Lilith hoping every day that just once he recognise her as the slave who make him tea whichever morning he come in from carousing. One afternoon Massa Humphrey make a trip to the kitchen huffing and puffing. Everything stop. Right behind him was Robert Quinn eating a banana.

—Goddamn if I won't see some British decency in this house, even if it's only tea at four, Massa Humphrey say.

—Then I's best be about fixing it, massa, Homer say.

—No, let her do it. The girl in the cellar. Her teas are particularly robust, if I remember. Not so, Quinn?

—Robust indeed, Robert Quinn say.

Lilith didn't look at the face she know Homer giving her.

THE NEXT MORNING, LILITH WAS IN THE CELLAR BRUSHING cobweb from a silver tray. The kitchen still dark as if no sun was coming. She look at herself and know that she never come 'cross no other woman with her colour eye save for Gorgon and Hippolyta, and they both ugly. She start to believe that Jack Wilkins really be her daddy and the road set before her was going to wind a different way than most nigger. That make her walk straighter. Three time she ask Homer 'bout her real mother and three time Homer go quiet. She wonder if her mother be like her, but without the green eye, of course. She wonder if she was short or tall or fat, or if she get kilt 'cause her spirit wouldn't dim like lamp. All she learn from Homer is that her mama dead the same time she born and that make Lilith feel bad. Mayhaps she was Jack Wilkins' chère amie and he did hold her soft while she dead.

Lilith have more question inside her heart, a dozen question all beginning with why, that she don't ask nobody. Plus she too 'fraid to ask Jack Wilkins and word was that him mind not be the same since he lose the overseer work. The only other soul who might know a thing or two be Tantalus the mad nigger, who was part of this arrangement too. She try to arrange her thinking. Jack Wilkins fuck her mother, her mother get heavy with niggerkin and dead giving birth. Jack Wilkins pass the baby on to Circe for mothering and put her to live with Tantalus for fathering. That don't make no sense and Lilith cuss. From down in the cellar Lilith hear something smash from upstairs, most likely the mistress' room. She smashing her Wedgwood china again. Mayhaps old age drive everybody mad at Montpelier. Mayhaps madness be the only thing that afflict white man and nigger alike.

—Lilith, potato waiting on you, Homer shout from the kitchen.

—Hoity-toity nigger deh 'pon the evening shift, say Andromeda. Lilith don't have nothing to say. Even Homer did turn around, waiting for Lilith smart mouth. But Lilith go over to her corner and sit down and peel potato with her back to everybody. That be near enough to throw the kitchen into 'ruption. Lilith smart mouth for all her rudeness did now become part of the house nigger morning rhythm and slave need a rhythm to carry through the day.

—Jesus Christ, is who break wind in here? Pallas say and look straight at Chiron.

—Me can't even break egg, he say.

—Smell like you just crack a rotten one with you arse, Pallas say and everybody laugh except Lilith. The laughing bring back the morning and lock Lilith out.

Lilith spirited from the day she first play with the other pickneys and call herself princess. This was Tantalus' fault for he used to show her the page from the backra storybook whenever she behave like a good little girl. She didn't know her head was high until other womens say so. But now her head hang low and the only thing that lift her up is the early, early morning when owl going home and nobody awake. That be the time she up and waiting for two riders to come back to Montpelier. And when Massa Humphrey ride up to the kitchen and fling himself into a chair and he and Robert Quinn ask for tea she ready already. She like even more when Robert Quinn not with him and he make conversation with her, even if that be about the damn sun that rise too fast or why Don Juan is lost on a whore and other things that she can only say yes massa to and wish she didn't have a slow nigger mind. When he laugh, she giggle like an agreeable girl even if she don't know what she laughing for. Lilith want him to take her up in the house and out of common negro life. Lilith hear about massas and they chère amie and she know she prettier than any other negro in the field or in the house. But she wish there was a nigger to teach her woman things.

Lilith peeling potato and pondering in a way that negro girl not supposed to ponder. She set her sight for the mistress at first but then her behaviour get uncanny and she call Lilith a big piece of black poo. But when the massa drunk and sprawl out and laughing to himself in the kitchen, Lilith start to see him in a new way. Just a drop more sugar, darling, is all he need to say and she carry that one last word for the whole morning, never mind that he call her a backward nigger cunt when she take too long and the tea too hot.

Lilith watch him from the kitchen window as he rein him black horse (white horse on a Sunday) and get dirt on him breeches when he lie down under the tree to the side of the conservatory, talking white people affairs with Robert Quinn. Lilith watch him taking him shirt off all the time. Him chest rise and fall when he laugh and him nipples surround by delicious pink the way a nigger own surround by nasty black. Lilith see him smile and think nothing evil could come out of that mouth. Lilith don't see that while he and Robert Quinn talking they have a negro whipping a slave girl hard for thieving out sugar to sell in Sunday market. The girl gagged so that she wouldn't disturb nobody with her screaming. Lilith see the road that goin' take her out of hard life but not sure what to do. Circe in the past would read her face and slap that stray thinking out but that woman dead. Lilith close her eye, shutting out the cellar darkness for her own and breathe in deep and try to remember what Massa Humphrey smell like. Then a quick thought run past her head. It run again and again until her heart beat fast and her temple kicking her ears. A nigger smart enough to know that any yes must be follow quick with a no. But this morning no gone on trip and not coming back. She thinking crazy-like and the crazy run through her. She wait for when Homer not looking and dash off to the hallway. Three doors down on the left be the linen closet.

The New Year's Eve ball was coming in ten weeks. Lilith not sup-pose to be upstairs but she grab bed linen from the closet. Lilith make it all the way upstairs to where the massa bedroom be, only to hear the dogs outside barking like they never bark before. Lilith keep on she gait and see a room door open and look in just as Massa Humphrey jump out of bed and dash to the window. Him body lean and dark on the limbs but white like porcelain in the chest, waist and hips. He turn and grab for him breeches and him penis swing and swing like it want to go back to the window. Massa member swing low like it hanging from a red tree that burst into flame like the red hair on him head. He pull the breeches over him bare arse.

—Hand me those, he say to her and point to the boots.

The dogs barking louder. Lilith drop her bundle to pick up the boots and forget that she did fix her dress so that her titties push like fruit that sell in the market. Though her own come first, she feel right there that other woman titty grown fast past her. She wish she did have some beet to rub on her lip and her cheek. Massa Humphrey grab the boots away from her and pull them on. The dogs getting more louder. Lilith looking round the room for him shirt and get lost in the big bed that command the middle, with four post make out of dark wood that raise all the way up into the ceiling that swirl round and round with naked baby angel. By the time she look back down to the floor, Massa Hum-phrey brush past her and gone. Lilith still. She grab the bed linen and almost give herself a start. She just stand there in the room waiting for the bed to give her something. She didn't hear when the dogs stop bark, but she hear the new sound. Sound that never come from the great house yet, that of a laughing woman in Montpelier. The woman laugh again. Lilith leave the massa bedroom and go to the stairs so she could see the door. Homer at the doorway.

Out in the courtyard be a black brougham carriage, big enough to seat four, with a negro at the reins dress up in a green suit and two white horse that get frighten by the dogs. Massa Humphrey run down the steps, and shoo away the dogs. Then he quiet the horse.

—Oh thank heavens, a voice say. A voice that belong to a young white woman. The massa surprise plenty 'cause nobody ever visit Montpelier just so.

—I thought hell's very hounds were about to make short work of me, she say.—And to think I've been such a good girl.

Massa Humphrey perplex. Lilith could see next to nothing. Homer go upstairs to Massa Humphrey room. Lilith watching the doorway and didn't see her. Then the woman in carriage yell out, Master Wilson! When she see him naked hand waiting to help.

—I daresay, Lord Wilson, that I shall not be seen speaking to a man in such scandalous undress! she say. Massa Humphrey look round himself 'cause he don't know what she mean.

—Madam? he say, looking down on him breeches that button right and tuck in him boots that did shine only last night.

—I repeat, the lady Roget shall not be manhandled by a man with no shirt on, sir, even if he is a gentleman, or claims as much, she say and sit back down in the carriage.

Lilith see Homer going back down the stairs and wonder when she come up. Massa Humphrey huff and puff and get red. Then he hear giggling in the carriage and smile. Homer, a shirt if you please, and a waistcoat, he say but Homer already at the door with white shirt, cravat, a shiny green waistcoat with a yellow flower pattern and Massa Humphrey favourite banyan that dark blue and shiny and flow all the way down to the ground and spread wide like wings when he walk. Massa Humphrey dress himself right in front of the carriage while the woman inside giggle.

—A thousand pardons, ma'am, I trust I'm far more presentable now, he say and bow low and grin like little boy.

—A little, the voice say and push out her hand.

The lady wearing a wide blue bonnet with a cream bow tie under her chin. Some of her hair tumble out and it curly and yellow. Her dress match her hat, blue with short sleeve and cut low in the front to show her bosom. The dress tie right above her waist with a cream ribbon and spread loose like brandy bottle. Montpelier never see nothing looking so lovely since Jack Wilkins' daddy come back from a trip with three peacock. She fanning her face. A small face, like a teacup that round like a heart with cheeks higher than the mistress' own. Two red lip and eyes an ashy colour. Massa Humphrey escorting her away when everybody hear a coughing from the carriage. An old woman hobble to the step wearing nothing but black.

—You're a cruel one, Master Wilson, to pay no heed to my chaperone, the woman say.

—Chaperone? Massa Humphrey say.

—Well, surely you would not expect a lady to come to a gentleman's abode all by her lonesome, would you? That would be irredeemingly improper, she say. Massa Humphrey instruct one of the manservant to help the chaperone, who didn't look too happy that niggerman was touching her.

The lady who come to Montpelier before breakfast name Miss Isobel Roget. She say her sorry for coming so early and blame the ninny nigger coachman who guess wrong the distance from Coulibre to here. Miss Isobel say she come on account of him distress. Seems everybody did know 'bout the legendary Wilson New Year's Eve ball and everybody also know that Mistress Wilson under the weather lately. Why, it's my duty as a lady to help, Miss Isobel say. Rumour was that the new governor, Sir George Nugent, would expect an invitation and him wife, Lady Nugent, never satisfied with anything. Miss Isobel repeat that it was her duty as a lady and a neighbour and as a friend to help in any way she can. Massa Humphrey perplex, but he didn't have nothing to say 'gainst woman reasoning.

—So we are agreed, Miss Isobel say.

Lilith get plenty time to see Miss Isobel, she the daughter of the massa of Coulibre. Massa Humphrey grateful for her, but is long time he living the island way and working himself back into a gentleman was a hard thing.

Since then Miss Isobel be coming to Montpelier every day of the week. The ball was coming and there be plenty thing to do. Lilith hatred turning to fever. She try to fix her dress to show even more bosom but since Miss Isobel come, Massa Humphrey cut down on the night carousing. Not long after, he stop coming at all, leaving Lilith in the morning to see how much she hate her own company. One morning she hear a sound in the kitchen and run up to see only Robert Quinn sitting by the table and looking out at the morning sky, waiting mayhaps.

She spend one whole night with a comb to straighten her hair, but the hair stay negro and curl back 'pon itself. Lilith go back to spending much time looking at herself in the silver tray in the kitchen. She grab the bed linen, which she not supposed to do, and run upstairs and go in the massa room extra early when he just about to wake up. She know he be sleeping naked like how he born. She know how some white woman think that be scandalous. Lilith come in just as he wake up with the bed linen in her hand and her bosom push up like she selling them. The massa walk right past her and go to the privy. She watch him not watching her. Lilith watch him shake it, then go back in him room and pull on him breeches, then stop, pull them back off and shout to Homer to fetch him clean clothes that gentleman receiving company should wear. Homer come in and step right pass Lilith like she don't see Lilith either. Homer go over to the closet that bigger than slave quarters and come out with dark green breeches and shiny brown boot that pull all the way up to the knee. She help him put on white shirt and cravat. Then him waistcoat.

—Will this please the lady Isobel? he ask Homer.

Homer look straight at Lilith.

—Me think it going please her plenty, massa, she say.

The massa rub him belly and growl like animal and Homer say, Miss Isobel be here already, so remember to act like a proper gentleman. Massa Humphrey laugh at Homer and step through the door, him banyan flowing like huge blue wings. Homer look at Lilith. Lilith place the bed linen in a red armchair by the door and leave.

Lilith stay up every night after that waiting for the full moon. The special full moon that big and gold and heavy and rise low over the Blue Mountain. When the moon finally come she sneak out for the cane piece. Then she remember that is crop time and plenty nigger would still be labouring. She head for the ratoon fields but the canes didn't grow very high. At some parts only shadow was hiding her. Lilith try not to think of the Johnny-jumpers. A white owl hoot-hoot and fly over her and give her a start so bad that she throw herself to the ground that damp from dew. Lilith go to cry but then stop herself. She look in herself and think about the sound of the cave, that nobody can find in the day. She think about the Blue Mountain that start at the edge of the estate. She think like how Homer would think if she have Homer mind. Homer run through the wild bush in the dark like a negro who don't need no eye. Lilith think of the dark and she think of the blindness. She think of how blind woman see.

Bufu-bufu
Backra riding through the bush

Lilith run in what she think be the right way. She run faster and faster and think what beating in her chest is her own drum. But her heart going one way and this beat going another. Double her time and beating like a clatter. She feel the beat under her feet and the sound getting louder. A beat and a clang. Then out of nowhere, a whinny. Lilith run faster and try to scream. The hoofs getting louder and closer no matter how fast she run. She try to make a turn to go deep in the cane piece but the loud, galloping hoofs come upon her. The last thing she remember is a blow, sharp and hard, clapping her in the back of her head and her eyes gone dark.

Bufu-bufu
Backra riding through the bush

The bird in the bush bawl *qua qua qua* and wake her up. Every time she blink, what she see get stranger and stranger. A shadow dance on the walk and frighten her so bad that she jump up and go to run, but stumble on the wood floor.

—And where do ye think yer goin', lassie? he say and the voice sound to her like is God or the devil.

Lilith eye don't wake up yet. Her hand start shake and she 'bout to cry. She spin round but can't see nothing that she remember. Lilith see two red velvet armchair like in the massa conservatory but is not Massa Humphrey house. The room smaller and every corner have a chair. Lilith see a wild animal head burst through the wall and she scream.

—It's quite dead, I assure you. Clipped that one myself, not far from the Cape of Good Hope, he say and throw a nut that bounce off the lion head and land 'pon the floor.

Lilith stop herself. She hear him chewing. Lilith spin around, past the painting on the wall of a white man and woman and two boy with a dog. Past the other painting of another man that look like Jack Wilkins, past the window that tall as the room and curve up top like the moon that waiting outside, past and going round like a circle, past the two armchair, past the old clock to the table that too big for the room, the table that Robert Quinn be sitting on, him legs up.

—And just what do ye think yer doing gallivanting all by yerself in the darkness? Not even the devil moves about at this hour, Robert Quinn say.

Lilith know when a answer worse than silence, especially to white people. The back of her head throbbing in pain and she wince. Robert Quinn watching her. Not like when the massa be watching a negro girl, but with him left eyebrow raise and head tilt like when dog want to know something. Robert Quinn black boots crust up with mud, but he have two foot up on the table with hands wrap round him knee, the left hand grabbing the right wrist, the right hand holding nuts. Robert Quinn hair black like night and long but him eyes lighter than the massa, so light that it look like he don't got no eyeball sometimes. This make Lilith more frighten.

—And what's yer name, luv? Speak up now, Robert Quinn say.

Lilith think this mighty uncanny, considering that he see her so often in the kitchen when he and Massa Humphrey used to come back from carousing. Every nigger is the same nigger to them sometimes, she remember Homer say.

—Lilith, sah. They call me Lilith.

—Who calls ye by that name?

—Everybody, sah. Me born to with the name waiting on me.

—Queer name for a place such as this.

—Yes, massa.

—I mean strange. Strange? Ye understand me, do ye not?

—Yes, massa.

—No, you don't. Too afraid to cross me, ye are.

—Yes, ma—

—Enough, I'm not yer massa.

Robert Quinn living in new quarters, a cottage smaller than Jack

Wilkins' own, not even five chains from the great house. Plenty time house negro hear he and Massa Humphrey cuss 'bout slave punishment, with Massa Humphrey saying Quinn weak now and Robert Quinn saying fine words from a man who can't watch the whipping he love to order. But Massa Humphrey and Robert Quinn too tight like thief to make cuss-out 'bout negro whipping split them up. Yet distance now between the two, and only one thing different in they affairs.

Miss Isobel Roget.

One of the house negro hear her telling the massa that it might seem a little improper, two unmarried men so close.

—I thought every negro had a Greek name, Robert Quinn say to Lilith.—I heard Jack Wilkins' father had a certain predilection for tragedy, he say.

—Massa?

—Ye must be something special. Or maybe Jack Wilkins named you. Is yer mum still alive?

—Me no know, sah.

—What do ye mean? How could ye not know? Was she sold? Speak up.

—Me no know, massa, me no know who me mama be.

—And yer father, yer papa?

—Me no know him neither, massa.

—Stop calling me massa. Mr. Quinn is satisfactory. Even Quinn. Could ye call me that?

—No please, massa.

Robert Quinn sigh. Lilith thinking that she goin' get whip for running around in the night after curfew. She start to wonder what a whipping feel like and if any man was goin' want her with scar 'cross her back. Robert Quinn lookin' at her like is the first time he seeing negro flesh.

—With those eyes of yers, only two men on this estate could've been your papa, now isn't that true?

—Me no—

—You no know. Confound it if you niggers know anything at all, save for Homer. Now remind me, where were ye heading this late, running through the cane piece? Weren't running away, were ye?

—No please, massa, no! Lilith shout. She look down and see her toes chopped off with blood spitting from her foot. She blink and they come back.

—Then where were ye heading?

Lilith don't know what to say. But she know she better say something or he goin' do her something. Chop off her toe if he think she running away. A whipping for sure. She look at him lookin' at her. Lilith is a girl who think like a girl. She wonder if she should push up her bodice and let her titties flop out. She wonder if he goin' whip her right there. Or if he goin' wait till daylight and call up the whole estate to see. Lilith think 'bout why she running through the bush.

—I was looking for Homer, she say.

—Homer? Flabbergasted I am, absolutely flabbergasted! Is every negro gallivanting in the dark? Had I known ye were all such night farers, I'd have put house slaves on field duty, Robert Quinn say and laugh.

—What makes ye think Homer was in the cane piece? The last time I saw about such things, she still worked in the great house, he say.

—Yes, massa.

—And what business do ye have with her?

—Massa?

—Why were you looking for her?

—I...

—You...

—Me, ah...

—Aye, if yer trying to save yerself from the lash, yer failing miserably.

—Ah beg you, massa, me no be doing it again.

—Oh, I'm sure ye won't, but this matter of negro running around at night and meeting disturbs me, disturbs me greatly. Plotting something, the two of you?

—No, please, massa! Lilith say. Robert Quinn jump off the table. Lilith heart jump. Robert Quinn coming toward her. Lilith step back until she couldn't step back no more. Her back run into the door. Robert Quinn come right up to her face, right up till she can feel him breath on her nose.

—What're the house niggers of Montpelier up to? he say.

Lilith thinking about what fire feel like. Her back start scratch her as if crying out from the beating already. Robert Quinn raise him hand 'gainst her face and Lilith try to scream but the scream vanish right as it about to leave her mouth. Robert Quinn touch her forehead.

—Yer forehead's bleeding, he say. Must've bruised it when ye fell. Sorry about that, but how was I to know who or what was running around in the dark. Him eyes light, light grey. Lilith try not to look shock that white man just tell nigger sorry.

—Should be thanking the lord for his blessing, that's what ye should be doing, he say. Lilith look 'pon him all perplex. Her head still throbbing.

—Yes, ye should be on your knees thanking God that the white man that found ye was I. And lately I've lost the taste for hurting negro women. As for yer secret, why don't ye keep it to yerself? Far more interesting anyways. Leave now.

Lilith grab ahold of herself and run to the door.

—Lilith, he say and she stop.

—I'll have my eyes on ye from now on, just so we understand each other.

Lilith run back to the house. The next morning she up working hard in the kitchen, so hard that Homer take notice. What a thing, me must did sleep and wake up white for you to be impressing me so, Homer say and chuckle. The other negroes in the kitchen chuckle too as they make the breakfast. Lilith laugh with them, but then turn back quick and continue working. Homer tell Lilith to go get some eggs from the hen house. As Lilith go through the door, Homer whisper something to her.

—Next time listen when people warning you, she say but Lilith look 'pon her perplex.

Lilith step outside but a carriage swing from round the bend with a bangarang and she jump out of the way. The cart full with red, green, blue and violet flowers. The cart stop and the negro driving turn round and look at Lilith.

Gorgon.

Gorgon smile like the devil. She say something without talking but Lilith hear it loud like a church bell.

Bufu-bufu
Backra riding through the bush.

· 9 ·

TANTALUS THE MAD NIGGER DEAD. HE MAKE HIM OWN FOOT kill him. Tantalus refuse to make anybody touch the chopped foot even though pus did pack it up and wherever he go, he stink up the place like a dead man. So Tantalus lock up in the hut. The man senses burnin' sake of fever. Tantalus' fever so high that the madness come back and he say things that would cause the massa to hang him in a flash. Even nigger start to complain so Robert Quinn go to Tantalus' bed one night, dress up in blue coat with shiny stripe that make him seem ready for the sea. Every time Tantalus fall sleep, the rotten foot wake him. Tantalus see Robert Quinn.

—Satan! Satan! Get behind me, Satan!

—Confound it! I'm a man, sir! Robert Quinn shout out but Tantalus keep calling him devil.

Tantalus say, White man, white man, ye be of your father the devil and the lusts of your father ye will do.

Robert Quinn raise him cane to strike Tantalus. Tantalus wail and pull off the sheet and when Robert Quinn see the foot he stagger back and nearly fall down. Robert Quinn see Tantalus cut foot moving and what moving be maggot. Robert Quinn call himself a hard Irish bastard who was never handed nothing in life but he grab him belly and vomit and when he couldn't vomit, he bowl over and hack like more soon come.

Soon Robert Quinn take to walking from him quarters to the kitchen at night like he haunted. Seeing Tantalus' foot make he sick to him stomach. Not many day pass before he sick for real. First he coughing then he wheezing then he shivering, even though the night hot like fire. One night he walk up to the kitchen in him nightshirt and see the moonlight shine through the window on a drum full of water by the counter. Robert Quinn dip him whole head in it. He look up with water running down him face and see a shadow lookin'. Quinn go to grab for a pot when he see the shadow be woman shape.

—Fer fuck's sake, does any negro sleep at Montpelier? What business have ye at this ungodly hour, Homer?

The next night he come through the door Homer ready for him. She sitting on a stool by the table. Drink this, she say and push a teacup across the table. Robert Quinn ponder a little but then grab the cup and drink. He spit out the whole thing and scream that she be witch trying to kill him with poison. He go to grab her but something 'bout Homer sitting up straight and not raising her voice make him stop. Homer go over to the stove and pour more in the cup. That tea not easy to make, she say. No more leave if you waste this cup, she say. He look at her for a long time.

—It not any good cold, she say.

Robert Quinn drink, rubbing him throat.

—God curse you if... he say to Homer and go back to him quarters.

He didn't come back for a while. But from the day he see Tantalus' foot, something come over Robert Quinn that make him eye darker and him voice quieter. Massa Humphrey don't like it. He ask if the man go take too much fancy for a negro wench, and who is the unlucky miss. But Robert Quinn not fancying no negro girl. Nigger see this in white man before, when he realise that he don't like how blood taste. They catch a boy in the boiling house stuffing sugar in him breeches, but Robert Quinn don't whip the boy, not even one little lash. Robert Quinn threaten to kill the boy next time but he don't whip the nigger. People too young to remember the last time that an overseer never wicked. Everybody but Homer. Robert Quinn eat in the kitchen with Homer sometimes and everybody but he find that mighty uncanny.

Then one morning Tantalus dead. Tantalus dead to everybody but one. Homer know who. Night come secret like witch and there be no moon to light up the kitchen. But he know the way by now. Homer at the table waiting for Robert Quinn, the goat weed tea steaming.

Massa Humphrey mother come out of her room when she think it be her birthday. Homer tell her that that day gone six months before and carry her back upstairs. Miss Isobel tell Massa Humphrey that there be places the mistress can go where she will be at peace. Now that she get the massa to buy all new decoration, she call for a seamstress to make all of the house slave new uniform with blue trimming. Miss Isobel choose a new set of slaves to serve at the ball and don't pick Lilith. Lilith fling some potatoes 'gainst the wall.

—But what the hell, Homer say.

—Is what? Is blind white woman blind?

—You must be the blind one to think you can lose temper in the massa house, Homer say.

—Me have wart in the middle of me face? Me eye them cross? Me fat like sea cow? After nobody can talk to white people like me, Lilith say.

The other nigger in the kitchen look 'pon her. Some laugh and Lilith see.

—Me give any of you stinking nigger joke? Lilith say.

—Stink me could be, but me still get pick and not you, Andromeda say.—Mayhaps is you who should smell under you arm again, she say and laugh.

—Go smell under you cunt!

—Lilith! Enough out o' you. You think the mistress owe you something?

—She not the mistress.

—Neither be you. Now go peel two potato and settle youself.

—She goin'—

—Me say go settle youself, damn girl. You must still be a pickney.

—Why you don't go breed another one and stop call me pickney. But that can't happen since you damn pussy dry up.

Homer silent. She open her mouth slow.—You sure you can handle big woman chat, pickney? You sure you ready for that journey? You think good before you answer. Because some people about to forget that me be the head bloodcloth nigger in here. Now, go peel two potato and don't draw me tongue out in this place.

—It not fair.

—Nothing fair, you dumb girl. Is nigger you be, Homer say.

Lilith think this was Homer idea to cut her down to size. Homer don't want to see anybody rise up from they station in negro life. She say if Homer have her way, she would be back in the field cutting cane and running from field negro who get tired of fuckin' cow. Homer say nothing. Lilith wait a little to go over to Homer and tell her that she want to come to the meeting tonight.

—You and me be combolo? Homer ask.—Why me must be going anywhere with you?

—Me want to come with you. Me want to meet you and the other womens. Me want to learn, Lilith say.

—Learn? Me did think you know enough already. What learning you want to be learning? Homer say.

—The things you say me must learn to put me over other woman, Lilith say.

—You didn't hear? There be three thing that don't come back. One is spoken word.

—Me not goin' beg you if is that you lookin'.

—Me not lookin' for a thing from you. They bury Tantalus yesterday. Right near where they bury Circe.

—So?

—Not a tear for Tantalus, eh? Not even a little sniff?

—Me don't care a damn 'bout that damn mad nigger.

—That be the pity. 'Cause he be the only nigger round here who did care for you.

Homer leave her.

Now the ball coming and Lilith mouth can't shut. Homer see what happening and let her stew. Every day Lilith saying how that clumsy idiot Andromeda can't handle china, and how Dido can't boil water and how Pallas can't be around backra company smelling the way she smell. She point out which female slave have too much wart, who too fat, who too skinny, who walk like duck, who lip too big, who smell like she don't wash her cho-cho and who just look like any common nigger. Lilith say she be better butler than Apollo and Chiron, even though Homer tell her that the mistress train them two herself. Homer tell her that if the matter burnin' her so bad, she should take the matter up with the new mistress.

—Montpelier done have a mistress, Lilith say.

—And lo and behold, she not you. Second time me telling you that, Homer say and look straight at Lilith until Lilith look away. Lilith go down to the cellar.

Homer used to teach Lilith how to read but stop when she turn her back to the womens who meet in the cave. Lilith hiss and say she don't need nobody but lonely feel worse than a night in Circe hut. Everybody hate her, and if everybody hate her, she goin' hate them back. Lilith was goin' to get the love she want. Lilith know from the day she see the page with the sleeping princess. Back then, she believe that one day she would wake up with gold hair. Lilith don't remember when she get green eye so she used to think it be true. Magic was goin' happen when she sleep. But negro girl can't sleep too long. Lilith see the new massa in him jacket, breeches and boots and go to sleep waiting for him to wake her up. Lilith don't tell nobody so nobody could warn her that she thinking crazy. Lilith don't want to accept things as them be, like a good negro.

Few days before Christmas, Lilith walking round the back of the house despite Homer warning 'bout Johnny-jumpers. Robert Quinn see her but he make her pass. She feel him watch her all the way till she reach the little dirt hill and turn around the corner out of him sight. Lilith walk until she come up to a row and row of pretty flowers and little trees all waiting to plant in the massa garden. The plants under a big shed that make out of a thatch roof and four post. A woman be watering the plant in the back, where the flowers and trees almost hide her.

—Uppity nigger bitch, I can smell you fishy from here, the woman say before she turn round and face Lilith, who clutch her dress and try not to look frighten. The woman study her from head to foot and hiss. How de mistress favourite nigger? She find special work give you yet?

Gorgon get up from the ground and go over to three clay flowerpot that just get water.

—Rose, Gorgon say.—My plant dat. Pretty like frock but will stab the shit out o' you. Like woman be sometime.

—Me never come—

—Den what you come for? Fi make friend, sister? Me no keep friend. See dem flowers? Dem be the only thing in the world that need soft hand to touch it. Hand that can't kill nothing. Dats why white man can't grow flowers, them kill everything dem touch. Even Papa Jack.

—Papa Jack? You call the man Papa Ja—

—What you want, nigger? Gorgon say.

.   .   .

Lilith go back to the cellar after she talk to Gorgon and look through her second dress that wrap in a bundle to use as pillow. She find two earring that Jack Wilkins give Circe, earring that she thief. Lilith go up to the kitchen and join the womens getting the lunch ready because Miss Isobel complain about saltiness two day before and Massa Humphrey slap Pallas and some other negro. Lilith see Andromeda over by the counter shelling gungo peas. Make youself busy, Homer say to Lilith. She grab a pot full of water and walk over to where Andromeda be. Just when she get near, Lilith trip and pot and water fly and slam into Andromeda back. Andromeda scream and slip and fall. Lilith scream she sorry, she sorry and grab Andromeda to pull her back up.

—*Bafan!* Fool-fool pussy-eye bitch! You ruin me frock, Andromeda shout.

—At least now it finally get a good washing, one of the mens shout out and everybody in the kitchen laugh except for Homer.

—Pallas, mop up this mess, and you, clumsy nigger, go fetch more water. Backra not here to wait on negro, Homer say.

Lilith go outside but leave the bucket at the well. She look around for Robert Quinn but he gone. She turn round the hill again and go back to the garden house. Gorgon waiting. Lilith pull the two earring out of her left pocket and a clump of Andromeda hair out of the right.

People think you light like you eye, but you blacker dan midnight, Gorgon say, then laugh. Lilith don't look at her for a while. Then she look up and green eye meet green eye.

Tomorrow, Gorgon say.

Next morning, Lilith wake up with fever and think Gorgon trick her. She go upstairs to see the sun come through the window and hit her in the face. Lilith know right away what a bitch this Gorgon be and regret that she go mess with her. Then she hear screaming. The screaming wake up everybody, but Lilith reach the slave quarters first.

Lilith jaw drop and she grab her mouth. Andromeda little girl scream-ing as she watch her mother on her mat. Andromeda mouth coughing up blood. Her eyes crying blood. Andromeda nose breathing blood. Andromeda dress hitch up over her waist and between her legs spitting blood. Andromeda cough up more blood and fall back on the mat. She jerk like she having fits, then stop. She dead. Andromeda little girl run out the room screaming until Homer catch her. Homer don't come in the room. Lilith turn round to see Homer looking straight at her.

· 10 ·

WORD SPREAD THAT ANDROMEDA DAUGHTER RUN ALL OVER the estate, screaming and cawing and dropping and rolling round in the dirt like mad goose. Homer try to hold on to her, but when she see Andromeda, death rattle in her throat already and Lilith looking over her, the girl pull away and run off, screaming down the passage and waking everybody up. Andromeda dead less than an hour, but her body already dark and bluish, as if she lying there for a day. Homer look at Lilith. Lilith know she looking and don't dare look back. The room still until Andromeda body jerk again and Lilith scream. Homer move in closer but not right up to the body and Lilith turn and leave so that Homer couldn't grab her.

Andromeda daughter running round in front of the great house making big commotion. Robert Quinn, who did very upset that he get drag out of him slumber, didn't even stuff him night shirt into him breeches before he step towards her with him musket. She flapping and bawling and when she see him turn to run. He chase after her and strike the back of her head with the musket. She drop flat on her face. Quinn grab her by the leg and start to drag her away, but then coming riding up be Miss Isobel, who frown at him.—I see the courting meth-ods of the overseer have not changed in fifty years, she say but Robert Quinn don't pay her no mind. Then Massa Humphrey come out on the terrace and say, Robby, what is that God-awful commotion.

—One of yer young slaves, Master Humphrey. Her senses have all but taken leave, I fear.

—Really? What could have caused such a thing?

Quinn look below the terrace and see Lilith running to the front door.

—I think I'm about to find out meself, Quinn say.

—*Confound it,* has it happened again?

—Massa Quinn?

Robert Quinn circle the body like Homer do before but don't move in close. One could never trust the bloody flux; even a dead body was—as some people think—more deadly than a live one. It don't take no time for a body to bloat up with gas and for the earhole, nosehole or pussyhole to spit blood at you. Word was that sometime the whole body explode and cover the room with blood and pus. Quinn make a step closer, then think better of it and step back. He look at the body again, then look at Homer. Sun was just getting up and orange light sneak in through the window. That's when Quinn see that he was stepping in blood.

—Oh, fer fuck's sake! he say and scrape him boots on the floor, cuss-ing still.

—God be damned should we have the bloody flux upon us, he say.—'Tis the second one, I said. Is it not?

—Massa?

—After the other one, Circe was her name, am I correct? Same thing, blood bursting from her insides. Upon me word, I've never seen such nasty, brutish business. And what's Lilith's stake in all this?

—Massa?

—Come now, Homer, I saw her running out as if to catch that poor child. This woman was the child's mother, yes?

—Yes.

—Horrible, of course, seeing one's mother die of the flux.

—Or perhaps something more nefarious.

Both Homer and Robert Quinn look round, like they both get stun by the same blow. Coming in the room be Miss Isobel with Massa Humphey running behind, like a papa trying to catch him young'un. Miss Isobel fan him away.

—Surely, Miss Isobel, this isn't the place fer the likes such as yerself.

—I'm well aware of my place, Mr. Quinn. Be so good as to remember yours.

Miss Isobel step in the room and when everybody see how far she be from upset, it upset everybody. She step closer to the body than everybody else, holding up her hand when Massa Humphrey step to her. She cover her nose with her fan and kick at Andromeda foot. Lilith in the hallway, not far from the door, but afraid to come in after Robert Quinn ask what she have to do with all this. She hate how him seem to know her, and scared too. From where she be, she see Homer standing still and both Quinn and Massa Humphrey protest every time Miss Isobel get closer and kick the body.

—Really, gentlemen, I hardly think she's in a state to make much protest, she say.

—Ma'am, I must insist that ye leave at once. Ye never can tell with the bloody flux—

—Bloody flux? she say very loud.—Surely you're not so ignorant of the island ways, Mr. Quinn. Were you not born in Barbados, then?

—I think I damn well know the flux when I see it, ma'am.

—Robby, Massa Humphrey say.

—If you think this is the bloody flux, then you're a bloody fool.

—Really, now, Miss Isobel, Massa Humphrey say. Both him and Robert Quinn getting redder because of her but mayhaps not for the same thing. Quinn getting redder like he about to stomp into the floor.

—How little of the island ways you know, especially for a man who all but grew up nigger.

—Then let us be friends, ma'am, seeing how identical our backgrounds be.

Miss Isobel quick to cover her mouth with the fan. She look at Massa Humphrey but he looking at Andromeda body.

—And you're convinced 'tis the flux, Robby?

Lilith look at Robert Quinn, who look at Massa Humphrey like he know the massa don't know the first thing 'bout the flux.

—Aye.

—And I maintain that it's not. This is not connected to any malady. Certainly none known by people with little understanding of island ways. Is that not so, Homer?

Is not every day that Homer jump. She look away from the three of them and clear her throat. Lilith look at Homer trying to not look at them looking at her. Lilith know she should leave. Right now, right then before they see her or before something evil happen. Andromeda body rising to spit blood in Lilith direction and mark her out. She start to tremble again. Her heart threaten to beat it way right through her breast. Miss Isobel say something twice, as if she know Lilith didn't hear it the first time.

—This is not flux, this is Obeah. Homer looks like the sort of nigger that can tell you all that you wish to know, and much that you wish not.

Quinn tell Homer to cover the body in a sheet and have two mens take it away through the back door. He still saying to Massa Humphrey that it be the flux but Massa Humphrey see Homer face when Miss Isobel say Obeah. Lilith watch him watching the two womens talk without saying a word. Man not fool. They know when woman, even a white woman and a negro woman, go off into their secret talking.

In the kitchen all hell about to break loose. Nobody did like Andromeda, but word spread 'bout how she dead and one woman already run outside the house screaming that Obeah deh 'pon di Montpelier Estate. Homer send one of the mens after her and tell the womens in the kitchen to shut they mouth. But whisper rise up and down and up again, and they look at Homer and Lilith and another woman lose her head. She grab a knife and point it at everybody and scream that she sooner kill whoever try to work Obeah on her. Pallas approach her for the knife but the woman try to jab her, saying that Pallas always smell like wild bush. Pallas duck and shift and clobber the woman in the head with a pot and she fall to the floor. Another woman say is not Pallas who smell like wild bush, and the kitchen go quiet around Homer. Lilith think to go back down in the cellar but don't want nobody suspect her of nothing. Lilith be thinking that Gorgon is who do this with her wickedness and malice. Gorgon who take her earring and give her what she didn't enter no bargain for. Gorgon who probably goin' make it look like this be Lilith own doing.

—Chiron, get me a big sheet of osnaburg, Homer say.

Lilith can't deal with her mind talking to her. She try to be the busiest in the kitchen but start to wonder if everybody watching her since she be the only one who can work when somebody marking off the Montpelier house niggers. Chiron then shout out that it must be a field nigger trick for they always be hating us, the uncommon niggerfolk. Couple nigger nod and agree, even Pallas. Or is the Johnny-jumper them trying a new thing, another one say and the room go silent again. Not a moment pass before Lilith notice that silence mean they all looking at her. She look up quick at Pallas and see her looking away.

—Lunch not goin' cook itself, Lilith say to nobody.

Outside her window a slave-driver ride past the kitchen on the way to the great house. The driver ride past again, heading back to the fields, this time with Robert Quinn in tow on him own horse. Homer enter the kitchen and go over to Lilith.

—Where them going? Lilith say.

—To the field, the first gang having trouble.

—Not 'bout this?

—Me not no town crier, Lilith.

Lilith go to say something but then Gorgon burst into the kitchen, out of breath even though she come by her carriage.

—Homer, ah yuh go tell dem fi make me carry Andromeda? Why yuh go set dis fuckery 'pon me?

—Next time, make sure you not the only nigger round here who ride carriage, then. Besides, this need to take care of quick before it spread to the field.

—Eehi. Of course. Wouldn't want no bloody flux to spread to the field, Gorgon say, but she look at Lilith. Lilith try to glare at her but look away first.

—Well, yuh too late. Yuh never see the overseer gallop gone? Two field nigger say dey see black coffin wid three wheel and two john crow on top rolling through de bush.

Somebody in the kitchen lose they breath. A girl younger than Lilith start to whimper then bawl then scream 'bout Obeah coming for them and why Obeahman choose to mark her when she be a good little nigger. She dart from left to right to left and start to see Obeah in everything, the bunch of herb on the windowsill, the pot that black from boiling green tea. Then she say last week she see lizard bones in the cupboard and start to bawl louder and louder. Homer march right up to the girl and give her one hard slap on her left cheek.

—Sort out youself, idiot!

The girl sink to the ground and whimper.

—Any more imbecile in here me need to deal with? 'Cause is the field all fool-fool niggers belong, so whoever want me to send them there, just show you hand. Nobody? Good, then get you lazy arse back to work!

Lilith look at Gorgon. Gorgon look back, her lip moving like she telling Lilith something. Lilith want to call her a murderous bitch but Gorgon face look like she saying the same thing. She don't know. Gorgon scratch her face but then, real quick, cover her lips with one finger and look at Lilith.

—Lilith. Lilith! Go set the table, Homer say.

At the table, Lilith hear them in the drawing room. Miss Isobel and Massa Humphrey, waiting on Robert Quinn to come back.

—Confound it that the age of reason should visit everywhere but the goddamn colonies, Massa Humphrey say. Lilith try to peep in the doorway and see Massa Humphrey walking up and down, Miss Isobel sitting by the window with her pink fan out.

—Age and reason have nothing to do with the colonies, Master Wilson—

—Humphrey, please, Miss Isobel. I despise formality almost as much as I do superstition. Goddamn it! Goddamn it all! Are there no ministers here, no priests? How in an age of Christ could so many be swayed by this…this darkness?

—It flows in them like blood, Master…Humphrey. I daresay it comes as natural to them as our lord and saviour is to us. I find the whole thing ungodly, but a wise master would do well to understand their ways. Even use them.

—Whatever on earth are you saying?

Miss Isobel look away.—Pardon me, my folly. This is not a matter as such that a feeble woman can solve.

—Oh, posh, Miss Isobel, I am an enlightened man of the age. I insist on your counsel.

Lilith hear footsteps. Robert Quinn stomping to the room, him hat in him hand. He change shirt but it so white and loose that it look like another nightshirt and he tuck in only the front. Quinn walk past

Lilith, not looking at her. Then he stop and turn around. Lilith quick to look away.

—What news, Robert?

—Like a herd of cattle they are, he say and step inside.—One says he saw this black coffin dashing down a path—with wheels, mind ye, like a carriage and driven by three vultures, then glory! 'Tis as if all have seen it. There was simply no talking to the fellow. 'Twere as if he'd seen the devil himself. Had to whip a few within an inch of their lives just to get them back to work.

—Damn! What is this then—Obeeyah, you call it? Is it like voodoo, Robby? Is it like that gypsy business we saw in Venice?

—Looks like stupid nigger superstition to me, that's all it is.

—This is not some nigger All Hallows' Eve, sir, Miss Isobel say.—It's a tad more serious than that. I've seen an entire estate go to a standstill over their superstitions. They took it with them from the dark continent, you know.

—Well, all I need is me trusty whip to flog some light back into their thick skulls, Quinn say.

Lilith watching. Massa Humphrey still walking up and down and don't see Robert Quinn getting redder and Miss Isobel almost smiling when neither man looking at her. Lilith can't bear to think 'bout herself so she think about Miss Isobel and why she smiling and hiding it. Robert Quinn say something about setting an example before it gets out of control and that's only way to eradicate it.

Lilith looking in on them with all her eyes and hearing them with all her ears so she didn't hear him until he clear him throat behind her. Lilith jump. She turn around and see him green eyes first. Lilith drop the fork. Him still tall but thinner than she remember in the cellar and he didn't bother to take him hat off. Him head bobbing and him neck loose and he seem weaker. But Jack Wilkins was like them animal who just because him weak don't mean him not vicious. This be the first time Lilith see Jack Wilkins since she hear that he be her papa.

He look at her like he didn't know. Or mayhaps she think he look at her like that. Mayhaps she did want to see something else in the green eyes, something that say she was more than just a slave and him was more than just the man who fuck her mammy. For sure he must know who she be, even if he didn't see her in the cellar. He looking down on her, she can feel it.

—You can never eradicate Obeah; you might as well eradicate the niggers themselves. But you can make your own Obeah seem greater, Miss Isobel say. Robert Quinn snort. Massa Humphrey looking outside the window, him hands behind him back.

—Are ye suggesting, ma'am, that we fight witchcraft with witchcraft? Is that what yer suggesting? Quinn say.

—And she would be right, Jack Wilkins say as he step past Lilith.

—Nobody asked for yer presence or yer opinion, sir.

—And when I need the permission of an Irishman, rest assured I shall ask for it.

—Enough, both of you, Massa Humphrey say.—What are you saying, Miss Isobel?

—This Obeah, it may seem to be about spells and witchcraft but it's really about their religion, potions and poisons. Even if these dim blackies believe that it's more than that.

—And how do ye know so much of their ways? Quinn say.

—The real question is how do you know so little, sir.

Robert Quinn stomp over to Massa Humphrey, saying, Humphrey! Then whisper the rest. Massa Humphrey nod him head over and over until he say *no* loud enough that everybody hear.—I shall hear what else Miss Isobel has to say, Massa Humphrey say, but he look at Jack Wilkins, who was looking around the room and smiling like he seeing a whole bunch of things he know too well.

—But Humphrey, this is laughable. We're men of science, men of reason. Might as well be gypsies if this is to be.

—Used to have your kind in chains before we switched to niggers, Jack Wilkins say.

—I would like to see ye try it, ye son of a bitch!

—Enough, Quinn! Massa Humphrey say.

—And how do you suppose we deal with it? Book learning? Science? That's lost to the negro. Might as well be the Dark Ages in the colonies, and you'd do well to think as such! Miss Isobel say.

Quinn look like he about to slap her. Instead he turn and leave.

—Oh, Robert, don't be unreasonable, Massa Humphrey say.

—Reason? Reason left this room a long time ago. Me, I shall trust to a good head and a better whip. Now I'll take leave of ye and yers, Quinn say and walk out. Lilith dash over to the table and rub a fork with her apron. Quinn see her and stop. He look at her for a while but then storm out.

—Let him go, Jack Wilkins say.

—Far be it from me to take orders from you, Jack Wilkins, Massa Humphrey say.—Miss Isobel?

—Yes, I know, I know, I'm too wise to their ways, but to be master over the niggers means having an intimate knowledge of their every move. You cannot sleep for a second, is that not so Mister...Wilkins, is it not?

—Quite indeed, ma'am. Quite indeed and yes.

—Now. Have you heard of the French Obi?

—No, can't say I have, Massa Humphrey say.

—This is the West Indies, Master Humphrey. We do things differently here.

Before the noon hour, three niggermens see a woman with some stick shove in her hair and shout that she goin' home to work Obeah. They grab her, was about to beat her when one of the men's calf explode.

The slave-drivers look and whoop and holler when they see that it be Jack Wilkins. They run to him, one of them even kiss him on the cheek and say, Wilkins, ya goatfucker! As me lives and breathes, to which Wilkins say, And you won't be doing the likes of both much longer if you don't git you goddamn paws off me, McClusky, ye sodomite! He then turn to the field niggers, including the man who just lost half of him foot and bawling like a little girl.

—Cursed hypocrites, the lot of you. Scared y'all are of the Obeah when it's set against you, but mark my words—you still goes to Obeah woman to work some shit against each other, yes you do, Wilkins say. Then he gather the drivers and tell them what to do.

Two hours pass before all over the estate slave-drivers whip out tallow candle from the great house and stick it on a fence, or stump, or table or ground or anywhere in the field that every slave could see it. Halfway down the candle they push a nail right through. The drivers light the candles. The cane field couldn't be more quiet if everybody was dead. Driver try to whip the slaves back to work but it be of no use. The candles burning for a good while and soon burn down to the nail.—Miss Isobel? She tell them 'bout that? Homer ask Lilith twice. Two time she nod yes.—Light a candle on them, she did say. Light a candle on them.

One candle did set in the kitchen by Miss Isobel herself. Robert Quinn see it and hiss. Lilith wonder if something was goin' happen to her, if Andromeda spirit was going come back and pick up the candle and fling it at her and catch her dress afire and burn her to ash. Pallas drop a pot and Lilith jump. Lilith look at Homer, who look at the candle. Lilith don't know much 'bout the spirits but know that Homer practice Myal, the blood enemy of Obeah. But both Myal and Obeah deal with so much darkness that even nigger from the Africa sometimes don't know which is which. Lilith wonder if they would catch Gorgon. Lilith wonder how much lash it would take to loose up Gorgon mouth.

Lilith wonder if she thinking too much 'bout herself and not Andromeda pickney and what it mean that she do.

Out in the field the candles burn. Field niggers gone back to work
but they quiet and the breeze whispering around them. Then a woman
drop to the ground like she having fit. Another one, stumpy and fat,
start to run, chattering balderdash that nobody can understand. In
another field a niggerman start to bawl out and rush to the candle to
put it out. Another man grab the candle and fling it in the field. Dry
bush catch fire and the drivers had to be quick to whip niggers put it
out with water from the pump. The man try to run into the bush but a
driver take him time and aim, then fire. The man drop flat in the dirt.
Before any candle burn down to the nail, seven womens and five mens
all get catch doing one thing or the other to put out the flame. Massa
Humphrey don't spare none of them the whip. But he leave such matters to Jack Wilkins and niggers did done forget how he wicked and
nasty. Wilkins have the driver tie them down to the ground instead
of hanging them up and he drip pig fat on them. Then he set fire to
they pussy and cocky hair, all the time chatting judgement which he
say come from the good book of Leviticus. Then he have the drivers
whip them chest and belly and back and face till they can't scream no
more. Wilkins then shoot one of the mens in the head as example to
the others. Miss Isobel watch the whole thing from the terrace even
after Massa Humphrey say he had seen enough.

Wilkins lead some drivers to one of the womens house. The Johnny-
jumpers take one look and run outside and not even the threat of a
whipping could get them to go back. The hut dark and clammy and
smell like an arse. In every crack or corner or section of the roof the
woman have rags hanging. Old rag, new rag, torn rag, some of them
be osnaburg but some be other material from dress that white woman
wear. She also have hanging bunch of feather, bone and things that
nobody could say. One of the drivers kick open a clay pot and a stink

rise up so gruesome that one say that is stillborn babies she keeping in there. No wonder I's never seen a puss in these lands, one of them say when they fish out a rotten one. In another clay pot be all sort of ball that make out of dirt, some rolled up with teeth and bone and feather and rags. In every corner of the hut she have brown and green jars. Wilkins shake one and see dead lizards spin around. A driver find an old jewel box and give it to Wilkins. Under a table by the window there be a small chest and inside be plenty eggs, too small to come from fowl. Wilkins tell the drivers to burn the hut to the ground. With the niggerwoman in it. They bound and gag her so that nobody would hear her screaming. Later on Wilkins stomp through the house to where the massa and Miss Isobel be. He say that you can bet that everybody knew who were Obeahmen and women and this was just the beginning. Jack Wilkins start to lay down what Massa Humphrey ought to do. Miss Isobel quiet. Massa Humphrey look at Jack Wilkins and say, Good sir, you are quite mistaken. I'd sooner vouchsafe my soul to the devil than have you back as my overseer.

Jack Wilkins stomp into the kitchen but stop when he see Homer.

—Homer, I would keep it for myself just to spite the son of a bitch, but it isn't his for me to take, is it?

—Massa?

—This, he say and show Homer the jewel box.—The mistress's isn't it now? I'm sure of it. That damn witch must have stolen it somehow.

—It don't look like the mistress own, massa. This look cheap, like what whore keep.

—And how would you know? And what's this inside, these earrings, could she have stolen them from the mistress?

—How would a field nigger get into this house, sah?

—Sod if I know, Homer, maybe she's in league with one of you. I would press further, and you know my ways, I'd get what I was looking for, but lucky for you, for all of you, that I couldn't care less if the Wilsons live or die. Pox on the whole fucking lot.

Jack Wilkins leave the box on the counter beside Homer. Homer open it and take out some single pearls, a ring and two earrings. Poor chile was trying to save up for freedom, it look like, she say, but Lilith grab her throat and cough and go straight down to the cellar. The earrings shine and wink and call out Lilith name. The same earring she give Gorgon two days ago.

EVERY NEGRO WALK IN A CIRCLE. TAKE THAT AND MAKE OF it what you will. A road set before every negro, from he slip through the slave ship or him mother pussy, that be just as dark. Black and long and wide like a thousand year. And when a negro walk, light get take away from him so he never know when he hit a curve or a bend. Worse, he never see that he walking round and round and always come back to where he leave first. That be why the negro not free. He can't walk like freeman and no matter where he walk, the road take he right back to the chain, the branding iron, the cat-o'-nine or the noose that be the blessing that no niggerwoman can curse.

Blood spurt on her face and wake her up. Lilith gasp and clutch her cheek. She scream in her hand when she feel the wetness and can't see nothing. She look around blind and whimper until she remember darkness. The wetness, sweat mayhaps. She run upstairs to wash yesterday off, wash off the blood that she can't see but know is 'pon her in some way, but gather herself as soon as she in the kitchen. Sun don't rise yet, nor the house with it. Lilith slip through the kitchen and disappear round the little hill. She come up to the garden house but don't see

Gorgon. She look left, then look behind her and step before looking in front. Lilith walk right into Robert Quinn chest.

—Holy Jesus Christ, she say to herself.

—Good heavens, our resemblance *is* uncanny, Robert Quinn say. Robert Quinn grab her two hands and study her. Not hard, but firm. Lilith try to look at him but him eye open too wide and they too grey, him hair too long, him nose breathing down on her too hard. Lilith look away and him look at her. He hold her for a long time.

—Homer's in the kitchen, if you've forgotten where to look, he say.

—Yes, massa, Lilith say. He still holding her two hand.

—Unless yer looking fer somebody else, he say.

—No, massa!

—Have a hankering to do as ye please, do ye? Disobey yer masters and treat a day as you see fit? Who waits fer ye? This is the second time I'm running into you.

Lilith in fear and trembling 'cause the Irishman be watching her. Lilith about to say, No! Me didn't want to kill her! Me only did want her too sick to work! But she couldn't say nothing. She look out into the sky and see the moon threatening to come and expose her.

—You enjoy being a house slave, do ye? Robert Quinn ask.

—Yes, yes, massa, Lilith say.

—And do ye think you'd enjoy the field?

—No, massa.

Then he grab her. By the chest right in the scoop of her bosom. He grab her hard with some of him fingers in between her breast and make a fist in her dress. Lilith shriek. Robert Quinn start to walk and pulling her behind him. He stride so wide that Lilith have to skip to keep up. Lilith start to cry. She look at him black hair blowing and him shirt hold tight under him vest and see the whip hanging from him belt. He dragging her and she buck her toe against a rock. She cry out but he don't stop. He take her back to the same flower shed but Gorgon still not there. Lilith want to bawl out No, massa! No, massa! But words failing to leave her lips. He yank her in the middle of the shed and she stumble.

—I've told ye how much I dislike the idea of niggers gallivanting as they please. Shall I send you to the field, then? Perhaps a spell in the boiling house?

Quinn pull the whip from him belt. It long and black like a thin dead snake.

—I sense something about ye, an insolence, an insolence, damn it, and I'll not have it. I'll not have it at all. Pull down your dress.

Lilith looking down on the ground.

—Pull down that feckin' frock or I'll rip it off! And God be damned if ye get another!

She pull down her dress and her two breast pop out. The dress fall to her waist and eventide blow a cold breeze on her back. She hide her breast with her hand and look at the ground. Robert Quinn look at her. Lilith don't say nothing. Robert Quinn look at her like he expecting something but Lilith look at the ground, her cheeks wet. Tears escaping, but she not sobbing or bawling.

—Yer just a child, Robert Quinn say.

In the kitchen everybody quiet and working. Massa Humphrey and Miss Isobel taking a late luncheon today so everybody moving slow. Lilith race down to the cellar before she could run into Homer. But as she reach the final step she smell mint and lemongrass.

—Can never find what I looking for in this cellar, Homer say. Homer back to Lilith as she search the shelf.

—Sugar jar empty upstairs, Homer say.

—A sack in the side room, Lilith say. Ants get in when it put on the shelf.

—Good thing you using you head, one ants in Miss Isobel tea and is a whipping for sure. Homer turn to go in the room.

—What other use you puttin' you head to? Homer ask.

—Me don't know—

—You don't know what you own head be doing? Maybe it gone free while you still slave. Anyway, make me find the brown sugar that Miss Isobel like. Uncanny, eh? You think she'd like white sugar the best. But she be white woman so she get what she want. Not like black woman, eh?

Lilith don't say nothing. She check if her cheek wet.

—Maybe is 'cause you part white, that why you not understanding black talk. Or maybe 'cause you part white you think you must always get what you want too.

Homer go in the room and say something else, but Lilith couldn't hear.

—What? Lilith say.

Homer come back out with the sugar.

—Me say, the thing with black woman, though, is that we don't get what we want and we never get what we need, but every nigger, I mean every nigger, get what she deserve.

Homer leave her downstairs.

—Potato not goin' peel itself, she say.

Lilith look down at her feet and see blood pooling. She have to blink it out of her vision. She hear Andromeda daughter screaming and turn around, lookin' to see where she be. Nothing but darkness. Lilith go over to her mat on the floor and stoop down, her head heavy and not together. Slave death is nothing new and a strong nigger learn to walk past it but Lilith look down on her own hands and keep seeing blood. Lilith wishing and begging that she can call up the white part of her, the part that can bear with killing a nigger like is nothing. She still hoping that her white half, her green eyes, can save her from her own looking glass that don't hang on no wall. To kill a nigger is like to kill a horse, she think. She invoking the white skin to come up and bury the black. She toil in the kitchen the whole day not seeing how all the niggers excited. It be Christmas Eve.

. . .

So much fussing go into New Year's ball that everybody near done forget Christmas. Nobody goin' take 'way Christmas from the field negroes, though. While the massa and the mistress and her friend in the house eating at table, the field negroes be putting on them good trousers and good dresses that only wear couple time a year. And they cook banana and yam and pork that is present from the massa. And they boil the cornmeal in banana leaf till it thick like pudding, and cook down the chopped coconut with plenty sugar and molasses until it dark, thick and sweet. All them things they lay out on a big table not far from the great house 'cause is the one time o' year when field negro can step anywhere near where backra live. Negroes eating and talking and playing and gallivanting 'cause this one day negro can forget that he be negro.

The banjo playing and the women commence to singing.

Moonshine tonight
Come make we dance and sing
Moonshine tonight
Come make we dance and sing
Me deh rock so, you deh rock so
Under banyan tree
Me deh rock so, you deh rock so
Under banyan tree

Then the mens and the womens commence to dance like white people at the ball. The mens in one line and the womens in one line. The mens rock then the womens rock. The mens spin then the womens spin. The mens tap one foot then the womens tap they foot. The womens stick out they hand and the mens take it. Then they spin. Woman and man at the back of the line join hand and skip to the front of the line.

Lady may curtsy
Gentleman may bow
Lady may curtsy
Gentleman may bow
Me deh rock so, you deh rock so
Under banyan tree
Me deh rock so, you deh rock so
Under banyan tree

Then the next woman and man move to the front and so on. Massa Humphrey love the excitement, he run down the verandah and join with a niggerwoman and dance. Then he see Miss Isobel fanning herself and go back to the verandah. New Year's be white people time but Christmas belong to the negro.

Then the drum thunder. John Canoe be coming. The pickneys jumping in excitement. The drums beat louder and a man and three woman start sing, *I want to go-oh, I want to go-oh-oh.* Then the negroes be dancing, but this not be no white people dance. Womens make *ulelele* and *click-clack* sounds with they mouth. Man grab a woman from the back and waltz her. Then John Canoe appear. He be wearing a red and white jacket with tails all the way down the ground. He be wearing white breeches, pink stockings and he face paint white like white girl dolly. On him head is a great house so big that he have to hold it with one hand. But him legs free. John Canoe dance and spin and then he sing, *I want to go-oh, I want to go-oh-oh!* and the negroes sing it too and the drummer beat the drum and player pluck the banjo.

Behind John Canoe come all sort of people in costume. Two horse head with petticoat body that look like rainbow. Two mens dress up like pregnant womens, in pink dress with no petticoat and wearing white mask. Man that cover from head to toe with strips of cloth put together so tight that they look like man who wake up one morning and all him hair grow to the ground. Then come the king, the little boy with a big crown who carrying him sword to kill all in the dance. Miss Isobel and Massa Humphrey and Robert Quinn and the chaperone clapping. Homer singing to herself. Lilith behind them doing nothing. Every now and then she look at Massa Humphrey. Every now and then she would look up and see Robert Quinn lookin' at her. Lilith turn to go back to the kitchen and see Gorgon going round the back of the house. Gorgon see her and run.

—Gorgon!

Gorgon try to run, but she short and couldn't get far.

—Leggo me hair, dutty bitch! Gorgon scream.

—You is a wicked, wicked dog. Me never tell you say me want the woman dead, me say me want her gone, Lilith say.

Gorgon laugh.—Me no tell Obeah woman how fi work. What yuh think? Me was goin' do it meself? Yuh drinkin' mad puss piss?

—You tell that, that damn woman say me want Andromeda dead.

—Me no tell her a damn thing. Woman never even know who yuh be, or Andromeda. All she do is call the Omolu. Is fi you heart it listen to, not fi me or fi she.

—What you saying, bitch? Lilith say.

—Dis bitch saying dat if yuh never want Andromeda dead, she'd be living right now. Omolu give you what you want in you heart, not what you say to me face, Gorgon say.

—Me never want her dead.

—Say dat over and over till it turn into sankey and yuh soon start believe it. Now leggo me fuckin' hair before you start spit pussy blood too!

Lilith let her go and watch Gorgon run off down the little road at the back of the house and disappear in the Christmas colour. Lilith trying to not ponder. She did come with guilt pack tight like a bundle of clothes to throw on Gorgon, but Gorgon throw it back on her. She turn round to go and there, waiting behind her be the Johnny-jumpers. Lilith try to run but everywhere she turn, she run into a Johnny-jumper chest that heave from shouting and cussing. Every turn she make, a hand grabbing for her hair or her neck or her titties. And they shouting and cussing. Lilith too frighten to look at any face. She just want to get away from the bare chest and nasty hands. And they cussing. They calling her murderess and witch and pussy-eye and they chests and they hands get closer and closer until one hand round her neck. Lilith hear a woman cackle but no womens be in they number.

—You's thinks you was goin' gets 'way after you kills me brotha, you cow? he say.

He shorter and fatter than the others. Him hair plait in two and curl under him ear like ram goat horn. Niggers still making up ruckus and the Christmas celebrating take up all the air so no room left for a scream. Lilith thinking that mayhaps if she imagine that she is Circe and if they don't beat her too much she can make the sounds that Circe make and do what she hear Circe doing. Mayhaps the first punch would knock her out and she wouldn't have to feel anything and she would wake when they done or when the last one pull out. Or mayhaps she would wake up and they would be long gone and Homer would clean her and tell what to do with her pussy now that man force her to become woman. Mayhaps after this they would leave her alone and then she can walk without looking behind her and maybe Homer won't leave her in the cellar no more and maybe the massa would see her and maybe she would know what freedom be for the niggerwoman. Mayhaps the way to go from this very day to the next wasn't around, nor above or behind, but through. Through this. Lilith close her eye to take what God goin' give her. The hand still round her neck and the Johnny-jumpers still laughing. Lilith thinking that if she be an agreeable niggerwoman things might end up better for her. She think that she thinking the way big woman supposed to think. Big woman who get wise about what every niggerman want. Not looking at any of the mens, Lilith pull down her dress so that her bosom pop out. The goat-horn nigger slap her.

—Whats you's doin? We no comes to fuck you. We comes to kills you.

The goat-horn nigger grab Lilith by the wrist and start to drag her away from the sound of Christmas. Lilith trip and fall and the man drag her same way. Lilith feel the dirt scraping her skin and every stone cutting through her dress. Every time she scream it vanish into the Christmas. She claw the man with her nails and he turn around and slap her 'cross her face. Lilith bawling. Her foot kicking up dust. Round behind a tree he stop and pull her up. The goat-horn nigger pull out a dagger that sharp till it pointed.—Ah goin' tek you titty shove in you mouth and you tongue shove in you arse, he say and scrape Lilith chest. The other niggers follow but then the goat-horn nigger stop. He buckle over, taking Lilith with him, and start hack and cough. He let go of Lilith and she can't move even though she crying. Then he clutch him belly and vomit burst like waterfall from him mouth. He stumble and roll in the dirt.

—Lef me alone! Lef—L—Lef me alone!

Lilith frighten as she watch the man rolling 'bout in the dirt like he getting kick by the devil.

—Lef me alone! Lef me alone! he say.

The other Johnny-jumpers step back slow from Lilith, then when they a good distance, run off. The goat-horn man stop coughing and get up. He look at Lilith and spit. He cough again and stagger off, tripping two time before he can run. Lilith look round for her, but see nobody. She run back to the house and hide in the cellar.

Six day till the New Year's ball. Robert Quinn don't feel like goin' in to town to rouse the slave trader for new negro and Miss Isobel don't have time to train any new negro on how to wait on people of refined social graces like the governor and Lady Nugent. One morning Lilith wake up to find a blue uniform beside her mat. Homer be waiting on her to wake up.—Andromeda bigger than you, so you better beg Pallas to take in the waist and hem the foot, she say and leave Lilith alone. Lilith look around the cellar, then she grab the dress like is her own pickney. Lilith jump up and put the dress to her chest and hold out the sleeve like a woman hand and commence to waltz. Not until she spin the third time that she see Robert Quinn watching her from the top of the stairs that lead down to the cellar.

—Pleased the dress meets yer approval, he say, then turn away.

· 12 ·

Since Miss Isobel start come every day to arrange the ball, Lilith don't see Massa Humphrey much. She get up early in the dawn and brew the tea and sit and wait for the sound of him boots staggering through the kitchen. Homer and Pallas keep telling Lilith that she be woman now and Lilith try hard to understand woman things. One time Pallas was talking 'bout a field nigger name Bellerophon and she talk 'bout how her own face flush and her heart beat fast and heavy and how plenty people just look at the two of them and know that something sweet be burnin'. You just know when you see some people, she say. Something that make you know that two body be of one head or spirit, even. When a man sweet for a woman and a woman sweet for a man, even slavery don't seem so bitter. Lilith look for sweetness every time she see Massa Humphrey and Miss Isobel together.

It come to pass one morning that Massa Humphrey walk through the kitchen door. The horse whinny and the door open but is the shouting that wake her. Lilith jump when she hear him stomp into the kitchen asking for that bewitching tea and the negress who make it.

She go up the stairs to see him staggering round the kitchen, grabbing the counter to steady himself.

—Damn it, an utter mess I am! A man of the most worthless sort, he say. He steady himself by the table and throw himself into a chair.

—Quinn! Where the blazes...where's Quinn? Only Quinn knows... he knows what to do.

The massa ask two more time before Lilith realise that he was talking to her.

—Good lord, I can barely stand....What hour is this, I wonder? Homer? Where's Homer? I...I can't have her see me like...Homer?

Lilith get into action. She work up a fire while the massa try not to fall back over in him chair. She listen to him talking about how he should not have gone carousing without Quinn. How Quinn is him conscience and him better man and the man who God has placed to save him from himself.

—Damn that man, he say out loud.

Lilith put the kettle on the stove and reach in Homer cupboard, the one that nobody go into, and grab the little brown sack that she think have comfrey tea. But she don't know. Lilith perplex. A woman like Homer could have any kind of bush. Bush to make you happy or sad, sick or well. Lilith don't know. Maybe brown be a good colour, and maybe she wouldn't keep the evil bush right in front. Maybe she put it in front just to spite whoever come to rob her. Maybe she should just mix him regular green tea. But he slump in the chair and don't know what to do with himself and the usual company coming for breakfast. Maybe if she help him, save him, he would look at her different. Not special, only different. Lilith thinking that she must think clearer.

—I's gone fix you up, massa, she say, but quiet and not to him. Lilith can't think of addressing the massa directly, certainly not without he asking first and even then the word slip out like little gasps. Massa Humphrey hair too fiery, him eye too blue, him shoulder too strong and him close-cut breeches hiding nothing. Lilith look away and listen to him breathing slow. She put back the brown sack and pull out a burlap bag. It smell of fever grass, the tea that bring peace to a troubled mind or belly. Or ginger. She hope. She put the bag back. Massa Humphrey nodding. She find tea in a purple bag next to a bottle full with white sugar. The kettle start to whistle.

Then a spirit fly up in her head and she don't know where it come from. The spirit dance in a drumbeat like it come from the Africa. Or mayhaps it be something she remember. Or mayhaps it be something Homer say to Pallas or Pallas say to Gorgon or one house nigger say to the other. A woman get whipped or killed if they even suspect her of Obeah. But the voice was a beat that match her heart. *Collect it, collect it quick,* she say. *When that hour come, that hour in the month, the time of womanness. Collect it in a jar and when nobody looking, mix it in him dark tea or peas soup. As soon as he drink it, he bound to love you and forsake all other. He goin' love you till love turn him into fool.*

—For the massa to drink, she say, but him already get up to leave. Lilith feel to slap herself for thinking what she not to think, but then he stagger again and grab the door before he fall. She run and put him arm over her shoulder. He heavier than she thought and they both nearly tumble over. But then she steady him by bracing her feet and they hobble upstairs. Midway they almost crash in the banister. He grind her toe with him boot and Lilith gnash her teeth to kill the yell. The next step nearly throw both of them to the ground, but she grab the banister in time. All the time he mumbling. They go, one tricky step at a time, up the stairs and Lilith wishing that Homer don't wake up. Him arm over her shoulder and she smelling him new, smelling the massa in a way that most nigger will never get to smell. She smelling old sweat and perfume and what must be liquor after the sweetness start to sour the breath. In the room Massa Humphrey throw himself on the bed, taking Lilith with him. Lilith feel herself sink into the sheet and into him. She thinking to stay but get up when she realise he mumbling again. As she rise him hand slide off her shoulder.

—Gifted as my clothes may be, they can't undress themsel . . . he say. Lilith hesitate. Then she step closer to the bed, but hesitate again.

—Get on with it, he say louder and lift up him right leg.

Lilith not used to no boot shucking and take a long time just to get the boot past the ankle. Massa Humphrey curse and say, Turn the other w . . . way, and twirl him arms until him eye start to swirl and he fall back on the bed. Lilith climb over him leg like she straddling a goat. When she finally shuck the boots off, he sit up again and take him coat off. He point to the cravat and she pull the bow and unwrap, trying not to look at him and thinking he must be looking at her when all of a sudden he lean and bury him face in her belly. Lilith don't move. Him breath was warming up her dress. Him forehead was right under her breasts. She look down at him wild hair that tempting, begging, commanding her to touch. He go to fall back in the bed and she catch him by the collar. She pull the blouson over him head and try to not look at him chest. Lilith wondering what a woman to do with a man right in front of her. He lean back down on the bed and pull down him breeches himself. Like many a young white man who get season in the colonies, Massa Humphrey don't fuss with underpants. Massa Humphrey climb on the bed and fling himself between a mountain of pillow.

—Good night, Lilith, is it not? Lilith? the massa say underneath the pillow.

—Y-yes, massa. Lilith them call me.

—Lilith. Liiiilith. Liliiiiiiith. Good ni . . .

—Good night, massa, Lilith say and leave the room.

Lilith try not to think too fast, too fast for the negro head. Lilith-Lilith-Lilith he say. He take her name, make song. He know her now. He say her name under the pillow. A whisper before sleep like her name be what come before peace. He call Lilith by her name three time. And he knew who she was in the kitchen and ask for her. And he look at her different, like he regarding a fine bird. And he look longer, so longer that she have to look away first. And he don't talk to her like he talk to the niggers in the day, but perhaps that just be him dawn voice. He know her name. Lilith slip down the stairs back to the kitchen, drunk on something else. *Opapala in you, the goddess of hunger*, she hear a voice say and look round for Homer.

Nothing.

Now for this whole day Massa Humphrey mother get back sense. And the woman angry like God at Sodom! Is three day before the New Year's Eve ball and Lilith hoping Miss Isobel arrive soon to get some of the wrath. Miss Isobel and her chaperone coming late for breakfast. Massa Humphrey, who she put to bed mere hours ago, still sleeping. The mistress up and running round the house wondering who put up these wretched green grotesqueries all over her house. Her voice spitting sense and anger but her near-white hair wild and her dress musty from never been taken off in weeks. She shout to Homer that there was no way a slave could have dared without permission and that she will flog the insolence out of the slave herself, even if it is Homer. Homer fan away her smell and tell her that it be Miss Isobel Roget from Coulibre who come over and change everything on account of the mistress being sick.

—That slattern Laeticia Roget dispatched her daughter here? To do as she chooses in *my* house? In *my* house? the mistress say. She furious now.

—We shall see about that! We *shall* see about that! the mistress shout. The mistress walk 'cross to Massa Humphrey room and don't bother knock.

—Humphrey! Humphrey! Get up this instant, she say. Plenty negro be near the door to hear the hataclaps.

—Humphrey! Humphrey!

—Mama? Oh sweet heavens, Mama, are you well?

—Clearly not! If this is still my house!

—Have a care, I beg you. Not so much noise.

—I shall be a shrieking harpy if I choose. How dare that hussy's daughter, that *Frenchwoman*, come into my house and change my things. Is she the mistress of this estate now, is that how you will have it?

—Good heavens no, Mama. How could you even ask such a thing of your son? You were ill and indisposed and rather than cancel the event, I—

—You had her come and change away as she saw fit.

—We haven't changed everything, dear Mama.

—Then pray tell me, why is there such an insipid green all over my ballroom?

Massa Humphrey sigh.

—Forgive me, Mama, I have been truly remiss. But we had it on good authority that the governor's wife absolutely despises blue. Surely you would expect us to be rid of it? I know you would take no pleasure in offending her ladyship.

The mistress stop huff and puff.

—I shall not bring any French flavour to my ball, Humphrey. I suppose next you will be marrying the Creole.

—Mother. I beg you, Massa Humphrey say and climb out of the bed.

—Good heavens! I see you sleep in the French fashion nowadays. And your poor mama!

She turn away from her son, but look a little.

—Oh, Mother, I daresay I didn't leave your womb in tails or breeches, he say. She don't say nothing but watch him go to privy.

—Now if you'll excuse me, I have matters of a natural function to take care of. You will join us for breakfast, won't you, Mama?

—Why, yes, thank you. Such a wonderful son have I, to invite me to breakfast *in my own house*. Next thing I know, I'll be getting an invitation to tea as well. I shall endeavour my very best to attend then, shan't I? the mistress say.

—That is all your loving, undressed son asks, Mama, Massa Humphrey say and close the door to the privy. The mistress huff and puff all the way down into the kitchen.

—I suppose soon you'll be marrying the Creole! she say in that whisper when people really want you to hear what they say.

Lilith and Homer setting knife and fork on the table for breakfast. As she set down a fork at the head of the table, Lilith look at Homer.

—You set Obeah 'pon the Johnny-jumpers? she say.

—What?

—Me say if you work Obeah 'pon the Johnny-jumpers.

—Listen, chile, I don't practise no black magic on this premises and anybody who say different goin' deal with me.

—You forget what you do with Circe? Me don't believe you.

—Well, me chile, me never care what you believe yesterday, and me don't care today, but who's to say how me goin' feel tomorrow, eh?

Now that Andromeda dead, Lilith take over her place in the dining room when the massa family eat. These days, Miss Isobel at every breakfast because the best work get done in the early hours, she say. Every now and then, Massa Humphrey will lose sight of the Miss and just call her Isobel, but nobody notice except Lilith.

Everything 'bout white people circle round bedroom, ballroom and dining table. The dining table near as long as two carriage and the wood dark like night. The edge curve around like circle and carve up with leaf and flowers in the wood. There be twelve chairs round the table, fourteen when extra company come calling. Homer say the cup, saucer and plate come from England. The last time anybody broke a dish was a slave girl back in 1784 and she get whip so hard she couldn't lift butter after that. Homer stand behind the chair at the foot of the table. Lilith and the other kitchen negroes stand beside each other on the left and right side. Supper can sometimes take up to ten course plus coffee, cake and nuts, but most times breakfast much simpler, with just one course of everything served at once. When the massa and family come in the room, the negroes pull out the chairs for them to sit and put the napkin in them lap. The negroes commence to serve. Lilith on the left side near the head of the table where the massa sit. But one of the mens pull out the chair for him. The chaperone grunt. Lilith remember her.

At the breakfast, the mistress chatting up plenty. She don't even eat much.

—I'm afraid we've not had the pleasure, Mr. Quinn, and my son seems to have taken leave of his manners, if not senses, she say.

—The pleasure is mine, Robert Quinn say and kiss the mistress' hand like he didn't meet her four time before.

—I've always had a soft spot for the Irish, even after that sorry business when you joined forces with the ghastly French in that ridiculous insurgency.

Robert Quinn look like he 'bout to choke. Miss Isobel put her fan to her mouth.

—A tiny fraction of me countrymen in County Mayo as it was, ma'am, and dealt with they were, he say.

—And how pleased I am to hear it. And you, young Miss Isobel, tell me how is your dear mother, Ludmilla?

—My mother has long been dead, ma'am. My stepmother, Laeticia, is quite well.

—Laeticia, Ludmilla, posh. At my age one loses track of the many merry wives of your father.

Then the mistress ask Massa Humphrey why he not in London for the season.

—Nowadays nobody takes the season seriously until March, Mama, he say.—Besides, with all that's to be done here I would not have much time indeed.

—Such a tragedy for you, for you're still young. In mind, at the very least. Ah, the season, I'm too old for such thoughts now, but when I was a young lady of betrothal age, I daresay I managed to win a husband after only one season. Ah, the times, the balls, the suppers, how other women were envious! And a West Indian planter, said my mama. I insist that you go back to London at once, Humphrey!

—But Mama, my place is here, with you.

—A young gentleman has no place with a West Indian woman. That is all I am now, I'm afraid.

—I shall never leave you alone, Mama.

—Please. To be a woman in the West Indies is to be alone. Isn't that so, young Elizabeth?

—Isobel, ma'am.

—I'm too old to remember or care, unfortunately. Anyway Humphrey, the season is the only chance you'll have for an ideal wife, of some decent breeding. I insist that you ship yourself off at once. And you, Mr. Quinn, are you married?

—No lady has blessed me with her hand yet, ma'am.

—Really? Has my house become a haven for young bachelors? Surely there must be a maid or serving girl somewhere who seeks to be made into a decent woman.

Robert Quinn don't say nothing, but look at Massa Humphrey, who sigh and nod. Everybody perplex. The mistress will remember which woman was wearing dress with pink lace trim and how it cause scandal back in 1779, but she will forget that her husband dead. She still talk to him. The mistress will know 'bout man things like war and how much slave must cost, but will forget that she must go to the commode to piss. And Homer used to think that the mistress be in her room writing letter until one day she pick up a page and see that she writing list. Nothing but list. List of name, list of animal, list of number, list of Bible chapter, list of list. And more list. Something of the mistress' mind lost in her room.

Soon everybody talking 'bout Saint-Domingue. Miss Isobel say it be a colossal, bloody tragedy on account that she still be having some sort of cousin over there.

—My family is at least half French, you know, she say.

—I think that makes you the enemy, Miss Isobel. Now speak true, are you a spy? Massa Humphrey say. They laugh like two little pickney up to mischief. The chaperone grunt like she be the mama. Robert Quinn don't say nothing.

—Serves those bloody Frenchies right, the mistress say. Too slack, that Code Noir. Way too permissive with those negroes. I swear, give a negro a free hand and he'll rub it all over you.

Massa Humphrey look at him mother hard.—What do you know about Code Noir, Mama? he say.

—More than you know about French-British relations, she say and look at Miss Isobel.

—Either way, it's a calamitous business, Robert Quinn say.—If we're not careful we'll be heading the same way.

—Whatever do you mean, Robert?

—Come now, Humphrey, he say and see the mistress and Miss Isobel glare at him.—Really, Master Wilson, Jamaica is about as stable as gunpowder in a kitchen.

—Quinn, I'll not have you scare the ladies needlessly. Surely it's not as bad as all that, Massa Humphrey say.

—Not as bad as all that? Are ye blind or stupid?

—Mr. Quinn! I'd thank you to remember your place, Miss Isobel say.

—Oh I'm well aware of it, ma'am. It has been made quite plain to me.

—Quinn, enough. As I said, I will not have you frighten the ladies, Massa Humphrey say.

—I'm not as easily scared as all that, Miss Isobel say.

—Master Humphrey, there has been a major uprising every year in this colony for the past five years. Montego Bay is still in ruins after being burnt down five years ago. I say, every month there's one conspiracy or another.

—Indeed, and the regiment always rises to the occasion. They dealt with those sorry niggers in Trelawney only a fortnight ago.

—Regiment indeed. Pansies, the lot o' them.

—Gentlemen! Surely there's another forum for this kind of talk? Miss Isobel say and nod in the direction of the negroes.—And you, Mr. Quinn, show some decorum if you're capable.

Quinn face get red.

—We're the envy of the colonies, Montpelier is, Massa Humphrey say.

—Besides, Mr. Quinn has not even been living in Jamaica a year, certainly not long enough to judge these things, Miss Isobel say.

—Trelawney damn near—

—Quinn, Massa Humphrey say.

—Pardon me. Trelawney almost became an African state in seventeen ninety-eight.

—What has gotten into you, Quinn? Is it some Irish propensity to exaggerate?

—Goes along with the British tendency to disregard the obvious, I'll wager.

—One is either British or brutish, as far as I can see, Massa Humphrey say. Quinn, him face still red, don't say nothing.

Everybody watching the two. Lilith watch the two man as both they skin get red. She watch the two man as they grip the knife and fork harder and talk lower and lower through grit teeth. Lilith watching man acting like how man act when chain not round him neck or scar on him back. Lilith think soon one goin' leap after the other and they goin' fight like wild animal on the floor. Lilith smelling expectation and it smelling like sweat. Lilith look at what she not to look at in way she not to look. Homer hiss and jolt Lilith. The chaperone not messing with man argument, she want more chocolate cake. Her third slice. Lilith nearly miss the plate because Massa Humphrey slam him hand on the table. The chaperone grab the plate. Robert Quinn hold him two hand up in the air.

—'Tis a fact, it is. As plain as day. The ratio of whites to negroes here is the same as Saint-Domingue, Humphrey, Robert Quinn say.

—And we have far greater control over them than Saint-Domingue, Massa Humphrey say.

—I hear the streets are covered in blood over there, Miss Isobel say.

—French blood, Robert Quinn say, and she look at him in a way that would shrivel the fountain statue.

—Well, I suppose now that you will have nothing to do with all things French, you have clearly resolved to a life of no French kisses, sir, Miss Isobel say.

Massa Humphrey blush. Then he laugh. Robert Quinn smile a little. The chaperone say, It must have been the wet nurse who taught you such vulgarity, dear, and everybody laugh some more. Everybody laughing so much that nobody see that the mistress did gone far back into herself. Not until she scream.

—One hundred pounds, not fifty! One hundred pounds, not fifty! One hundred pounds, not fifty! the mistress say.

Homer and Lilith hear her first. The others still rocking back and forth from what the chaperone never mean to be joke.

—How many times must you be told! say the mistress. This time everybody quiet.

—Tell us what, Mama? Massa Humphrey say.

—One hundred pounds, not fifty, one hundred pounds, not godforsaken fifty, the mistress say and throw away her fork.

—What hundred pounds, Mam—

—Oh, to hell with it all, you were never really cut out for slave affairs, selling a healthy buck for fifty pounds. I truly wish you were a man, Patrick! Sometimes I truly do!

Massa Humphrey shut him eye and grab the edge of the table hard. Robert Quinn and Miss Isobel look away. Only the chaperone didn't know what the story was.

—Who's Patrick, madam? she ask.

—And what business have you to be inquiring about my husband? the mistress shout. The chaperone shrink. Massa Humphrey look at Homer.

—Patrick! Get down here this instant! Patrick! Patrick! the mistress say.

Massa Humphrey face bury in him hand. The mistress quiet for a little bit, so quiet that the wind start whisper in the window. But then she scream. And scream and scream again. Robert Quinn leap from him seat, but Massa Humphrey head still hiding in him hand. The mistress start flap her hands like they be wings that can't fly and tip back with the chair. Lilith rush first and catch the chair, but the mistress coming down so hard that they fall to the floor anyway. Homer rush to the mistress to pull her up but the woman in hysterics, screaming to butcher the horse that kill her husband. Miss Isobel hand in her lap and she staring at the tablecloth. The chaperone too. Robert Quinn throw down him napkin and go over to the mistress, Homer and Lilith. Robert Quinn reach down to help but Homer shout out to give her air and him pull back. The mistress' head fall back in Lilith lap and she still like a corpse.

—Take her away, Massa Humphrey say.

The mistress room look like evening even when is noon. Lilith go to pull back a drape but Homer shake her head no. Robert Quinn and Homer put the mistress to bed, but as soon as she hit the sheet she wake up. She weak. She saying word that don't sound like no word. Then she look over and see Lilith.

—Who are you, one of Jack Wilkins' bastards? she say. Lilith don't know what to say. She look up and see Robert Quinn looking at her. The mistress nod off. Then her eye open again.

—I will not see my son betrothed to a Creole half-Frenchie coster-monger's daughter, she say. Not on my life, such as it is.... Patrick! Is that you, Patrick! Put a stop to this childish nonsense and come out of the closet! Patrick! Patrick!

Homer tell Lilith and Robert Quinn to go, for she will deal with it and it not right for a lady to be seen like this. Quinn open the door for Lilith and she step through queer-like, her hands touching her shoulders. Outside the door be Massa Humphrey.

Robert Quinn say Homer is taking care of her but Massa Humphrey cut him off by raising him hand.

—I will not hear you speak ill of the French when Miss Isobel is around, Quinn, Massa Humphrey say.

—Maybe you've forgotten, Master Wilson, that we're at war with the French, Robert Quinn say. Massa Humphrey walk away. Lilith watch him leave, following the creak in the new boot, the colour of the new breeches, to the waistcoat that shine, to the hair. She turn and see Robert Quinn looking at her.

THE BALL COME. LILITH READY. BY HER LONESOME LILITH hem her dress, since Andromeda was taller, and take in the waist, since Andromeda was fatter. The needle and thread she thief from Homer. Lilith don't have no real sewing skill, not even after fixing the mistress' petticoats on several occasion, so the hem uneven and the waist too narrow. Homer watching Lilith and not saying nothing. Sometime Lilith see Homer watching her and cut her eye. Lilith 'fraid of what Homer itching to say, but Homer don't say a peep. Andromeda daughter now so crazy since her mama dead that Massa Humphrey sell her to a white man from Kingston who judge how plump her pussy be before he judge her face.

Two night in a row, Lilith wake up and see a woman watching her. The first night she go to scream but catch her mouth. She first think it be Andromeda in the shadow but this woman thin. Her hair wild and natty and her skirt spread wide like bat wing. Lilith can't make out the face. She don't see no eye, only the blackest black. When she leave something visit Lilith mind and don't leave for the rest of the day. *Six tell six tell six,* she remember the cave and the words like a chant.

—Stop come near me bed, she say to Homer the next day.

Homer hiss.

—And you funeral frock don't scare me neither, Lilith say.

—And why me would a-come to a mix-up nigger bed, girl chile? she say. Lilith hiss too, like she don't believe but she know that Homer too proud to lie to any negro girl who beneath her.

The following night Lilith didn't sleep, thinking that the woman was some sort of dream witch that wouldn't come if she stay awake. Lilith pace round the cellar and count wine bottles and stomp the dust out of her mat and search the cellar for rats with the tallow candle. She listen as the great house go to sleep. She try to stand up but her blinking getting longer and heavier. Lilith go upstairs to the kitchen to wash her face and look around. She lift her dress to wipe her face and the night breeze make her legs shiver. Lilith cover herself and turn to leave but at the doorway be the dark woman. Lilith jump back and her head clap a pot hanging over the counter and that pot hit another pot, that hit another pot and set off a ringing like Sunday church bells. Lilith grab after the pots, her heart beating hard as she wait for somebody to wake up. She fearing and hoping somebody wake up. Nobody. At the cellar doorway, the dark woman gone. Lilith stoop down to the kitchen floor, watching the doorway. Tiredness and fear fight for so long that as soon as she close her eyes she would jump up, giving herself a fright. Tiredness soon win. Lilith fall asleep on the kitchen floor.

Morning come and Lilith realise that she wish she had somebody to talk to. Certainly not them six woman who did want her to join them. Some she don't see since that night, but others when they see her act like they don't know her, even Gorgon, who only nod when nobody else looking. Even Pallas, who work right beside her in the kitchen and sometimes had a good word, don't say nothing no more. One time Lilith go outside to throw away water and see Iphigenia passing by in a coffle of artisan slave that Massa Humphrey rent out to the Worthy Park Estate. Even on the way to the hot sun, Iphigenia still cover up in long sleeve dress, still wearing neck scarf. Iphigenia look right through Lilith like she make out of breeze. Lilith tell herself that she don't care, she goin' change her heart to wood. But she perplex. Is hard work after all, hardening heart for nigger and then softening it every time Massa Humphrey pass by.

Cooking commence from early in the morning. There be mutton and pork to roast, ham to bake, beef and fish to stew, chicken, duck and goose to fry, and crabs to pickle. There be bread yam to sear, plantains to boil, pawpaw sauce to stir, potatoes to steam, carrots and cabbage to chop. There be chocolate batter for cake, flour and corn for pudding, cheese to slice and wine bottle to wash off from the cellar dust and rum and whiskey to get from the liquor merchant. Pallas boiling the soup. All of a sudden the kitchen go off in silence, one negro then another, except for one of the mens who ears hard. Homer slap him shoulder and the man look up and shut up. Miss Isobel in the kitchen. Lilith look behind her for Massa Humphrey, but she come by her lonesome. She walk round the kitchen looking over what cooking. She nod and smile when she see the cakes cooling and put her fan to her mouth when she see the chicken get pluck.

—Mornin', mistress, one of the mens say and bow down real low. She nod.

She check the lamb shoulder and the pork loin and she check the greens, touching things light, then wiping her hand on a kerchief. Miss Isobel ask for a spoon and go over to where Pallas cooking. She dip in the pot and blow over the spoon, then she sip a little. Pallas in fear and trembling. Miss Isobel face screw up and she spit in the pot.

—Ghastly! Positively ghastly! More salt than in the Dead Sea, she say. You'll have to begin again, surely, she say and leave. Pallas perplex. She cook the same soup the same way, two time a week for the past three year. Homer raise one eyebrow.

—Do what your, I mean the mistress tell you, Homer say. Pallas go to pull off the pot but Homer nod no.

—Put in three potato to suck up the salt, chile, and add two spoon of sugar, she say. Everybody look 'pon Homer, but Homer just go on with what she doing.

Lilith like how her dress fit even if she can't breathe right. Christmas is for nigger and New Year's Eve is for backra, but Lilith not hearing that. Because of the night before, Lilith doze off to sleep in the kitchen. She peeling potatoes and almost cut her finger, for her head elsewhere. She want to go to the ball and that be white people affairs and she not white but mulatto, yet at Montpelier mulatto no different from nigger. Lilith want to go to the ball and impress Massa Humphrey but she not sure what that mean exactly. Perhaps she too young and not ready for woman things and Massa Humphrey don't take too kindly to young flesh. Lilith tell herself that she want to see what the white womens goin' wear and see how the white womens goin' look and hear how white womens laugh in the colonies. She think of white flesh and black flesh, that really be brown flesh by blood and the two flesh melt into one flesh that don't know colour. Then Lilith wonder if she dreaming because dreaming is one thing God never allow negro to do. For that she blame Circe for living like a free nigger only to have the Johnny-jumper take that away. She start to blame Circe for giving her white woman expectation and hatred for negro life. Putting the blame on Circe make her feel righter 'bout Massa Humphrey. She wonder 'bout what Pallas say 'bout feeling sweet for a man. That be what she born for.

Before the evening ball come the morning church service. The negroes gather near a clearing by the field. The preacher 'fraid to go any further 'cause he not too long off the ship from Liverpool (and him heart went out for the hell-bent negroes that be on the ship) and the massa tell him that snake and leopard live in the bush. The preacher red and fat like a choking pig, but him pocket fatter from the guinea and shillings that he just get from Massa Humphrey. The preacher wearing a black hat that wide at the brim and hide him face until he look up.

Him eye little and squinty and lip puck together like a dainty woman. Him jacket black and breeches grey and too tight and him crotches wouldn't behave. The preacher burnin' in the sun so much that him pick up that one-day-old hog smell that only white people pick up.

The negroes get preaching ten times a year. The last time was All Saints' Day. Although they preach the same thing every Christmas and New Year's, niggers don't understand what a baby in the bush can do. Seem that if baby get left in manger he would scratch up, bite up and dead by the third day. But white people think this be the greatest thing. The baby grow up and they kill him, and white people think that be even greater. It make plenty sense that white people would get so much mirth and joy out of this 'cause nobody kill for fun like backra. Preacher tell nigger that God is man and baby. Then he say that God is baby in December but man only four month later. But then he say God is father and he is son and he is spirit. That sound like he breed himself to get himself, then kill himself. White man God perplexing like the white man. Then when it be Easter, they say that people kill him and then he rise up from the dead and he in heaven now. We still don't know what all that have to do with a God. God supposed to be God of things people can be or use or be 'fraid of, like Asaase Yaa or the terrible Ogun or the Imilozi bush spirits. Preacher say there be only one God right after he explain that there be three God and look up in the sky when he say so. Some people wondering what God doing up there so long and how come he no fall down yet.

Other people pleased like puss over white man God. They not fidgeting and scratching in the heat. They not hissing or leaning on right foot, then left. Preacher say they's goin' get reward in heaven and they screaming and wailing and falling down on they knees saying, Thank you, Jesus! Preacher man tell them that the Bible say them to stand firm in they suffering 'cause that is they lot for being the cursed son of Noah. That Jesus don't care for slavery but for the heart of the slave. That Jesus goin' reward them in heaven for being a good nigger. The preacher look at Massa Humphrey as he ride pass and start sing "All Glory Be to God on High," and start to pick up him belongings. Even as he leave and the negroes scatter some still be singing the hymn.

Lilith couldn't wait for the preacherman to leave. Everybody have to resume the cooking and the cleaning and the preparing 'cause the ball start at seven o' clock. Lilith go in the kitchen and see it empty, save for Homer. Lilith try to walk past her to go down to the cellar.

—What a thing, eh? Some people pleased like puss, Homer say.

Lilith don't say nothing.

—Some people in happiness and rejoicing when they should be in fear and in trembling, Homer say.

—That must be old people talk, 'cause me don't understand you, say Lilith.

—So it go, he who don't hear must feel after all. Lord knows what happen when a nigger girl not satisfied with her lot, Homer say and walk away.

Lilith still for a little bit. Then she hiss and go downstairs. Lilith say that she is big woman, but when she put on the dress she feel the most girlish. She don't have no looking glass, but in the silver tray she lookin' just fine.

Five o'clock. All the negroes have to assemble except the cooks, who getting everything hot and ready. Homer standing by the soup that Miss Isobel spit in. She have all the negroes line up for Miss Isobel to inspect. Four fat negro woman in the line, follow by Pallas, another woman, Lilith, then three mens. The women in white frock with black skirts that spread out 'cause for the first time they wearing petticoat underneath. Everybody hair push back in a cap that Miss Isobel sketch herself. Only Lilith dress showing bosom, which make some people look twice. Miss Isobel step in to look over the negroes. She don't say nothing, but she nod to Homer and leave. They soon hear a horse whinny. Miss Isobel gone back to Coulibre to dress in what Homer call her finery.

About an hour later Massa Humphrey and Robert Quinn come back home from horse riding. Homer at the door to tell both that they so late that they must be going to some other New Year's Eve ball. Massa Humphrey remind her that that kind of talk begging for a whipping, but Homer say nothing. Robert Quinn whisper sorry to Homer when Massa Humphrey gone off too far to hear it.

—Send one of them to prepare my bath, Homer, Massa Humphrey shout.

—A female this time, Homer.

Lilith make a small step.

—Not you, Homer say.

Homer point to Pallas, who frown. Lilith remember that Pallas be her sister and never show any malice towards her, but that don't stop the disliking.—Some people think 1801 goin' be different from 1800, Homer say, to nobody.

Miss Isobel come back looking like is heaven she just come from. She float down her brougham carriage all covered in white. She take off her mob cap and her yellow hair part in the middle and pull back from her face except for two curls that spin up her cheek. Nobody ever wear a dress like this in the colony for sure. It white but white like milk, a deep colour that look like you could drink it. Right on her bosom wrap a cloth that hide and show at the same time. Look one way it white, look another way it clear to see through, look another way it shiny. The cloth go all the way around her shoulder and back. Right below her bosom there be a green ribbon that shiny like the silver. Her sleeves big and puffy and cover all the way to above her elbow. From her elbow down cover in glove that stop at her palm and show off her pretty fingers. Massa Humphrey take aback when he see her step in through the front door. The negroes take aback when they see him.

The last time anybody ever see the massa dress so gentleman-like was when he come here from England. The massa in a black coat with tails that brush the back of him knee and him white cravat cover him neck all the way up to the ears. Him breeches and stockings white and shiny but not as shiny as the black shoes he wearing, a first for him.

—Good evening, ma'am, Massa Humphrey say to Miss Isobel.

—And a good evening it is, but we've had this discussion before, Master Wilson. *Ma'am* refers to my mother, Miss Isobel say.

Three hundred guests of the most proper class and breeding expected. Confirmation come from the Earl of Warwick and Lord Cheltenham and Dowager Baroness Essex. Massa Humphrey and Miss Isobel in the hallway to greet the guests after one of the speaky-spokey negroes announce them. Some of the white people think it peculiar, but they say how much they admire a planter who could manage to get so much refinement out of a negro. Miss Isobel mother and father come. Is years since they come calling to Montpelier. Massa Roget come in black like he in magistrate clothes with long white curly hair running down him shoulders like woman who ready for bed. The mistress in white looking near like her daughter. Governor Nugent and her ladyship late. Robert Quinn come to the ball dress up in him old navy uniform. The gold button shine 'gainst the dark blue and gold fringe cover both shoulder. Him breeches light grey and him boots black. Quinn come alone.

Andromeda was the one who get the training so it hard for Lilith to keep up. She moving too slow with the dishes, walking from right to left instead of left to right when crossing the room, and bouncing into two negro already. Watch where you goin', fool! one of the womens say when they go back into the kitchen. By now, the ballroom full with people. The governor and Lady Nugent come and every white man and woman try meet and make friend. The governor look like he just come to the island, which mean to say he whiter than everybody else, and redder too from mosquito bite and sunburn. Him eye so blue that it look like they come from water. The governor dress like Massa Humphrey except that him breeches blue, stockings white and him shoes little and shiny like woman shoe. Him brown hair cut short with curls all over him face, as is the latest fashion. The governor smile with everybody, but Lady Nugent look around mostly at the negroes. She didn't stop looking at negroes the whole night, especially the mens every time they talk. The womens all gather near Lady Nugent to see what a woman of peerage wearing for the London season. Her dress white like Miss Isobel, but the sleeve and the sash blue. Lady Nugent nose so straight that when she raise her head to look down on people, all you see is two nose hole. She talk only one time to ask some of the womens who gather what is a chère amie. One woman cough and two womens blush, but Miss Isobel say, I think she is nothing more than a consort, in the biblical sense, of course.

—A mistress, you mean, say Lady Nugent.—I see the British appetite for the common law is quite pronounced in the colonies. Permit me to say, in the few months I've been here I've seen so many bastards and so many regarding this as a natural state of affairs that I have begun to doubt the legitimacy of my own children! Lady Nugent laugh, but only Miss Isobel laugh with her.

Massa Humphrey ask Governor Nugent, How was your first Jamaican Christmas? The governor look like he just smell fresh shit.

—I'd fain forget this infernal island sooner than later. That much I will offer, he say.—This was my first Christmas without sleigh bells. But, dare I ask, is it true that wedding bells may be in the offing? Surely I will not be denied some entertainment soon?

Massa Humphrey face turn red and he say that he would have thought Spanish Town so exciting that nobody would have time to concoct rumour.

—Exciting? If there is only one thing I've come to understand about the colonies, my dear man, it is that one does nothing here but wait. That is all.

The governor go on to say how he grow up hearing about the exciting exploits of Jamaica but he was disappointed that he didn't run into a single buccaneer yet. Massa Humphrey laugh and say that when he come here he was hoping to see a mermaid. The governor laugh. Lilith watching from the hole in the kitchen door. Lilith wondering what to do to get the massa attention.

—Move along, girly, Pallas whisper behind her and push. Lilith almost trip inside the kitchen. Pallas grab a tray and go back through the door. Lilith decide to rest her feet.

—The ball pleasing you? somebody say. Lilith jump. Homer. She standing by the table pouring soup into little bowls all on a silver tray.

—Some people come late, yet they still want all nine course, she say.

—Everything so pretty, me never see nothing like that yet, Lilith say.

—Yes, yes, outside nigger only see a little. Then sometimes they see too much, Homer say.

—Me not no field nigger, Lilith say.

—Must be my mistake. Forget say is in midwifery you born, not bush. That be your mama, Homer say.

—What you playing? Why you talking so now? Me hear enough 'bout mother and father fi know me no care for either.

—Me not playing nothing. Me just saying that some people born under curse. Curse to do exactly what people before them do.

Lilith stand there fidgeting, she look down at her bosom and feel like covering it up.

—The massa say anything to you yet? Homer say and Lilith look up, surprised.

—W-why him goin' say nothing to me? Lilith say.

—Look like you be waiting for somebody to say something, Homer say.

—Me don't know what you labba-labbaing 'bout, Lilith say.

—Eh-eh, you using word from the slave ship? Then so it must go, everybody using mouth more and more and ear less and less, Homer say. They quiet again. Homer pour soup in the bowls.

—We meeting tonight, she say.—'Bout serious, serious things. You can come if you want to. The backra goin' be so tired that we can meet till morning. We can help you with more reading. You remember reading? You remember the little that me teach you? Remember Joseph Andrews? Him in all sorta mix-up now, that be a fact. When we done you can even scratch out you name.

—Me already have two mama and two daddy and neither serve no damn use.

—Me never say me want to be you mother, chile.

—You finger be the last thing me want in me pussy.

Homer eye shock open and her mouth quiver. Lilith think is the first time she ever see Homer shake.

—H-h-how about, how about a fist in you mouth, then? she say, but her eyes didn't mean it. Lilith look down like she shame. But then she raise her chin high like white woman.

—Carry these to the grand table outside, Homer say and point to the tray. Lilith stand up like she don't want to carry it.—Make sure the governor get serve pumpkin soup, not pepper pot, Homer say and Lilith hurry up and grab the tray.

—Careful! Homer say, remember you never get Andromeda training.

—Me not no fool, me can carry a tray, Lilith say. Lilith pick up the tray and it wobble a little, but she settle it. She go to the kitchen door and one of the mens open it.—You welcome, he say and frown. Lilith sail through the door.

—And remember to offer Rogets first, Homer shout. Lilith look back and hiss.

Then she turn round.

Too late.

Too late see that Miss Isobel's chaperone was licking her lips for more soup right in front of her. Too late. Lilith walk right into the woman and the whole ballroom hear the crash. The silver tray ram into the chaperone like a bull. The bowls shatter and porcelain cut through the chaperone dress. The soup, boiling hot, splash all over her dress. The soup spread over the chaperone neck, bosom and belly like fire. She scream. She scream again and again, like an animal, like something burnin' in hell. She scream and fall back on the ground. Five white man rush to her. One grab a pitcher of water and try to wet her with it. Some of the white womens screaming and some look away. The mens try to hold the chaperone, but she screaming and bawling and soup and porcelain on the floor. Massa Humphrey run over and Miss Isobel rush to the woman, who jerking like she having fits. Massa Humphrey face red like God at Judgement.

Lilith couldn't move.

Lilith tremble and she couldn't move.

Homer run to the chaperone.—The conservatory! Quick! Quick! She say to the white mens.

Lilith couldn't move. She looking but she not seeing, she listening but she not hearing, all the sounds come like one sound and she can't hear nothing. She don't even see it, when Massa Humphrey take all the rage of the lord and slam him knuckles in her face. Lilith stagger back, but she didn't fall. Before she can even think, he punch her in the chest, then straight in the mouth and she fall and spit blood. He about to pounce 'pon her like animal, but Robert Quinn jump in and catch him first. The force of Massa Humphrey so mighty that he nearly throw Quinn to the ground.

—Humphrey! Fer the love of God, man, not in front of yer guests! Quinn say.

The girl head jerking and blood running from her nose. She bawling and coughing. She on the floor trying to get up. Massa Humphrey look around at guests all looking away. The pianist stop play. The governor whispering something to her ladyship, who hide her face with her fan. Massa Humphrey look around again, step back and leave the ballroom to go upstairs. Robert Quinn look down at the girl. Deal with her! he say to a slave-driver who dressed up, and that driver nod to three of him cohorts. The girl try to run but she weak and pain overpowering her. And she can't see good. A slave-driver grab her by the hair and drag her outside round the back. Quinn point to the pianist and the violinist to commence playing. People talking and whispering and mumbling, but nobody leaving. Quinn go join Homer in the conservatory.

Outside, the girl spin round two times and laughter rush in one ear and outside the other. The darkness giving her nothing. She can't make out shapes. Her left eye swell and her cheek wet from either sweat or blood. A driver they call McClusky grab her and she stop spinning. He set her good. The girl standing now but she teetering. She didn't see it coming. McClusky punch her straight in the face, between eye and nose. The girl fall back flat on the ground and near knocked out. She bite her tongue.

—Jaysis, Charlie! Y'were s'pposed ta catch tha pussycat, y'were, McClusky say. The other drivers laugh. The girl only seeing a blur of white hands and faces and the faces have no eyes or nose or mouth. A hand grab her by the foot and drag her for a bit. Dirt scrape under her skin and rock cut up her legs. A hand grab her wrists and pull her up again.

—Shall we play us a nigger game, mateys? A right spot of ketchy-shooby? McClusky say.

—Wot says you, pussycat? he say to the girl.

—Always up for a fair sport, ye is, McClusky, say another.

—Well, mateys, why waste me time with something that me dingus can put to better use, eh?

The girl hear laughter running in and out of her ears again. Two hands grab two ankles and she try to scream through all the blood in her throat choking her. More laughter and singing, *Oh, she is a gal down in our alley, now, she is the gal that I spliced nearly, way, hey, bully in the alley, down cock alley, the wench fair sally.* Two hands drag her to what look like the stable. They pull her up to her feet again and start to push her from one set of hands to the other, and again and again and up and down until she lose balance with the ground and fall again. Two hand catch her. More laughter. The girl feel her dress rip off her body and cold air rush into her bruises. More laughter. McClusky say something about first and another voice say something violent. The girl hear a scuffle and a shout.

—Mince her up, a voice say.

One hand grab the girl left leg and the other grab her right and pull them as far apart from each other as sun and moon. She feel the air crawl between her. More laughter. A man pull down him pantaloon and slap him cocky till he ready. He throw himself on top of her to more laughing and shouting. The girl feel the whole weight of the man crushing her chest and forcing between her legs. A man with yellow hair, straight and sour. He grab her neck and her eyes go black.

The ball still going and people still eating, drinking and merrymaking. Robert Quinn leave Homer to overseer things but Miss Isobel take over, even making Lady Nugent laugh with a comment about chère amies. Quinn gone with the chaperone to a doctor in Spanish Town. Massa Humphrey lock himself in the bedchamber and don't come out. The girl on the ground in the stable not moving, the dust making more sound than her.

· 14 ·

Homer squeeze blood out of the rag and dip her hand in the bucket. She squeeze some of the warm water out and rub Lilith face careful. She touch Lilith neck, then forehead. She wipe the dirt and dry blood from Lilith mouth. Lilith between asleep and awake. She sputter little bit, then cough. Homer look up and search round her quarters. One candle burnin' in the room with a dim orange glow. The light make the shadows jump. Lilith on Homer bed, which used to belong to Massa Humphrey when he be a little boy, but he never did come to the estate to sleep on it. Now Lilith on the bed as Homer washing her. Lilith eye open. The right one. The left eye swell and shut. She start bawl.

—Hush now, girl chile, hush, Homer say. Don't make them give you reason to cry more.

Lilith see shadows on the wall moving. There be more womens in the room. Somebody fussing with her foot but she too weak to move. Bitch too heavy, Gorgon say. Lilith feel Gorgon touch her and jerk.

—Her body have seven or eight bruise but nothing broke. But is like dey was tryin' skin de gal neck, Gorgon say.

Homer cut some sinkle-bible plant stalk and scrape the clear jelly out of the middle. It cool and tingle like mint. First she rub some on Lilith face, then neck. Gorgon rub down her breast and Lilith flinch. Gorgon scrape some jelly out of a stalk and rub her belly. They roll her over and Lilith bawl out. Homer and Gorgon rub her. Pallas and Iphigenia on the lookout.

Miss Isobel is the last guest to leave. Quinn come back that night cursing, since the hotel in Spanish Town didn't take too kindly to mens of Irish descent.

—Ye'd think I was a bloody Jew, Robert Quinn say to nobody, although Homer be in him quarters.

—What news 'bout milady, massa?

—I have no knowledge, unfortunately. Doctor Willhew would have her stay the night. He may move her to Kingston tomorrow.

—Lord have mercy.

—How does the lass? he ask Homer.

—She do as well as the lord allow, she say.

—Maybe that's not as good a thing as ye think.

—Sah?

—I've witnessed this in him before, that Humphrey Wilson. More than once and 'twas not a pretty sight. Not at all, but I've said too much.

—Lawd Jesus.

—Vicious thing, that temper of his. Quite mean. I've seen him unleash it on many in Europe, even those of the fairer... There was this time... Good God! I am remiss. Go now; I shall not discuss this with the likes of ye.

—She deserve it, massa, Homer say.

—Aye, ye'll get no argument from me there. Couple estates in this very colony she would have been shot for what she had done. I hope the lass is made of strong stuff.

—Pardon me asking, Massa Quinn, but strong for what? Homer say.

—Because of this, this episode, woman. She brought out the absolute devil in Master Wilson and he'll never forgive her for letting him show it. Alas, she has been whipped and disciplined by the driver and that should be enough.

—Whipped, massa?

—Well, what was the lass expecting, a wee spank on her little arse? A firm fifteen lashes she had coming for starters, maybe twenty.

—No, massa. They...

—What did they...?

—Massa...

—Speak up, woman, what's holding yer tongue?

Silence come between the two. Quinn jaw drop.

—Good God, certainly they did not...

—They do what one expect from a man, massa.

Robert Quinn jump up and march to Homer quarters. Homer rush behind, almost having to skip to catch up. Quinn march right up to Homer room and push in the door. Gorgon jump up and Callisto leap through the window. On the bed, blubbering, was Lilith.

—Jesus Christ, Robert Quinn say.

Morning sun come and wake Lilith up. One eye open wide and the other just a little. Lilith not knowing where she be and start cry again. Nobody not there, so she make the breeze hush her. Lilith hear a screaming but see nobody in the room. Lilith hear again and see herself seeing the chaperone. Lilith shift in the bed and yelp as her shoulder burn. She start to cry again and see the dark woman in the corner of the room. Homer? Lilith whimper, but the dark woman don't move. Lilith close her eye tight, then open them again. The dark woman gone.

Lilith see moonlight and think the day silver. She see sunlight and think the night yellow. Some morning she see Homer touching her face, some time she see Gorgon or Pallas or Iphigenia and flinch. The room close up and in the dark she think she see the dark woman but is only Callisto, looking up to the ceiling and whittling with her knife. She close her eye again and wake up to see Pallas.

—Is, is morning? Lilith say.

—Still night, Pallas say.

Lilith don't say nothing.

—Is me did find you, Pallas say.—You lucky too, 'cause dem cum was all over you. Me clean you off and wash out you pussy before me call Homer. You remember that, Pallas say. She pull a green pawpaw out of her apron and cut four slice with a knife.

—Now eat this, she say.

Lilith don't want to eat or talk or do nothing with she mouth.

—Eat it!

Lilith eat one slice and go to spit. She put back the rest.

—Listen to me. Plenty man rape you tonight. One of them seed must did get in you. So you goin' eat the green pawpaw until up in that womb clean out, you hear me? Don't have no dutty stinking white pickney.

Lilith eat the rest.

—You eat. And you goin' eat for the next couple day. Week and month if you have to. And if anything leave you pussy, just catch it in a cloth and tie it up and hide it. Don't look, girl, me talking to you! Don't look at it, you hear me? Don't look at it.

Lilith don't say nothing. Pallas open her mouth then, like she 'bout to say something, then don't. She turn away from Lilith.

—Fuckin' backra bastard sons of bitches. Sometimes me think the only reason they give me this goddamn one-bullet musket is because so much of them deserve kill that me could never make up me mind.

Lilith try to look at her.

—Enough goin' soon be goddamn enough, she say and gone in the dark before Lilith notice she stop talk.

.   .   .

Homer upstairs by Massa Humphrey door, hearing Robert Quinn tell Massa Humphrey that most of the broke-up porcelain did stick through the chaperone clothes but never cut her flesh. But the soup did burn her skin raw, her neck and bosom something awful.

—And good show, Master Humphrey, how gentlemanly of you to act like a wild beast in front of your guests, Robert Quinn say.

—Oh, don't you get all British with me, sir, Massa Humphrey say.

—I fear ye've driven them all away. I'm as British as ye've got left, Quinn say.

—Lord in heaven, I thought this sickness was gone. I swore t'was the result of some malodorous European air, Robert. I've been doing so well these few years, haven't I? Haven't I? Massa Humphrey say. Quinn nod.

—Goddamn!

—Humphrey.

—Robert Quinn, you're here to save me from myself, he say.—I haven't forgotten Venice, and that woman. This is why I have never whipped slaves, Robert. I swear to good graces, I don't know what malcontent comes over me, he say.

—Nor I, Quinn say.

—Is my standing in society quite ruined?

—Oh please, sir, yer a rogue quite like meself and that ye shall always be. Yer no better, no worse than the Prince Regent himself. I daresay yer standing was quite awful to begin with.

Massa Humphrey look stern at Robert Quinn for a good while, then laugh a little.

—Goddamn, Robert, I feel this thorn is in my side for good.

—Well, thank heavens for virtuous women whom ye shall drive yer thorn into. And Miss Isobel? Robert Quinn say.

—Isobel! Isobel! Dear Isobel! She is furious, quite furious. At the slave and at me. Curious, she wants me to apologise for my...explosion but she also thinks the slave has not been disciplined enough. I shall endeavor to satisfy her as is in my power, Massa Humphrey say.

—There is another matter, Humphrey, Quinn say. Yer man McClusky figures into it. He figures into it very badly. Seems he and the others had a fair bit of sport with the lass. She's near half-dead now from look of things.

Massa Humphrey don't say nothing for a while. Then he look straight at Quinn.

—Her misfortune then, is it not? he say. Quinn stunned but he say nothing. Homer listening.

—She'd have wished herself dead had I gotten to her.

—Good heavens, man, hasn't she had...a saving grace, I reckon then, that she's not from Venice.

—You'd do well to remember who issues the bank notes around here, Robert Quinn, Massa Humphrey say.

Homer burst through her door and light explode in the room. Ache fly up in Lilith head and she shut her eye tight. Lord have mercy, lord have mercy, Homer say. Homer run to the back of her room and pull open a trunk. She dig in and pull out a piece of red cloth wrap tight. She tear it open and coins fall out.

—Lilith, get up! She say. Lilith awake but she asleep.

—Lilith! Listen to me when me talking to you, chile, now get up, the devil waiting.

—Lilith!

Homer go over to the bed and pull Lilith. She bawl out little bit, but get up. She wobble. Homer hold her up by the door. Homer wrap the coins in the red cloth and shove it down between Lilith bosom.

—Now listen to me, chile, Homer say. Lilith start to blubber and Homer slap her. Lilith bawl out again.

—Shut you mouth and listen! Round the back of the mill be a passage, it don't look like no passage sake of no carriage pass round there no more, but look good and you can still make it out. Go down that trail and turn at the river, you have to run through the river so that you lose you smell, so the dogs, Lilith listen! So the dogs can't follow you. Then come back from the river, don't cross it, come back and go south. Continue south and you'd soon see a hut. Stay there till nightfall when me send for you. You hearing me? Stay there! Stay there till we fix some other—

The door swing open and slam against the wall. Robert Quinn step in. Homer quiet herself and step back.

—Take those off, he say.

Lilith don't know what he mean.

—Take those off at once! Robert Quinn say. Homer and Lilith never hear this voice before. Robert Quinn don't wait. He go over to Lilith, grab the dress by the bosom and pull. The dress rip and Lilith two breast tumble out and coins sprinkle 'pon the floor.

—Lawd o' massy, have mercy 'pon the chile, Massa Quinn. Have mercy, Homer say and run toward him. She touch Robert Quinn shoulder and Quinn strike her hard, so hard that she stagger back.

—Don't assume familiarity with me, woman, Robert Quinn say. Homer touch her chin, her eye wide open.

Lilith pull down the rest of her dress. Her waist wrap with white cloth. Her neck have so much bruise that it look like a quilt. Lilith did turn into a full woman and nobody knew. Her body beat down and her eye still swell, but her breasts strong and pointed. The two stand up where her eye would have. Robert Quinn see. Robert Quinn get to see that nigger flesh will find even the slightest thing to stand up, even a maggot-full, rotten chop-off foot. Robert Quinn grab Lilith by the hand and push her out the door. He go to the doorway but swing around quick.

—Do not follow, Quinn say.

—Me remember where me place be, massa. Me and the tea, Homer say. Robert Quinn pause for a little, then step out.

Outside, three Johnny-jumper grab Lilith. One grab her two arms and the other grab for her foot. A third negro, short, fat and squat, move past her foot and grab Lilith pussy. Lilith kick him with her free foot. The squat negro go to thump her but a whip crack across him back and put a stop to that quick.

—Shall I be whipping one nigger this day or two? Robert Quinn say.

To the right of the great house be a cotton tree where all the negroes gather. This was three days after New Year's Day, and white folk and nigger folk have different expectation. Massa Humphrey sitting on the terrace with Miss Isobel. The two negroes carry Lilith to the cotton tree. She struggling and she bawling and she screaming. Work stop and all the negroes gather to watch. Some of the womens don't look. They bind Lilith hand tight with a long piece of rope. A Johnny-jumper throw the long end over a high branch and the other two pull her up. Lilith scream again. Homer don't leave her room. Lilith muttering and chattering. Some of the negroes look at her like somebody they just remember to forget. Robert Quinn nod.

—This be for the uppity nigger who be thinking he or she can be hurting the massa and him folks. This be proper disciplining right here so, the fat squat negro say. Robert Quinn nod again. The taller negro curl out the whip like a long animal tongue. Bullwhip. Negro rather burn from the breath of Satan than get that. Miss Isobel looking. One or two nigger smile when they see Lilith back smooth for the last time. The tall negro swing and the whip lash Lilith straight cross her back. Lilith scream so hard that she cough. The negro lash her again. Lilith struggling 'gainst the rope and her legs swing wild like hanging man. Some people watch her face, some watch her breast, and some watch her arse and pussy. The negro lash Lilith again and her eye start to go back into her head. The new pain wake up the old pain that the massa done give her. She bawling like a girl, not a woman, and she screaming.

The negro swinging the whip wide and it curl round her back and slice her breast. Robert Quinn go up to the tall negro and slap him head with the thick end of the whip.

—The back only, ye stupid coon, Quinn say. Some laugh as the negro thank Quinn for the lick. Lilith close her eye. Seven more lash and she stop scream. Lilith swing and the rope creaking. Thirty lash and they cut her down. She fall in the dirt and stain the ground with blood.

Lilith get ten lash every day Miss Isobel come calling, which be twice that week. Now that the ball be over, it didn't seem proper for a lady to come too often to a gentleman house, not even a lady from the colonies. But as be the way of other things in the colony, some rules of Mother England get toss away like crinoline. Plus, she didn't have no chaperoning as that woman take to bed even after the injury heal. She bawl 'bout her injury all the time as reason not to leave bed and Miss Isobel confess to Massa Humphrey that she was not a even a little sad to be rid of her.

Lilith know that each day getting darker and darker for her. After a week, negroes stop come to her whipping, even them that glad she get what was coming to her. Everybody just know the scream. The frighten wild beast scream that ring throughout the estate and the field and the boiling house and the kitchen, twice a week at around the two o' clock hour. The negro scream that white people don't hear because it never stop late lunch or early afternoon tea. A negro scream be like a pig scream. A negro scream be like a dog whistle. A negro scream be like wind. Soon she stop scream. When the time come for the whipping she don't even need nobody to get her. She go to the tree early and raise her hands up. She stop cry and only wince when the lash too hard. She used to look in the sky, but by the third week she look straight at Robert Quinn and watch him look away. When they cut the rope, she drop to the ground and pick herself up. She stand and stagger a little, but still stand. Lilith raise her chin and walk over to her bundle of clothes. She put them on herself and Robert Quinn see fresh blood press through the old blood on the dress. Lilith don't say nothing and go back to the cellar. Every three of four step she limp, and one time she nearly drop, but her chin still raise.

Two nights a week, six black womens go to Homer room and mix brine, comfrey and sinkle-bible to rub into Lilith back. Even Callisto. Homer and Pallas sing a song in a tongue that be known only to them. Then they sing like negro.

Fi me love have lion heart
Fi me love have lion heart
Fi me love have lion heart
Only fi you

And the other womens come in on the back of the song.

Fi we love will never die
Fi we love will never die
Fi we love will never die
Only fi you

Lilith will hear the song and feel the drum click on they tongue and heal her back. The womens light a secret fire and spirits dance on the wall. Olokun, owner of the seas and god of water healing, and even Anansi, the spider god and trickster. The womens call on Oya, the river goddess of the Niger and wife of Shango. They call on the river mama to plead to the god of thunder and lightning to cast a thunder-stone from the sky to the field and give them powers. The womens go to the river where Oshún be waiting. The time be the night, but the moon big and bright and the river and the trees dress up in silver. The womens down by the river with Homer, all who come from slave that lay with Jack Wilkins. The womens who all have white and black in they blood with the power of two.

Then later than that, Homer read to the womens and teach the womens how to read. Homer take out the book that she steal from Massa Humphrey library, *Joseph Andrews*. Right where the Lady Booby first try to get him to see 'bout her cho-cho, but Joseph blind to her intentions—or so it seem. But there always be a time, some time winding before daybreak when the talking slip past Lilith. When though she be amongst them, she not with them at all. *Six tell six tell six.* When they talking get inside every woman but she and they be conversing 'bout deeper things. She listening but she can't hear. Homer do most of the talking while the other womens nod or say yes, but is not schooling or church. *Six tell six tell six.* Sometimes a word or a bunch of words would slip through like a night snake and gone as soon as it come.

—Word from Worthy Park?

—Word be dem rising but dey did have to tell couple man.

—Man. Shit. Me can't abide manfolk, y'know. Me don't like it.

—Dem don't have womenfolk like we. Most of dem fool-fool or breedin'.

—You can't trust a man.

—Homer, you worried 'bout Worthy Park? Jackson Lands worried 'bout we.

—They say that?

—Me hear it. Ever since Circe dead.

—Tell Jackson to worry 'bout Jackson and mind they bloodclaat business.

Lilith perplex. She know she seeing Homer but not sure she hearing Homer. Her eyes red like fire and her mouth too. Homer don't cuss. Homer is Homer because she don't cuss like common nigger. They talking 'bout other estate and she don't understand it.

One morning Lilith feel roughness on her skin and wake up. She scream. Four or five white man with whip round they neck and no clothes all over her, biting into her skin. The whips turn into snakes. They all have straight hair, one brown, one yellow and one red, but nobody got eye or nose or mouth. Two spread her legs and jump between her. Him skin cold and scaly and the snake slither off him neck. As the snake set to bite, Lilith wake up for real.

People come to know Lilith as the woman with the quilt on her back. One day, soon before whipping time, Lilith look out the kitchen window and see two people stirring up dust as they march toward the house. Wilkins got no call to talk to nobody since the Obeah business, so most people look twice when they see him. Homer go outside to look and Lilith follow her. As they pass the kitchen, Lilith see Jack Wilkins wearing a wide straw hat followed by Mrs. Wilkins, who protesting he should not be moving about in this weather or fussing about the massa business.

Jack Wilkins limping. Him face red like beet and he lookin' both skinny and apoplectic. Jack Wilkins don't look at Lilith, but Mrs. Wilkins, once she see her, didn't take her eyes off her, not until she walk right into her husband back when he stop. Lilith not sure what Mrs. Wilkins' eyes telling her. Perhaps something that be woman things, perhaps shame or anger or jealousy or something she don't grow into yet. The two go up the great house steps, where Jack Wilkins demand that he see Massa Humphrey.

—On what business? Robert Quinn ask, since he be on the terrace.

—Nothing that concerns the likes of an Irishman, Jack Wilkins say. Neither Lilith nor Homer see Robert Quinn face after that remark. The two go up the stairs and step inside. Nobody know what correspond between Jack Wilkins and Massa Humphrey, but they know this. After the two meet, nobody ever whip Lilith again.

Soon Lilith take to wearing clothes that look like Homer hand-me-down. Lilith look at Massa Humphrey and Robert Quinn and see the same thing. Robert Quinn see her looking at him different and don't say nothing to her no more. One time when Lilith was passing by with rubbish from the kitchen, the same Johnny-jumpers who whip her start to mock her. Lilith say to nobody in particular that scar only make the skin stronger but there be no whip, in hand or in a pants, that goin' knock her down again.

The fat, squat Johnny-jumper don't know what she mean but he don't like how Lilith get uppity as if she better than he. He ask her them same words, you think you better than me, cow?

—Me don't know what call you have to use word like *think*, Lilith say.—After all, dog like you never think once.

The man jump up from him stump and the other mens stop laugh. He stomp toward Lilith but as he go to grab her, the fat squat man stop and stagger back. Him eye blaze white and he start tremble something awful. He yelp like a sick dog and run away, still yelping as he drop two time in the dirt.

Lilith foot thinking before her head. This be the early morning hour but the sun already hot and burning down a nigger back. For a long time Lilith try to not take stock of what she know, what Homer and the other womens tell her. But for the longest time, even before white man whip a quilt on her back, she feel something missing, something she don't know if she to look for. Mayhaps a man. Whether that man be a pappy, massa or lover, she start to wonder. Maybe she just want any white man to be close. Maybe she just want something that make her eyes make sense. Lilith wasn't expecting no more deep thinking. Her life did boil down to two things, workin' and whippin'. But Jack Wilkins make himself present one day like he just appear out of the dust and the whipping stop. Surely, she say to herself, sure even now you know to stop read anything in the action of white people. Surely. But there her two foots be, making up they mind when her own mind not doing nothing. The foots stop. She tell herself that as for she, she would never come to this place, what with every white man having the hankering to whip her, but there she be.

Jack Wilkins' house.

—Took your own goddamn nigger time, he say.—Neither whip nor cat'll teach you monkeys anything about haste, that's your tragedy.

He seated out on the porch like he be waiting for her all this time. But that be him custom from the days when he reign over the estate. Lilith look at him looking at her. Now he have no control over Montpelier, but he still out on the porch every morning, looking out and waiting for him pitcher of lemonade mix with rum, and cuss 'cause the wife can't make it as good as Homer. Wilkins' hat off and the top of him head bald. Him shirt open right down to the waist but him white chest hair so bushy it look like he got another shirt underneath. He leaning back in the chair with him foots up on the balustrade. Wilkins look like everybody know he old save he.

Lilith still. She at the foot of the step and can feel the dirt under her foot. The shadow from the step cool. She can't think to say nothing so she just still. Lilith force herself to look up but he not looking at her.

—Only the almighty knows why he set me up with a woman more barren than Jesus' wilderness, he say.—Instead, he gave me a litter of niggers. Guess it's my fault for not keeping me sticker in me breeches, eh?

Lilith don't say nothing.

—I remember your mother, yes I do.

Lilith look up at the man. He not smiling.

—She . . . Like the bloody second plague. Never knew I could go sick from the sight of blood. 'Tis a wonder that you're not red yourself. Why have you come?

—Me . . . me . . . me don't know, massa.

—I hope 'tis not looking for a pappy to buy you gifts and marry you off to a gentleman. For if that's what you seek, then you're an even darker nigger than you look.

Lilith don't say nothing. He look at her for a long time. She don't know for sure, for she not looking at him, but she can feel him on her. Not like a pappy, though; only Tantalus did do that for a little while. He all over her like a man and she feel naked. She feel him testing her skin and prying apart her arse and grabbing to check how plump her pussy be. She feel him looking on her like a massa.

—Ever heard about me father? he say.—He would have been stunned by the likes of you, he would have. Didn't take very kindly to the abuse of niggers, as I recall. No, an upstanding gentleman he was, given to calling niggers Africa men, if me memory serves me right. Mind you, memory doesn't serve me naught these days.

—Weak. The son of a bitch was weak.

Lilith don't say nothing. Her mind waiting, for what she don't know. Her mind a-taken, like it be when she first start think 'bout Massa Humphrey.

—Lilith. Named you meself. Did you know Adam had a first wife before Eve? Called her Lilith, but the bitch was too headstrong so got rid of her, he did. Headstrong, another word for uppity. You uppity?

Lilith don't say nothing.

—Speak up! Damn you.

—No. No, massa.

—Then why in all fuckery do you think you can come to me house unsummoned? Do you think I owe you something then, is that what you're thinkin'?

—No, massa.

—A wicked son of a bitch, that's what the lord will call me. Not even the devil ever met the likes of me, I'll tell you that much. But God, there's a sum'bitch if there ever was. Saddle me with a barren bitch of a wife and nothing but niggers calling me pappy. Your mammy didn't want nothing in this world but for men like me to leave her be. Now I . . . I couldn't get the blood off. No matter what I did, I couldn't get her blood off. I couldn't get her . . .

Lilith look up again and see him, it seem like for the first time. He take him legs off the balustrade and try to stand up, but either he weak or he drunk or he both. He lookin' like a man who need help. Lilith don't know what to do. Her mind still waiting for something from him but she don't know what.

—Begone! he say.

Lilith don't tell nobody where she go. Not even Homer.

A morning come whereby Homer rush in the room all fussing and Lilith, who just wake and heading to the kitchen, don't know why Homer acting the way she act. Homer head usually high and her chin straight and her voice even. But this be the second time she flutter high and low like a girl who don't know the wise ways of woman yet. Like she 'fraid.

—What is to be done? she say. What is to be done?

Lilith don't like when she talking that way. Like a fussy white woman.

—It must be according to your strength, Homer say.

—All they goin' do is open up a old scar when they whip me, Lilith say.

—They not goin' whip you, girl chile, Homer say.

—Oh, so they goin' kill me now for sure. Me good as dead anyway, Lilith say. I know I wasn't goin' be too long for this world. Watch me if I don't curse every single one them backra bastard for—

—Hush you mouth, chile. They not goin' whip or sell you, Homer say. They sending you to Coulibre.

Joseph Andrews

· 15 ·

Knowing what to expect if he hand Lilith back to the slave-drivers, Robert Quinn drive the carryall himself. Robert Quinn work them horses like is hell they driving out of, he in the box seat and Lilith in the cart at the back. Lilith have to grab the side of the cart to hold on. Robert Quinn hit one bump after the other and they throw Lilith up so much that her back hurt. He whip the horse for them to ride faster. They burst a turn round a cliff and Lilith gasp when she see the gorge below. Coulibre seem far, very far for a place that Miss Isobel leave every day to come to Montpelier.

They set out from late morning and now the hot sun threatening midday. That be what Lilith thinking when she give herself allowance to think. Most time, her thinking be like her talking, which be nothing at all. Sometime she look at Robert Quinn in the front, him wide back pressing against him shirt and him long hair whipping up in the air like is black flame. Robert Quinn don't say nothing other than a grunt when he whip the horses. The carryall ride up the hill and Lilith grab the side so she don't roll out. Lilith look out into the wild bush and try to be Homer, listening if the bush have any secret to tell her. Not a word. The hill go on for five minute or so.

As Lilith was tying her bundle together to leave, Miss Isobel come into Homer room like she float in there. She shock Homer so bad that the woman back stiffen up. A purposeful nigger, that be what Miss Isobel call her.

—You are to pack your belongings, such as they are, and head to Coulibre, where a nigger will learn soon enough how to behave, she say to Lilith, but look at Homer. There's no overseer to beg for you there. It's a good thing I'm here to help out Master Wilson, poor man is still too much of the Englander. He knows nothing of the society of negroes, she say.

Then she sit down on Homer bed.

—He's been far too lax with the lot of you, you know. No Coulibre nigger would have made the terrible mistake you made and live to make another. Are you an Igbo?

Lilith and Homer quiet.

—Speak up, you stupid nigger, are you of the Igbo blood?

—Me did know her mama, mistress, she be Akan descended, Homer say.

—Splendid. I'm not one for niggers who kill themselves. Messy business, very heathen-like. And those Coromantees are far more trouble than they're worth. Akan, you say? Well, she is to be sent directly to Coulibre, where my mama will teach her some social graces. Despite her horrendous behaviour she may still be of use. I will certainly have use for her in the near future.

Homer and Lilith perplex.

—I shall make a little lady of you. Aren't you thrilled to hear it, Lilith? she say.

Lilith don't say nothing. Homer try to nudge her without Miss Isobel looking. Lilith stand still looking at the ground. She don't say nothing.

—Yes, ma'am. She plenty joyful, ma'am, Homer say.

—Splendid. Just splendid. I have been watching you, Lilith. Watching you very closely.

—Ma'am? Homer say.

—Oh, yes. Of course you would never have noticed, occupied as you were, watching somebody else.

Lilith say nothing. Homer say, Me no know—

—That's the lot of all niggers: little knowledge, less sense. Some of you even think you can aspire to something greater than your fate. Do you know what aspire means, child?

Lilith say nothing.

—She never did born too righted, ma'am, Homer say.

—Just as well. I trust that there was nothing about her behaviour she understood, nevertheless, she'd do well to remember her place if she knows what's good for her.

—Mistress, me don'—

—And another thing, Homer, since the fool can't speak for herself. That...dress she wore with her bosom all tumbling out and embarrassing decent people? Get rid of it. She's so clear to me she might as well be glass. A woman knows another woman's heart, eh? Well, Lilith, you failed, and it will be my task to remind you of that failure. And of your place. In quick time you will be my shadow, Lilith. I've decided to keep you closer than a brother. Very close, she say.

The hill flatten out and the carriage come to a stop. A breeze cold like rain make Lilith shiver. She look around and see the place for the first time.

Coulibre.

Lilith was thinking that Coulibre was goin' look like Miss Isobel in some way or the other. Coulibre look down on her through sixteen black window and a wall that not whitewash in a long time. Coulibre not like Montpelier that have a ground floor that cut from stone and two top floor that make from wood. Coulibre is all stone. There be a ground floor all seal up except for the wide staircase that run from the ground, over the ground floor and up to the first floor, where it end in front of two big black door. Four window on the left and four window on the right and all of them dark. The next floor have nothing but window, but they a little lighter. The roof was dark brown to black and point to the sky like church. Robert Quinn waiting on her.

Lilith grab her bundle and jump out of the carriage.

—Be a good negro to yer new masters and misfortune shall not befall ye, Quinn say. Lilith stare at the ground. When she look up he turn away from her quick. Lilith start to head to the door.

—Lass, unless ye want to begin yer stay by meeting the cowhide, I suggest ye use the rear, say Robert Quinn.

Lilith step down the front step. Robert Quinn rub him palms. Nobody look at nobody. Good day, he say and turn round the carriage and leave. Lilith turn to go round the rear of the great house and hear the carryall stop. She know he looking. Lilith walk a wide length from the house and hear nothing. Just right then a negro girl, her hair plait tight and her dress white and torn, burst through a side door and run down the steps. She lose her foot when she near the bottom and trip. The girl pick herself up and still crying. She push past Lilith, who did walk to the steps to help her. Lilith watch her go to the shed nearby and hear noise inside the house. She step inside slow.

—Come now, you stinking child! A fortnight it's been, high time for a bath. Good lord, smell those dirty arms and feet! Abominable! Just abominable! this white woman say. The little boy she talking to have hair yellow like Miss Isobel. He jumping up and down naked even though he much bigger than baby. Spots all over him face that white people call freckle. He bawling and screaming because the white woman hand grab him ears and twist.

—God's words! Do you take your mother for a stupid nigger? she say. The boy still be screaming.—Speak when you're spoken to, answer when you're called. Do you take your mother for an imbecile? she say.

The boy shake his head.

—Well, relieved am I to hear such a thing. Now, upstairs with you, and have yourself a good proper cleaning before I take the switch to you, she say. She let go him ear and the boy grab it and sniffle.

—I hate you! the boy shout.

—Nor do I find you agreeable myself, but God has yoked us together, so together we shall be. Now, off with you, you little shithouse, before I grab the other ear, she say.

The boy run off and a little old negro woman run after him, clutching her bosom that flap up and down hard under her frock.

—Heavens! So you're the unseasoned nigger my daughter has foisted upon me? From Montpelier? You're a full day early! God's words, what am I supposed to do? the woman say. Lilith don't know what to say. She remember somebody saying this be Mr. Roget second wife but didn't remember that she look so much younger than Massa Humphrey mother.

—You, you girl who just stepped inside my house, she say, pointing with her finger. The other negroes in the room look. Lilith look at the negroes dressed so good, only black skin stop them from looking white. Two negro mens by the window putting up a new curtain. One chubby negro woman on the floor trying to hush a baby. One old negro woman over by the big table in the middle of the room taking more curtain out of a chest.

—You, you nigger by the door. Yes, you. Are you deaf as well? Is there no limit to the trials my stepdaughter will put me through? Does she not know how much I suffer? she say.

—Ma'am? Lilith say.

—God's words! It speaks. At least that's one thing I shall not have to whip out of you. For, make no mistake, I shall whip you in earnest as soon as your master bids me! Do you know why you are here, girl? she say.

—Yes'm.

—Well, at least you think you do, if you blackies think at all. Quite the problem you were at Montpelier. Nothing but source of trouble and humiliation, not to mention grievous harm to Isobel's chaperone, Miss Holliflower, the incident which I saw myself. You had every single lash coming to you, and mind you, I shall show the fullest extent of my discipline if I ever sense such defiance again. Uppity nigger indeed. To think you're estate born, yet still you need to be seasoned. I tell you, I've never heard of such a thing. But seasoned you shall be, and sooner rather than later too. Do we understand each other?

—Yes'm.

—Of course not, your negro head has never been to a Christian school. And...oh, hurry up, Bessy! Hurry up!

The old negro woman put down her bundle of curtains and run out of the room.

—Now you. Work and work hard, harder than everybody else, and I shall be kind to you. Do otherwise and I shall be most unkind and— Oh goddamn, Matraca, will you shush that damn little hellion!

The chubby negro woman on the floor with the baby look up. Her eye wide open and her mouth tremble.

—L-l-lawd, mistress, he, he, he don't want be hush, mistress, she say.

—For heaven's sake! the mistress say and go over to the negro woman and the baby. The mistress put the baby on her shoulder, then she slap the negro woman in the face.

—Imbecile, the mistress say.

The negro woman grab her cheek and cry quiet. But she look up two time to see if the mistress was looking at her and scowl when she see only Lilith. The negro mens put the curtain on the window, and the old woman come back with a chest full of more. The mistress walk over to Lilith and shove the crying baby in her hands. Lilith grab the baby quick, lest she drop him and start the day with a whipping. Lilith cradle the baby soft in her arm and the baby cry a little, then stop. As the baby stop the whole room go quiet.

—You may be of some use after all, the mistress say. Now off to the kitchen with you, she say and point to a door behind her.

The kitchen half the size of the one at Montpelier and look like not much cooking be doing in there. All sort of pot and pan hang from the ceiling and the counter make out of the same stone as the rest of the house. The room be hot from the brick oven. Lilith have her bundle in one hand and the baby in the other.—Set down wherever you choose, the mistress don't care, somebody say. Lilith look round and don't see nobody. The kitchen door swing open and in she step. She taller than Lilith but thicker, like a young man almost, with wide shoulder but thin waist. Her hair in all wild direction but it direct eyes to her face, the prettiest Lilith ever see on a negro. Lilith didn't know God portion out them kinda prettiness to negro people. Lilith perplex a little, 'cause the girl lips thick and dark and her nose flat till it disappear between her eye. She didn't have good hair and her skin too dark. But the girl was the prettiest woman Lilith ever did see. Lilith perplex, 'cause the arrow from ugly to pretty was from black to white. Her bearing not like a Montpelier negro. Plus, she dress in a deep blue frock, complete with petticoat and lace trim. Not even a chaperone dress up like that.

—Set down you things and grab dis here bucket, she say.

—The baby? Lilith say.

—Cain't see he making much protest, the girl say.

Lilith set the baby on the table and take one of the buckets from the girl. The thing so heavy that she near drop it on her toe.

—Montpelier cain't even give a nigger some shoes? the girl say. Lilith wondering why she wearing such stoosh clothes just to go fetch water. Lilith grab the bucket and set it on the counter.

—Dem call me Dulcimena, but everybody done call me Dulcey, she say.

—Lilith, Lilith say.

Dulcimena pour milk into a pot and set it to boil.—To kill out the nastiness in it. White people drink it straight from the cow, the nasty bastards, she say. As soon as she set the milk 'pon the stove, she turn to Lilith and ask if she suckle. Lilith don't know what she mean.

—Me mean if you did breed lately, Dulcimena say.

—No, baba, me never do them things, Lilith say. Dulcimena take one look at Lilith then throw her whole head back laughing. Lilith relieved. This woman look at her too long when she ask a question, long enough that Lilith sweat feel cold.

—Excuse me, please? How you manage dat deh miracle with nasty backra and nasty nigger around? Down dere sew up?

Lilith don't say nothing.

—Not even de overseer fuck you? Dulcimena grabbing her waist now.—Not even de slave-driver? You means to tell me that plenty mens look 'pon pretty gal laka you and no try to take de pussy? You diseased, gal?

—No!

—Dis no sound right. Eh-eh, dis mighty peculiar. Well, anyway, God know best, or God don't know a raas.

Dulcimena laugh again. She laugh haughty and loud and the kitchen shake with her. Lilith laugh but it come out soft. Dulcimena look at her so long that she look away first. Lilith wonder why she thinking of a sour white man with yellow hair and cold sweat and sailor speak. Dulcimena did call her pretty. She take the baby off the table and plop a titty out of her dress. She hold up the white baby to her black nipple and the baby grab quick and greedy and suck so loud the whole kitchen feel like it soon get suck in. Lilith have to push her own mouth back shut.

—Jesus Christ! They make you do that?

—Dem people would sooner give him donkey milk if it be more easy. Dem don't care and he? He nah remember ten, fifteen year from now when he same one whipping de life out o' me.

—How come you have breast milk? You have a young'un too?

—Did have two. Twin. Massa Roget sell dem last fortnight. Or he kill dem, me no know.

Dulcimena give Lilith a chuckle but it weaker than before and she look away from Lilith quick, dart back and look away again. Then she let out a loud laugh, though the kitchen didn't shake.

—Nigger life! What you gone do? she say.

Dulcimena boil the milk, then set sweet potato on the stove. Dulcimena go outside to feed the chicken in the coop and tie off three goat. Dulcimena rub down and feed Massa Roget special black horse, throw scrap corn give the hogs, then go upstairs to prepare the bed for Massa Henri Roget, the son who ears did get a proper squeezing not long ago. Then she come back to the kitchen when the sun gone and give Lilith a pan with sweet potatoes and a jar of cow milk. Eat now, Dulcimena say. You going be sleeping over there, she say, pointing to the floor by the kitchen door. Lilith look 'pon the woman like she mad and the woman laugh.

—Excuse me please, you was expecting bed? The mistress like her nigger to sleep where dem work so dem can work early, Dulcimena say.

Is night and the great house quiet. Homer did say Coulibre was an estate but is not an estate at all. No sugar be growing in this place, nor tobacco, nor cotton neither. Massa Northbert Roget work in Kingston as magistrate for the crown. He make him money from that and from what Dulcimena say is one thousand a year that he get from him papa who dead long ago and eight hundred a year that he get when he married him second wife near ten year now. Isobel was little girl when the new mistress come, a year after the old mistress dead and Dulcimena never say how she know so much 'bout massa affairs, except that the man take to talking too much any time she suck him proper.

There be seven slave at Coulibre. Sacco and Thunder, who work the grounds; Habakkuk, who clean and drive the barouche. Bessy, the old nigger woman with a hump in her back, do little things, but mostly nothing. Matraca, who take care of the young massa and him baby brother. Francine, who wait on the mistress. Then there is Dulcimena, who do everything else, including all the kitchen work, cooking and whatever the other niggers forget to do.

Lilith on the floor by the mistress' stairs. She 'fraid, but not of the dark woman who come to her in the night. Lilith 'fraid 'cause she don't know what to be 'fraid of. Homer did warn her that Mistress Roget very French in her ways, but Lilith don't know what that mean and Homer didn't have time to make it clear. Night moving on and Lilith listening to nothing. She hear one and two sound from upstairs, a woman fussing. The mistress not sleeping. Some time later she hear a man voice. Must be the massa, Lilith think. They talking loud like it be everybody business.

—Dulcimena? Dulcimena? Where is that nincompoop!

Dulcimena get up quick.

—Yes, mistress! I's be in de kitchen, mistress, she say. Lilith watch her rub her shoulders something terrible.

—Have you staked the cows? You know Mr. Roget prefers when you do it and not those stupid boys, the mistress ask.

—I-I, I's goin' get to it, mistress, Dulcimena say.

—You going get to it? say a man voice so loud that it just come down on the kitchen like thunder.

—Dulcimena, come to me at once!

—But I going do—

—Now! the man say.

Dulcimena stop dead. Lilith watch her as she step slow. Too slow. Massa Roget come down the steps and step over Lilith in him night-shirt. He short and fat round the waist, him hair long and white and curl down him shoulder and him face fat so till the chin bounce when he step. In him hand he carry a horsewhip. Dulcimena try to run, but nowhere to run in the kitchen. He back her up in a corner.

—Suggestions now I'm giving instead of orders, is it? Master over me now, are you? he say.

—No, massa, me was just going to do it, massa. Lawd God, massa, please, massa, ple—she say, but he cut her short with a lash clear 'cross her shoulder. Dulcimena scream. He tear into her and she flip right and left, but he slashing her whichever way she turn. He lash her back, her shoulder, her neck and two time he whip her in the face. Dulcimena fall to the floor between the counter and the kitchen table and Lilith can't see her no more, but she see Massa Roget over her, whipping and whipping and she screaming and screaming, Me dead, massa, me dead, you done kill poor Dulcey.

Massa Roget whip her until him hand give out and he couldn't whip no more. Dulcimena crying. The massa red like choking pig. He step past Lilith and go back upstairs. Lilith so frighten she couldn't move. She stay on the ground, her eye wide open, until Dulcimena pick herself up and go through the door to stake the cows. A good while later Dulcimena come back in and she still sniffle. Lilith watch her as she take a brown bottle out of a cupboard, pour something onto her hand and wipe her face, chest and as far on her back as she could reach. She lay out her mat on the floor of the kitchen and go to bed. It was February and the shortest month suddenly felt like it goin' go on forever. Lilith didn't fall asleep till near morning.

· 16 ·

LILITH SEARCHING HER MIND BACK AND FORTH TO FIND A word stronger than perplex. Flabbergast? She roll that word on her tongue quick, but spit it out when she remember that is Robert Quinn she hear it from first. Robert Quinn, who say he lose the taste for whipping negro womens, then turn round only to make slave-driver manhandle her, then whip her every week. Flabbergast can go to hell and take him along, she think. Perplex, she settle on. Perplex. Lilith perplex cause Dulcimena just wake her up.

—Wakey, wakey, cooking and bakey, she say as she nudge Lilith.

As Lilith roll over and rub her eye, Dulcimena hopping, skipping and jumping round the kitchen and singing and dancing as if she doing the quadrille. She hop, all dainty-like, from one window to the other to let fresh light and new air in the kitchen. She sing a song that sound like what Robert Quinn sing unawares. She spin two time and stop, and only then Lilith see the dark blotch under her left eye and the mark on her left arm. For a moment Lilith did think last night was a dream.

—Miss Dulcimena, you feeling poorly?

—Me lookin' poorly to you?

—No, but...

—Call me Dulcey. Me halfway out the door by de time you get to mena.

Lilith think it best to not say nothing. Dulcimena go over to the water bucket on the counter, dip her two hand in and wash her face. She lift up her dress to wipe her face but jerk when she touch her eye. She dab slow around it and smile when she see Lilith. Lilith watching Dulcimena face. And her little belly and thick legs that shiny with morning sweat and her pussy hair that plenty bush up. Dulcimena smile wide but wince, so she smile narrow.

—Come, pickney, massa and mistress soon wakes up and if breakfast tardy, you goin' get what de duck get.

Dulcimena and Lilith in the barn, not far from the house. She set Lilith 'pon a stool beside the cow. Dulcimena push a bucket underneath the udders, then stand back and look at Lilith. Lilith watching the sky go from pink to orange and the flowers as they wake up and the land that, unlike Montpelier, lead to a fence. Anything but the cow.

—Lawd, pickney, de cow cain't milk sheself.

Lilith don't know what to do. She try to remember if she ever seen anybody at Montpelier milk a cow. She hiss. Is not as if cow keep in the cellar. Lilith grab an udder hard and the cow jerk. Lilith so frighten she push herself back and tumble over the stool and land flat on her back. Dulcimena have to clutch herself from laughing so hard. Lilith hiss.

—Make haste, pickney, de massa soon wakes up, and we still have egg to collect.

—Me no know how to do them things! Lilith say.

—Excuse me please? How come you is nigger and you don't have nigger skill? Look here, pickney.

—Me don't name pickney, me name Lilith.

—Eh-eh, excuse me please, whatever you name. Dulcimena don't say nothing else. Lilith set herself back on the stool and grab a cow udder. She squeeze again and milk, right in her left eye.

—Cho bombocloth!

—Pardon your French! Dulcimena clutching herself again with laughing.—Pickney, if you keep dis up me soon start hiccup. Come now, she say and sit down beside Lilith.—Like so, she say. Dulcimena take an udder in her hand and glide her finger down as she squeeze. Milk spurt in the bucket.

—Slow, slooooow, but firm like when you pullin' the massa ding-dong.

—W-what?

—Excuse me please. Me forget say is in church dem grow you, Lady Virgin. What a ting, eh? Massa Roget goin' puppalick when he hear say nobody ride through you bush. No bother look 'pon me like you don't know nothing. Somebody must was taking Massa Montpelier lobster if is not you.

—That is not my affair.

—Uh-huh. Me think is you. Dat's why dem send you to Coulibre, don't it? Tings was getting out a hand. So tell me now, Massa Montpelier, him buddy big like banana or small like bean?

Lilith jaw drop again and Dulcimena almost fall over the stool with laughing.

—Why you so hoity-toity? Montpelier must be some different place to rahtid.

Lilith look at Dulcimena. Dulcimena think Lilith shock over what Dulcimena say, but she shock over how she saying it. Dulcimena full with so much mirth and laughing that Lilith begin to wonder again if she did dream what happen the night before.

—Grab a cow cocky! Dulcimena say and she start to sing, I want to go-oh, I want to go-oh-ohhhhh. Lilith can't help herself. She grab an udder. Soon after that she singing I want to go-oh too. Dulcimena did say she pretty.

. . .

Massa Roget come downstairs before everybody and Dulcimena have him breakfast ready. The man dressed in black coat, black waistcoat, black breeches, white wig, white socks and little shiny black shoes that look like they be for womens. Massa Roget bald and he have him white hair in him hand. Lilith have a start, but only a little. Old white man have more wig than woman. Dulcimena pass him on the right to spoon out eggs on him plate and he slap her hard on the arse. Dulcimena jump and shriek a little, but giggle real quick.

—You is mischievous boy, massa. Mischievous, mischievous. Dulcimena smile wide and motion Lilith to bring the teapot. Lilith set the teapot down on the table but don't look at Massa Roget.

—And who have we here? he say.

Lilith don't say nothing.

—Dem call her Lilith, massa. She send over from Montpelier Estate.

—Ah, yes.... Word has come ahead of you, my child—none of it good, I might add.

Lilith don't say nothing. The two womens stand while Massa Roget eat. The whole time he using him right hand to shove food down him mouth, he using the left to lift up Dulcimena dress and stroke her arse. Dulcimena looking at her finger like she about to bite her nails. Lilith inch back to the stone counter behind her. Even with the sunrise coming through the kitchen, the counter still cold. Soon Massa Roget finish him breakfast and after he done search Dulcimena arse Lilith see the front of her dress shifting up and down. Dulcimena mouth sound like she enjoying the feel-up but her face already out the window. Massa Roget gulp down a cup of coffee, then set out. He ask Habakkuk the carriage driver to bring round the barouche, saying he is still lord of this house and his daughter is just going to have to make do without it today. Then he set he wig lean and Dulcimena stop him and straighten it. After he leave, Dulcimena set bread, eggs, coffee, white yam, strips of goose, strawberries, banana and pear on a tray and hand to Lilith.

—The mistress take her breakfast in bed, Dulcimena say and point upward.

Lilith upstairs. The banister is wood, but the steps is out of stone. The walls is out of stone too. Lilith never see an entire house that look and feel like her cellar back at Montpelier. She let the noise of Mistress Roget lead her to the room door.

—Enter!

As Lilith open the door, all stillness come to an end. Francine at the closet holding a petticoat like a baby. Lilith never pay her much mind since that first time when she run past her crying just as she was coming to Coulibre. Francine skinny like a stick, with hair pull back into a bun, like black woman hair forcing to be white. She wearing a brown dress that touch the floor. Lilith remember her bawling but can't remember her voice. Dulcimena say that Francine be there to wait on the mistress, but Lilith don't know what that mean, for it seem too easy work for them to give a negro. Mistress Roget sitting up in the bed like an invalid but she not sick at all. She in a light blue gown with her hair tie up. Though is early, still her lip red and the beauty mark move from the left cheek yesterday to her chin today. The sun coming through the glass window that look much bigger inside than outside. At the center of the room be the bed, with a dark wood desk to the right wall and another to the left. Right in front of the bed is four armchair, with purple cushions, all put to face each other like a cross. A rug with white baby angels cover the whole floor. On the right wall be a painting of a woman who look exactly like Miss Isobel but the clothes she have on not the latest fashion. The yellow-hair boy from before running all over the room shouting.

—I'm a kite, Mama! A kite I am, he say.

—And do kites try their parents' nerves, Henri?

—Woooooooosh! Woooooooosh!

—Henri, Henri. Down for breakfast you go now. And try, my dearest, not to wake your brother. Follow...what do they call you?

—Lilith, mistress.

—Yes, follow Lilith. Off with you.

Lilith place the tray on the bed and leave the mistress.

—We shall have to get you a new dress. Mister Roget would have a conniption should he see you in those rags. Has he seen you yet?

—Yes, ma'am.

—Really? Hmmm. Nevertheless, let Dulcimena lend you one of hers. Coulibre boasts the best-dressed niggers in Jamaica. As for myself, I'd sooner die than see a nigger unclothed. Does that fill you with pride, young girl?

—Mistress?

—Does that make you proud? Oh, how I hate repeating myself. Gives one the fear that one is not being listened to.

—No, mistress.

—Good. Now leave me. One more thing. I'll leave the baby in your charge, so please take him away from that guttersnipe Matraca, I can hear him crying already. God's words! I've slapped her so many times about her confounded stench!

Lilith walking down the corridor to the pickney room. It strike her how this house so hard with all the stone, but every room noisy and light cover all the walls. Montpelier is wood mostly, but no noise come from that house except for the early days when Robert Quinn take him female company home. Sometimes Lilith wonder if she hate Robert Quinn because at least Massa Humphrey never promise her nothing. But Robert Quinn didn't promise her nothing either, not really, and whatever white man say, they contrary enough to take back anyway. Maybe this be one of the things Homer was teaching her that she didn't listen to. Lilith wonder what they plan to teach her at Coulibre.

. . .

Dulcimena have lunch ready with Lilith help. Lilith hold the baby most of the day and hand him to Dulcimena when he need feeding.

—Francine can talk? Lilith say.

—Who? Dat lil' bitch? She sing when she ready. Matraca hate her because she get the mistress' old clothes first, then Matraca second.

—She ever come downstairs?

—She? Dat girl be the only nigger who get send off the premises, 'pon errands for di mistress. Ride the mistress' little carriage herself. She even go to Montpelier one, two time, you never see her?

—No.

—Well, the only time that nigger leave the mistress is when massa feel fi fuck him wife for a spell. Eh-eh, di baby do a stinkee, Dulcimena say and hand the baby back to Lilith. Lilith wrinkle her nose.

—Then what you expect me to do with it?

—Dat a your business, pickney. But you might want to go back to him room and grab two cloth. And the basin upstairs should have water. Or just give him back to Matraca. She love baby shit.

The baby grin at Lilith like he don't care. Lilith try real hard not to grin back.

The mistress still in bed, but Dulcimena say that is nothing out of keeping with how the mistress usually behave. Unless guests come calling or she go on visit or go to town to visit the good stores.

—Miss Isobel don't take luncheon here? Lilith ask.

—Excuse me please? Most time she don't even take breakfast. But you should know dat better dan me.

—What you mean, Dulcey?

—What me mean? Come now, pickney. No Montpelier she head off to as soon as cock crow? Or town or Morant Bay or God-he-knows? White woman do as she please in de colony.

Miss Isobel take supper in her room and ask for Lilith to serve it to her. Neither woman say nothing. As she getting ready for bed, Miss Isobel do her toilette, then sit at the mirror for Lilith to brush her hair.

—Eh-eh! A new dress this? Miss Isobel say. Lilith thinking she don't hear correct.

—I mean, is this from Maman? The dress, girl.

—No, mistress, Dulcimena loan me.

—Really? Can't imagine Maman having that at all. She will get you a new dress before the week is out. Coulibre niggers are the best dressed in Jamaica.

Lilith commence to brush Miss Isobel hair. She look up and see Miss Isobel staring at her hard in the mirror.

—Do you know what I admire in you niggerwomen?

Lilith don't say nothing.

—I do believe I'm speaking to you, Lilith.

—Yes, ma'am.

—Then speak when you're bloody spoken to.

—Yes, ma'am.

—I said, there is one thing I admire in you niggerwomen.

—Yes, ma'am.

—That good, trusty nigger resilience. I dare say you blackies could survive Armageddon with no loss of life or limb. God must be wise in giving every living thing just what it needs. I mean, look at you. Why are you here? You tried to use the mind, the brain, but you silly girl, those things are lost to the negro. What you have is a back that won't break, a skin that won't crack, legs like an ox and teeth like a horse. How fortunate you are that we found each other, Lilith!

—Yes, ma'am.

—All you Montpelier niggers, gallivanting like goats. This is Humphrey's influence, of course. Actually not him, but that beast from which he takes counsel. What think you of that man, that Robert Quinn?

—Ma'am?

—Robert Quinn. What do you think of him?

—Me don't have no thinking towards him, ma'am.

—Well, personally I must say I find him loathsome, absolutely loathsome. What should one expect from the Irish but the very worst? And quite the nigger lover, is he not? Lilith, I'm sure you're well-versed in the black arts, what magic does that stump of a man have over Humphrey?

—Ma'am?

—I swear, you are tiresome. Look at those bull shoulders and thick hands of his, trying to squeeze himself into a gentleman's wardrobe. And that silly navy coat of his, he probably bought in some fish market at Port Royal. Athena tells me that the brute doesn't even wear an undergarment! Can you believe that? Mr. Quinn and his Irishman lobbing to and fro in his detestable breeches.

Lilith think to say that neither do Massa Humphrey, for the most part, but keep silent.

—Yes, ma'am, she say.

—Me no kno—I, I don't know what's to come of that estate without some sense brought to it. It's little more than a stable now. The only ray of hope is Homer. Of course, she's clearly practicing Obeah.

—Yes, ma'am.

—I'm quite the Creole myself. I know some of the darker aspects of colonial life.

—Yes, ma'am.

—Yes, Montpelier needs quite a bit of work, it does. But soon things shall flow as smoothly as Coulibre. But first we have to deal with his ghastly maman. I swear, she swooped down to luncheon only this afternoon reeking of wee and asking for Lady Nugent! The governor's wife! Of course, I feel so terrible for Humphrey. I told him, you know, of places in Spanish Town, for a woman in her state, but, he will not part with his maman and I shall take that as a good sign. Is that wise, Lilith? Am I being prudent?

—Yes, ma'am.

—Yes, ma'am. You is a damn fool. And yet there is something in you, isn't there? Must be those ghastly eyes of yours, I swear, it is as if I'm being watched by an owl. Any more brushing and you shall pull my hair out. Leave me now.

—Yes, ma'am.

Lilith hear Miss Isobel brother in the room as she pass. He not sleeping, even though Matraca begging him to. At every five pace or so, there be a lamp burnin' on the wall and a large circle of orange, and yet the passageway and the stairs still dark. Lilith at the bottom of the stairs looking up at stone. She walk to the kitchen. She come through the door and see Dulcimena hoist up on the counter, with her legs spread gone to two county and her dress pull up over her titties. Between her be Massa Roget, who white wig fall off as Dulcimena rubbing him head. The massa breeches down to him ankle and him arse peeking out of him coattails. Lilith hearing sweaty white flesh slapping sweaty black flesh and grunting and moaning. Soon she notice Dulcimena looking at her. Her mouth all hissing and moaning and cooing and catching breath, but her eyes near gone to sleep. Then Massa Roget push her away from him and lose control of himself. Dulcimena looking at Lilith. Lilith think she smile but not sure. Massa Roget jerking slowing down. He pull up back him breeches and grab Dulcimena by the neck. She say nothing. He let go and leave Dulcimena, walking right past Lilith but not looking at her. Dulcimena, her two leg still spread wide, use her dress to wipe Massa Roget off. She hop off the counter and set herself down on her mat and go to sleep.

One day Sacco, a young nigger who take to leaving flowers in the kitchen whenever he see Lilith, carry a bunch of pink hibiscus to the mistress' room. He leave one on the counter beside Lilith and she hide her smile. Sacco pick a whole branch and carry up to the mistress' room. The mistress don't take too kindly to some flower and sneeze and cough something dreadful. She wheeze and sneeze and run down to the living room yelling and screaming that Sacco trying to kill her. The other two negro run Sacco down, tear off all him clothes, tie him up and leave him hanging round by the stable in the hot sun, so that Massa Roget would see him first when he come back. But that not be enough for Mistress Roget. The mens go in the kitchen and take Dulcimena honey jar. Dulcimena sit down and bury her face in her hand. Lilith go to see what going happen but Dulcimena grab her hand and shake her head no. Lilith pull her hand free and go outside while Dulcimena go back to head burying. Lilith hear Sacco screaming. She run to the stable to see honey on Sacco nakedness from head to foot. Sacco bawling and screaming so much that other nigger get a cloth and gag him. Afternoon sun still hot. Lilith almost vomit. She run back inside. The other niggermens go back to what they was doing. Soon Sacco muffle scream get as loud as a real scream. After nearly a hour of cutting up carrots and potato and being interrupt every time he yell into the gag, she go outside again, not listening to Dulcimena shout, No, Lilith!

At the stable Lilith stop and couldn't move for a spell. There be Sacco, writhing and shaking and yelling into the gag, him feet, back, chest and cocky all cover in black ants. They traveling all over him body and biting every inch. Lilith think to run first, but stop. Lilith run to the horse trough and dip the bucket nearby in water and wash him from head to toe with it. She run to the trough for another bucket full and wash him again, rubbing him skin and feeling the welt rising from ants biting. She cuss her mind for noticing too much that she touching a naked man and rubbing some places that another Lilith wouldn't touch. Some of the ants break off him and bite her. She slap them off and look at Sacco. Lilith hear of this before. Honey on the skin, ants in the day, mosquito in the night. When he finally wash full the other niggermens come back. They look at Lilith with the same wide-eye fear that they do the massa. The two mens run away. Lilith furious.

—Little pussy like me still have bigger cock than the two of them, she say. She pull the gag out of Sacco mouth.

—What you gonna do, Miss Lilith? You and me, we's dead now, he say.

The whole night Lilith in the kitchen but elsewhere. *Dem cum was all over you*, a voice say to her and Lilith jump. She turn around but there be nobody but her. Lilith take a candle out of the cupboard and light it with a stick of wood in the fire. As she set the candle down on the table, she look around at the orange walls and the black shadows jumping. A shadow move away from the others and go into a dark corner. Lilith have a start but catch her mouth. The woman again. The woman who belong to darkness. Lilith go to run but feel the weakness that been taking over her of late. She try to think of something Homer would say, or the womens by the river. The woman don't move. Lilith move backways into the table and grab a knife.

—What you doing? Dulcimena say as she enter the kitchen.

—Nothing, me not doing nothing.

—Maybe not to me, but dat knife out for somebody.

—No.

—Suit yourself. Next thing you start chat like dem mad nigger.

It take two day for Lilith to see that Sacco gone, and one whole week to see that he not coming back.

· 17 ·

LILITH LIVING AT COULIBRE FOR THREE FORTNIGHT NOW.
When she not working in the kitchen, washing, baking, and feeding
the little animals, she waiting on Miss Isobel when she come home
every night.

—We are to be married, your master and I, she say one evening
when Lilith by the dresser brushing Miss Isobel hair. Miss Isobel look
at Lilith through the looking glass when she say it. Lilith say, Yes,
ma'am, and that be all. Miss Isobel screw her face.

—Did you hear me? Your master has asked for my hand in marriage,
she say.

—Yes, ma'am.

—Well, are you pleased?

—Pleased, ma'am?

—Yes. Are you happy?

—Me sure everything is the lord will, ma'am.

—I'm sure. Don't pull me goddamn hair so tight, cain't you do nothing right?

—Sorry, ma'am.

—Good heaven, just listen to me. I should be the one apologising. Goddamn indeed, where is my tongue this evening? I'm too much in the company of negroes, yes I am. Way too much. You have all but ruined me with your nigger ways. But anyway I'm very pleased, Lilith. I've heard reports that you've become quite the well-behaved little nigger. Maman is putting in a good word and she's so difficult to please. And my, how you have taken over Dulcimena's tasks. So easy as well, that it's as if that poor negro was still here, Miss Isobel say.

Lilith think hard 'bout this. One fortnight ago, Massa and Mistress Roget kill Dulcimena. It start when Lilith hear commotion up in the massa and mistress bedroom. How dare you come in here stinking of that damn nigger's sweat, the mistress say. Lilith look over to see if Dulcimena hear it too but she just roll over. One door open and slam and then another door open and slam and that was it for that night. But then morning come and it look like Dulcimena forget to lock the goat pen from the night before. The goats let loose in Mistress Roget garden and eat nearly every flower in sight. When the mistress wake up and look outside her window, she scream like somebody killing her. She run outside in nightclothes to the garden and still screaming. She try to shoo the goats from the flowers but they just run from one plant to the next.

—Dulcimena! the mistress bawl out.

—Dulcimena!

Dulcimena run out from the kitchen to see two niggermens shooing the goats back to the pen. The mistress yell to the two mens to grab Dulcimena and forget the goats. They rip off her dress right there and Dulcimena start to bawl. They drag her off to the nearest tree and tie her up by the hand and pull her up till she swinging. Dulcimena begging for the massa to save her but Massa Roget ride right past her to go to Kingston.

The mistress wield the cart whip herself. Lilith always hear she do such a thing but never see for herself before. She flog Dulcimena as hard as she could flog, swinging the whip wide and lashing Dulcimena back till the skin tear into flesh and the flesh tear into blood. The mistress get tired and rest for a few. Nobody beg for Dulcimena. Every time the mistress get tired, she sit down for a spell and have the new grounds nigger whip her till she ready to flog her again. Dulcimena get one hundred sixty-six lash that day and the mistress say she would have derby-dose her too if any of the negroes was setting to pass shit. When they cut Dulcimena down, she fall hard on the ground and never move. Dulcimena scream right through the night and Lilith didn't have nothing but water to wipe her. Lilith have to gag her when the massa shout out that he was coming down there with a musket if she don't shut up.

Dulcimena never get up from the floor again, even after the massa walk in and kick her two time in the side and one time in the pussy and call her a lazy, lying cow. Lilith try to help her, but Dulcimena didn't want to help herself no more. In days she swell and swell with so much pus and water that she just burst and dead. As soon as Dulcey dead, all her duty fall on Lilith.

That be when Lilith starting to see that while she frighten, fear would rush out like sea tide and something else would roll in. Something that make her cook with the devil in her heart. Lilith did still have spiritedness 'bout her, but this time she keep quiet and make the spirit work secret-like. Lilith start to imagine what white flesh look like after a whipping. What white neck look like after a hanging and what kinda scar leave on a white body after black punishment. She think of the little Roget boy, Master Henri, of tying and hanging the boy up by him little balls and chopping him head off. She make the thoughts of white blood work into a fever. She have to snap herself out of it before she cut her own fingers with the kitchen knife. She think of these Coulibre niggers who loyal to the massa and work against each other even though he killing them off one by one, and she think of Massa Humphrey and of blood and what sound a white body make when he fall from fifty feet.

Lilith don't know what to do with her head. She think to cut it off so that her mind would stop haunt her. Dulcimena, no matter what wrong with her, could still laugh like God did wish a niggerwoman joy. Seem that when Dulcimena dead, the noise in the house dead with her and the corridors feel colder. Lilith cook the meals fast, so she have plenty time to think about how she no got nobody. One day, she so sick with herself that she go from room to room downstairs looking for something to make her mind flee from herself, even if that mean more work. She open a door that never open before and smell something that leave her memory a long time ago. She close her eye and breathe in long and deep. She breathe out long and slow and breathe in deep again. That scent, like tobacco, or an old batch of spice.

Books.

Wall and wall and wall and wall of nothing but book.

Massa Roget library.

Nigger got no reason to mess with books, not even to clean them. She pull a blue book out, open it and then clap the thing shut. There be something in the sound that make her giggle. She pull another one out and blow the dust off the top and feel she just clear away a secret mystery. Books. She grab one book because it red like a cherry and another because it red like blood. Lilith run her fingers along a shelf of brown book that feel like the skin of a shoe. Leather. She pull out one and carve in the front is a ship, while at the back is a half woman, half fish. Lilith never see the like of which before. In the book was handwriting but the writing too tight for her to make out any word. And Lilith did more spelling than reading so making out words was still not easy. Some words she know without thinking, others she had to call out the letter until the shape fit into her mouth and she know it. At the end of the same shelf of leather books she pull out the last one. Behind that book was another. Lilith go the door and look east and west. The mistress was asleep and Matraca would never leave that room upstairs. The massa was a good four hours away. Lilith go back to the shelf and pull out four to see which books hiding behind them. One say *Fanny Hill*, one say *Moll Flanders* and one say something that look like it write by the devil. The next one spit out dust and make her cough. She put them back and her finger brush another book, with a rough skin like linen or osnaburg. She look outside at the sunset and pull the book and gasp when she open it.

Joseph Andrews.

Massa Humphrey come to supper at Coulibre after dusk. Lilith watch him as he seat Miss Isobel first, then sit down beside her. Francine seat Mistress Roget, then stand behind her. The supper table not longer than Montpelier's but it dress more fabulous, with lace mats and shiny silver candle holder in the middle and blue and white plates that Dulcimena used to say worth more than a brand-new nigger. Miss Isobel and Massa Humphrey to one side. Massa Roget at the head and Mistress Roget at the foot. Before they even commence to eating, Miss Isobel tell her father how Montpelier niggers be getting away with so much murder that nobody goin' surprise when they commit the act.

—A nigger not be like, I mean is not like, a man, Humphrey. Papa says that in his ways he is more like a cockatoo. Was that not what you said, Papa, was that not what you said exactly? They can imitate us, but above that they are still beasts that'd even kill their own? Miss Isobel say over roast goose and stuffed fowl.

—My daughter speaks my exact words, young sir. They are beasts that kill their own. I had a kitchen slave who killed her own twins, several months ago. Gave the poor bastards a Christian burial myself. Killers, the lot of them.

—Then in that regard they are more like us than we care to imagine, Massa Humphrey say.

—God's words! Why must blood be brought up at the table! My

husband and daughter are so insufferable, the mistress say, but nobody listening to her.

—Oh, no, young sir, they are nothing like us, they have no interest in the finer arts, knowledge, literature and science, nothing that man has put in place for his own advancement. No, sir, Massa Roget say.

—Neither do we, for the most part. In the colonies for certain, I must say. Present company excluded, of course.

—Good sir, you flatter me. I've certainly had my share of intelligence, but we were speaking of these unfortunate negroes.

—Some of his slaves choose when to have their own meals, Papa, Miss Isobel say.

—What? Good sir, surely my daughter speaks false.

—I think a negro is quite capable of knowing when he is hungry, sir. And truthfully, I don't much care. Production is up and Montpelier continues to be the envy of many.

—That may be so, Master Wilson, but how do you know you're not on the brink of rebellion? No, milord, take some stern words from a man who's endured a lot more than you. You weren't here for seventeen sixty. Oh, that was a year. Sixty good souls murdered all because these bushmen wanted to set up their African state! Confound it!

—Tacky?

—So you *have* heard of Tacky and his little revolt?

—I've heard of him and of seventeen sixty.

—A dark year for this island. Your father was involved, sir, surely he must have told you. I fought by his side myself!

—My father was never one to have me in his confidence.

—I see. Well, as we are in the company of such fine, gentle ladies I shall not bring up that bloody, tragic event.

—Please refrain from such, Mr. Roget, for you shall aggravate my poor nerves, Mistress Roget say.

—I daresay there is nothing poor about your nerves, Mrs. Roget, certainly not to this purse, Massa Roget say to him wife, then turn back to Massa Humphrey.

—No, sir, slaves cannot be trusted to do anything themselves.

—Not even eat, sir?

—What are we doing right now, Humphrey? Speak up, boy.

—I will not be called a boy, sir.

—My apologies, good sir, I am remiss, Massa Roget say, looking at Miss Isobel.

—Well, unless my vision serves me wrongly, I'd say we were eating.

—Eating and what else?

—Really, sir, I wish you'd get to the—

—Eating and talking, sir, we're talking. We are in discourse. And who's to say your negroes aren't doing the same? A chance to talk in numbers is a chance to gossip, conspire and plot. Most estates have one gentleman or lady to thirty to thirty-three niggers, Humphrey. Thirty-three sullen, lazy, rebellious negroes, many unseasoned. Have you been to the dark continent, sir?

—Oh, no, Venice was as dark as my travels got me, I'm afraid.

—Well, curse me, I've been. So savage a disposition is the blackie that many cook and eat their enemies! The heart they find a particularly tasty dish.

—Mr. Roget! Mistress Roget say.

—Mrs. Roget. The truth shall never be an unwelcome guest at my table. Not at all. As I was saying, they, meaning the negro, have a ferocity in manner that must be tamed. At all times they must fear you, Master Humphrey, they simply must. Because they are capable of thought, some anyway, and once you have them thinking beyond fear of the cowhide, they will see strength in numbers.

—My negroes are quite docile.

—Your negroes are plotting. You must tame these beasts, young sir, you must never, ever let a slave forget that you are master. At least those Maroons have begun to behave themselves accordingly—well, as accordingly as wild rutting beasts can possibly be. Raided us all the time, they used to, and who can blame them? Why raise chickens when you can steal them, after all? Even they were of little use in seventeen sixty.

—Seventeen sixty, you say? Pardon me, I've just realised. My father had never even seen Jamaica before the seventeen seventies.

—Really? I could have sworn...nevertheless, I shall not ever forget that year, sir, even though I was quite young myself when it happened. I shall take it to my grave. That Tacky was a demon. That—that...

Massa Roget didn't finish the sentence. He start cough little, then hard, then he start trembling and grabbing him left shoulder with him right hand. He fall back in the chair and him face red like beet. Massa Roget eyes gone.

—Good lord! Massa Humphrey say and jump up. The mistress and Miss Isobel rush to him too.

—Dearest Papa, what's the matter? Miss Isobel say.

—Water! Water! Get him water! Mistress Roget say. Massa Roget coughing and him eye getting redder. He squeeze him left arm with the right and he shaking all over. Everything he say come out as a cough or a wheeze.—He wants water! Mistress Roget say. Him face get redder. He cough up something dreadful. Miss Isobel grab her father, and almost push the mistress out of the way. Everything quiet save for the wheezing sucking in and out of him chest. Francine pour water from a pitcher to a glass and give it to Miss Isobel. Miss Isobel hold the glass to her father mouth and he gulp down the water and cough. Plenty time pass before he stop breathing queer-like.

—For heaven's sake, sir, do you need a physician? Massa Humphrey say.

—I already know the great physician, Massa Roget say and try to laugh but the laugh turn into a cough.—Probably just the wind leaving me for a second, not for the first time either. Fret—fret not, young sir, this too shall pass.

Massa Humphrey look at him for a long time. Lilith was by the door watching Massa Roget. She didn't look at Massa Humphrey.

Mistress Roget, who was red herself from not getting to talk, finally say that while Lilith has come a long way, she still have a disturbing spiritedness that must be tamed. So the Roget family get new permission to whip Lilith. Lilith get whip and hit so much that she could tell just from the sound what a nigger was getting beaten with. Lilith know the sound of cowskin on young flesh and how different it be when it lash old flesh. Lilith know the difference between the smart of the rope, cowskin, cart whip, bullwhip, slap with wedding-ring finger, punch, box, and hot tea throw on her dress. Most of the whipping, pinching, hiding, scraping, cutting, thumping and punching Mistress Roget do herself. Even though otherwise she never come out of bed, sake of the hard birthing she do for the young'un, or so she claim to anybody who would hear, even negro.

Lilith take her beating in silence. But fire going off in her head. Blood spraying and flesh tearing. Lilith can't sleep, not 'cause the cuts from the whip burnin' her, but because darkness burnin' in her own heart. Ashanti blood racing through her and she can't stop thinking about white people shedding theirs. Even the two young children. Lilith count how much lash she get each time and by who and she remember it. She think of Mistress Roget getting tie to a tree and getting whip till she raw. She think of dashing salt in her gashes until the mistress smell like corned pork. She think of a cornstalk thick like black man cock ramming up Massa Roget arse so hard that he piss blood in him own bath. Lilith having dark thoughts and think the devil taking control of her. And there be no Homer to know without Lilith telling and help without Lilith asking. There be only Joseph Andrews. There be only one man, one soul, that can make her laugh and he be neither black nor real:

He was of the highest degree of middle stature. His Limbs were put together with great Elegance, and no less Strength. His Legs and

Thighs were formed in the exactest Proportion. His Shoulders were broad and brawny, but yet his Arms hung so easily, that he had all the Symptoms of Strength without the least clumsiness. His Hair was of a nut-brown Colour, and was displayed in wanton Ringlets down his Back. His Forehead was high, his Eyes dark, and as full of Sweetness as of Fire. His Nose a little inclined to the Roman. His Teeth white and even. His Lips full, red, and soft. His Beard was only rough on his Chin and upper Lip; but his Cheeks, in which his Blood glowed... Add to this the most perfect Neatness in his Dress, and an Air, which to those who have not seen many Noblemen, would give an idea of Nobility.

There was a time when she would reckon a certain white man in this certain way and not think it uncanny. She think of perfect legs, sturdy and strong like a wonderful horse, legs that only behaving as they should inside breeches that can't deny what pack tight and loose where the two legs meet.

She need him every night. After working through a page, she would wipe away tears from laughing quiet-like and feel her face. The soft skin would surprise her. Something about her new days make her expecting that one day and one day soon her face would feel hard as rock. Hard from dark thoughts. She take the book out at night when everybody gone to sleep and try to read with piece of a candle. In time, reading wasn't even too difficult and she come to understand Joseph Andrews in a way that perplex her about other white man. Joseph Andrews never do a cruel thing, but he also didn't know negro flesh. But sometimes she wonder if this Joseph, being as him be, was a real man after all. For he take after no kind of man she ever meet. Not even Robert Quinn, and it anger her to think of the Irishman and him damn *wanton ringlets down his back* and him ye's and fer's and lasses and feckin'.

She read this over and over and the more she read, the more it perplex her.

Ever since *Joseph's* arrival, *Betty* had conceived an extraordinary Liking to him, which discovered itself more and more, as he grew better and better, till that fatal Evening, when, as she was warming his Bed, her Passion grew to such a Height, and so perfectly mastered both her Modesty and her Reason, that, after many fruitless Hints, and sly Insinuations, she at last threw down the Warming-Pan, and embracing him with great Eagerness, swore he was the handsomest Creature she had ever seen.

Joseph in great Confusion leapt from her, and told her, he was sorry to see a young Woman cast off all Regard to Modesty; but she had gone too far to recede, and grew so very indecent, that *Joseph* was obliged, contrary to his Inclination, to use some Violence to her; and, taking her in his Arms, he shut her out of the Room, and locked the Door.

How ought Man to rejoice, that his Chastity is always in his own power, that if he hath sufficient Strength of Mind, he hath always a competent Strength of Body to defend himself: and cannot, like a poor weak Woman, be ravished against his Will.

Betty was in the most violent Agitation at this Disappointment. Rage and Lust pulled her Heart, as with two Strings, two different Ways; one Moment she thought of stabbing *Joseph*; the next, of taking him in her...

She throw down the book, for no man she ever hear of would refuse a woman of such fairness who so want a man to be a man. Not even a preacher or a magistrate. Certainly not no Massa Roget or Wilson or Quinn. Or the yellow sour-hair man who appear only in dream and make her pussy feel clammy. She throw down the book for she stop believing in Joseph. She don't want to. Man did become a thing to Lilith, a black thing, and here come a man who didn't even breathe to grey her up.

One night in reading when her mind was perplexing something awful over the word *heterodox* that Barnaby just say to Mr. Adams, she hear the stairs creak and jump. She shove the book under her dress. But it was Massa Henri asking for milk. She reach for a pitcher of milk that boil that evening and pour some in a glass for the boy. As she hand him the glass the book drop to the ground. She look at the book and at Massa Henri. Lilith couldn't read him face.

—You just had a book baby! That was a lark, indeed it was! Quite like when Ivory, my horse, had a horse baby!

—Shhh, Massa Henri. You mother would have a fright if she know you up and about.

—Does it have pictures of horses and rainbows?

—No, Massa Henri.

—Oh. That's dreadful. Is it a nigger book?

—Shhh, Massa Henri. You mustn' tell nobody.

—'Tis a secret? I love a secret.

—Is the secretest secret. If the mistress hear, she goin' wring you ears again. You not goin' like that, I should think.

—No.

—So be a good little boy.

—I'm not little!

—Shhh. Be a good big boy. Off with you.

—I should very much like a piece of cake, I think.

Lilith look at the boy. He not smiling or angry, he just look at her straight. She try to find the massa in him, but see the Miss Isobel. They let him hair grown down to him shoulder now. She cut him a slice of pound cake and he run back upstairs.

Lilith come to realise that Miss Isobel lie. Massa Humphrey don't ask for nobody hand in marriage yet. Lilith know this because she know the white man way be for the man to ask the father to hand over the daughter and Mistress Roget not be screaming in joy yet. But things was smelling of something else. Lilith not sure what until one day when Homer pay a visit. Homer come by carriage with Francine 'cause Mistress Roget poor nerves aggravate again. Homer come through the kitchen door, dress head to toe in navy blue, a frock and a blue bonnet from long ago when Massa Humphrey mother was young belle. As Homer step into the kitchen, Lilith rush to her. Then she stop. She open her arm to hug, but feel that might be too much. She reach out the hand to shake, but feel that too little. Come here, chile, Homer say and grab her up like a baby cat. Lilith go weak in her arm.

—You light like a feather, chile. You eating? Homer say.

Mistress Roget shout from upstairs that several guests coming for supper, so Lilith need to add more to the cooking. Lilith kneading flour while Homer boiling cerasee and comfrey leaf in a pot. The stove heat up the room and Homer take off her cap. Homer hair more white than Lilith remember even though Lilith be at Coulibre only two months or so. Homer go over to the counter where Lilith was kneading and write this in the flour:

A.M. Cum Isobel.

Lilith read what Homer write.—Come, chile, me know you get enough learning to read that, Homer say.

—Me can read it, Homer, Lilith say. But them things not be word.

—Things say more than what word can tell, Homer say.

—Well, is only you they talking to, 'cause me not hearing nothing.

—Massa Humphrey write it in him journal.

—What A.M. mean?

—Not just A.M., A.M. Cum Isobel. Wake up and smell the sheet funk, chile. They fuckin'. Massa Humphrey cunt-struck like man dog. Most time when he write that in him book is when he gone carousing and is always some woman name write after cum.

Right then, young Massa Henri run in, shouting, Sweets! Sweets! Like sweets be code word for him breeches being on fire. He run up to Lilith and wrap him arms around her. They move over to the cupboard with the boy little foots riding Lilith's big foots. Lilith take out a big jar of molasses and dip a big wooden spoon while he hold out him hand. She pour molasses out in one streak, making a big X in the palm of him hand. Massa Henri giggle and run out. Lilith and Homer look at each other for a good long time. Then they burst out laughing. Homer laugh with a whisper that sound like she heaving with the breathing sickness and Lilith cover her mouth, slapping the dough.

—Bitch getting treat like nigger, Lilith say.

—How you mean?

—How you mean by how you mean? You say he be fuckin' her. That mean he hold her down and take 'way. No so he do with nigger girl?

—Chile, hush you mouth. Backra no use same plough with white woman bush.

—Eehi? All me know 'bout white man is they seize a woman and shove it in and ram and jam till he start to whinny like horse.

—So white man be with nigger. White woman is another story. Unless she not worth a shilling. Besides, from what Pallas tell me, is she do the seducing.

—Right. Me'd think that was improper, as Miss Isobel herself would a say.

—Chile, watch when clock a-strike. She find some way to go in him room, saying she looking to have fourposter bed made for her maman and want to see what him own be lookin' like. Pallas say is 'bout half hour or so the two come back out with them clothes mess up. Pallas say she never know two white people could a-work a funk like what she smell in that room after.

Lilith laugh.

—Hush, Homer say.—Plus me sees them.

—Lying bitch.

—Who you be that me have to lie to you?

—All right! All right, talk you talk.

—Listen to me. One time they so frisky like young rabbit that they forget to close the door tight. Me passing by to drop the new sheets and lo and behold, me hear sound like cat and dog a-fight. So me be thinking that two of massa dog get loose in the house. Me push the door little and it creak.

—And?

—Well, when door creak and nobody hear, you know them be busy.

—Ah suppose.

—Suppose nothing. Me open the door little wider and what should look at me but massa backside. There them be, him breeches down to him knee, coat throw to the ground and shirt all tie up. All me see of Miss Isobel is one leg spread left and one leg spread right, and there be massa ploughing the middle.

—Raas!

—Me chile. He moaning and she hot breathing and them try to come all quiet-like. He write this too in the book, *Sed non bene.*

—What that mean?

—Me no know.

—White lady suppose to lock it up till wedding ring come to open it.

—You don't know what time clock strike. Them white woman be more shameless than nigger girl. Watch out for that one Miss Isobel, you hear me. She know more 'bout negro ways than you think. Every now and then she even have to catch herself chatting like nigger.

—No man going go 'pon top of me ever.

Lilith go to say again, but her mind catch her mouth.—Me kill him first, say.

—But see here. And why you come to that understanding, me chile?

—How you mean? All me see is white man or niggerman using one more thing to get on top of you. Me tired of that. Sick and tired.

—Me hear you. Me hear you. But sometime fuckin' sweet, though.

—Homer?

—Hello, what you think me keep down there, cobweb? Me used to be a woman, you know. I know what you think, I know what all of you think, but there used to be one time when me was woman.

—And man lay down with you?

—Three.

—Massa?

—No.

—Who?

—First one name Benjy. When Benjy coming toward you and open him arms is like a tree spread wide in front of you.

—You did love him?

—Stop talk like white people.

—Then what?

—Then nothing. When that man hand wrap round you, you feel safe even if he was just another slave, just like me.

—And you make the man fuck you?

—That wasn't fuckin'. And the man never make me. We make each other. That be what them call the making love. He slow and say pretty word like it be singing he singing. You must be the first person me telling this to.

—What making love feel like?

—Making love? Like the longest sweetest tickling. Then it turn into something else and bump come up under you skin and is like one wave hit you toe and wash all the way up to you head, sometime one, two, three time. You never know two people could make that one feeling. With Benjy, me used to shake and move so hard because he do it so good. And you pussy? It feel like it just get bless. Making love is good thing, Lilith.

—You use to say you don't meet no man who could handle you.

—He almost, but in the end he was just a nigger.

Homer don't say nothing after that for a while. Lilith look at the pot on the fire.

—He dead?

—I don't know. Time come when me belly get big and as soon as Massa Jack see say the baby was goin' be Akan and Coromantee he sell it already, before it even come of me belly. He...me not talking 'bout this. Then Jack Wilkins make more mens rape two pickney out o' me.

—Me no understand. After all that you come tell me that sexing good. Sound like it come at cost.

—Maybe, maybe not. Me tired of man misery. At least you seem righted now anyway. How they treating you?

—Homer, even nigger treat you like nigger here. And since Dulcimena, the kitchen woman, get killed, her work be my work. The rest of the niggers here worthless and stupid and chat you business to the mistress. Me do the cooking, the washing, the cow milking, and minding Miss Isobel stinking little brother, even the baby.

—Lord, me chile. They whip you?

—Any time she wish. The mistress do it mostly. Sometime for no reason, ever since Massa Humphrey give her permission, cowhide turn into her third hand. Me back have new scar take over from the old one.

—Lord have mercy.

—No. Lord don't know mercy here, so he can frig right off. Homer, I think I goin' run 'way.

—Lord God, me chile, don't do that. Don't make it worse.

—*How the bloodcloth*—Lilith slam her hand on the counter. She breathe deep, quiet herself and say, How it to get more worse?

—Coulibre not but twelve mile from Accompong. Twelve mile.

—Accompong?

—Maroon town, chile. Them niggers will smell you as soon as you set out. They have settlement not twelve mile from these parts. Better white man keep you than Maroons catch you.

—What the Maroon do to you, Homer?

Homer look like she 'bout to fall. She pull the stool from by the doorway and sit down.

—What them didn't do to me, you should ask. That would be nothing.

—Don't give me one of you Homer kinda answer. Me see you back already, Homer, one day when you washing yourself. Is all right. Now me have the same back just like you.

—Indeed. Indeed.

—What the Maroons do to you?

—The same thing Benjy do to me. The same Benjy me just talk 'bout. I tell you already that me and Benjy did sweet for one another, but me did lie. Me did love him, yes. Love him like how white girl say they love man in storybook. Mayhaps even more than that. That man use to rub me belly all the time when he see me was with chile. Then Massa Jack get wind of it. Talk 'bout how he see money in breeding and my baby with the sense of Akan and the back of Coromantee bound to catch a good price—even if is a gal. Me no know, something in me just break. Mayhaps every nigger reach that place where she say that done be enough now. Me tell Benjy that me running 'way and he come with me. Tell me that we should go west and head for the Maroons. We know they still under treaty, but they still taking niggers, especially one as strappin' as Benjy.

Me still remember the night. Damn grounds so hot there be nothing for nigger to do but sit down and cuss. Massa Jack just buy fresh pussy off from Spanish Town slave market so he busy seasoning her. Everybody up to them usual business and even the mistress gone to Kingston. We never take nothing but weself. We go through the ratoon fields and the provision grounds—lord God, me never see so much rat in me life. Snake too. But nothing was goin' stop me from having a free nigger baby. Not a damn thing. And Benjy. Every time he touch me belly is like the man grow some more. Me never tell a soul me was goin', not even Pallas. Well, we make it to the west and in the hills where the Maroons be. Before we find them they find we. Remember, this be after the treaty.

—What that mean?

—That mean that they grab we and kick we like we is nigger. Benjy tell them that me in the family way and them don't business. White man can make you feel plenty bad, but me never dream that nigger could make nigger feel worse. Call me lanky titty donkey. Say that the massa might not even want me back. One of them lift up me frock and shove him hand in me pussy to see if me tight enough to keep. Sum'bitches. Goddamn sum'bitches. Me was right. Them was looking for strapping nigger so they keep Benjy, but they drag me back for they two pounds. And not before they beat me first. Beat me so much that see me own pickney give up first and fall out of me womb. A girl. You understand what me telling you, chile?

—Y-yes.

—No, you don't understand. Is not even losing the pickney that kill me. Is losing meself. Them Maroons make me feel like no nigger deserve freedom. No nigger must be man or woman. They think they free but they base and wicked and fucking goat so long they don't even know woman. Me did think a woman not a woman unless she be free and they take that from me. Take 'way me womanness. Is better they did rape me than send me back. Benjy, that same Benjy who tell me that me birthmark is like island and me skin is sea. That same sum'bitch don't even say nothing and couldn't even look. Me even feel sorry for him, for what nigger love be compare to free? And that Jack Wilkins, he make an example out of me. He been waiting for that all he life. All he life. You think you get whipping? Me get the worst whipping ever in Montpelier. The worst of the worst. Beat me with whip and tree branch and then brand me with iron across me back for every day me did gone. That one be the mistress idea. She take great interest. When Wilkins run out of back she tell him to brand me front. Hear me own titty cook like a goose. Smell me own self burning. Then she have me wait on her hand and foot since then. And even that, Lilith, even that wasn't the worst. The worst was when him set six man 'pon me to fuck me so that me can breed again. Two time he do it. You know how it feel to take out this mash-up thing to feed you chile? Every time me look down, me think me chile suckin' some animal.

—Jesus Christ, Homer. Jesus Christ. Lilith clutch herself.

—No, you just tell him to go frig him own backra ass.

—You cussing again.

—All them leave me was me mouth. And me become a good-behaving nigger. The best. Me so best that near everybody done forget what happen to me, except the white people. But that fine. That sweet and dandy. Me been friggin' up the mistress mind with me tea for years now. She soon mad as raas. And this one. She think this tea goin' cool her nerves but it goin' do more than that.

Lilith shock again and look at Homer for a long time. She look again at the hair and the dress and wonder how it take her so long to see that is woman she looking at. Lilith say, Homer.

—Homer?

—Huh?

—Me have me ways too.

—Really, now.

Homer get up and have her arms akimbo. She straighten herself and wait for the old Homer to come back.—What ways?

Lilith take the pot with Homer tea boiling off the stove.

—This kinda ways, Lilith say and hike up her skirt. She crouch good over the pot but high up that she don't burn herself and piss. Homer laugh. When Lilith done, she put the pot back on the stove. Homer spit into it.

—Sometime, when the recipe call for molasses, me slip some dog shit in it too, Lilith say.

—Cow shit! Cow shit for me, Homer say.

—White man be one strong bastard with all the shit he eat, Lilith say and they laugh again.

—You different, Lilith. You have more darkness 'bout you now. You turning into woman, Homer say to her.

—Me turning into something, Lilith say.

18

EVERY NEGRO WALK IN A CIRCLE. TAKE THAT AND MAKE OF IT what you will. But sometimes that circle start squeeze in on itself and get smaller and smaller and smaller like a mark, or a head. A head so small that the negro have one chance to stomp it with her foot and stomp it good. Lilith know. She learn and she learn it good. Plenty things be a sin, but every sin come with temptation and chance.

One night Lilith on the kitchen floor trying to sleep. Her mat softer now that she get Dulcimena sheets to pile on top of hers. Lilith thinking 'bout how no matter how much people come in and out of her life, she be alone. Sometimes Lilith like lonesomeness, sometime she hate it like poison. Lilith lie down on the sheets and stare in the dark and the moonlight that come through the window. One spot of silver that surrounded by darkness. The house quiet but she wait and listen to the silence for a good while. The only thing making noise is cricket. Lilith feel something coming on her, that feeling of the devil. She reach for *Joseph Andrews* at the bottom of the cupboard in the darkest corner of the kitchen but didn't open it. Joseph want her to be a woman of the sort that she don't want to be, she sure of that now. Or she think she sure. She don't know and don't like how this man who don't want to use him cocky as befits a man should make her think deep into herself. Lilith breathe in the night for she know what coming. But then she open her eyes and sigh. She get up and look in the direction of where the moon coming through the window. She know the night woman be there, standing and looking at her.

The black woman dressed in black dress like she coming from God funeral. Lilith still. Is long time since she see her, and not at Coulibre. For a while she still hold that it was one of her five sister. Pallas, Iphigenia, Callisto, Gorgon, Andromeda—no, she wasn't one...Hippolyta.

—Callisto? Lilith say. The woman say nothing. Lilith feeling cold. Then the woman raise her right hand with one finger point up. She point the finger at her own heart and tap seven time. Lilith look at her own chest where she think the heart be. She look up again, but the woman gone.

One time when Lilith was a little girl Circe tell her about the Abarra. Plenty people claim they see one. Abarra is a tricky spirit. Something white man would call demon. When the Abarra come after you, she take the form of somebody you know but she can't talk since the Abarra got no tongue. Lilith wondering if she seeing the same spirit but she don't look like nobody she know. She wonder if is somebody she supposed to know. Or somebody who know her. Lilith thinking she can't sleep in the kitchen but if the mistress ever call her and she not present, she goin' get a whipping for sure. Even Abarra can't whip nobody. Lilith lie down trembling. A roach run across the floor and she jump. Lilith pull up her knee and curl like baby until she go to sleep.

Miss Isobel step over Lilith and wake her up by slapping her forehead with a horsewhip.

—Is six o' clock, you indolent bitch, Miss Isobel say. Lucky for you, my horse is the only animal getting thrashed today. I shall be back by the afternoon. Tell that to my stepmother when she asks.

—Yes, Miss Isobel. Me commencing breakfast right now, missis,

Lilith say, but Miss Isobel gone through the door already. A horse whinny and then gallop off. Lilith rub her eye and get up. She make one step and feel *Joseph Andrews* under her foot. Lilith shudder. Surely if Miss Isobel did see the book Lilith would be halfway up a tree to be whipped right now. Lilith grab the book and hide it in the cupboard. Joseph want her to look at him, to laugh like a white woman who have the right to.

But she not a white woman. She not Lady Booby or even Betty, the servant. This not England. And there be no man in the colony like Joseph Andrews or him very dear friend Mr. Abraham Adams. And even if there be white mens of such quality, they only be so for white people. There be no love for the nigger. Lilith cup some water and splash on her face. The coldness wake her up. She check the stove if any piece of wood left to start a new fire. As soon as the fire catch she would go outside and commence milking the milk cows and setting loose the fed cows so they can graze. The chickens wake up late. Even the sun haul herself out this morning like she don't want to come out to work. In two hours the mistress wake up and the pickneys goin' to start make all sort of noise. Homer did leave some comfrey tea leaf with her the other day and these days is only a drink of it that prevent her from losing herself. But she still seeing blood. And the more they whip her, or she see somebody getting whip, the more blood she seeing. And Joseph not making her laugh no more. Lilith search her mind for something in the book, something to make the day light. But *Joseph Andrews* lying to her, making her wish for a place and time that never goin' come. No Mr. Adams waiting for a nigger. Nothing in this book a nigger can use. Lilith spend so much time looking for light under a man heel that she shock when a woman speak to her. A woman in the book by the name of Tow-Wouse. A woman with *that Piece of Flint which that good Woman wore in her Bosom by way of heart*. She set three pot of water on the stove to boil.

Time for the massa bath. He always wake up and bathe early. Earlier than him wife wake up, because, he say, he have to leave for court in Kingston. After the water done boil Lilith take some to the bathroom and pour into the tub while she wait for the massa. The massa come in and pull off him nightshirt. Without the wig, him head near bald like a newborn young'un. Lilith watch. She watch him pregnant-lookin' belly that flap down and him shoulder that cover in little spots. She watch him penis and balls jiggle into each other. Is a good two week since he have reason to whip her.

—Confound it, woman, how many times must I ask if the water's warm enough? he say.

—Yes, massa, it warm enough, sah, Lilith say.

—I don't recollect you testing it, Massa Roget say.

—Yes, massa, I does that now, sah, Lilith say.

Lilith dip her hand in the big white tub but the massa climb in the same time and splash the front of her dress. Lilith get up and go for a bucket of warm water. She pour over the massa head slow and listen to him moan. She look at how the water part the little bit of hair left and show a white point in him head. He lean forward and Lilith take the cotton cloth and scrub him back. This be the only time when Lilith not thinking of man to be a devil, this time when she not seeing him face and he cooing like baby. Massa Roget grab Lilith by the dress and pull her round to face him. He smiling already and suddenly she wonder 'bout Robert Quinn. Long time since that face come up in her mind and she surprised that she wondering 'bout him. Lilith pull out of her thinking just in time to dodge a slap. Massa Roget close him eye and lean back so that him cocky rise out of the water. Sometimes him hard, sometimes him soft, sometimes him hard again, but all the time him blame Lilith.—Stupid black goat, you're not shucking corn, he say. Lilith thinking about what she can cook in the little time she goin' have left after this. She yanking him slow. Massa Roget breathing heavy. Him face wet. Lilith don't know if is water or sweat.

—For heaven's sake, my wife wakes with the roosters, him say.

—Then shuck you own cock, Lilith say almost like whisper, so quiet that only when she look up she see that the massa hear.

Both she and Massa Roget eye open wide. Before she could jump away he grab her hand and squeeze, the fingernail digging into her skin. Lilith struggle 'gainst the man. He call her an impudent, treacherous slut. Inside her, a Lilith shouting that she must stop stop stop the uppityness and take what white man giving her. This Lilith pointing to the reward for uppityness and she see her body swinging from a noose. Then burn by fire. Then shove in river and drown. The water splashing. She pulling away, he holding firm. The inside Lilith take over her skin and she twitch and shake as the white flesh overcome her. Everything inside tell her to just lie down, lie down right now on the floor and mayhaps the cowhide won't be so hot this time. Mayhaps the kick to head will hurt for two day instead of three. Mayhaps if she beg like a girl and not like a woman, if she whimper and cry, massa take pity 'pon fool-fool Lilith, he would only slap her across the face with him ring and by next day she good as forget. Lilith look at him, smiling as he squeeze her arm skin off and she kill that woman inside her. Then she spit in him face. The massa let go one hand and punch her right in the cheek. At that second she feel two other white man punch her in the face, one with red hair, one with sour yellow. Lilith claw Massa Roget cheek and skin come off. He yell and grab her hair and yank her to the tub. She grabbing for anything her hand can reach, slippers, shoes, the pail, loose brick. He raise himself to stand up but freeze. Lilith struggling to get away and slip out of him hand sudden. Massa Roget eyes fly up in him head. Him whole body start to quiver and he grab him left hand with the right. He losing breath.—H-h-h...elp, hhhhh, he say. Massa Roget legs buckle and he fall back in the tub, clapping him head hard on the rim. He sink below the water. Massa try to push himself back up and slip and go under again. He coughing now.—H-h-help, he whimper. Lilith step slow to the tub like she 'fraid. Massa push himself out of the water, coughing and still shaking. Lilith reach out to him chest.

Massa eyes red and Lilith never see a white man looking so frighten. She put both hands on him chest, feeling the hair between her fingers, and shove him back down in the water. Massa Roget fight, but she pin him harder. She on her feet now, using all her weight to pin him down. Massa Roget not weaker but him jerkin' and the water making him slippery. Lilith looking at him eye that wide open and red and frighten like a pickney. Like a nigger. He grab after her hand and miss and grab one of her breast. Lilith yell. He push himself up above the water again. Lilith don't know if him eye red from water or tears. He groan like he about to say something, but jerk again. She try to push him under, feeling the darkness growing under her skin. Massa Roget trying to get up but him chest exploding on him. Lilith pull away and thump him in the chest. Then she thump him again. And again. And again. And three more time. Seven, the number that a woman tap in the dark. Massa Roget croak and slump down in the tub. Lilith pin him down again, shoving him under until she feel a bone crack and one last bubble leave him nose. Massa Roget still. The tub water settle and she look at him, looking at her with black man fear on him face. Lilith feel a new thing under skin, something that tingle as her heart jump up and down. It never beat so fast and so loud. True darkness and true womanness that make man scream. Then she hear a scream for real. At the door be the mistress. She go to scream again but a cough come out. She run from the door.

Lilith not thinking, Lilith not frighten, the only sound she hear is her heart beating like a drum in her ears. *Boom. Boom. Boom.* She hearing the drum beat. Seven drumbeat. Seven tap of finger from the Abarra woman. True darkness and true womanness that make man scream. Now she know what the woman in the dark want.

Blood.

The woman want blood.

Lilith run after her. Mistress Roget screaming and bawling, Lilith almost catch her. Blood pumping hot through Lilith and her temples pound like they goin' burst. Lilith catch up to Mistress Roget by the stair balcony and push her hard. Matraca coming up the stairs and scream. Two scream, but Mistress Roget's scream get cut when she burst over the wood balcony and fall to the marble floor and crunch her neck. Blood spread from under her back like two red wing.

Lilith turn to the pickney room.—Lawd, sweet Jesus father deliver me, not the pickneys! Not the pickneys, Matraca say. Lawd have mercy! Lawd have mercy! Matraca run past Lilith and beat her to the pickney door. Lilith hear a door click. Lilith cuss, but then remember Miss Isobel. Her heart pumping so hard that she feel it goin' burst out of her bosom. Lilith done think. Lilith be the beast that backra saying she be from she born. They bound to kill her now. Miss Isobel soon come back to see her family dead and they goin' roast Lilith slow over the fire. Two dead body—white body—make Lilith blacker than ever and more frighten. She want to live and she want to die and she shock when Robert Quinn appear in her head again. Lilith start to cry and whimper like a dog. She start to rock like when Tantalus' head fly up inside him. When Miss Isobel come back, they goin' roast her slow over a fire so that she scream for one week straight. They going stick hot coal up her pussy so that she can smell her own burnin' flesh. They goin' whip her until her fingers pop off. True darkness and true womanness make her want to live, make her think that goddamn, this nigger goin' live longer than what white man say. Than what God say. Lilith let the spirit take her back into the kitchen. She have to hide and the only thing she can think of hiding in is fire. She don't think. She chanting in her head. Lilith grab some stick from the kitchen stove. She look out the window and then go back upstairs. In the mistress' room, be plenty curtain, drape, bedsheet, carpet and paper. Lilith touch each with the stick and fire take birth. First it crackle, then it spread, climbing up one curtain and scooting across to the next, then spreading across rug, then twisting and turning through paper. Soon the fire roar. Lilith hear the roar and understand it. *Opapala in you, the goddess of hunger.* Lilith leave the room. At the doorway she step out and a cloud of smoke follow her like a army of spirits. She go by the pickney room and throw the burnin' stick by the door.

But as she step down the stairs the same fire strike Lilith back and she jump. The fire cackle and mock her and leap for her skirt. She scream again and again as the fire hiss. She run down the rest of the stairs and trip and fall to the floor and get up to find her shoulder and chest soak with the mistress' blood. The fire coming after her, hopping down from step to step like a impudent pickney. Lilith run.

19

MISS ISOBEL FALL TO THE GROUND AND STAY THERE TILL Massa Humphrey come. She bawl out, Lawd! Woi! like a nigger girl. One of the two mens who see her riding back to Coulibre say she scream all the way until she reach the house. She nearly fall off the horse and try to run to the door, but one of the mens hold her back. She screaming and fighting them off and cursing all kind of word 'bout niggers messing with her.—Don't touch me! Don't you dare touch me! she say and bawl out her little brother name. She scream, Maman! Maman, oh God! Oh, God! She try to run into the house again from the back but the mens hold her.—No, Miss Isobel, it too late, the fire bound to kill you for sure, he say.—I going to kill you, I'll kill you all! Miss Isobel bawl again. She bawl until she keen and keen until she drop. The mens look at her on the ground but 'fraid to touch a white woman. One nigger jump on her horse and near fall off. He steady himself little bit and ride through the gate.

Coulibre burnin'.

Fire raging and hissing and cussing and bending and climbing and racing like a yellow-red-yellow snake from one window to the next.

Fire run up to the ceiling and spread across like a spill to run back down one wall then the next and then a painting then the next. One window explode, then another, then another. Black smoke fly out the window like house spirit fleeing. Fire crackling like lightning and like laughter. So much in the white man house to burn. Carpet and curtain and book and letters, and chairs and tables and flesh. Fire hop out a window and climb up on the roof. A cloud of black smoke make the noon dark.

Two hour later the slave come back in a cart that Robert Quinn driving. Massa Humphrey ride him horse over and reach little earlier. The river too far and Coulibre have too few nigger to form a line to carry bucket of water. Massa Humphrey run to the house but Robert Quinn reach in time to stop him. The two struggle, but Robert Quinn stronger.—Damn it, Humphrey, I will not have ye make a corpse of yerself! he say. Massa Humphrey push Quinn off when he see Miss Isobel in the dirt. He lift her and put her in the cart, scowling at the niggermens who stand there and watch. Lilith see them. She wonder if they did see her first. A fit of fear did hit her when the fire take over the house and no matter how far she run, the heat chase her. Flame catch her back and some of her clothes burn. She watch Massa Humphrey trying to be gentle with Miss Isobel, wiping her face with him handkerchief. She look around to see Robert Quinn watching her. Robert Quinn left eyebrow raised, asking question. But Miss Isobel wake up screaming and he rush to the cart.

Miss Isobel screaming for her mother. She faint again and Massa Humphrey hold her like a baby. Robert Quinn whisper something and Massa Humphrey look up right away at Lilith.—Come here, you, he say. Lilith gulp. She move to them slow, feeling her bare foot cut through the grass. Robert Quinn lookin' at Lilith, then whisper to Massa Humphrey again.

—Lilith? he say.

—Yes, massa.

—Of Montpelier.

—Yes, massa.

—Explain what happened here. At once, girl!

Lilith don't say nothing.

—I said speak up, damn you.

—Me . . . me don't know, me don't know, sah.

—You don't know? You don't bloody know? What are you, the daftest nigger cow God ever let loose to torment me? Let me enlighten you, Lilith, there's a little fire raging behind you, or are you blind as well as stupid?

—Yes, massa.

—How did this happen?

—Me . . . me was milking the cow, massa. Me didn't even know the house be burnin', sah, till me come back.

—You didn't even know.

—Humphrey, it's quite possible that—

—I'm capable of asking my own questions, Quinn. So, Miss Lilith—

—Me try to run in for the pickneys, massa.

—Don't you dare interrupt me, you damn . . . Did anyone . . . Couldn't you have . . . Had none of you the heart to . . . oh, Jesus. Kill us, that's what you wish to do. You wish death on us all!

—Humphrey, Robert Quinn say and touch him shoulder. Massa slap him hand off. Quinn stare down massa but then look at Lilith. She wish down to the bone that she didn't just jump. She know her jaw drop. She know it and he seen it.

—And yer sleeve? Did ye hurt yerself?

—Me was . . . me was trying . . . the pickneys—me was trying to save the pickneys but board fall 'pon me, sah.

Quinn go towards Lilith but Massa Humphrey stop him.

—Oh, for God's sake, Robert. We have other priorities than a bloody nigger!

Quinn turn away but look at her again. Lilith feel like he might rip off her clothes and throw her into the fire when he see nothing. She walk away backward and stumble. She get up and run off.

By evening nearly every planter, attorney, infantryman, priest and clerk in the county pay visit to the Coulibre house. Terrible business, some say. The preacher pray. Massa Humphrey send Miss Isobel off to Montpelier and give the mens instructions for Homer.—You stay, he say to Lilith when he see her heading for the cart.

The wall was stone and they stand firm though they black with soot. Everything else burn to nothing, including the roof. Some parts still burnin' but most was now ash and rubble. The little fire that left in the corners and under the floorboard hiss. In what was the sitting room, half of a red chaise longue stand out around black and grey. Things that use to have shape in the world the day before is just mound of ash now. The bathtub fall from the top floor to the bottom. Robert Quinn see it first and step through the rubble to look closer. He cover him mouth quick. Massa Humphrey walking over but Quinn jump in the way.

—Humphrey, there are things ye can't unsee once you've seen 'em, Quinn say. Massa Humphrey step past. Quinn grab him hand, but the massa push him away.

—I'm not a goddamn boy, Robby, he say. But when he see what left of Massa Roget, him legs get weak and he almost fall. Robert Quinn hold on to him tight until he done throw up.

Matraca wouldn't leave the pickneys so she dead too. Bessy too old, so by the time she could wake up to feel herself burnin', she burn to death too. Francine, the mistress lady in waiting, was not on the premises but didn't get far. A soldier see her just as she turn her carriage around to ride away. They ride her down and demand to know where she was trying to get to with the mistress' carriage. Then they beat her, even though she scream that she was coming, not going. They round up Habakkuk and the niggermens too, saying they was trying to rape Miss Isobel. More hour later the commander of the militia say they suspect that Francine was part of the plot and was trying to run away. People beginning to wonder how come neither the massa nor the mistress could save themself. They wonder how come nobody even try to run for the door and why Massa Roget body was in a bathtub.

For the next two day they strip all them niggers naked, wet they skin and whip them with the cowhide. They whip Francine leg first and she scream and bawl, then her back, then her belly. They push her down on the floor and pin her with they boots. She bawling that she didn't do nothing. The commander say she should be a credit to her race and stop being a lying nigger cunt. The commander have the soldiers light corn husk and scrape off the burnin' bits so that fire rain down on her belly, face and titties. Francine still screaming that is not she! Is not she! So they heat a poker and start to brand all over her body. When she still didn't talk they spread her leg wide and brand her pussy. People at the far end of Spanish Town hear the girl scream. When she could finally talk, she beg for mercy for all her wrongdoing. Then they do the same to the mens, branding they balls or they arsehole. Every nigger confess. The commander lock them up in the gaol for trial.

Friends of Massa Roget storm the gaol, pull them out and beat them some more, blinding the girl in the right eye with a club. She scream so much until she could scream no more and all that leave was her mouth agape. Two white womens spit on her but even they couldn't stomach what happen next. The men folk drag them all to the center of the Spanish Town square as evening come in grey. They pull them up with rope and the niggers swinging from a cotton tree. Then the mens stone them until they start to swing. The girl dead before they set her on fire. The mens did still alive but too weak to scream. The sour stink of burnin' negro invade every window and doorway in Spanish Town. Lilith return to Montpelier.

She come back the same way she leave, in the back of the carryall that Robert Quinn drive.

—Are ye happy to be back, lass? he say.

—Yes, massa, Lilith say.

—Well, how anyone finds cause to be happy amidst this terrible business mystifies me, of course. Then again, much about negroes mystifies me.

—Yes, massa.

Robert Quinn sigh. Terrible, terrible business, he say. Miss Isobel is beside herself, of course. Do ye feel sorry for her, Lilith?

—Yes, massa. Me feel terrible sorry for her. And the poor pickneys.

—I'm sure ye do. Lucky you were to be out milking the cow and not asleep.

Yes, massa. Lucky.

At the estate, Homer and Pallas was in the kitchen.

—Look who come back, Pallas say, but Lilith didn't say nothing.

—You good, girl chile? Homer say.

—Yes, Lilith say, lookin' down on the floor.

—Look like you goin' need two kinda tea tonight, Homer say.

—One to sleep and one to forget, Pallas say.

—Me don't have nothing to forget, Lilith say.

—Of course, Homer say. You have you bundle? Lucky you manage to save that in time.

Lilith don't say nothing.

—You hear the news, Homer? They kill them Coulibre niggers that do it. Burn them right down to nothing. You know her, Lilith, the girl they say start the fire? Pallas say.

—Me and she was not friend.

—Me sure you and she wasn't enemy, neither. Anyway, Homer, the white mens catch her trying to run 'way. Next thing you know, they say she confessing to starting the fire. Yes, me dear, they lock her up, but of course you know what happen when nigger get lock up in gaol.

—Lynching.

—Lynching is correct. No trial for that bitch. Not a baby killer. No she used to take care of the pickneys, Lilith?

—No, that be Matraca.

—Where she be?

—Dead. Where me sleeping?

—You forget already? Where you always sleep. You space waiting on you, Homer say. Lilith step past her and go down the cellar steps.

—Welcome home, Homer say.

Morning come and Miss Isobel wake up in a fit. She clutch herself quick as if to make sure that she have on clothes. Miss Isobel jump out of bed and run down the stairs. Passing through the hallway, her movement wake up Massa Humphrey, who be sleeping on a chaise in the sitting room.

—Isobel? Isobel? Is that you?

—A heartless one you are, that's all I can say about you, Humphrey Wilson. A heartless, heartless one.

—Pardon me?

—How could you, Humphrey? How could you have let me sleep in your room through the night? Do you know what would happen should this get out? A lady still needs her honour, Humphrey, her entire family's standing rests on it.

—But Isobel.

—I must have lost all good sense, doing what I'm doing with you. Allowing you to have you way with...You must think me no better than the niggers. And look at me, maybe I'm not. We are sinning, Humphrey Wilson.

—Isobel, I beg you.

—No, we have forgotten ourselves, Mr. Wilson, and you have dishonoured me once too many times, but even this is going too far.

—Isobel—

—Oh, let me leave, Humphrey.

Isobel fix her dress bosom and head for the door. She nearing the doorway and stop. Just stop still, like Lot wife that turn back.

—Isobel? Massa Humphrey say. He run in time just to catch her as she nearly faint. Miss Isobel start screaming again. Lilith hear the scream from downstairs, the woman scream that she hear before from Massa Humphrey mother. *Serve her right, the bitch,* Lilith whisper to herself, over and over and over till she believe it.

Lilith wear the anger through the day, like she gnashing teeth. —Me peeling as fast as me can, pussyhole, she say to Pallas when Pallas ask her for the potato to put in the soup. Homer don't say nothing and Lilith make sure not to look at her. Pallas put food on the tray and tell Lilith to carry it up to Miss Isobel. Lilith say she busy.

—Twiddling thumb don't count as busy, Homer say, and that be that.

Lilith open the door to Massa Humphrey room. She don't see Miss Isobel. She put down the tray with the soup and go to leave. Right then, Miss Isobel come out of the water closet.

—What is that you brought? Miss Isobel say.

—Soup, mistress.

—Soup? Who said I wanted soup? Tell Mr. Wilson that I do not have much of an appetite, not now.

—Yes'm.

—Maybe not ever.

—Yes'm.

—You killed them, didn't you?

Lilith jump.

—You and all the others. You killed them. You watched my family die. Burn to death like...like...oh! Did you not hear a scream? Not a single scream?

—Ma'am?

—Nor a shout? Not even a whimper? You heard not one cry for help? Were you not in the kitchen?

—I...I was out milking the cows, ma'am.

—You telling me that you're the one nigger in creation who don't know what a scream sounds like? You want me whip the bloodcloth out of you so that you remember?

—No, please, ma'am! I try to save...I try to save. The doorway fall 'pon me...I...

Miss Isobel climb off the bed.—What kind of monster kills a baby? What kind of demon lets him die? Answer me that question! Answer...Miss Isobel knees buckle and she sit back down. She look overcome. Lilith backing away to the door.

—Weren't you friends with Francine? Don't you all share your damned nigger fantasies? Would you have killed them too? Answer me!

People hearing. Footsteps approach the door.

—You were on the grounds! You were...oh, God.

Lilith stand still, lookin' down on the ground while Miss Isobel cry again.—I'll bet you're not even sorry, she say.

Lilith feel like she about to cry herself.—Me plenty sorry, mistress. Me plenty sorry.

—You know what I wish? I'll bet you don't. You think right now, right at this very moment I'm wishing God returns my family? You think so? Well you're wrong. Wronger than the devil.

Miss Isobel get up again, but she wobble when she walk. She still wobble and hobble over to Lilith as Lilith step backways and backways.—Try to guess what I'm wishing for. Me say *guess*, bitch, not run!

Miss Isobel close in on her by the door before Lilith could slip through the doorway. She close enough for Lilith to smell oldness on her, that sour mildew mixed with perfume smell. Her eyes red and her cheek hollow and dark. Her breath foul.

—You know what I wish? I wish I was strong enough to wield an axe. I wish I could take an axe and chop every nigger in my sight. Chop you from the feet up so that you scream all the way. Chop you all up into bits and feed you to Humphrey's dogs. That's what I wish.

—Me sorry bad, mistress.

—You're sorry? What for? Isn't this what all niggers want? You think me don't know how you stay? Mind is you even set the fire.

—No, please, mistress, me didn't have nothing to do with it, mistress.

—All the time now. I hear them all the time. I'm hearing them right now.

—Me wish me could bring them back, mistress.

—That's not what I wish. I wish I had the bare hands to choke you or a knife to cut your tongue out. I wish I wasn't a lady or a woman, but a nigger like you. Can you imagine that? Can you imagine me envying a wretched nigger like you?

Massa Humphrey rush into the room.—Isobel, are you all right?

Miss Isobel lose herself in him arms. He shout and catch her and take her to bed. Lilith can't move. Before she know it, he in front of her.

—What were you doing to her? he say. Lilith about to say something but he slap it out of her mouth.

—Get out.

Lilith in the cellar hiding in the dark. Babies crying around her as they skin burn. Lilith try to think about the quilt on her back, the reason for what she do. Lilith trying to think of a deeper, more angrier reason. Lilith thinking that this is just eye for an eye and tooth for a tooth. Lilith think that if she say it enough time, maybe ten, maybe twenty, maybe the number after that it would leave a mark in her head like Robert Quinn's tattoo on him knuckle. Eye for an eye and tooth for a tooth. Lilith thinking about the anger that boil her blood and why it leave her. Why it put fire in her eyes then stamp itself out, leaving this heaviness. The fire that did say this is what she be and this is what she do. The fire that not red, but black like skin. True darkness and true womanness that make a man scream. But if this be the true womanness, then she don't want it no more. Mayhaps true womanness was to be free to be as terrible as you wish. Like a white woman. Mayhaps true womanness mean to let the terribleness run loose and wild like river flood. True womanness be the seed of destruction like plenty whorish woman in the Bible. Mayhaps a woman be a beast indeed and everything the white man say 'bout a niggerwoman being left to her own devices be true. Lilith don't want to be no woman no more. She want to go back and run through the ratoon fields, even to Circe, whose wickedness was never wicked like the Rogets. Nobody deserve to be dead more than Massa Roget, except that now the man really dead. And the two pickneys and Matraca. Blood don't taste like wine, Lilith learning. Homer in the kitchen.

Lilith walking down the corridor and pass a looking glass on the wall, big as the paintings of the dead Wilsons. It didn't make right and the mistress keep it away from people. Lilith watch the looking glass looking at her. The looking-glass Lilith have a flat head top, a chin that point all the way to the ground and eye so big Lilith can see another Lilith in it. She looking at the looking-glass eye holding her secret and wonder if maybe anybody can find out if they look hard enough.

—*I beseech you, Isobel,* you must eat, Massa Humphrey say. He at the door of him own room that now be Miss Isobel room. Near two week gone since the fire. Massa Humphrey living in one of the guest rooms. The day before, he go to him mother to tell her what happen, but she didn't seem to hear. The whole time she asking her son where the father go when he go riding, since nobody in town ever see him. Her room smell of dead flowers and piss. The mistress thin and her lips chap up. Massa Humphrey about to leave the room when the mistress say, Poor, poor Ludmilla, before she go back where her mind usually go. Homer wipe sweat from the woman face.

Now Massa Humphrey at another door trying talk to another woman who lock herself in. The massa look ragged, blue shirt not tuck in breeches and no shoes on him foot. Him hair wild. The two womens wearing him down.

—Isobel, really, I will open this door, he say.

—Do as you must, she say. Massa Humphrey open the door. Homer behind him. Lilith behind her carrying a food tray that still steaming and crackling with frying oil.

The room smell different to Lilith. Not just the perfume that woman use in between bath, but also the lighter sweat that come from woman flesh. Massa Humphrey pull back the drawn curtains and light pounce 'pon Miss Isobel, who look like the bed swallow her up.

—Oh, a pox on the lot of you! Miss Isobel say. Her eyes puffy from crying and sleeping but she still dressed ready to go in her one light purple dress with the petticoat showing and her shoes still on.

—Isobel—

—And you, sir, stepping into a woman's bedroom like I were some parlor whore!

—I have been criminally remiss, Miss Isobel, my apologies. I'm only concerned—

—I do not want your concern, nor do I accept your apology.

—Miss Isobel.

Miss Isobel climb out of the bed dressed head to foot, like she just coming in from the country.—I'm just like them, you know. Did you know I was no better, Humphrey?

—Forgive me, Isobel, I don't understand.

—No better than negro I am, no breeding nor bearing, no education on how one becomes a proper lady. Have you not heard what Edward Long has said about us? Even we backward Creole women have heard of it. Seems he think we are ignorant blackie lovers who are to be pitied. Do you pity me, Humphrey?

—Isobel. This is a tragedy, a real—

—Please. You think it's a tragedy for them? Look at them outside this window playing at remorse. You don't know them like I do, Humphrey, but how could you? How could you know what goes on in the mind of these niggers? Get out.

—Isobel?

—Them! Me don't want no stinking nig—I don't want to be around any goddamn nigger laughing behind my back. Get out. Get out! *Get out!*

—Really, Isobel! There's no call for—

—You think I'm a witch, don't you? You think I'm a hellion. I'll bet you weren't thinking such when—

—Isobel!

Miss Isobel sit back down on the bed, with her back to everybody.

—Just get them out, Humphrey, my stomach grows sick from the sight of niggers.

—And I don't want any goddamned nigger food, Miss Isobel say. Massa Humphrey point to the dresser bench for Lilith to put the tray.

—God is punishing me for my sin, Humphrey, surely he is.

—You're sick with grief. It's only fitting that—

—Oh, enough with your patronizing! I know how much of a family's honour is tied up in the daughter's purity, Humphrey, even if you don't. Thank God Papa died before hearing news that I was a degenerate. That would have killed him.

—I don't think—

—I dare ask, do you ever think at all? Did you think what you were doing to a poor lady when you had your way with—

—Had my way? Had my goddamn way? I don't remember putting

you in shackles and dragging you into my bedroom, the room you're sleeping in right now, may I remind you. Not for the first time, may I remind you. And if you really want to pass bl— Oh, will you set down that blasted tray and get out!

Lilith put down the tray so swift that the teacups tumble. She and Homer step out of the room quick, only Massa Humphrey face was getting red quicker.

—You have certainly defiled me, sir, was the last thing Lilith and Homer hear before Massa Humphrey slam the door. Lilith back at the crooked mirror looking. Lilith wondering if the mad version of her goin' jump out again, maybe right there. She wonder if it is all this heavy thinking in her head that drawing her cheeks down so till she start to look meager. Lilith turn to go back downstairs but Homer grab her hand and pull her over to the door. Massa Humphrey and Miss Isobel don't finish yet.

—No, Isobel, you are not yourself, Massa Humphrey say.—I will not. I will not! Isobel!

—Then get out! Miss Isobel scream. The door swing open and another *Get out* fly through before Massa Humphrey. The massa so frighten he don't even notice Lilith and Homer tumble down on the floor as he step past. Lilith peek inside and see Miss Isobel readjusting her dress.

Massa Humphrey finally convince Miss Isobel to go through with the funeral, almost a month after the fire. Homer hear the massa talking to Robert Quinn 'bout the father body that burn so stiff in the tub that they have to break it up just so he can fit in a casket. Robert Quinn say they found what they believe to be the mother and they should just take whatever they find, put it in two casket and call that the children. Lilith hear Homer tell Pallas and Callisto. Lilith run through the kitchen around the back of the house and vomit.

At the funeral everybody expecting Miss Isobel to break from the pew like wild goat and run to the coffins. Lilith expecting her to bawl and wail and keen so loud that the church roof rattle. She expect bawling that drown out the bell. Loud enough that them God would come down and point Lilith out as the evildoer and drag her straight off to the lake of fire where wicked negroes burn. But instead Miss Isobel was a stick. People expect Miss Isobel to be in black but she wearing the same purple dress, even though Massa Humphrey said he would buy her a whole new wardrobe or have Homer make her something.—I'd rather burn in hell than be draped in something a nigger made, she say. Almost every woman have a veil covering them hair but her.

Since the fire, Lilith feel wrong whenever she eat, and don't have no desire for it. She will eat the boil potatoes and milk and throw it up every time she think of two baby flesh burnin' into one with a negro who trying to save them on top. Lilith wonder if she kill them first, gentle-like, before they feel any burn. She wonder again what kind of spirit give her madness, then take it away for her so that she see what madness did. Lilith bedding soak with tears and when she think 'bout how she not to cry and how every white devil get what he or she deserve, she soak the bedding some more. What only Lilith know is that Miss Isobel all cried out. Soon, burned baby start to follow Lilith. A stump of ash that try to cry from what fire melt together. The stump follow her. Behind it another stump with ash crackling and bits falling off. Behind it another stump of ash, bigger than the two, with the belly fat and a head with a wig. All screaming and coming after her. Lilith wake up.

Homer wake up early to see Lilith already working on breakfast. —With all this energy, you might as well be a field nigger, Homer say. Lilith say nothing. Lilith stay in her corner and peel yam and potatoes, cut up fruits, boil vegetables, scrub the floor on her knees and clean out Massa Humphrey mother's chamber pot. Lilith working hard in the mother room and when she run out of things to do she do them over.

When she come back down to the kitchen Lilith so tired that she barely notice that one and two womens quick to step out of her way. She turn to grab the washbucket and see womens look away from her quick. One of the mens come in with a bunch of banana and leave it far off in the corner for Lilith to pick up herself. Lilith look to see if Homer looking. She go up to the mistress room and stay long because the mistress blank face is the only one in Montpelier that don't have no judgement in it. Lilith working like mule until she so tired she can't even move. Lilith on the kitchen floor sleeping until Homer drag her to her mat.

In deep night, Lilith wake up. But then she see her and rage fly up in her head. She grab the nearest thing to fling at the dark woman in the corner, a silver plate that wear down and rusty now. As she go to fling it, the woman not there anymore. Lilith cry till she cough. Then she stop all of a sudden to check if anybody hearing her through the dark.

She hear a whimpering and know is not her. Then a scream. Then the smell of burnin' flesh, sour like dirty hair and stink like roasting goat. Lilith feeling sweat run down her face or mayhaps it was tears running without her say-so. Francine dead in her place and in the most wickedest way. Three man too but all she can see is the girl. But which nigger would make choice to take that punishment? Lilith is not Homer, a woman who look like she would have dignity if death come for her. She hate herself for being frighten like any nigger girl. She want to forget her name. Francine ash come all the way up from Kingston and settle down on her, Lilith can feel it. She try to think of true womanness and true darkness but neither come from thinking. A girl killed in the most cruelest way. And two baby. Two baby who was goin' grow up wicked anyway. Two baby.

She go outside. The moon shy tonight, only showing half her face. Lilith walking to where she think the cave of the six womens be, but frown when she remember Callisto and Gorgon and Pallas. But maybe they have the potion, the magic, the spell to make a woman forget. Something stronger than the most secret tea. She turn to go to them, but stop. They goin' want to know what she trying to forget. Homer in particular. Lilith walking the estate and seeing the fields. Before too long, be crop time when the negroes work night and day. She fearing the Johnny-jumpers but she hoping too. Maybe she should get punishment and maybe they would deal with her body the way nobody know to deal with her head. Just then when she looking over the field, she see something jumping up and down, rising above the bush, then down, and then above again. Lilith run to hide behind a old cart. She hear before she see who. The sound of hoof on dirt. A horse. A dark horse with a rider to match. Lilith go to scream but catch her mouth. Nigger know all 'bout creature of darkness riding horseback at night. But then the rider yell at the horse and the dark hat, dark coat and dark boots show who, even as the shadow under the hat hide the face. She gallop through the gate and gone.

Miss Isobel.

Nightwomen

· 20 ·

BAD FEELING IS A COUNTRY NO WOMAN WANT TO VISIT. So they take good feeling any which way it come. Some time that good feeling come by taking on a different kinda bad feeling. Near three month now, first every day, then three time or twice a week, then whenever she wish, Miss Isobel leave the plantation, riding out on horseback on a real saddle, like a man. Most night, Lilith awake and outside hiding behind bush even though sometimes several day pass and she don't see her. There was a spell, almost for two fortnight, when she seem to stop altogether, but then she start up again one week in September and start back in earnest. Sometimes the sky so bright with moon colours that Lilith see that she wearing man clothes. Massa Humphrey's, mayhaps. Lilith then go back to the kitchen and wait till Miss Isobel come back. Sometime Lilith drop asleep, only to jerk herself back up. Most time Miss Isobel come back just as the sun start peek up in the sky.

Lilith have a hard day's work ahead of her, so she start. Lilith work so hard that Homer say she must be missing her days at Coulibre. Sometimes in the early morning she see Robert Quinn. Sometimes Robert Quinn see her before she see him. Them times she would back away from the window and watch him face. Quinn stop taking care of him hair these days and he belly start to poke in front of him, but him jaw still strong and him eye still bright like a cat. He would look in the kitchen window for a while, then turn and go off, the horse waiting as the field slaves file down the road. Lilith know why they marching so. This be October 1, the first day of crop time, and five months later when all this finish, at least a fifth goin' be dead.

Even white man come to crop time in fear and trembling. The overseer shout louder, the slave-driver drive harder, the Johnny-jumper whip longer and the negroes work they fingers down to a stump. The massa worry himself till he fool and like the field negroes he don't sleep. Most time the field negroes work all through the night cutting cane, trashing the leaves, dodging rat and snake, and piling the cane together to send to the mill. Crop time is where the slave reap the cane and the massa reap the money. The overseer too, with his commission of every hogshead over one hundred twenty. On Montpelier, crop time is what keep the estate going. Next to rumor of rebellion, crop time is the only time a white man lose sleep.

—How much worm you catch this morning?

Lilith jump. Homer step in the kitchen, wearing the blue dress that she put on to go out. Lilith clutch her chest trying to settle herself.

—You heading out somewhere?

—Into town with Massa Quinn, he want some drapery and things to make him house look decent and since he don't have no white woman company, me be the next best thing.

—What 'bout the breakfast and luncheon?

—You used to cook at Coulibre and nobody never dead. At least not from that.

—What you mean?

—Me don't mean a thing, girl chile, other than you can cook the food and manage a kitchen, so do the two of them like we woman always call to do.

—Them not goin' hear me. You see how they all treatin' me like leper. You can't say you no see it too.

—On the contrary—

—What that mean?

—It mean on the contrary. Something tell me you not goin' suffer no difficulty.

—But—

—Butt is what you get from goat. Can't keep backra waiting when him deh on haste. Homer put on her blue bonnet and step through the door. She stand up outside long time and wait. Lilith look at her.—Do you work and stop watch me back, Lilith, Homer say even though she didn't turn around once. Lilith step away from the window.

Near a hour later, Lilith step timid-like into Massa Humphrey room to see Miss Isobel fast asleep. Lilith set the tray of food down on the table by the window and pull back the curtains.

—What de bloodcloth! Blow it out! Blow it out, Miss Isobel say, half into the pillow, and half into the air.—The curtains, the curtains, curse you, Miss Isobel say.

Lilith draw the curtains and darkness sweep over the room again. Lilith see man clothes on the floor, white blouson, white breeches and black boots messed up with mud and grass. They peep out from a white sheet that messed up with mud also. She pick up the breeches and it smell like a drunk man, with liquor, tobacco and something she can't fathom. She pick up the sheet, which smell the same, with marks that look like hands all over it. Miss Isobel in the bed, her back to Lilith. A knock on the door wake her up good.

—Isobel? Isobel, it is I, Massa Humphrey say.

That give Miss Isobel a start. She roll over the bed quick to check the ground and gasp. She look up at Lilith with the clothes in her hand.

—Isobel? Massa Humphrey say.

Miss Isobel and Lilith look at each other for a long time, her hair down and flowing over her shoulders. Lilith take off her apron and wrap the drunken clothes. Miss Isobel still looking at her.

—Isobel, may I enter, Massa Humphrey say.

—A minute, if you please, a minute, Miss Isobel say.

The two womens look at the boots. Lilith kick the pair under the bed. Miss Isobel set up in the bed.

—Come in, Miss Isobel say.

Massa Humphrey step in with him shirt untuck and no boots on. The massa step with long stride first, but when he see Lilith, he stop and move slower.

—Really, Master Wilson, I'd sooner take you for a common peasant.

—My apologies, Miss Isobel. My concern for your well being, well,…it overrides my attention to decorum. Leave us, he say to Lilith.

—Stay. She was just about to hand me my breakfast tray, Miss Isobel say. Lilith set the bundle on the floor, grab the tray and put it on the bed over Miss Isobel lap.

—Well, it does my heart good see you eat, Miss Isobel.

—Three hurrahs for your heart, then. Now you may go, Miss Isobel say to Lilith.

Outside, Lilith linger for a little bit. Long enough to hear Massa Humphrey say, I will not, Isobel. Lilith turn to go downstairs but slip in the room next door.

—I am nothing more than your trifle, your Creole courtesan, then, Miss Isobel say.

—I must entreat—

—Oh, will you quit speaking so pompous, Humphrey, your head will soon explode.

—Pompous? Pompous! My dear woman, are you aware that when you speak you—

—Have a little of the colony in me? Yes, Humphrey, yes, 'tis like a taint on my own damn blood, if you must know.

—I will not take advantage of someone grieving—

—I do not need to be comforted, Humphrey Wilson, I need to be fucked. Rutted like a common cow. Does that shock you? Are you quite horrified? Do you find me improper? Why should you? You made me this way and now I'm nothing but a leper to you. Is that what you want to hear? Do you really wish to know how base I can be, Humphrey? I'm sick of feeling like an orphan—even a whore's lot is better than mine. I would kill my family again to swap grief for pleasure!

—Isobel! You're not making sense—

—You're the one not making sense, you hypocrite.

—I . . . I shall return when you're civil.

—Return when you're hard, I have no use for anything civil.

Massa Humphrey storm through the door and leave it open. Lilith pass Miss Isobel door to see her pouring something from a metal flask into her tea, then gulping the whole thing down like a thirsty nigger. After midnight, Miss Isobel gone out riding again, this time with no moonlight or clouds to show the way. She wearing the man clothes, the same clothes Lilith wash and dry and put back in the room that afternoon while Miss Isobel act like she sleeping.

The next morning Homer up before Lilith.

—Lawdy to clawdy, ah tired! Homer say when she see Lilith coming into the kitchen.

—Tired from what? Lilith say, trying not to act surprised.

—Tired from honest living, she say. Massa Quinn take me all over Kingston yesterday, to shop after shop after shop. Me'd almost think me shopping with the mistress if he didn't know so little 'bout drapery. Two time the man pick up osnaburg cloth and ask if it can make curtain. Me have to remind him that only nigger wear osnaburg. And now me and the womens have curtain to make. Them teach you how to make curtain at Coulibre?

—No.

—Too bad. Could use another hand. Massa Quinn look like he in a haste.

—In a haste for what?

—That be him own business. But I tell you this, the way Massa Robert fixin'-fixin' up the little overseer house, you'd think he expecting a wife.

One night Lilith still awake from working, but this be different work. The great house dark except for a dim lamp Lilith holding up with her right hand, that colour the walls orange. She set the lamp on a table outside the bedroom door and step in. Miss Isobel lying in the bed and the only sound in the night be her breathing. Lilith set down the boots that she polish and shine herself, and leave. The next morning, she go back to the bedroom early and grab up the same boots, now soiled with mud, and the same man clothes on the floor that stinking up the room. Miss Isobel fast asleep but on the floor, peeking out from under the bed, be the metal flask. Lilith pick it up slow and careful-like and twist the cap off. She smell it and frown, closing it back quick. The something-else smell, the thing that all over the stinking clothes was in the flask too. Whatever it be and whatever Miss Isobel do, taking care of her was Lilith work now. She didn't know how much work a nigger must do to forget. How long a nigger must work until she feel debt pay or punishment enough.

Massa Humphrey learn to treat Miss Isobel bedroom like a whole 'nother house. He don't go in there much no more and when he do, he don't stay long. At one point he ask Homer where Robert Quinn be and she remind him that is crop time. Oh, yes, massa say and touch him lip. Little time later, Massa Humphrey on horseback galloping down to the cane field. Homer at the window seeing them ride back together, slow-like, with the horses trotting. Massa Humphrey burst out laughing and slap Robert Quinn on the shoulder. Robert Quinn laugh too. When Massa Humphrey come back through the kitchen, he look 'pon Lilith for a good while with one eyebrow raise. He step to her, then stop, then turn and gone 'bout him business. Couple nigger notice. Lilith don't look at them, but stare out of the window until she sure they not looking at her. Her palm sweaty, she know.

Night time come and Lilith in the cellar, her nerves worse. She think about what she can do now that them find out her secret. Lilith wonder when he was goin' strike her again, Massa Humphrey. She wonder how he find out about her and why he taking so long to beat her. Lilith sweating on this and remember something Homer say about when a puss catch a bird. The massa was looking at her all queer-like, so why not come to her that very instant and beat the lying out her frame? But he be white man, after all. Taking they good time to move in for the kill is they most favourite thing. Lilith tell herself she don't care, she dead from the day she born.

Lilith look around the kitchen. She blind in the dark, but know where everything be. She know where the knife keep. She know where Homer keep the razor to shave Massa Humphrey, like she do most Sunday. A house nigger deal with herself that way one time and Homer say that if you cut across your wrist right you don't even feel pain, but a slower kind of feeling, like when you smoke certain bush.

Down in the cellar Lilith think of blood and on the cellar floor, Mistress Roget blood spread like wings. Mistress Roget eye open wide and she scream hellfire. Lilith shake her head out of it. White man God say vengeance is mine and he always ready to judge the quick and the dead. The night woman don't come back no more. Maybe she be neither Anansi or the Abarra but the Ogun, who Homer say negro womens must never talk 'bout. Homer make Ogun sound like man, but maybe Ogun pretty and terrible and shift like hot wind, a she not a he, who always and never the same.

Then Lilith see blood on her hands and have a start. She run upstairs and buck her toe on the step. Lilith run into the kitchen, feeling her way through the space that she know. By the counter under the window, the open barrel of water be where it always be. She scrub her hands in the barrel. Then she cup some water in her hand and bury her face. The coldness snap Lilith right down her back. The splashing make noise and she didn't hear the first step. But she hear the second. And the third. Lilith run over to other end of the kitchen, dodging pot and pans that hanging above and banana bunches that lie on the floor. Four and five step. Too late to run down the stairs back to the cellar. Lilith run into the darkest corner and make herself like shadow.

Sixth step. In the room. Miss Isobel yellow hair push up in a hat. She wearing man tails and man breeches that too loose on her hip and boots. Lilith look at Miss Isobel face and see a mask, shiny like she coming from a costume ball. Miss Isobel halt. Lilith still. Lilith pushing herself in the corner trying to make herself smaller. Between Lilith and Miss Isobel be the counter in the center of the kitchen. Miss Isobel turn to the door and let herself out.

The next morning Lilith rise again and go to the kitchen. The sun don't rise yet and not even cock crowing. As she reach the top step, she stop. In the kitchen be Homer at the table, and making noise as he drinking tea be Robert Quinn.

—Speak of the devil, massa, Homer say.

—Aye, lass, the person I've been expecting, Robert Quinn say.

Lilith perplex.

Robert Quinn gargling the tea.

—Massa Quinn, he have good news for you, girl chile. Good, good news, Homer say, but the smile come too late and go too early. Lilith don't like the look of it.

—Massa Quinn come for you belongings. You goin' live with him now, girl chile.

· 21 ·

EVEN THE DIRTIEST, SMELLIEST, POOREST, MOST GODFOR-
sook, black teeth, worthless Cockney bastard know that white skin
carry God power. White people say something to that sort all the time.
Usually is planter and other rich white man talking 'bout they fellow
white man who poorer, who come to Jamaica and see that there be nothing like danger in black flesh to make all white man realise they have
the same standing. Good money wagering that this not be how things
go back in the London, or Liverpool, or Birmingham or whatever ham
or hell the white man come from. But even fool-fool white man know
that he worth something as soon as he take foot in the West Indies.

The truth be this. They's scared of the negroes. They scared of the
arms that can grab three stalk of cane in one grip and chop it straight
through with one swing. They scared of the fingers that sprinkle something in the soup that might be pepper today, poison tomorrow. They
scared that the hand that can wring a chicken neck can wring a lady
neck. They scared that what between negro man leg goin' battering
ram up in white woman and leave her loose with niggerkin, and ruin

her. They scared that deep in the blackest pussy more bewitching than opium.

There be thirty-three negro for every white in Jamaica. And when most of them negroes be Ashanti, there goin' be more hataclaps in the colony than in hell itself. 1702: Rebellion in the east county, not far from Montpelier. 1717: Twelve rebellion in the east and west, so much so that the king send more militia to the colony and they didn't leave. 1722: Slave rebellion in Montego Bay so bad that the governor have to send for the Mosquito Indians to fight the negroes. By now, the negroes take to fleeing to the hills and joining the Maroons. Maroon take residence and beat the British so much they turn fool. 1734: Rebellion. The backra sack Nanny Town. 1738: Rebellion. 1739: Rebellion. 1740: Rebellion. 1745: The plot to kill all the whites. 1746: Rebellion. 1758: Rebellion. 1760: The worsest rebellion under Tacky—sixty whites and four hundred blacks get killed. 1765: Rebellion. 1766: Rebellion. 1771: Militia discover a new slave plot and find there be five hundred negroes plotting. 1777: Rebellion. 1782: Rebellion.

White man know that there never be a safe day in the colony. So they whip we. One hundred, two hundred, three hundred lash and whatever number come after that. They burn they mark with hot iron on you chest, breast or arse cheek. They chop off a foot if you run away, a hand if they think you thief and a balls if they showing you a lesson. They derby-dose you, stuff you mouth with nigger shit and wire it shut until you swallow it. They beat you if you sick, they beat you if you well. They make a well man sick. They shoot you in the head if the cane don't cut right, they shoot you in the arse if you not moving with haste. They step on you after the whipping and rub salt pickle, lime juice and bird pepper in the wound until you cry blood. They make one negro piss in another negro eye or mouth. They rub molasses on a naked negro so that fly set 'pon him in the day and mosquito take over in the night.

They take a mama new young'un and kill it in front of the mama.

They take a mama new young'un and give it to other negro to suckle. They take a mama new young'un and sell it before it reach six.

They say black woman titty lank like goat and black man head low like rooster. They say you lazy, lying, thiefing, lusty, savage, wicked, ungodly, stink, rank, sweaty, vile, stupid, backward, sickly, worthless and brutish. They say you eat negro flesh, drink negro blood and rutt you own father, mother, brother and sister. Then they look at you breast and watch they own crotch rise. They work you from before sunrise to after sundown and in crop time, through the night.

They takes you from the Africa. Plenty negro born on the estate, but in 1800 plenty negro still come from the Africa. They pile six hundred negro in the ship beside and on top of each other, lying down with a chain on they foot for three months. They take the negro out and talk to them in a tongue they don't understand and wash they shit and rankness off with sea water and whip two or three for amusement. People think the Igbo negro fool, but the Igbo have sense to wait until they take up all the negroes on deck for cleaning and whipping, and he or she would tip over the edge of the ship and drown and take the baby too. Six hundred negro sail from the Africa, four hundred negro living when the ship dock. Lilith have a quilt on her back, but there be a bigger quilt, a patchwork of negro bones that reach from the Africa to the West Indies.

But sometime, a negro get tired of white man stomping so he grab the foot, twist and break it. Sometime a negro say, Enough done be enough now.

The year of our lord, 1784. December. Jack Wilkins get correspondence that a Coromantee nigger they call Bacchus run away to the swamp. Rage fly up in Jack Wilkins' face that get red like annatto. He storm into the dining room where Massa and Mistress Wilson taking tea and say one rude nigger gone take it 'pon himself to run away and this is what happen when they look at a white man and see only weakness. The massa look down on the ground, but the mistress say that if

Jack Wilkins so strong, then he should get going and catch the negro, since they don't pay overseers two hundred pounds a year to stand up and chat about how brutish a man of lower birth like him can be. Jack Wilkins storm out of the house with him face redder.

Jack Wilkins get more correspondence from the same house nigger that Bacchus be seen on the west end of the swamp, waiting for sunset to flee. Jack Wilkins head to the bush and see Bacchus right away standing in the swamp with grass that tall like tree, and tree that swinging with green vine, and vine that swimming in the swamp river that giggle and gurgle. The sun setting and sometimes light slip past a tree branch and stun Jack Wilkins. Jack Wilkins coming, but Bacchus not running, not at all. Jack Wilkins cursing 'bout how he going chop Bacchus member off, but Bacchus still standing, up to him calf in swamp water. Jack Wilkins 'bout ten or twelve paces from Bacchus and uncoil the whip. Bacchus smile. Jack Wilkins crack the whip but the swamp tree too plenty and every time he swing the whip, it coil round a branch. Jack Wilkins struggling to pull the whip and making noise in the water. But Bacchus quiet like a mouse.

Cronos even quieter.

Jack Wilkins didn't see Cronos until a big black hand wrap round him neck and start to choke him. Jack Wilkins push back and the two of them stumble into the water. Wilkins trying to pull off Cronos' hand but Cronos too strong. Cronos squeeze down on Wilkins' neck as if he goin' crush it before Wilkins strangle. The whole swamp hearing the sound of him splashing in the water and coughing cause he can't breathe. Wilkins hand flay and flay until he manage to pull out the musket he keep on him chest. The gun damp but not wet. Wilkins manage to push the musket up under Cronos' chin and pull the trigger. One click, then nothing. Cronos laugh.—Jus' like a backra, fi have gun that can't shoot, he say. Cronos choking Wilkins and swinging him around like a dolly. Wilkins look like all blood squeeze into him head and soon bust. Wilkins try again, two, three time, he try so hard that he didn't know that Cronos dead until blood start flowing down him white cheek. Cronos' death grip tighter than the strangle and Wilkins make great effort to push the nigger off. But musket only have one shot, and Bacchus know.

By now, plenty slave out surrounding the swamp and watching. Just watching. Nobody come in the swamp, but stay outside, just watching. Wilkins stumble and try to run but the water too shifty, the mud too deceiving and the trees too plenty. He turn west but Bacchus chasing after him.

—I's gone kill you, you bombocloth! I's gone chops off you cocky and cut you a new-fangle pussyhole! Bacchus say.

Wilkins push him off and run. Bacchus swing the cutlass but strike a tree. Wilkins running to the setting sun, but the west is deep water.—Come back, backra! Come get you judgement, Bacchus say. Wilkins run and stumble. Wilkins cry out for help but none of the negroes move. All the negroes watch. Wilkins cry out for help again and promise double portion of food to the slave that help. The negroes watch. Wilkins can't see no face. He turn around and Bacchus jump him. They twist and turn and roll and struggle like two crocodile. Bacchus swing the 'lass and slice Wilkins right near the knee. Wilkins try to grab Bacchus' throat but him neck slippery. Bacchus set down the cutlass in the water and grab Wilkins' neck. Bacchus push Wilkins under the water so far that only him legs be kicking and splashing. Wilkins kicking and Bacchus still have him under the water. Wilkins make one last kick and hit Bacchus square in the balls and Bacchus yell and fall back in the water. While Bacchus groaning and clutching him belly, Wilkins find the cutlass. The baby crocodiles wake up to the smell of man blood. The whole fight take twenty minutes or so. Only one man come from the swamp. Jack Wilkins take Bacchus' chop-off head and go straight back into the dining room, where he slam it on the table right in the massa plate. The mistress swoon and the massa throw up.

—This is law and order according to the tropics, Jack Wilkins say.

Later that night he shove Bacchus' head on a stick and plant the stick right in front of the slave quarters, where Bacchus stay until he rot off. Knowing who Bacchus' sister be, a house slave who not yet fourteen, he drag her from great house to the stable, where he rape her and leave him seed in her. Eight month later, in a birth that kill the mama, come a girl black like pitch with the prettiest green eyes anybody ever done see. Word was that Wilkins see the girl lifeblood on the ground, making the way from the boiling house to the midwifery, get full up with pity when he hear she dead, and put Lilith to live with Circe and Tantalus the mad nigger, under a sort of arrangement that make Circe all but a free nigger. That was the last good deed Jack Wilkins do for the rest of him life.

From that day in the swamp Jack Wilkins carry two musket. Many slave take the heed, but some stay spirited. One of the little boys that the massa was teaching to ride pull a knife on him and scrape him cheek a little. Jack Wilkins have him gibbeted for attacking a Christian. Two negro slave run away to go live with the Maroon negroes in the mountain, but when Jack Wilkins set the dogs after them, they leave only pieces of meat to eat later.

But even negro woman was showing sass. They talk back and they act poorly and they mimic the mistress. Plenty get whipped, two or three get chop, one get gibbet and one get red-hot iron poker ram up her pussy, which kill her in one day. Wilkins tell the massa that it lookin' like he weak and if he keep up in this fashion the negroes was goin' soon rebel like they do in the east county and kill every white man within three hundred miles. Wilkins say they must teach the negroes a lesson.

That Saturday, the negroes get the learning. In the morning when the womens washing before they go to the field, Wilkins ride up and grab Leto, a girl who not be sixteen yet. Leto scream. One hour or so later he summon all the slave to one of the empty fields.—This is what happen to you when you cross with your master! Jack Wilkins say. In the middle of the field was bundles of stick and bush. In the middle of the bundle was a tree trunk. Tied to the tree trunk was Leto who screaming, pleading and crying. Jack Wilkins wave him hand and a Johnny-jumper come with a burnin' stick. Behind the negroes go the sound of *click*. White slave-driver and black slave-driver all pointing gun so that nobody can even turn away. The only choice was to close the eye and hear the scream, the likes of which nobody hear before or again. The only choice was to hear the scream and pray she catch fire quick and knock out and wait until the grounds full with the smell of burnin' negro.

Montpelier negroes behave after that. The estate get good name for having the most docile negroes and even the Coromantees learn to be obedient. They behave even after the massa die and Jack Wilkins get replace and they behave good now with Massa Humphrey and Robert Quinn. But some fire don't go out, they go quiet under the ash, waiting for one little dry stick to feed. So the white man sleep with one eye open, waiting for the fire next time.

That fire coming.

· 22 ·

LILITH SET DOWN HER BELONGINGS AND WATCH THE MORNING rise on the curtain and colour the room red. Robert Quinn house change plenty since the last time she be there, but that was in the night, so she not really sure. But she remember looking out the window and seeing sky, so the red curtain must be new. The floor clean and there seem to be one or two new chair in the house. The wall wear down from old age so they look grey. Two paintings still on the wall and a map that say Jamaica. Lilith remember the table and she remember him sitting on it, with him eyebrow raise, trying to get to the bottom of what she all about.

—Since I have no wish to dine with the Wilsons, I expect a hearty supper when I get back, he say to her as he leaving. She listen to the horse riding away from the house. Only she and the breeze left inside. Lilith stand still in place and don't move for a long time. The house bigger than she remember. Lilith go down the corridor and find what supposed to be the bedroom, but the curtains draw and the room dark and hot like August night. She nearly stumble two time as she go over to the window. Lilith pull back the curtain and light rush in past her without permission. She can see the estate, the mountains and even the sea to the far west. She turn around and look about the room. The bed so big that there not be room for much else, and clothes all over the floor. She pick up all the boots—more than the massa—and match them, then set them in the closet. She pile all the dirty clothes outside the room and set to spreading the bed with new linen, linen that set aside on the chest of drawers on the other side of the room. The linen smell like the curtain, like perfume and new things. She use a old sheet to dust the room, then spread the bed with the new sheet that deep red like wine. The sunlight agree. The bedpost shine and the chest of drawer change from black to brown.

She leave the room and find another room on the other side that not bigger than the mistress closet. There she set her belongings. In another room down by the corridor be a trunk and old clothes and horseshoes and other things man put in house when no woman be there to say no. There she find bucket. Half day later, the whole house spotless. Lilith set down her blankets on the kitchen floor and go about with the cooking, killing a chicken from the pen and cooking it down in salt, pepper, thyme, ginger and green pawpaw, a trick she learn from Homer.

It dark before Robert Quinn come home. He look around the house couple time and eat the food hearty, but say nothing. Lilith standing by the wall and quiet. Robert Quinn kick out a chair from under the table and point to it for Lilith to sit. Lilith still until he point again. She move to the chair.

—You'll need a plate, he say.

Night come heavy and Lilith washing dish in a half barrel with water. She look outside the window and think she see a star dash through the sky. She look again until she feel a cold hand on her shoulder. The hand move down her arm and grab her wrist. Robert Quinn take Lilith into the bedroom. Lilith stop for a little, but he pull her. Outside pitch black save for the little dots of light coming from the slave huts, that look like a bunch of firefly holding still.

Robert Quinn behind her. He pull the lace in the front of the dress and hold on her titties, hard at first but then softer, rubbing them and squeezing them. Lilith frighten but feel woman shouldn't show fear. Lilith feel the cold air on herself. Woman must come to man like she like it. He pull down the dress first, but then pull it back up. He lift up the dress this time right up to under her arm and Lilith can feel breeze ride up from her leg to her back. She still. She can hear him undressing behind her. He kick away a boot and she jump. Slow-like, he push her on the bed, but grab her by the hips and hoist her arse up. Cold air wet Lilith thighs. This goin' commence, surely. Lilith set still like woman, like her heart not pounding through her chest. Robert Quinn grab her arse and push himself in her pussy and Lilith yelp. Lilith head in the bed and not knowing what she feeling. Quinn feel rough and thick like him shoulders be and Lilith don't know if she supposed to feel it hurting a little. She try to imagine the face that making the man sounds she hearing. He grab her hips tighter. Lilith look out the window to watch the lights, but then she feel what Homer call the everlasting tickle. Lilith moan and wonder where the moaning come from. She feel a little shame and she feel a little pain, that a wicked woman mustn' feel good. But she feel the tickle growing inside her. The two of them making sound like neither could believe it, on and on like stopping would be the wickedest thing. Robert Quinn lean on her back, wetting her dress with him sweat. He wrap him hand round her waist and start to fuck her faster. Him saying things that sound like Irish speak. They moving like a two cog in the mill and Lilith never hear such a sound coming from a white man voice before. Like he weeping or laughing gentle. That be what please her the most, more than even the sexing, and it shame her as it sweet her and she try to hold on to hating Robert Quinn. The sweat rising on her skin make her dress feel cool and loose. She trembling little but not like him, he make more and more noise and he grab her shoulder and start to ram her one, two, three and four times, then he pull out. He moan louder, even though he not in her anymore. Then he still and breathing hot breath into her back. He hold her for a long time. That frighten her more than the fuckin'. She was expecting something different, something with more pain, big pain that punish her for her wickedness. But he didn't give her pain at all, other than little bit that she try to remember but it gone. Then he break away and climb into the bed. Lilith looking at what just go up inside her and it swing thick and bouncy like it be 'bout it own business and don't care 'bout nobody. It look like him. Robert Quinn roll over till him back be to her. Lilith stand there for a long time, trying to hold on to hating Robert Quinn. She go back to her room.

Lilith wake up early and leave Quinn's house, run through the greathouse kitchen and upstairs to Miss Isobel room. She grab the man clothes on the floor and take them away before Miss Isobel wake up. She look at Miss Isobel for a little while and wonder if the miss feel the same way when she lay with the massa secret-like, or if she was to expect more. She think to talk to Homer but something about Robert Quinn make it feel wrong to talk about it, or to take it, make joke. Plus, she did like the feeling, is just that Homer and every other nigger make it feel that fuckin' was like talking to God and hearing an answer. Lilith wake up thinking something would tell her that she be woman now, but that didn't happen. Something already tell her that she was woman now, something that come to her in the sour smell of a white man yellow hair.

Lilith go down to the brook and wash Miss Isobel man clothes. She hang up the blouson and breeches and head to the kitchen, but then she think about what she doing. She live in other house now, with other master. She taking care of new man now. Taking care of new man. How wicked man must be to enter a woman like a thief and rob her womanness away from her. She know she must hold on to hating Robert Quinn. Only worthless nigger make a fuck turn her into fool. But plenty womens get fooled, even Homer one time. Lilith think of her back and she think of him and how the night before he couldn't even look at the scars he cause. And yet plenty man, white and black, do worse to her than Robert Quinn. And when him hand did touch her pussy bush she think 'bout him being her master forever even if that be only while they was rutting. No, fucking. No, rutting like animal, like the animal all white man think black woman be. But he say something when he coming and he hold on to her so weak like she be the master and is all he can do to hold on. He call her lovey. Lovey. Lilith run back to the overseer house. She break some eggs in the pan and fry them up. She take some corned pork out of a barrel and wash the salt off. That she throw in a pot too. In another pot, she brewing comfrey tea, which she learn from Homer that he like. Robert Quinn groan and step into the room. He see Lilith and stun for a minute, like he don't know why she there. Then he look down and see that he naked. He turn quick to go back to the bedroom, but then stop and turn, and raise him chin, but don't look at her. Lilith lookin' at him.—Tea, he say and Lilith hand him a mug full with comfrey tea and drop two thick spoonful of molasses in it.

—How did you kn—

—Homer, Lilith say.

—Aye, Robert Quinn say.

Robert Quinn walk over to the window. Lilith look at the man who was inside her the night before. He shorter than Massa Humphrey but thicker and hairier. Him shoulder wide and broader with him shirt off and black hair rest on him back. Him legs thick with hair also and him arse that he scratching tight like he do plenty hard work. An Irishman don't look like a Englishman, not even Massa Humphrey, who look more strapping than she suppose an Englishman would be.

But he didn't take off her clothes even though he was naked. Lilith think of her back and the big scars left from whipping. She feel sorry for him but hate him same time since he be the cause. He be the one that drag her out to get whip, and who stand there while slave-driver and Johnny-jumper whip her, and who count each lash till it be enough. But that hate always threaten to pass, quicker than she wish. When he turn around and him Irishman dangle up and down like it have other plans, she laugh. Maybe Homer right, she think, maybe a cock just be the second version of a man that he keep in him breeches. Robert Quinn cock be like Robert Quinn. Thick and stocky and maybe mighty, judging from the way barmaid and field niggerwoman both used yell out from behind him room door. But Lilith didn't scream out or bawl out, just moan little, then a lot, and the thought of that make her back itch. She go back to watching it flop and bounce all over the sitting room and chuckle so much that she had to remind herself that she hate him. He throw himself down in the armchair and Lilith watch it flop up and down on him belly like a dog resting on him master. She look up and see him grinning at her. She remind herself that she supposed to hate him. She wish she could see her back in a looking glass. Anything.

Lilith didn't know that is so often man want it. She also didn't know that the time come to pass when she want it too. That surprise her in a way that she couldn't tell Homer. So Homer fish it out of her.

—So how you like woman things? Homer say couple day later when Lilith in the kitchen helping her make lunch.

—Me was woman before whatever you talking 'bout, Lilith say.

—No. You did have darkness but not womanness. You still have that darkness, though, Homer say.

—I don't have no darkness 'bout me, me sick of people thinking me carrying wickedness, Lilith say.

—Well, throw stone in pigpen and who bawl out is who it lick, Homer say.

—You go on with you double talk, Lilith say.

—Twice and thrice, Homer say. So, Robert Quinn fuck you good?

—Homer!

—Lawdy to clawdy, is shyness set 'pon you now?

—I don't have nothing to say 'bout Robert Quinn.

—Raas! So him fuck you sweet, then.

—Me think me like you more before you mouth and you pussy turn friend.

—Me and my pussy was never enemy. Just me and stupid woman who think pussy have power. Take power over the cocky. Then you have power.

—You never had to do that.

—Things change, but man don't. You good to remember that now that you have Robert Quinn right where you want him.

—I don't know what you chatting 'bout now. He is the massa second man. Plus, me hate the man, him same one make them whip me. Hope pox kill all of them.

—Really, now. You full of fire this morning. Still, though, hate and love be closer cousin than like and dislike.

—Mayhaps you read too much damn book.

—Mayhaps is time you learn how to have power over them kinda man. We meeting tonight. Is like two year pass in the two months you gone.

—Unu still meet? That must be one big book.

—Stop play fool, you know full well what we was meeting 'bout when we come every night to fix you back.

—I don't know.

—Me not asking twice.

Lilith walking down the hallway with her bosom push up like she proud, thinking 'bout what Homer say about her having power, but when she see Miss Isobel she sink again. Lilith step into the doorway leading to the conservatory and watch her walk past. Miss Isobel look like she falling apart and pulling together at the same time and Lilith think about her own hand with Miss Isobel family blood on it. Days pass, month pass, yet Lilith couldn't tell if she getting better or worse or what better or worse supposed to look like. Miss Isobel walking to the living room and swinging so hard she stop two time to stand up straight. She almost run into a vase before Massa Humphrey catch her. Massa Humphrey try to take the flask out of her hand, but she hold on to it tight and yell and wouldn't let go. He pull and she curse and try to slap him with the other hand. Massa yank the flask away but it slip from him and fall to the ground. She run after the flask and scoop it up like a dropped baby.

—What in blazes has taken over you? Massa Humphrey say.

—Judgement, Miss Isobel say. Massa Humphrey try to take the bottle again but Miss Isobel slap him and run halfway up the stairs. She trip and land on the step hard. Massa Humphrey go over to pick her up but she push him away. Massa Humphrey hold her hands but she struggling still. She spit on him and he slap her face.

—Goddamn you! he say and get up.

—Goddamned indeed, she say as she pull herself up and stagger the rest of the way. Then she stop. Massa Humphrey look at her.

—I'll need to be taken care of, Humphrey Wilson. I'm without a future. You and God have seen to that, Miss Isobel say.

Night time come heavy, like a woman ready for baby dropping. Lilith watching the moon in Robert Quinn bedroom window. She wait as it sail from east to west. West was when to move. Homer teach her things about being a woman and she teach the Irishman. So after Robert Quinn climb on top of her and fuck her and she say it good so much that she realise that it really good after all, she roll him over like a baby about to get him nappy change. He say what a man say and do what a man do, like he will not stand for perversion and lecherousness and decadence and other sort of big word that Lilith don't care to understand. But she learn what man think he know, when a no mean yes. Man can never tell the difference if they reasoning with they cock, but a woman know. A woman know when a man's no mean not yet or not now or not in that way, or not until me drunk or not until me too tired to pretend me care. So Robert Quinn nooooooo turn into ohhhh as soon as she take him Irishman in her mouth.

—You goin' own him after that, Homer did promise. He goin' hate you for taking the power, but he goin' love you too 'cause giving up power never sweet a man so.

Is like he turn into woman under her. On the bed he moan and moan and spread him legs wider and arch him back. Most time him head so far back that all Lilith see is Adam's apple and chin. Other time he look at her and Lilith can't tell if he bawling or laughing or something else. He grab her hair couple time but let go, him hand grabbing the sheet or clutching him head. She scoop up him balls and tug and he take to moaning most unmanly. Lilith picture herself as a mill, something that must do the same thing over and over, to keep her from stopping, for the way Quinn behaving stunning her out of her wits. So she suck everything into her mouth of him and how he taste. He sound like Massa Roget when a cool wash of warm water run down him back. But Quinn do more than oohing. He ahhing and ohhing and holy feckin' Christing like the devil giving him something he not supposed to get. Lilith feel like there be Robert Quinn, right in her hand middle, and all she need to do is make a fist. But no. A man can breathe and sigh and moan and whimper and take over a woman by making she think she take over him.

Sexing sweet the Irishman so much that he take to cuddling her in the bed like she be white woman. She lie on top of him and let Quinn wrap him arm round her back. But then him skin touch her scars and they both realise what they touching. He flinch and she flinch too. Suddenly they turn back into slave and master and they both know. He look away. Mayhaps if she think of the whipping he give her, she'll forget the wickedness she do to white people. Maybe wickedness match wickedness and clean her head out. She watch him face wither a little as him hand slide off her back and rest on her arse. Lilith look at him mouth that close and wonder if this is how they goin' talk and no word would pass between them in the night, and maybe no word ever need to. She lie down on him chest. Him arms slip off her arse. The moon waiting in the west.

Lilith know where to find the cave this time. The cave is the same but the moon colour inside grey. She waiting for the cave to show magic, but it stubborn and stiff.

—Come in, Lilith, Homer say.

Lilith stand outside. Inside be the womens. Fire-hair Pallas, neck-scarf-wearin' Iphigenia, tall, bony Hippolyta, one-eye Callisto and mad midget Gorgon.

—Is who bring dem fishy cunt in here? Gorgon say, but Lilith look at her and she back way into the dark.

As Lilith step past, inside something shoot by her and she jump. The knife jam into a tree root and bounce.

—Pardon. Think you was something else, say Callisto.

Lilith body still shaking but not her mouth.

—Aim little lower and maybe get the midget next time, Lilith say.

Lilith expect Gorgon to charge like roaring lion. But Gorgon don't even look at her. Callisto look at her good, though. Lilith don't like that, so she look round the cave. Smaller than she remember, but the table in the middle still big like it belong in a better house. Homer move over by the entrance and look out. The other womens settle by the table. Only three chair in the room, so Pallas, Iphigenia and Gorgon take them. Pallas have on her headwrap ever since Miss Isobel say her white woman hair make her ill. Iphigenia cover up from head to toe in her red frock with her scarf round her neck. Lilith wonder what kind of funk that woman work up when sweat run. Hippolyta go over by the other window and almost give Lilith a start. Is then she see that Hippolyta wearing black from head to foot, even a black bonnet. Over by the window, Hippolyta eye disappear in the dark. Lilith feel like rubbing her own eye. But Hippolyta didn't look at her once. If she be the Abarra, then nobody know it, Lilith wonder.

—Every estate swift like a hawk but we, Homer say.

—What she doing here? Pallas ask.

Gorgon hiss.

—Gorgon, give the girl you seat. You don't see she tired? Callisto say. Gorgon look as stun as Lilith and both lip gape open. The other womens say nothing as Lilith take Gorgon seat and Callisto stoop down beside her.

—Sunrise coming, Homer say.

—Pallas, Homer say and point. Pallas raise her two hand and the room go quiet. Callisto shoulder almost touch Lilith knee. Lilith squeeze her legs together but they touch Callisto anyway. She expect Callisto to turn round with her eye like a knife, but she don't do nothing.

—Jackson Lands again. They hear that we adding one again, seven instead of six.

—What the bloodclaat? Nigger presuming to give me order 'bout number? Me have six plus one, all that mean is more ready for blood when the time come. Tell them to take speck out of they own eye first.

—Me not you one, Lilith say, almost like a whisper.

—You one already, backra killer, Callisto say, not wicked-like but meek, almost happy. Lilith don't like it.

Then Pallas start sing. And the womens ululate with they tongue and stomp with they feet. The sound bounce from ground to top, from wall to wall and go out one passage and come through the other. Soon Gorgon and Callisto and Pallas jumping and singing. Lilith know what they singing and don't know at the same time. She seeing some shadow jumping from the candlelight and some jumping a different way. Everybody singing, it seem, but Hippolyta. The voices die down and they sit down, except for Homer, who go over to the fire burnin' in the corner and stir the boiling pot two time.

—Time to get in readiness, Homer say.—Time coming to judge the quick and the dead. Lilith, nothing you hear is to leave this place. If you fixing to tell it, the spirit will deal with you before you open you mouth.

Homer take the pot off the fire and put it on the table. Hippolyta put a bowl on the table that Lilith didn't see before, a black bowl that look like wood with a lid that point up. The lid carve through with pattern that Lilith can't make out. Homer pour some mixture from the pot into the bowl and Lilith watch the steam rise. The room get full with a bitterness that touch her tongue.

—Tefa, Homer say.

—Tefa, the womens say.

—Call the seventeen Odu, call the Osetura, Homer say.

—Call him, call him, the womens say.

—Osetura make one with the Meji Odu, Homer say.

—Omu Odu, witness creation. Raise the Omu Odu, the one and two hundred.

—This is the Ifa bowl, Homer say, looking at Lilith. From this one and two hundred spirit goin' rise.

—Rise for what? Lilith say.

Homer look on her serious.

The womens talk for little more and then leave one by one. Gorgon almost scrape off her back the way she press 'gainst the cave so not to touch Lilith. Then Callisto get up and look at Lilith from head to toe. Then up and down again. Lilith want turn away bad. Callisto lookin' her in the eye, she don't smile but she don't frown neither. The sun outside threatening to come up. Pallas leave, looking at Lilith, and Hippolyta leave, with Lilith looking at her. Tall, skinny, black dress and black bonnet. The room quiet with Homer and Lilith alone.

—What you working at? Lilith say. You six up to some mischief. Even when me was...when Massa Humphrey...anyway, you six doing something.

—Hmm. You niggers who didn't come over 'pon the slave ship don't know a damn thing, Homer say.

—That sound like an answer to you? Lilith say.

—Always too much sass with you. Too, too much sass.

—What you playing at, Homer?

—You still have scar on your back, Lilith?

—What you think?

—Well, since you be a thinking woman, you think you not goin' get whip again? You think them not going beat you till they kill you or somebody else? You think them not goin' rub salt and lime juice on you back? How long you think you goin' go till they hang you for some foolishness?

—Homer? I . . . I don't know.

—Don't be a fool. You damn well know. No black woman safe as long as white man alive. Plenty years me be here and that is the one thing that don't change. This goin' on long before you come this house and still goin' on even when you gone to Coulibre. Set youself down, girl chile, and let me tell you something.

Lilith take her time to go back to Robert Quinn quarters but she still pant like she was running hard and long. She go into Quinn room and look at the man lying in the bed. She look at him head and the long black hair that cover most of him face. She study the overseer body, especially the hands that touch her softer now. She watch him shift and the black hair fall away from him face. Lilith think she see a grin for an instant. Whatever it be, she look at him and think about gentleness, about the strong hands that stop Massa Humphrey from killing her that night. Robert Quinn open him eye and smile. He take her hand and pull Lilith on to the bed. Lilith lying on her side with her back to him and he curl up behind her like a spoon and go back to sleep with him warm breathing down her neck and him hand between her thighs. Lilith listening to him breathe heavy. She feel the up and down of him chest on her back and him knees up under hers like she sitting in him lap. He mumble something but she didn't hear.

Lilith eyes open wide and she hope he fall back asleep soon. Things like these was making Lilith forget that the white man be a monster. That is not what Homer want. Lilith remembering what Homer say right before, and the heaviness lick her so hard she feel she going fall right through the bed.

—You planning something. All me hear is what you want. Me no hear nothing 'bout how you and them niggers goin' do it. Six tell six tell six, me arse. Tell them what? How-de-do?

—Chile, Irish cum juice block you ears? You hear anything people tell you?

—Homer? You mouth so—

—Me mouth being what a real nigger mouth must be. Don't watch it. Watch what goin' on round you. Planning was three years ago. Doin' is what commencing now.

—We call the spirit of one and two hundred. One and two hundred spirit we calling on to help we in the journey.

—To where?

—Journey that be like the wind and the word, two thing that don't come back.

—You talking even more foolishness than usual. Me don't have time for perplexing nigger. Because if you want me in it—

—Every nigger done in it one way or the next. Even you, when you did still fool and a-chase after the massa, you did already in it.

—Me didn't chase no—

—Enough. Learn this, and take it as God-swearing truth. We goin' kill them, girl chile, every single white son of a bitch within hundred mile. We goin' kill them all.

LILITH THINK TO TELL ROBERT QUINN 'BOUT MISS ISOBEL'S night riding. She don't know why. Sometimes she feel to tell him everything. Like some of the things Homer say. But black skin have black secret and you don't tell if you say you black. Robert Quinn gentle sometimes. One time he ask her how was her day and Lilith didn't know what to say so she smile and he smile back. Two day after the womens meet in secret, he call her lassie. The day after that, the food so hot it burn him throat and he shout at her. But that night he didn't fuck her, just pull her down on the bed and sleep with arms round her waist. Lilith didn't sleep the whole night.

She start to doubt her true womanness. She wonder what kind of nigger she be and why her stomach don't go sick every time the Irishman drop him drawers and suck her titties. She wonder what kind of nigger she be that turn fool every time Quinn take up lodging inside her. She no better than old niggerwomens who used to swear for Jack Wilkins. Lilith hate him, she know she do, she just didn't know that hate was goin' be just like what Homer say love be like. That she would have to guard it, lock it up in a pen like wild animal, for every chance hatred get, it flee. More times she have to just tell herself that she hate the man, she hate the man, she hate the man, goddamn.

He touch her back in him sleep. Lilith curse herself. She is the one who get whip but he is the one she feel sorry for. She must be the most crossed and mixed-up nigger ever. But is a diabolical thing when a white man show kindness. Even if he wicked for seven day and good only one. She try to hold on to the Quinn that make her get whip twice a week. But whenever she think of whip she think of blood, and when she think of blood she see white woman blood and white pickney and black woman who face she can't remember. Her hand is as bloody as any white man, that she know. But not a single slave would blame her for what she do. And the Rogets was devil in the flesh who gone back to the hell they come from. She already do what the womens planning. That must be why they so pleased 'bout it, they don't know how the smell of blood can sick you. Blood and burning flesh, so sour and heavy it make her belly heave. She roast a goat head once to make soup and the stink of burning hair make her vomit. Damn them, damn even the babies who was goin' grow up to kill nigger just like her. Damn Miss Isobel, who whip her in the face. Goddamn the whole of them. Lilith feeling good and righted. She tell herself that she feeling good and righted. But if Quinn touch her hair or moan or whisper lovey, everything broken. She would have to work up the hate all over again. Something fly up in her head and say, *Kill him now. You not a woman until you do.*

Morning come, then noon. One week pass since the womens meet and nobody talk to nobody. Lilith run into Callisto again behind Quinn quarters as she carrying five cutlass. Callisto look like she about to talk but say nothing and vanish into the cane. Miss Isobel continue with the riding too. Lilith wondering what she get herself into. She keeping secret for Miss Isobel, the negro womens in league and herself.

She straighten her back and think she can bear it. But then Robert Quinn come home early.

—Supper ready yet, luv? Robert Quinn say as he come through the door. Lilith frighten. It not usual for him to come home before night-fall. Lilith thinking about how she just call him house home like it be her own. She don't hear him the first time.

—Cat got your tongue, bat got your ears, which is it? he say.

—Massa?

—I said, have I come too early?

—No, massa, I mean yes, massa. I...Lilith fidget.

—Well, can you fix something quick? I'll have to head out again. I fear I shall not be coming home tonight, he say.

—All night? Lilith say and look away.

—That's what I said, Robert Quinn say. Lilith fold her arms and rub her shoulders.

—Crop time, t'will devour us all, I tell you. Damn if it won't make a slave of me as well. Well, don't tarry, lass, fix us something.

Lilith have bread that bake from morning, two small loaf. She was cooking pepper pot soup for herself but know how much he like it. She pour some in a bowl and watch the green callaloo and cabbage go to rest on the bottom and the peppers poking up. She set the soup and the bread at the table with a spoon. Quinn take a big gulp and cough hard.

—God feckin' damn! he say and cough again. This is from the devil himself, I swear. Good show, Lilith. Good show.

He call her by her first name and break her.

—Sweet Christ, are ye weeping now?

—No. No, massa.

—Well, maybe yer eyes have different plans from the rest o' ye, but I'd say yer weeping. What is it, this cause for all this melancholy? Is this because I shouted at ye?

—No, massa. Something fly in me eye, massa. Lilith run to her room. She look behind her, thinking he might follow. She turn, waiting. He don't come. Plenty time pass. She think he gone. She get up and go into the kitchen.

—Ye composed enough to tell me now? Robert Quinn say. Not my practise to ask women more than once.

Lilith look at him. Ever since he take her to bed she don't know what to say to him or how to say it. He talk to her sometimes with a voice that white people don't give black people and sometime not to white people either. Things would be easier if she was just a whore or a tool that get use, then put back in a box. But him want to hold her in bed even when they not sexing and he want to talk, and him talk to her in white people voice. She listen to him sometimes and think of milk flowing. Him smile. Negro people not to fuss about what white people thinking. Negro people not to think that they is anything more than a dog or a parrot to white people.

—Lilith?

He call her name again. Lilith want a woman to tell her about man things. What man want and if she must desire him, desire as the Bible say. But her head heavy. She have three burden and have to let go at least one.

—Fine. Keep yer business to yourself, then, he say and rise up. —Have supper ready when I get back. *If* I get back, the way crop time is lookin', he say and leave.

Lilith go to her room and look through her belongings for the piece of looking glass. The one time she go back to Coulibre after the fire, a time she go with Robert Quinn, she find it sticking out from ashes and ready to cut her foot if she did step without looking. Lilith pull out the looking glass in the dim light. She look at herself, at the one thing that make her not black. She not black, she mulatto. Mulatto, mulatto, mulatto. Maybe she be family to both and to hurt white man just as bad as hurting black man. Lilith wonder if green eye is the only thing she seeing that any good. Maybe she should use the piece of looking glass to cut her eyes out so that she can't see herself.

Maybe if she start to think that she not black or white, then she won't have to care about neither man's affairs. Maybe if she don't care what other people think she be and start think about what she think she be, maybe she can rise over backra and nigger business, since neither ever mean her any good. Since the blood that run through her both black and white, maybe she be her own thing. But what thing she be? Even Robert Quinn look at her queer-like sometimes cause he can't look below the eyes. Lilith used to think that green eye put her one step higher than other nigger; she think it put her on a perch so that Massa Humphrey could see her better. But then he have man beat her till she near dead, and since then he is monster to her.

Since then, anything to do with loving make her sick and angry, but then Robert Quinn take her in. They eat together for the most part and she bathe him like a boy on Saturday morning and find nothing sweeter than when he say ahhhhh as she pour warm water over him head. She think of Massa Roget the first time, but when she realise afterwards that all he want from a bath was water she didn't mix him up with that fat sum'bitch again. Lilith would get up from the table when she done eat and Robert Quinn would hold her and pull her back gentle-like because he don't want to eat alone. Lilith trying not to count, not to add up. The same day she meet with the womens he walk up to her in the kitchen with him shirt off and slap him big belly two time and say that she is to be blamed, she and that heavenly cooking of hers. She say, What a way backra get fat so quick, then shut her mouth for giving him backtalk.

—On the contrary, I do nothing faster or slower than need be, he say and smile as he go back to the bedroom.

—Have you ever ridden a horse? he ask when he come back out, and she shake her head. He promise to teach her one night when he is home.

Home.

Lilith need a new way. She tired of thinking that she have to hate

Robert Quinn. Need to hate him. She tired of knowing what she supposed to do but not doing it. Tired of guarding her hate and forcing her hate and thinking that if she just tell hate to come and stay, it goin' come and stay. Mayhaps she hating too big. Hatred still be like love, stronger when what you hate right in front of you. She remember that between Massa and Mistress Roget be a monstrous hatred, but they don't hate one big thing. They despise little things, like how he fart and how she stupid, and them little things add up, spread out like plague. Mayhaps that be the way. Under him arm can smell like a dog. He leave the most unholy stink in the outhouse. He shout at her when the food not right. And when he piss in the commode, everywhere wet up but the commode itself.

—Here's wot methinks. Methinks I's going ta sail right down that cockstream o' yers. Sounds right nice, ennit? Does that sweet ya, pussycat?

Lilith watching herself in the looking glass so long that she didn't hear the man come in or see him standing in the doorway. Is not evening yet but the man look like a shadow. He tall and skinny like scarecrow. Him yellow hair wild and poking out from him hat like hay. Two teeth missing and the others yellow when he smile. He smiling plenty. Him shirt dirty and boot cake up with mud and him breeches brown. The man grabbing himself through the breeches. Lilith know is who.

—Quinn downright built a love den fer us, yes 'e did, pussycat, yes 'e did. The gentlemanly sort that Quinn be, the gentlemanly sort, always looking out fer 'is fellow man, the man say.

—I'd give me last quid to vouch fer 'is character, that I would, he say.

Lilith look around but there be nowhere to go.

—Keep ya noodle down, pretty, keep ya noodle down and nobody needs ta get 'urt. All of us're just doing as the Bible intended, innit? the man say as he step inside more.

—The Good Book says that a man, a strapping man like meself, can't be burning of passion. Say so right there in the Good Book, it does. If man got some passion in 'im 'e gots ta release it, ya know? We gots ta release it now, doesn't we? he say.

—Ah, quit with the crying, dearie, I'll be right sortin' ya out in a minute... or two.

The man shift to the side and pull down him breeches a little. Light peek out from behind him and Lilith try to run and push herself past him, but he catch her.

—Now, where do ya think yer goin'? Eh? Where do you think yer goin'?

Lilith try to push him off but he grab her by her two arm, push her back in and slap her across her face. Lilith claw him face, but he smile and all she can see is the blackness beyond him yellow teeth.

—Jaysus Christ, behave yerself now, pussycat! he say.

Then he pounce on her like cat 'pon rat. She scream but he slap her again.—Enough of that, he say. He pinning her down on her sheets with one hand and pulling down him breeches with the other. Then he hike up Lilith dress and push him way between her legs. Lilith close up but then he start to slap her, saying, Open up, nigger bitch. Lilith bawling and fighting but the man strong and him hard. Then she hear music. Music starting and stopping and starting again. Music coming from inside as she feel stone underneath her outside. She smell a sourness, a sourness from white man hair and a sourness from the music. The music was inside. Outside. Outside was the yellow hair, straight and sour. Sour and yellow, like the man who was on top of her before she black out. Sour and yellow, like the man of top of her now. Lilith scream and scream and scream. He slap her on the cheek. Lilith feel him miss her pussy at first, then feel him taking him hand to guide it in so that he don't miss.

—We're pickin' up right where we left off on New Year's, darlin', innit? the man say.

Then the man scream but the scream drown out with a thunder-crack. He scream loud like a girl and he screaming louder and louder.

—Goddamn! Goddamn! Ya damn fuckin' killed me, oh my God, oh my God!

He jump off Lilith and grab the back of him arse that full with buckshot.

—McClusky, I barely scratched ye. *Now* I'm going to kill you, Quinn say and hold up him musket.

—Oh my God! Oh my God!

—God can't help the likes of ye right now. Is this the full day's work Master Humphrey get for a full day's pay? And how come I can't remember inviting you to my house?

—Blazes! Me apologies, sir, me apologies. Oh lordy, the pain, sir! Lordy, the pain!

—There's more where that came from, ye son of a bitch!

—Pardon me, sir, pardon me. Me thinkin' there was a free meal to be 'ad 'ere, sir, that's all.

—Really, McClusky? Who in all fuck gave ye so wrong a news as that?

—Aye, sir, I means you no offence, sir, that be all to it, yeah?

—Maybe you didn't, but yer dingus here had other plans. Maybe I should shoot the little fucker off?

—Oh, lordy no, sir, please sir, 'tis the only dingus I 'ave, sir, kind sir.

—Aye. But since you're so burning with passion to dock yer dingus, I tell ye what. How about I shoot ye a new arsehole so that you can fuck yerself. How does that suit ye?

The man look like he goin' cry. Lilith pull down her dress and run out of the room.—Get up, Robert Quinn say. Lilith in the kitchen, the man run past her, limping as blood drip on the floor. The man turn east outside and vanish.

—Goddamn worthless East End scum! The goddamned nerve to set into me own house. I'll have him in irons, by all that's holy, Quinn say.—Perhaps I should get a dog. What do you think, Lilith?

Lilith on the floor with the water bucket and a brush. She scrubbing the blood off the floor, moving from one spot to the next. She don't look up. Robert Quinn move over to her and stoop down.

—I was talking to ye, luv. I said, What do you think of a dog? Quinn say. Lilith still scrubbing the floor.—Enough, Quinn say and touch her shoulder. Lilith scream and pull back. She push away from him like crab running sideways.

—Jesus, lassie, I'm not out to harm ye, he say. Lilith push herself over to a corner in the kitchen. She trembling like she just come back from white people weather. Quinn walk slow over to her and she push herself deeper into the corner until she can't push no more. Quinn right in front of her. Him face next to her face. She turn away from him, her eye shut tight and her face set as if he about to punch her.

—Oh my stars, lass, you have nothing to fear from me, he say.

He touch her cheek and she yell again and scramble to her foot and run into her room.

Darkness fall and Quinn still in the house. He supposed to go back out 'cause it be crop time, but Lilith didn't stop bawling until he promise to stay. Quinn on the right side of the bed, reading a book from Massa Humphrey. The lantern beside him throw light on him nose and cheek when he smile. Lilith didn't know that he wear spectacles. She look at him for a while, look at how he just get older before her. She wonder if he do deep thinking. Quinn look up and see her.

—Are ye talking to me now, lassie? Quinn whisper as he put down the book and look at her.

—That son of a bitch McClusky has been dismissed. You have nothing to fear from the likes of him again. But I'll wager you were troubled before that bastard set foot in here. Please don't look at me like that, darlin'.

—Massa?

—Like, like that. Ye looked at me like yer seein' him. McClusky. Jesus, lassie, I'd never harm ye. It wasn't in my power before but it is now, so help me. Were it up to me nobody would have ever laid a hand on ye, not once, not even when that Coulibre bitch demanded that they whip you every week. You probably think I've forgotten but I have not, luv. So what is it? What is it that yer not willing to tell me?

Lilith push herself to talk.—Nothing, massa. Nothing.

—Come here.

Lilith start to pull off her dress.

—Good heavens, Lilith, I'm a man with a dingus, not the other way around. Come in the bed with me. Have ye ever laid eyes on a book, luv?

—Yes, massa.

—Aye? And have ye opened one as well? Do ye know how to read?

Lilith look 'pon the book hard and long but she know what it say, *The Faerie Queene.*

—Nigger don't know them things, massa, she say.

Some time pass with Massa Quinn teaching Lilith word. She act like she don't know anything. One time he read a line that go *A floud of poyson horrible and blacke,* and she frown 'cause she know is not so poison spell, nor flood, nor black.

—That no right, she say, but go quiet when Robert Quinn look at her queer-like.

—'Tis not right? What's not right?

—Ahhhh, er, that the, that the woman so nasty. All that nastiness coming from her mouth.

—Aye! Indeed, nasty indeed. She's quite the harridan, she is.

Lilith still perplex, for them words don't sound like nobody she ever hear. Them way too speakey-spokey. And spell wrong. Even a dim nigger would know that son don't spell like sonne. Quinn don't even need the book, he just talk the book and tell her that everything that mankind ever needed to say Spenser say in *The Faerie Queene.* He nod off and she think he think she don't understand. She about to say that she know what he mean without telling him that she know a Faerie

Queene that still be sleeping until a man wake her, but he answer with a snore.

Lilith slip outside. She run to the broke-down wagon and hide. She think she hear a gallop but nothing come of it. Mayhaps Miss Isobel sleeping tonight. Most night she go but some night she don't and Lilith can't find no reason behind it. She wait. No moon in the sky.

A hard hand grab the back of her neck. Lilith jump. Robert Quinn.

Even in the dark she can see he furious.—I knew you were haunted by something, he say.—And if it's freedom yer looking fer, I have half a mind to send you to heaven, how's that fer true freedom? Lilith mouth wide open but no sound coming out. She know he looking at her. Then a sound catch her and him too. Quinn notice that it catch her first.

—Who's there? he say to her.—Your lover? Is it some goddamned nigger? Running away, are ye now? Or perhaps you seek to make a cuckold out of me? I should have left ye for McClusky, that's what I should've done!

Lilith feel him squeezing her neck. This not be the man who call her lovey and was talking to her from *The Faerie Queene*. The galloping getting louder.

—Feckin'...you await a man on horseback? No slave knows how to ride. What in blazes is...

Lilith stoop, grabbing him hand still round her neck, and pull him down. He cuss and try to pull her up, but the galloping getting louder so he stoop down. Him hand still on her neck. From the stables the hoofbeat coming. Quinn let go of Lilith and peek out from the wagon. Miss Isobel ride past them, her yellow hair flying and her horse kicking up dust. Robert Quinn look at Lilith, him jaw dropped low like stunned goat. He look at her till she look away and she wish he would say something and wish he don't, for whatever coming out of him mouth won't be pleasing. He leave, running to the stable. Lilith can't move. She still behind the wagon when he ride past.

Lilith stay awake all night till it be morning and the rooster start crow. Lilith thinking about how her head not as heavy as before, but she still carrying things like a chain round her neck. She glad he know. Lilith tell herself that she didn't owe no white woman nothing anyway. Miss Isobel ride past her window. Not long after that, Robert Quinn come home from the other way, so that he can see the morning shift of slave take over from the night shift. When he come through the door, Lilith yawning.

—Awake all night, luv?

—Yes, Massa Robert.

—Might as well make me some breakfast, then, and it better be a good, hearty one, fer I'm still very cross with ye, Lilith.

—Yes, massa.

Lilith set about getting the pot and pans ready.

—And Lilith?

—Yes, massa?

—About Miss Isobel, have you spoken of this to anyone?

—No, massa.

—Good. Let it remain so. Do you understand?

—Yes, massa.

Robert Quinn sit down by the table and take off him boots. She listen to the boots banging on the floor and him fingers tapping the tabletop. She don't look. He whistle and she look around to see him nodding him head over and over.

—Goddamn. God feckin' damn.

· 24 ·

ROBERT QUINN NOT GIVING UP NO ANSWER. NO WAY IN BLAZES after Lilith try to keep Miss Isobel night affairs away from him. He ask her how long she know 'bout Miss Isobel. She couldn't remember if it was a fortnight or a month but it before October. A quietness come between them, and Lilith think that the silence would make her happy, but it don't. Even when she wash him hair and rub him scalp with her fingers, he moan and breathe deep but don't say nothing. Even when they sexing, he grunt and groan but don't say nothing. Not even lovey. Sometimes when he come home early and she still cooking, Lilith would look up and see him looking at her. At night time she in bed with him and can feel him looking when her back turn. Looking, mayhaps waiting for her to do something again. But he never strike her and more than anything else, Lilith was looking to be struck.

Lilith don't know. She thought that this was what she want. It easier to hate him now. It easier to smell him field smell and think it stinking up the sheets and the curtains and the room and the wall and everything. It easier to think like Homer or Gorgon or Pallas. She don't have a single care 'bout him goddamn Irish flesh and don't have to think anymore when he lie on top of her, but still she wish he would remember that he say he was goin' teach her to ride. She wish he would talk like the Faerie Queen or teach her a word she already done know. Lilith never know that the day would come when she would rather hear lovey than her own name, a day where she be the perplexing nigger. She clean him shoes and hand he him clothes and watch him leave. She wish he would even pat her on the head like a dog and know she be the most worthless nigger for thinking such.

Gorgon ride her carriage past the Robert Quinn house and shout to Lilith in the kitchen, telling her that Homer say they's to meet tonight to go over the next banquet menu.

—They's no banquet coming, Lilith say.

—Banquet coming, Gorgon say and ride off. She don't look at Lilith once.

Last week in October a trunk come for Miss Isobel from Kingston. She run down the stairs herself and grab the chest and cry like is a coffin. —Up to my room at once, she say. It take two strapping negro to carry the chest all the way up the staircase to Massa Humphrey room, that be her room now. Lilith just come in the kitchen, fixing to talk to Homer.

—Lilith, to my room this instant, Miss Isobel shout.

Lilith go to the room to see the chest fling open and all sort of dress tumbling out. Miss Isobel wearing a riding outfit, a dark red dress. She say she finally feel like a woman. Lilith thinking that at least she going stop wear the massa clothes now and she won't have to come in the morning to wash nothing.

—Oh, Lilith, have you any idea how happy I am! How rootless a woman feels when she has nothing of her own!

Miss Isobel still looking at herself in the mirror.

—Lilith, you've been such a dear, you must help me unpack, Miss Isobel say.

A little later, near to the hour, Lilith come back in the kitchen with a bundle under her arm.

—Nigger Christmas come again, what a thing, Homer say.

Lilith don't have nothing to say to Homer.

—I goin' to fix Massa Rob—Massa Quinn lunch, she say.

—Yeah, why you don't go take you bundle and go fix Massa Robert, Massa Quinn lunch.

—What me do you now?

—Me? After you can't do me anything. Is what you doing to yourself, you need to ask.

Other womens in the kitchen and Lilith don't want to talk nothing 'bout her business in front of them, 'specially with one or two still lookin' at her uncanny.

—I gone, Lilith say.

—Little later, me chile, Homer say.

Night come. Is still crop time, so Robert Quinn may or may not come home. Lilith want to see him something bad. Out in the dark, six women goin' be waiting. Lilith ask if things not risky to be meeting during crop time and Homer say, Risky for who? And go back to her business. Lilith imagine them right under Robert Quinn room window, plotting.

Robert Quinn come home cursing something in Irish tongue. She run to him and jump him, wrapping her arms round him neck and her legs round him waist. Lilith push her hand down him breeches. Quinn carry Lilith to the bedroom. But Quinn tired. He near scold her to leave him alone. Lilith was hoping he be him usual Irish self and sex her most of the night. She try to talk to him, but he wasn't in no mood for talking. Not to her. He still carrying ill will 'gainst her, not massa-slave ill will, she see that now, but man-woman ill will.

—Tell me 'bout the Ireland, she say, looking at him back and watching the window.

—Go to sleep, he say. He silent for a while, but then he turn round and face her.

—I thought you and I had an understanding. In this house, in this place, I had it that ye understood me.

—Massa.

—You've got no cause to see me as yer enemy, Lilith.

—Massa, me don't know, is what she say. But not what she think.

—But you do know. That's the whole point, isn't it, luv? How could you have kept this from me? I think about it all the time, how you kept it hidden, and now I'm no use in the field, no use here, all because the negro who has become my favourite keeps secrets. But I should have known.

—No, massa.

—What else are ye keeping from me?

—Me not hiding nothing, massa.

—I remember ye comings and goings all times of the night. Think I've forgotten, have ye?

—Miss Isobel must be doing something wicked, wicked.

—That'll be my business, the goings of Miss Isobel, thank ye, not yours.

—Yes, massa, Lilith say and get up to leave.

—Where're ye going?

—Me know you don't want to see me face, massa. Only way to please you is to leave you be.

—Why in feckin' blazes would I prefer a cold bed to a warm one?

Lilith go back in the bed but she don't touch him.

—I'm not different from you, ye know, Quinn say. Lilith don't know what he talking 'bout and think she didn't hear him correct.

—In these colonies Irishmen are held in even lesser esteem than negroes.

—What? Foolishness that!

Quinn look at her.—Ye'd do well to think twice before you call your master foolish, even if he is an Irishman.

—Sorry, massa.

—Oh, not me, I couldn't care less what ye call me. You don't understand, lassie. At least a slave has some value to the master. An Irishman has none. They hate the lot of us, you know. They say, Aye, what's an Irishman? A nigger turned inside out. It burns me that ye should keep things from me. It burns me so.

—Me sorry, massa.

—And for God's sakes, stop calling me massa. I'm no massa to them, just a potato eater. Every soul thinks less of the Irishman, even that Creole bitch, who you'd reckon has no cause for malice against anyone.

—Miss Isobel?

—That would be her. Would ye like to know where following her led to? I'll bet in blazes that ye do.

Lilith keep talking until him answer get shorter and shorter and a good time pass before she see that he asleep. She remember what Quinn say 'bout Irishman lot being the same as nigger and hiss it off. He never did mention nothing 'bout where Miss Isobel riding to.

Ever since Quinn teach her how to read the timepiece, she find a new way to tell how late the time be. Quarter past two. Close to the hour, the womens will be gathering. Lilith curl up behind Robert Quinn, fitting herself around him shape and letting him body hair warm her. When she wake up again, the clock just strike six in the morning. Lilith don't know what to look forward to in the day. But Robert Quinn sleeping in the bed, and man can look like baby when he fall asleep, or a puppy, or just something that no evil could come from, and he roll and turn and grunt and there be something 'bout the morning, and him, and the smell of clean hands with no blood on them that just seem right.

Quinn leave early, saying that he still concerned about the crop time yield. Lilith in the house waiting. Quinn did leave the watch with her and on occasion she look at the hands move and listen for the click. A click come but not from the watch. Then she smell mint and lemongrass.

Homer.

She behind Lilith in the kitchen, not saying anything. Lilith wonder where behind her Homer be, if she over by the passage that lead to Quinn bedroom or if she right behind her, breathing near the back of her neck. A quick wind dash past her right ear and she jump. The knife jam right into the cupboard and bounce. Lilith gasp. She turn around to see Callisto holding another knife by the blade, ready to throw. Lilith straighten herself even though she so frighten she almost piss.

—And where you bulldog be? Lilith say.

Callisto smile.—Dagger go deeper than dog bite, she say.

—The two of you have eye, so you see that me busy cookin'.

—For who? The man o' yard gone go whip nigger already, Callisto say.—Maybe you forget that that is what him do, eh? Maybe you think that the whip on him belt there to hold him breeches up. Maybe—

—Callisto.

—Don't Callisto me, Homer. Me did think...me was hopin'.

—What me name, Jesus?

—Me did hope Coulibre did done change you. Make you a real woman finally.

—Callisto, Homer say.

—No more with no damn code, woman! She come back here all quiet-like, like we don't done know her business. Like we couldn't smell it 'pon you.

—Me don't know what you talkin' 'bout. Massa Robert don't—

—Fuckin' hell, you know what Massa Robert do? You deh with him all day? You see him last week when him whip poor Mother Hera who too old fi work?

—Lying bitch—

—Wash them scar off you back yet? Callisto say.—Every day he put a new one on another nigger back. The day me see you come back, me say finally this nigger know what is what. All of a sudden you did have what Gorgon can't get even though she try and try. Then one pigskin fuck you and—

—Homer, tell her to get out of me—

—Is true she talking, Homer say.

—Lie that.

—Girl chile, don't turn into no fool. You do that before.

—Pallas say, every time backra smile with you, you pleased like puss, Callisto say.

—Me want the two of you to get out. Now.

—Or what? Cho! Right now I feel to cut up you up in here so—

Callisto dash after Lilith like a mad animal. But Lilith stand up to her. Callisto right after all, once you kill five people or more, not even the devil frighten you. Callisto swing but Lilith catch her hand and twist it round Callisto back. Callisto hiss, then laugh.

—If me did know that is so she was, me'd befriend her long ago, Callisto say.

—Enough! Homer say. Lilith let go, Callisto still smiling.

Lilith run for the wall on the other side of the kitchen. Homer go over to Lilith and touch her forehead. Lilith spit in her face.

—Dead dog cunt, Lilith say.

Callisto laugh again. Homer raise her hand to halt Callisto just as she grip the knife to hurl straight into Lilith back. Homer wipe off the spit. Then she slap Lilith on the left of her face. Then the right. Homer grab Lilith by the shoulder and push her hard.

—You! You is the devil own woman! Lilith say. You is the devil! Wait till Massa Quinn come home. You just…when he see this, he goin' know…and—

—Look 'pon me and look 'pon me good, fool nigger. Me look like me 'fraid of Robert Quinn? You worrying 'bout him seeing bruise, how 'bout me make it that he see corpse? You forgetting who be the head nigger in this bloodcloth place. That be me. Me! Now you listen to me, chile. If you want to fool yourself again so that man beat you down, that be your business, but next time me call you to a meeting, you drag you dry backside there or is me you goin' deal with.

—Me . . . me not 'fraid of you.

—Then you is a friggin' fool. You want me to give you something to 'fraid of? You think 'cause you make woman bleed to death, you is bad? You think me kill Circe sake o' you?

—What you talkin' 'bout? Everybody done know the bitch try to kill me!

—You, you, you. Circe couldn't kill flea! That be her damn problem from the first day. All mouth and no act. Circe never try to kill you, she couldn't even stay in her hut, sake of the Johnny-jumper blood you shed in it. You, on the other hand, was a different story. Me know that from the day me walk in there and see you with the cutlass.

Lilith stun.

—From the day me see what you do that boy, me look 'pon Circe and know that me rope in the wrong nigger. Beside, the bitch was goin' be a turncoat nigger—you hear her youself. No, better she did gone and gone quick.

—Circe never try to kill me?

—Circe was goin' frig up the struggle with her mouth. You know how long we waitin'? How long we plottin'? We planning this since 1796, five year after Saint-Domingue free itself. Before even that!

—Circe never try to kill me?

—Wise up, woman! Circe was goin' tell the massa 'bout you and the whole o' we. Me take one look 'pon you blood-up face and know which woman me did want.

—And you make it look . . .

—All the better for the struggle.

Callisto mouth stiff but her eye wide open.

—You is a wicked bitch! Lilith say. A wicked, wicked bitch. She was me mama! She never set no Sasabonsam 'pon me. Is was you. Is was always you!

—You need to know which side you on—

—You not on nobody side! Your side goin' to hell. You worse than she ever be, you dutty stinkin' bitch! Me hate you.

—Look 'pon me good. No hate you can bring that me can't handle. You think you bad? You know who the pussycloth you taking step with?

—You don't know 'bout—

—Trust me, fool, there be nothing about you that I don't know. You know why I make them hang that other girl, Francine, when me know full well that is you set the fire? Homer say.

—Is...is not me—

—Quit the damn foolishness, idiot! The girl was running errand for the mistress. The mistress tell me that herself, how she wish she had one slave as sensible as Homer 'cause that idiot Francine don't know herb from weed. She tell me that some morning she send Francine out but all she can do is pick fruit and don't know nothing 'bout bush. Poor girl, think she be somebody 'cause she ride carriage like Gorgon. The mistress send her to me so that me can teach her what to pick and how to brew it. Time o' the fire, she just left Montpelier with some herb tea for the mistress' nerves, so me know is not she do no burning. Me give her the tea meself! You think is arsehole me push out of when me born? Look yah, girl, you better start acting right or you goin' drop down dead before me even touch you.

—You could have tell on me. Why make them kill that girl if...if is me do it?

—Because that was the best she could do for the struggle. She not cut out for nothing else. But you, you different. Me always know, but me sure now, after you kill four white people just like that.

—Me never mean to—Jesus Christ, you think me did mean to?

—All the better. Don't come talk to me 'bout Circe when inside you blacker than pitch. You can't even control it. That be why we goin' use it. You hear 'bout Saint-Domingue, Lilith? That be the all-negro republic. Nigger want freedom and they take it. Nigger want land and they take it. Nigger want blood and they take that too.

—Nowhere no name so.

—Me learn you to read so read, you fool. Saint-Domingue nigger no better, no worse than we. No, no. They better, they grab the whip and whip the backra. All my life white man boot in my back. Well, time it done, don't make—

—You don't know what you talking—

—I say, no more white man boot goin' be in my back again, you hear me? Me ever tell you 'bout me pickneys? You want to know what happen to them?

—No.

—The boy, he get send to Bermuda, then Turks and Caicos to dig for salt. The boy never strong, so they kill him. Work him to death. Want to hear what nigger from Clarendon say 'bout me daughter? Didn't even reach sixteen birthday before she make me a grandmother. Then she make the pickney a goddamn orphan two weeks later. Who reckon a girl could live after two hundred fifty lash, eh? A whole week she live, my girl. A whole w . . . But not even she strong enough to withstand whipping one week after a baby. Nigger say she didn't even have blood left to bleed.

—Homer.

—How far, Lilith? How far backra must ram up you pussyhole before you see that he fuckin' you?

—Tell her, Homer. Tell her.

—Shut up, Callisto. Who goin' get kill next, eh? Who goin' dead? Me? You? Enough, you hear me, eeeeenough. Nigger from Saint-Domingue better than we, them woman have sense and them man have balls. Them don't take nothing from no devil no more. Our time now.

—How you can do anything? This is nigger life. What you one can do?

—Chile, is not me one. Not me one at all. Anyway, me done talk. Don't think you not in this, woman, because I know 'bout you. And if you don't want me to start talking 'bout that fire again, you better get your nigger backside to the cave next time me call meeting.

—What you need me for? You say things planning nigh five year now.

—Because you still don't seem to know what in you. But me know. Callisto know, even Gorgon know—that be why she 'fraid of you these days. Don't act like you don't see.

Homer turn to leave, but then turn back to Lilith.

—Robert Quinn still out there beating and killing niggers. He go to Spanish Town to buy two fresh nigger only yesterday. You remember that, she say.

Them leave her. Lilith set about preparing the lunch. Massa Robert goin' come back for a lunch and a smile, she tell herself. She goin' get some beef and some potato and make a soup that the Irishman like. The pot set to boil and Homer voice come back to the kitchen. *Robert Quinn out there beating and killing niggers*, she say. Lilith try to blow the word out of her head. Lilith grab potato from the sack and cuss when her hand get stuck. The more she pull, the more her hand stuck until she scream, Goddamn raas cloth! And pull so hard that the sack tear and potato fall out and run across the floor. One roll to a dark corner of the room. Roll right up to where the woman foot be.

Lilith still at first. Is the first time she seeing the tall dark woman in the day and she know for sure now that is not Hippolyta. Lilith frighten a little, but angry more.

—Who you want me to kill now? Who you want me to kill now, bitch? Maybe me should kill meself? You find that agreeable? Eh? *Eh?* Lilith grab a plate off the kitchen counter and throw at the dark woman in the corner. She disappear before the glass fly into the wall and shatter up into pieces. Lilith try to cry but fear and rage well up in her and she shudder so bad that she near have a fit.

Lilith brushing the shatter plate into a piece of paper. She sit down on the floor and feel the heaviness come down on her. Mayhaps more spirit was goin' visit her before the day done. Mayhaps a burnin' pickney and a burnin' young'un and a burnin' Matraca, and the three burn down into one that wait for the john crow to take it.

She can now tell what sorta mood Robert Quinn in just by the hop and drag of him foot when he come home. Maybe she shouldn't be so happy to see him and maybe she should punch her chest where her heart be so that it stop jump every time he step through the parlor. He pull off him shirt and rub him porcelain belly. Maybe he be white man first and Robert Quinn second. What can a white man be in the colonies but the enemy of all negro flesh? From they takes us from the Africa; who they don't kill by the work, they kill by the whip. How can a white man smile mean any good? What it mean when he turn you over in bed so that him face meet your face? That he want to see your pleasure and your loving and your tears or that he can't stand to see the scars on you back that he cause? What it mean when he hold you gentle-like and whisper word that not be word and can't eat unless you eat too and promise to teach you to ride? What it mean when lass turn into luv, then lovey, then Lilith?

Robert Quinn step into the kitchen and the whole house hear the crunch.—What the . . . , he say and pick up piece of the plate, piece that have pattern on it.

—What's the meaning of this? he say. Lilith jump up from the floor real quick. She rub her hands and start to step back the more he step forward.

—Lilith, what's this?

—Me never mean to do it on purpose, sah, me never mean to do it on purpose. Lilith still stepping back, Robert Quinn still stepping forward.

—Don't…Out with it at once. At once!

—Lawd o' massy, sah. I broke a plate, sah.

—You did what? Lilith jump. Robert Quinn back her into a wall. You…fuckin'…have ye got butter sticks fer fingers!

—No, massa, me sorry, massa. Don't kill me now, massa! Don't kill me and go buy new me in Spanish Town!

Robert Quinn stop. A new Quinn come over him face, one she never see before. He look away from her.

—The brown or the blue one? The brown or the blue, damn you!

—The brown one, Lilith say.

Quinn sigh.—Oh, good, good, he say. He rest him hands on her shoulder.—Didn't mean to give you such a fright, lassie. But, those Wedgwood plates are the last of my mother's in me possession. Would break my heart if I were to lose one. Robert Quinn kiss her on the forehead.

—Fix us some supper, lovey, he say.

Word was that Miss Isobel was grumbling about how Lilith take up with Robert Quinn. She'd been grumbling about it for a good while now. She don't like it one bit. That be exactly what she say when she summon Lilith to her room two day later.

—I don't like it one bit, Lilith, she say.—I suppose you're his chère amie now?

—Ma'am?

—Stop play fool to catch wise. You forget that I grow up here too. Me know what kinda tomfoolery you niggers up to.

Lilith hear Miss Isobel chat like nigger all the time, but never on purpose.—There's nothing under the sun that you tar babies can fool me with. Can't catch Harry catch him shirt, eh?

Lilith look at Miss Isobel, perplex.

—Or should I say massa?

—Mistress?

—Oh, please, Lilith. Perhaps it's better that the times are such as they are, I daresay we almost sisters in our purpose. But you're Quinn's woman now. See what happens when a nigger remembers her place? See how virtue is rewarded? Mind you, virtue is a land I have no wish to visit. Tell me, since 'tis only through trick of fate that we're not sisters, does he fill you?

—Sorry, mistress, me don't understand—

—Oh, come now, Lilith. You niggerwomen are so lucky, having as you do *le petit mort* without having to marry first.

Lilith still perplex.

—Oh, for heaven's sake, imbecile, does the Irishman please you with his loving? Does he have a real brute between his legs? Do your toes curl? Do you take him in the mouth?

—Mistress!

—Please save me the outrage, Lilith. You and I are colonial creatures, different though you certainly are. For your information, I do not fool myself as other women do. As for you and I, we're cut from a more blunt cloth. At least I am so. Now I insist that you tell me. I shall not go into marriage with Mr. Wilson without fair warning of the male sex.

This perplex Lilith more. Homer never lie and Homer say Miss Isobel and Massa Humphrey be fuckin' up to the day before Coulibre burn down. Maybe this be another white woman game. Say one thing but mean another. Black woman game too.

—Is he enough for you, I said. I mean, you niggers with your bottomless cunts. He must be rather, ahem, mighty for you not to swallow him up.

—Nigger cho-cho not bigger than white woman cho-cho, mistress, I don't reckon.

—Who was speaking of size? But you darkies have your ways of bewitching our men. I have already accepted that when I marry, I will have to share whatever hangs below his belt. How can a lady compete with your bestial ways?

—I don't know what that—

—Trouble not yourself, Lilith. I daresay, though, I'm glad I'm a Creole girl. A little of your black magic has rubbed off on me as well. Me Obeah him, you know.

Lilith never know one set of word could stun her twice. For one instant she think a third woman was in the room, another woman talking to her that sound black. But it was Miss Isobel opening her white lips so that a black voice come out. Then there be what she saying, thing that nigger even in them deepest blackness don't talk 'bout in daylight.

—Me say me Obeah him, Miss Isobel say again.

—Miss Isobel, you not to be messing with them things.

—And why not? Seems to work fine for you niggers. Works fine and dandy. I told you, Lilith, that's why you can fool people like the massa but you can't fool me. I know all about your ways.

—So you go to Obeah woman, Miss Isobel?

—I am already wise to their ways. I should have collected it in a jar when we women have our times of the month, and mixed it in his soup. Not that I would ever do such a thing. Not that it would work. Somebody—

—Who, ma'am?

—I fail to see how that's your business. Someone suggested I sweat him. Can you believe it? Of course, I knew all about it and only pretended shock, but certainly I was not about to wear food in my . . . my regions and then have it cooked. So much for Obeah. Black magic indeed. Anyway, Lilith, I must insist that you come and attend to me at once.

—Yes'm, Lilith say.

—I will arrange it today.

—Yes'm, Lilith say.

Not even two evening pass before Robert Quinn see red. That happen the very next morning. Lilith didn't hear or see, but Homer did. Homer laughing when Lilith come into the kitchen. Lilith was still plenty afraid of Homer but wasn't about to act that way. She walk up right beside her.

—Who did know that white man would lock horn over black cho-cho?

—What you chattin' 'bout now?

—No you, Miss Precious. The two man lock horn like man bull a-threaten boy bull. Massa Humphrey and Massa Quinn, Lilith. Seem Massa Humphrey did want to move you back in the house to wait 'pon Miss Isobel. Humph! Robert Quinn did get very Irish is all me goin' say.

—How you mean?

—Me don't chat 'bout people affair, but me will say this. Any time a white man start fight for a nigger girl, it mean he liking her too much and that bad for both him, but worse for you.

—Robert Quinn only glad that him belly full and him bed warm.

—Mayhaps is so, but me never see a man so hopping mad as Robert Quinn. He storm right into where Massa Humphrey sleeping. *Tell that Creole bitch to stay out of me damn house*, he say, right there to Massa Humphrey face. Massa so frighten he didn't even defend Miss Isobel honour. He just say, *Of course, Robby, of course*. That was that. Robert Quinn storm out just like he storm in.

—That be him own business, Lilith say.

—Yours too, Homer say.

—Me no care what white people want to fight for, Lilith say.

—Really, now? Well, make sure you heart take kinder to what negro people want to fight for, Homer say. Lilith say nothing. She don't want to be near Homer.

Lilith don't say nothing to Robert Quinn and Robert Quinn don't say nothing to Lilith. Evening come and pass with him still in the field. Night come and pass with nothing but her ghost as company. Lilith wondering why the thin black woman keep coming to her. Maybe she not asking to kill but warning that a killing bound to happen. Maybe the woman be on her side and guarding her like the home spirit that come from the Africa or what the church call angel. Same thing, she think, one just get burn by more sun. Maybe the woman was angel warning her to not sin with wickedness. Or maybe a devil.

Or maybe the woman be the spirit of the head god and the fire of revenge, and maybe is she and not Lilith doing the killing and she, not Lilith, who deserve the blame. Lilith wondering if her burden would be better if some god was in it. Even Homer believe in something, though Lilith don't know what that be. The only thing she can remember believing was the page from the picture book and the sleeping girl, who different from her in every way but eye.

But now Lilith perplex again. If the girl was sleeping, how she to know the colour eye? The picture coming back in her head but not clear. Is long time that Lilith have to think about what the page really be, what at the edge of paper, what word did on the page that she could read now, but not back then. She think 'bout the white man who dress in a black jacket and who, now that she think, don't look nothing like Massa Humphrey. She wonder why she used to think so, that maybe there be something in man that make them alike other man, and that thing not be how them look. Maybe is how them stand, maybe is how them walk, or what them say. Robert Quinn still out there beating and killing niggers, Homer did say.

Two day later, right before dawn, three man on horseback ride wicked into Montpelier. A rap come from the door like somebody set to knock it down and Quinn jump, grabbing him musket under the bed. Lilith frighten but Quinn ask who is it and go to the door. Then he come back in and pull on him breeches, grab him boots and leave. Before sunrise Lilith dash out to the great house to hear Homer telling

Pallas that Massa Humphrey ride gone with the mens too. Ride gone to Kingston. In the wee hours somebody set fire to Kingston Harbour. Half of the walk burn down and crash into the sea. No ship can dock or set out to sea from Kingston. They have reason to believe that it be the work of negroes. Homer hum a song. She didn't look happy, but she didn't look sad neither.

EVERY NEGRO WALK IN A CIRCLE. TAKE THAT AND MAKE OF IT what you will. But sometime the circle not be the negro's but the white man own, and white man circle full of hill and valley and things they say that mean something else. Black man wake up to find circle make for him, beginning with the shackle that lock round him neck. White man circle come by him own choosing. Plenty have choice to walk straight and away, yet plenty come back to where them start. Others never leave. And if you the negro get take up in the white man life, you travel that circle too.

After the Kingston Harbour fire, word spread to the backra that he must be unceasing in him vigilance. Seventeen niggers get round up by the infantry. Most of them get whip, hammer, derby-dose, beat, bludgeon, burn, whip, gibbet or arse fuck with a red-hot poker. The rest get shot, so no slave alive to stand trial. That don't stop Miss Isobel night riding. Lilith stop going outside to watch her, but Robert Quinn go outside and come back laughing so hard that he throw himself into a hiccup. He go to sleep for a little, but then wake up early to go back out to the cane field. Lilith didn't sleep. In the evening Robert Quinn come home just in time because Lilith mind was haunting her again.

—God feckin' damn! he say and throw down two stalk of cane that he take to peeling and chewing.—God feckin' damn! The man's lost all claim to good sense. Kingston damn near burns down, something is afoot and all he thinks about is marrying the bitch!

—Massa?

—There's no place for the militia to be dispatched, no place for merchant ships to dock and take his precious sugar, mind ye, and all he speaks of is finding a feckin' ring!

—Find ring for what, massa?

—Lilith, do ye think there could ever come a day when ye call me Robert?

—N-no, massa.

Robert Quinn sigh.—This must be a warning, to myself, he say. I should guard my heart after all, he say.

—Massa?

—Huh? Oh, I was...

—Who getting married, sah?

—Yer master, that's who to goddamn. She's finally bewitched him. Deceived is more to the matter, totally and horribly deceived. I tell ye this, he cannot, simply cannot, marry that woman.

—Why, m—

—If ye call me by that word one more time.

—Why, M...Ro...Lilith don't know what to say.

—Because...I regret, I cannot tell you this. Good lord, should I tell him? I haven't really considered this.

Robert Quinn sit down on the table and pull him legs up. He wrap him arms round him knees. He look at the ceiling, he look at him knees and he look at Lilith.

—Goddamn, what do I do? I ask ye, what am I to do?

Lilith shrug.

—A devil of a thing, keeping a secret, isn't it? Devil of a thing. 'Tis like God or some blimey bastard just picked ye to be the innkeeper of all this...this...truth, so that everybody else can go about lying. Devil of a thing, man. The very devil.

—If you say so, massa.

Robert Quinn sigh again.—I wager a negro, especially a house slave, would be bowed down by a life's worth of secrets.

—Me don't have no secret, sah.

—Of course, and me mum named me St. Patrick so that I'd marry Catholic.

Lilith bow down her head.

—Seems to be our lot in life, I fear, he say and smile half-like.

Lilith stare at the ground for a long time. The she unbutton her dress and make it fall to the floor. She half smile but not for long. Robert Quinn look at her with him left eyebrow raise.

—Not the intercourse I was hankering for, he say and get up and go to the bedroom and shut the door. Lilith still in the kitchen, feeling a nasty breeze on her back. She pull up her dress and go to Quinn room. He on the bed shucking off him boot. Lilith open her mouth to ask a question but don't. He see her.

—That question ye just thought better of asking, what was it?

—Nothing, massa...Quinn.

—Yawning you were, then, were ye?

—Yes, m—

—Come in, Lilith, and shut the door.

Lilith close the door and watch him pulling off the right boot. She grab the left one. Him toes wriggle but him foot stinking something awful.

—You foots need washing, massa.

—Do you want to wash them, luv?

—They need cleaning or they goin' stink up the bed.

—That's not what I asked of ye.

—Massa?

—D'ye want to? Do you have any desire to lay yer hands on me stinky feet? Do you want to or are yer afraid of me and feel ye have to?

—I . . .

Quinn pull her down on the bed beside him. He looking straight at her.

—Tell me the very thing you were about to say before you quit, he say.

—Massa.

—Lilith. I demand to know.

Lilith quiet. She rubbing left hand with the right.

—No, I do not. Lilith, I don't demand it. If it's yer wish to tell me, please do; if ye don't, that's fine as well. I would like to know, though, if ye please.

—Massa. Massa . . . I . . . You, you have to . . . I don't . . . When you . . . we can't forget. We can't forget.

—Forget what?

—Who be the massa and who be the nigger. Lilith wrap her arm around herself and bow her head. Quinn quiet for a while.

—Aye. Aye. I ask ye, though, who sees us in this room, other than God?

—Nobody, sah.

—Nobody. That's correct. That's correct. I'll strike a bargain with ye, an arrangement, if you will.

—Massa?

Quinn touch her knee.

—This room, these walls, d'ye see 'em, luv?

Lilith say yes.

—Once we're in this room, inside this room, what if you could say to me whatever comes to ye? Call me whatever you wish. Call me Robert and I'll call you Lilith. Can you do that, Lilith?

Outside the wind was threatening to answer.—No, massa, she say.

—I'll beg ye if I have to, he say.

—Backra not supposed to beg nigger nothing, sah.

—And yet here I am, watching you make a beggar out of me. All right. Since you must be this way, I order it, then.

—You commanding slave to be free?

—Yes, I command it. You must call me by the name me mother gave me when we're in this room. I'm just a man and yer just a girl. And you must say anything you wish or nothing at all if you please. As long as we're in this room and the door is closed. D'ye understand me, luv?

—Yes, massa.

—No ye don't. Not at all. The door's closed, Lilith. And I'm Robert. Robert, Robert, Robert.

Lilith know she can hate a massa, a Massa Quinn or even a Massa Robert. But she can't hate a Robert, or a Humphrey or a Isobel, for that matter. Him spinning her and she like and dislike what him do. Why a white man want to be nice to a nigger, only to be more wicked later? Why white man love give thing, only to take it back later? She get up quick to leave but he catch her hand and pull her back.

—Look around you, luv. Nothing here but the walls and the dark.

—And what outside?

—I don't give two shakes of a rat's arse what's outside. I'm in here with you, luv, and yer not leaving until you call me Robert.

—Robert.

—Not like I'm yer horse, damn you.

—With all the riding that go on—

—That go…what? Dear heart, could ye just finish one goddamn sentence? D'ye think I'll whip you if you speak yer mind? D'ye think I'm a liar, Lilith?

—No, ma…No, Robert.

—Good. That's good to know, at the very least.

—Robert.

—That's my name. Pleased to make yer acquaintance, Lilith.

But she know. She know as soon as he start playing with her name, taking Lilith and Lovey and getting Lily and then going back to Lovey. From he start touching her face and lying down on him back in full clothes and pulling her on top of him. From he hold her and start laugh and never go to take off her clothes even though she feeling him grow. From he start talk like he just come back from wherever the Faerie Queene was hiding them long weeks. She know that her mouth could still say what her heart can't swear. She know that the loose tongue, more enemy than friend, be all that save her. The same heart that should want to give all to Robert Quinn say no, or mayhaps it can never say yes. So she cry. She cry long and loud and Quinn weep too because mayhaps he think this be the bawling that woman do to cleanse themselves. The bawling that mean she free herself from whatever did bound her and just like a woman she need tears to wash it all away. But Lilith cry because her heart couldn't cleanse, because she couldn't wash away nothing and what he want she could never give him. She don't know why. Mayhaps that be what Massa Humphrey teach her by making them mens nearly kill her. She wanted to give everything to him, she could say that to herself now. But she can't do this again for he white and he be the overseer and he control the whip and he white and he Irish and he soon tired of her and he white and he be the overseer and some things don't mean to be and he white. And a nigger girl must be sensible 'bout white man behaviour, for it set like the sun and sunset always different on any given day. She could give herself like she do before and this time never get herself back. No. No. No. She bawling and Quinn think it be tears of joy. And that is what they be, in they way. For a man can make a woman know her true self and what she be is nothing that belong to Quinn. She know that now. So she cry.

The next morning, Lilith get summon to Miss Isobel room.

—Oh, Lilith, if only all women could share in my joy! If only, she say. Then she pause herself for a minute and burst out a laugh that sound dirty like a whore.

—Share indeed. Pox 'pon de stinking, backstabbing, petticoat-shedding lot.

Miss Isobel drive the carriage to Kingston with Lilith beside her. Lilith so frighten that she can't remember when last she so frighten. Massa Humphrey did say it not too safe for two womens to be riding all the way to Kingston with no man for protection, for that would be going all the way down to the harbour and all sort of drunkards and worse were down there—wicked men, licentious women, perverted sailors who have not seen a woman in months. Indeed, it was the most disgusting city in the empire. Miss Isobel say that she going to Kingston, not Port Royal, and have no fear, no pirates have been seen for ages. Miss Isobel insist, saying she can use a musket and a cutlass better than most man and to get her they would have to catch her first. Massa Humphrey look like he about to take a stand but Miss Isobel would have none of it. He look at Lilith like he sorry for what she about to get into. Robert Quinn tell Lilith to stay away from Greenwich on the harbour, since it be in ruins and populated by the most desperate sort, as if she be the one doing the riding. As she and Miss Isobel ride off, Lilith see Robert Quinn touch Massa Humphrey on the shoulder and whisper. Robert Quinn look at Lilith for a second but then he disappear. Miss Isobel swing the carriage round a corner and them gone.

Kingston. Miss Isobel ride straight down to the harbour that Massa Humphrey warn her about. By Lilith reckoning, they ride for twenty or so miles and when they get to Kingston it be noon. Lilith never before see the place. Is the noise that lick her ears first, the noise of one thing mixing with another and fighting with something else. The noise of coloured and mulatto pickneys, wearing shirts or trousers but never both, and yelling and laughing and screaming as they dodge carriage and cart, and market women, some of them nigger, some mulatto or quadroon or mustee, all selling by the roadside with they basket full of orange, yam, cassava and banana. They turn down Orange Street that litter with even more people moving up and down like mad ants. Most be white mens, but a good few coloured, some wearing loose shirt, old breeches or pantaloons with dirty boots or shoes. Some dress up in fine coat with tails. Some carrying cane, others books, others paper or handkerchiefs, which they use cover they nose when they pass a stink place.

Sometimes the people pack so thick that Miss Isobel halt her carriage and cuss. They turn left and go across two lane to King Street, then head down to the sea. Lilith can see two ships at the harbour. The buildings rise higher on King Street, some having three, four, even five floor. Some even more lavish than a great house, with window even in the roof and columns tall as a tower and wider than the carriage. The buildings colour like the sky or fruit or white woman skin, with French windows bigger than doors. But they stand tight together. Unlike Orange Street, womens be all over King Street, white womens especially. The womens all dress like Miss Isobel but in white clothes or yellow or blue or a plaid pattern. And some don't have on petticoat so the dress fall flat. Some walk up and down the road, two by two and they stop and talk and whisper when they see one another. Lilith didn't know that there be white woman who walk. Miss Isobel ride through a little ditch and almost splash a woman in red dots, who then cuss out like a nigger. Some of the womens in buggy and carriage like Miss Isobel. Some of the carriages draw by a niggerman or by a white woman with a negro housemaid in the back. They all hide they nose with a handkerchief when they pass a stink place.

At the bottom of King Street, nearer to the harbour, be the shops. They smaller, and even tighter, most with two floors, the shop at the

bottom and what look like living quarters at the top with curtains in
the windows. From the shops and stores come all sort of pretty smell.
Perfume and powder from England and France that Miss Isobel say we
still at war with. They ride past a tall building with a Christmas orb for
a roof that name Batty's Emporium. Lilith almost say it 'loud but catch
her tongue. Lilith wondering if it slip before to Miss Isobel that she
can read. She could always say that is Robert Quinn teach her and that
wouldn't be no lie. Lilith keep her mouth shut for the rest of the ride.
They pass two store and one more by the name Emporium. They pass a
shop with a green and bone wall and a tobacco smell that jump out the
door and greet the carriage. Some buildings have a balcony that hang
over the street with white mens, some of them in red uniform, looking
over like they standing guard. Lilith looking at the negro womens selling by the roadside, not far from the shit water, and wonder if they be
slave or free for is not Sunday, when slave get leave to sell. Then they
pass a building and Lilith read these words quiet-like:

SLAVES, BOUGHT AND SOLD.

She think that Miss Isobel see her this time, but Miss Isobel busy cussing people to get out of her goddamn way. The carriage can barely
move now, sake of the crowd of people. Lilith didn't notice when they
start swimming in this sea. Mens, mens and more mens, some dress up
in hat, coat and tails and shiny boot, some in blouson and pantaloon,
some dirty like nigger even though most white. Most huddle in group
of two or three and they talking, whispering, laughing, shouting, but
mostly looking forward to the platform. Negroes.

—A fine buck is what we 'ave 'ere, gentlemens, a fine buck! the auctioneer say and he open him tight collar to free him fat neck.

A negro man and a negro woman on the platform. The two naked,
save for chain round they neck and another binding they wrist. Both
shiny from palm oil that carry scent right up the street. The auctioneer

grab the woman little titty and squeeze. The woman yelp and try to run but the man grab her by the hair. A white man whisper something to another white man and the woman beside them slap him, playful-like, on the cheek with her glove.

—A ripe one, this lassie is, not yet fifteen, methinks. Aye, I'm sure of it. An exotic princess was she back in the dark continent, a boon to any household. And fine gentlemen such as you are surely you know a good value, so lets start at one hundred, do I hear one and twenty? the auctioneer say.

One by one hands rise up and Lilith hear what negro woman go for. Montpelier be an estate for three or four generation now and there be so many slave that Lilith can't remember the last time she see one that come straight from the Africa. Plenty on the estate, but they work the hardest part of the field so that they can get seasoned quick and none allowed to work in the house, sake of how they brutish and chat bad. She look at they body and forget palm oil and wonder if is so they come from the Africa, so shiny that they body glow. But then Lilith see something in the Africa man that she thought was only in the colony nigger. The hunch in the shoulders, the sinking neck. Just off the ship and the Africa man sinking into nigger pose already. He already buckling under backra weight. For all they funny talking and funny smell, Lilith did imagine the African back as always straight, the African leg powerful and the African eye big and wide. But there they was, a man and a woman, and already they body twist into question mark like what Massa Humphrey write.

—One hundred ninety-five, sold! say the auctioneer.

The auctioneer talking 'bout how hard the negroes goin' work but he point to the negro woman breast and bottom and stuck him finger in her mouth to show her white teeth. He make the man spin round couple time and use him cattle prod to poke the man balls and lift up the man cocky so that it jiggle.

—A right bounty of negroes will be sprouting up from that seed, gentlemen, you might mistake him for a stallion. You may never need to buy a nigger again. Spiting me own self out of business, yes I am. Shall we start at two hundred?

Again, plenty hand shoot up one after the other. Lilith looking at the white mens buying and the black bodies shining and didn't notice they eye. When she see the woman, the woman was looking at her already. Lilith see them eye before. On Andromeda daughter when she watching her mother spit blood till she dead. But she see it on white man too, on Massa Roget when she pin him to the bottom of the bathtub and he realise he not coming back up. Lilith think she know what frighten is, but didn't know it until she see the woman face. But is more than frighten, is something else, mayhaps in the eye or the eyebrow, Lilith don't know. Something else that her mind answer before the question ask. She know the answer. She can't help nobody out of white man power, not even herself. The woman eye still asking. Lilith don't know how to fix her eye to say no, so she look at the man and the same question come over him face.

The negro man and woman look round and round, frighten by the dog barking, horse whinnying, wheel crunching, goat mehhhhing, donkey heehawing, womens cussing, mens shouting, pickney playing, cat jumping, whip cracking, people pointing, ladies blushing, flags flapping and sun rising. Lilith watch as they get the frighten eye, the mark of every negro.

—Two hundred ninety pounds! the auctioneer shout and the woman jump. Lilith jump too. A church bell ring from the south and Lilith look at the two negroes again. Lilith wonder what running through bush with no chain on you foot or dog coming after you feel like. And what it feel like to know all of that, then lose it. Do losing feel different from never having? Do a captured nigger be a different nigger? Lilith gone from perplex to melancholy. She surprise that she never talk to a Africa man or woman before. Except Homer. And even Homer, who talk more Africa tongue than most, still don't talk 'bout the Africa land much.

Miss Isobel yelling that if they don't let her through, she going to giddy-up her horses and let come what may. The men give her pass. The auctioneer yell, Sold and two white mens come for the negro man. He bolt. The white women stiff and screaming. A naked negro man let loose in they company set off a terror. Some of the womens swoon, some try to run, some hide behind they mens. But the negro man run only so far before the chain yank him by the neck and he drop flat on him back. The auctioneer go to strike the Africa man but stop, perhaps because he remember how much the slave worth. Some of the womens still hide behind they mens. The Africa man make a sound and the white mens laugh and call him beast and monkey. But Lilith know the sound even though she never hear the wail before. She know what he bawling for and force herself not to look in him eye, for she know he looking at her. The carriage take her away.

Lilith look at Miss Isobel. She sweating even though the Kingston air cool, and trying to catch her breath even though the horse doing all the work. Two white mens step in the carriage way and Miss Isobel hide her face quick with her hand, not even watching where she going until the mens dash to the other side. The taller older man cuss but the younger man say nothing. Some of Miss Isobel hair fly out of her bonnet and she grab it quick with her right hand, almost letting go of the reins, and push it back underneath. Miss Isobel looking straight ahead but Lilith look back. The younger man was looking at the carriage and Lilith know she seen him before. She ain't never been to Kingston and Massa Humphrey don't keep no friend so it must be a man who did be at the Rogets' funeral. Plenty mens was there but she remember him now. Miss Isobel did take more notice of him then and he tip him hat to her. Lilith surprise that she remember and Miss Isobel forget, for he wearing the same purple coat—the only one on the street—and the same brown top hat tilt to the left to show him black hair. The carriage take them away but even as he get smaller and smaller he still looking.

Lilith and Miss Isobel come back to Montpelier at about one o' clock. Robert Quinn waiting at the step when Miss Isobel drop Lilith off. Robert Quinn and Miss Isobel don't look at each other. She drive off, the back of the carriage full with parcels.

—Fer her wedding dress, luv?

—Yes, massa.

—Yer not helping the cow, are ye? Robert Quinn say.

—Me don't know how to sew, massa.

—Good. Good. Ye shall have nothing to do with that poppy-show, he say.—Do ye hear me, Lilith?

—Yes, massa.

—Now fix us a proper lunch, will ye? he say.

The next morning, Lilith in the great house kitchen early. Robert Quinn leave out before dawn. Nobody in the kitchen but Homer.

—Me pass a place where they was selling negroes, Lilith say.

Homer put down the knife and the potato she was slicing. She don't say nothing for a while.

—When you see that? she say.

—Yesterday on the way to the dry goods merchant. They was having auction for negroes.

—Do tell. Me did hear that slave ship come in on Tuesday. How them look?

—How who look?

—The slave them, the Africa mens and womens.

—Me only see two, a man and a woman. The woman go for a hundred ninety-five pounds and the man two hundred ninety.

—Nigger price goin' up like everything else in this world. How them look?

—Frighten.

—Frighten. Poor sum'bitches don't know the meaning of frighten yet.

Homer go back to her potato peeling.—But is all right. White man goin' know the meaning of frighten soon and very soon.

Then she start sing.

—Soon and very soon, we are going to meet the King. Soon and very soon we are going to meet the—

—Me see white man frighten out o' him wits already.

—What? What you talking 'bout?

—Me see white man frighten before. Frighten like God catch him a sin. Back at Coulibre.

The knife fall from Homer hand.

—Jesus the father. Me did know you was the one.

Homer cover her mouth with one finger and say, Shhh. She look round, outside, out the door and out the window.—You burn down the Coulibre house, she whisper.

—You sound like you never did sure.

—You sound like me was asking question. Me just saying things as they be. What me don't know is how you manage to burn them up without them trying to escape.

—Me kill them first, Lilith say.

Homer pick up the knife again but pause. She pause long. She turn to the window. She look at the floor. Then she look at Lilith hard.

—Me know you have the darkness, but me didn't know it so black, she say.

—Blacker than midnight when me ready.

—How you kill Massa Roget?

Lilith go over to the kitchen window to watch slave coffle pass and singing work song.

—You wasn't at Coulibre the first time Massa Roget heart take set 'pon him.

—No, but me know 'bout it.

—Well, him heart take set 'pon him again. Right when me was giving him bath and him want him cocky jerk. Him 'bout to get out when him heart sick him. Fall right back in the tub and slip under the water.

—Go on.

—Him pull himself up and wheezing and he begging that me must help him. Me help him, all right. Me help him right back down under the water. Me hand on him chest, him trying to wring me titty, but me keep him down. Then me eye see him eye.

Homer silent.

—Sometime he slip from me and sometime he try to grab me hair, but him heart was on my side, the son of a bitch. Him own heart. Me hold him down until him nose start suck in water and bubble come up. Me hold him down until all him cocky stiffen up. Best cockstand that devil ever manage.

The kitchen quiet. Homer look at her hands and Lilith look through the window.

—How long it take him to dead?

—Too long.

—And how it did feel, chile?

—How it did feel? You asking me how it feel? Me don't know.

—Killing people not an easy thing, you know. Bothersome.

—No, you don't understand. Killing too easy. That is what me telling you. That is what bother me 'bout it. The mistress walk in 'pon we, so me chase after her and she just screaming and screaming and fall over the balcony.

—Jesus Christ.

—Me never was intending that one.

—You didn't intend to kill her?

—Not that way, me think. But me don't know, is like when you see what two hand can do, you just want to do more. It just come over you like anointing. After that, me know it was soon before Miss Isobel come back and the only thing me could think of was to get rid of any trail linking them to me. Fire was the only thing me could think 'bout that could hide everything. Just burn down everything like judgement. Or me wasn't thinking, me don't know.

—Hell of a thing to kill a white man.

—Like you would know.

—Me know death, that for sure.

—Knowing and causing it be two different thing. Night and day, as you would say. That's why me not killing no more.

—'Cause you like it too much?

—'Cause me probably won't stop.

—Good. Good. Wonderful good. Time we teach these bombocloth devil a lesson. Saint-Domingue point the way and we need to stop skylarking.

—You really don't know nothing 'bout killing, don't it? You think 'cause you work Obeah—

—Myal. Me don't work no Obeah.

—You think 'cause you work magic and somebody get sick or drop down dead is the same thing? It not like killing with you hand, Homer, not a raas claat. You want to know how it feel? You really want to know? Nothing in this world like killing a man. Your skin on him skin, you tearing him chest hair off. You kill just one time and you know why God save murder for himself. Wicked, wicked, wicked. And good. Good. Good. Too good. You understand me? It better than full belly or when a man fuck you good. You do it and you know why white man be master over we. Because he can grab a nigger and kill her just so. Just like that. Only white man can live with how terrible that be.

—You living.

—Me is a murderess. You want that kinda living, then take it. Every nigger have reason for the white man to dead. Me more than most. You can talk all you want, but me shed real blood, and me not shedding no more. Me not killing nobody.

—Them people is not somebody. Me don't know what them is, but them drain of all peopleness, that must be why they skin white. Lilith—

—Me smell them, you know. The pickneys. Me smell them burning all the time. And me sees them. Me sees them.

—Me have a tea that can fix that.

—Me don't want it to fix! Me want to remember. You don't understand. Me want to know why me must never do nothing like that again. Besides, how we to do anything? Them have gun and them is master over we.

—Few years back. You still living with Circe.

—You head take you again, woman? What you talking 'bout?

—Seventeen ninety-five. That's when me find out that me two baby dead. Hear it from Jack Wilkins only because the man that buy me son come for him money back. When me hear him dead, first me think that something in me just go. Then me realise that whatever in me gone long time. Go to market the next Sunday and see two mens and a woman me know from Jackson Lands. One whole year pass before they tell me 'bout they plot. Every time a nigger plot fail, other nigger take heed and learn. By the time them tell me, nigger on seven estate already plottin' to kill every backra within a hundred mile.

—All this time me did think is you come up with this.

—Me never come up with nothing. All me did want to do was draw blood. Pallas be the first woman me bring into it. Then Iphigenia, then Callisto, who bring Gorgon. Then Hippolyta. Six tell six tell six. Make freedom news spread like brushfire. Look round you, girl chile. There be thirty-two nigger to one white man on this estate alone. Some is thirty-five to one. The real thing you should be pondering is how come they master over we for so long.

—They have musket.

—Can only fire one shot. Fifteen white man, fifteen shot, and even if them shoot straight, that be only fifteen slave get shot, and even if the fifteen get kill, that still leave near two hundred more.

—You thinking this hard.

—Me born thinking. Look 'pon you. One nigger you be, yet you bring one whole estate down. Cho! You think them better than we?

—No, me stop think that long time ago. Is we not better than them.

—Don't be damn fool, chile. Black man could be wicked like the devil and you can still find a white man that worse. Them don't even know how to grow sugar right. Negro man could 'ave teach him to grow cane two times the length if they did only treat we right, but no. Freedom goin' get musket now, but me talk too long and wall have ears. November soon gone and more talking to do tomorrow.

—Homer...

—Tomorrow, Lilith.

—*Because we are to be* mother and father, damn you, Robert! Press me no further, Massa Humphrey say and slam him hand on the kitchen table.

Robert Quinn pacing from one end of the kitchen to the other. He stop at the table and touch Massa Humphrey on the shoulder. —Humphrey, I entreat you, he say.

—No! Enough of this, damn you. I will speak of it no longer.

—Yes, ye damn well will. I will not stand by and watch ye—

—Then leave, for God's sake. Nobody's strong-arming you to stay.

—Aye, nobody is doing that, indeed. Is that how it will be? After all I've been to...after Venice?

—You'll hold that above me as long as I live.

—You're the one holding yourself to bondage, Humphrey. Do not marry this woman. You don't know.

—I damn well know all there is to—

—No, you don't. Trust the voice of a friend. You do not—

Robert Quinn see Lilith at the door and stop. Him red skin get redder.—God feckin' damn, how long have you been there? he say.

Lilith look away.

—I said, how long have you been there?

—Me just come back, sah, me—

Robert Quinn stomp over to Lilith and Lilith make one back step into the wall behind her. Then he slap her.

—I will not have a goddamned slave sneaking up on me, he say. Lilith grab her cheek and her mouth drop. She look in him eye and don't see Robert Quinn.—Go to your room! he say. Lilith run. In the room a tear run down her face. But she not crying, she not sobbing and she not wondering if this is Robert Quinn too. She feel something that she don't feel in a long while. She feel black. Her door still open.

—Don't ye walk out on me, Humphrey Wilson, I'm not done with ye yet.

—I'll do as I damn well please, Quinn. Don't forget who's in whose employ. Now, I'll thank you to remember your place and speak no ill of the person who's to be my wife.

—But...

—Or find some other means of employment. You are rather skilled for an Irishman. You'll not be wanting in opportunities, I assure you.

—Humphrey, fer God's sake.

—I bid you good-bye, Quinn.

Lilith listen to the boot stomp across the floor and out the door and down the four steps. She hear the footsteps on the dirt, the horse whinnying and galloping away. She hear another boot step, slower coming into the room. She hear him getting slower and closer. Robert Quinn touch Lilith shoulder and she flinch. She don't look up to him face. Robert Quinn hiss and leave the room.

Lilith get up before dawn and go to the great house kitchen. She push the door but it lock. She push the door again, for Homer always up before dawn. Lilith knock and the door open. Homer frowning but she let Lilith in. Inside be Pallas and Callisto. Pallas shove something inside her bosom.

—You forget one, Pallas say and Callisto pick a bullet off the counter.

—Make haste, Homer say. Callisto unwrap a piece of osnaburg and reveal a musket. Pallas wrap it in banana leaf and put it in her basket. Lilith go to ask but say nothing. She slip past the door and leave through the main entrance. She go down the steps and look out at the sun that still trying to come over the hill. In the kitchen she brewing tea and boiling pudding. Robert Quinn come in huffing and puffing. Him left eye dark with bruise and getting darker. He sit down at the kitchen table and quiet. Lilith quiet too but don't know what to expect.

—Ye won't be making tea for me much longer, lovey, Robert Quinn say.—Appears I've been dismissed.

Oriki

· 26 ·

December. With near all of the militia down by the harbour and some inlands, few did by the barracks at Up Park Camp that night when fire break out in the mess and spread from one barrack to two. Infantryman in two barrack burn to death—it seem that both barrack was chained up from the outside. Word be that it was the work of Maroons who itchin' to start another war, but the Maroons quick to deny it. Seventeen new nigger get purchase from Kingston to replace the seventeen old ones, all of them kill by firing squad that very morning.

Robert Quinn thinking of what to take of his belongings. He pace round the home, eye him drapery and saying that coming with him. —No fair chance of that, I'm afraid, he say when Lilith ask if he and the massa can't let bygones be. He rest him chin in palm and tap him face with him fingers but wince when he tap too close to the black eye.

—I have said the unforgivable and he has done the unforgivable, he say. He 'bout to say more but right then they hear the march of the slave coffle. Quinn go to the window and watch as they pass. Lilith go to her room. Couple minute pass as Lilith hear talking. She hear Quinn voice getting louder and louder.

—This is still my house, so get the feck out, Quinn say.

—I kin do wot I likes, methinks. Gonna be my 'ouse now, yes it will. Gonna be mine, the other man say.

—Not yers yet by any stretch, McClusky.

—Will be in 'alf a mo', says I. Wot says you? Methinks we'll be keeping the fair nigger wench as well, that's wot methinks. I kin make sure of that. How's 'er arse? Didn't get very far with 'er poxy cunt, second time around.

—Why, you—

—Careful, guvnuh, don't want you leaving in a coffin now, does we? Does we have to give you a good taste of my cutlass?

—Leave by yer own choosing or so help me, ye'll leave in a box, McClusky.

—And who or wot's gonna make me?

Lilith step in the room to see Robert Quinn standing with him hands on a chair. McClusky, the same man who was on top of her once and try for twice, pointing a cutlass at him. McClusky hear a click. He look at Lilith and jump. Lilith step towards Robert Quinn holding the musket.

—Now, hold on now, dearies, surely ye knows jesting when I plays it.

—Ye know the business with muskets, McClusky, how they always jam and misfire or blow up in one's face or just plain misses a fair target?

—A-aye, Master Quinn—

—This ain't one of them. Now fer the last time, get the fuck out.

McClusky look at Robert Quinn still holding on to the chair and Lilith beside him with the gun. He laugh a little but limp away quick. Lilith hand the gun to Robert Quinn but he don't take it.

—First thing the son of a bitch does, he hires the man I dismissed. Maybe I should've let ye shoot the cunt, he say.

Lilith feel the weight in her hand. She know that a bullet in the musket, for she see Robert Quinn load it himself. She could even load the musket herself if she try, she thinking. Robert Quinn out there beating and killing niggers, somebody say. She can't remember who say he killing and who say he beating. Two saying be one thing and she look at him turning him back to her, a slave with a loaded musket.

—Planning on shooting me as well, lovey?

—N-no, massa.

—Good to know. Lord knows yer the only fair thing left to see in this godforsaken place.

Him back still turn to her.—Make us some lunch, luv. A fine corking one.

Robert Quinn stay home all day. He go outside twice to see if he can see the slaves working from up on him terrace. He watch the smoke rising from the boiling house. Twice or thrice he look over left to the great house and Lilith imagine he get a heaviness in the heart.

—Fine and dandy, Quinn say when he come back in.

After lunch Quinn sit at the table for a long time. He reach for the almanac that Lilith read sometimes when he not there to get better at word knowing. She hear *blam!* and see him hand still swinging from throwing the book. She wash and cure and cut the chicken in two, then season it with pepper, thyme, sea salt and a powder Quinn get from one of him sailor friend that they call curry. That make the chicken look like gold and spicy, the way he like it. She boiling yam and potatoes and dasheen and roasting breadfruit. Lilith cooking up plenty and she know Robert Quinn watching her.

He at the kitchen table and she feel him all over her. He on her as she walk to the water barrel, he on her as she grab the curtains to take outside, he on her as she sweep the little dust down the step. Lilith find herself wishing he wasn't there and find that peculiar. Other times when he not there she want him to come home, and she used to find that peculiar too. But now with him here through the day, she don't feel free. Not slavery-free but woman-free. He step past her in the kitchen and reach for the rum. Robert Quinn take a swig and cough hard. He bowl over and cough so hard that Lilith thinking he coughing him tongue out. Him face blaze red quick-quick.—God feckin' damn, he say and strike him chest. Lilith laugh.

—Ye laughing at me, lovey?

—No, massa. Not at all, massa. Not at—

Lilith bowl over with laughter again. Robert Quinn look at her queer-like, with one eyebrow raise, and start laugh too.—Is this how it will be? Am I to be your laughingstock? he say but laughing again. He put down the rum bottle and put him arms around Lilith. Lilith see him moving in to kiss her and pull back. He look at her. White man supposed to lie with negro woman, fuck them and even squeeze them. Sometimes they even love them. But no white man supposed to kiss a nigger. That be love things, things for white woman, and proper white woman at that. Robert Quinn hold her firm, close him eye and try to kiss her again. Him eye close but Lilith wide open. Lilith can't remember what a man lip feel like, so she reason that she never feel a man lip before. Him lip soft, she expect pink lip to be soft, but not so. He sucking her bottom lip, then her top one and Lilith do it too. He pulling her in tighter and they kissing and pecking and licking and sucking. Her eye wide open. Him leaving. Him leaving soon. Can't she . . . ? Then Quinn work him tongue into her mouth and she feel like she lose another maidenhead. He feel rough and soft at the same time. She tasting rum and rum sweat and rum tingle and be the most wonderfullest thing. Her eye still open, him eye still close. He cup her face with him hands soft, like he catching a feather. Quinn lean him head left and roll him lips and tongue inside her, then he lean right and roll again. He pull away, kiss her lips flat and work him way back into her mouth. She seek him with her tongue too. Him arms round her back and her arm round him. Lilith finally close her eyes.

Friday, long past midnight. Saturday. Lilith watching Robert Quinn sleep. *He beating and killing niggers*, a woman say. Maybe she didn't say it. Maybe Lilith didn't hear right. Maybe the womens full of evil and want to take 'way a girl happiness. Happiness? Lilith thinking deep. What nigger girl know 'bout happiness? What shape that come in when the skin black like tar and death is a whipping, a chopping, a burning and a hanging away? Lilith more than perplex, Lilith feeling happiness and sadness fighting in her chest and fear coming in like he never did leave. Robert Quinn roll over in the bed like sleeping giant. Man have magic over woman when he don't even try. Lilith watch him bushy chest rise and fall and hair sticking to him forehead with sweat.

The womens ready. She come back from the meeting in the cave two hours ago, but the voices running in and out of her head like she still there. *Nobody do a thing before the abeng blow.* In one week be the day. The hataclaps. *White man goin' think is the great tribulation itself,* one of the womens say, but Lilith couldn't remember who. She did trouble enough by how far and how cold Homer thinking. *Nobody move before the abeng blow. Then all hell goin' broke loose.*

Lilith watch Robert Quinn as he shift again. She love to watch how him face turn first, then him shoulder and then him thick legs and she giggle when he rub him belly in him sleep. Robert Quinn kissing her now. Signs and wonders is for white woman; nigger must take things as they be and don't look no deeper. But him hair slide away from him face again and she see something not pretty like Humphrey Wilson but more beautiful nonetheless. Lilith cuss herself, like them word make for nigger to say. She feel herself going back to what she was when she try her very best to hate him. But he leaving. He never goin' see her again. She too happy that he goin' to live to be sad that he goin' be gone. Mayhaps now she can...

Word from Worthy Park, McIntyre Pen, Ascot and Jackson Lands. They ready, but what 'bout we?

Gorgon be one of them special worker niggers, the only slaves with true business to travel from estate to estate spread the news. Her carriage carry flowers and correspondence and whatever people from one estate want to share with people from another. Homer trust her to be her own mouth on other estate and Gorgon spread the word far, meeting with the other people who plotting from estate to estate. Homer and Callisto meet with other negroes at Sunday market when slave free to shop and correspondence. Gorgon carry message through the week. *Over by Ascot a Judas nigger get trample by three horse. Hoof to the head or crowbar, nobody can tell the difference*, she say.

The evening before when Robert Quinn kiss her, he hoist her up on the kitchen counter and kiss her some more. She kiss too. Then he pull away and start spin and dip and Lilith laugh when he claim he dancing.—'Tis the very latest, I assure ye, he say to her. He pull her to him and show her dance step, telling her, No, this way, and then spin and then curtsy and No…yes, like that, darlin', like that. He grab her again and lift her up and say that he should take her to the next Montpelier ball just to see the look on everybody face. Lilith can't take no more of this, so she say the food about to burn. He put her down.—Of course, of course, he say. That evening the supper sweet him so much he start sing, as be the custom with Irishman when he happy. He start sing some song 'bout a woman who wait so long for her sailor man to come back that even when she dead her ghost still out by the seashore waiting. She ask him why him singing sad song if he happy.—One's never far from the other, him say. *McIntrye Pen, twenty-two white, three hundred black, fifty unsure. Cutlass sharpen and the womens ready. Two o'clock be the hour. Right before the lunch bell. Niggerman of no use if they belly full.*

At two o'clock. Right before the lunch bell. Hungry man is angry man, for sure, and Homer want them plenty mad. By two o'clock the slave-driver also at them tiredest after being in the sun for long that they slack off or rest off even though they not supposed to.

—How you expect field nigger to take instruction from house nigger? Lilith ask and watch Gorgon growl.

—They only hate nigger who forget where they come from, she say. They only hate negro who start to think they white too.

—So you tell them that you half white, sister? Lilith say to Gorgon.

—De only white be full white, fool. Whether you mulatto, mustee or octoroon, you still nigger. Some o' we forget dat, Gorgon say.

—How, with you to remind we all the time? Who remind you, Papa Jack?

Gorgon look 'pon Lilith hard, but Lilith lookin' at Callisto to see if she watching.

—Is not nothing. Me no talk to him unless him talk to me, Gorgon say to Callisto with her head low. Callisto playing with her knife and waiting for Homer to talk again.

—At the two o'clock hour, the abeng goin' blow. Then all soul stop work, but keep the hoe and axe and pick and club ready, she say.

—Why in the broad daylight? Why not at night when everybody asleep? Lilith say.

—Night sound smart, yes, but that is what mash up the seventeen sixty revolt. Night help the fighting good, but then day come and the militia have a whole sixteen hour to run down negroes. No, we start in the afternoon and use night to get 'way. By the time the militia reach, this whole county goin' burn down. Now make we get particular. Some nigger goin' get shot with the musket them driver carry. But most of the bullet goin' miss and if one or two get shot, so it go. But we need the field nigger to kill the drivers still in the field. We will deal with the ones who go back to rest. Tell them to run backra down, use the pickaxe or the hoe, no white man must get 'way. Nor Johnny-jumper too. When abeng blow, we all stop work. Nigger from Jackson Lands say best to set fire to they great house first. All wood, burn quick. Poison set for massa, mistress and all nigger who eat from the same pot. Callisto deal with Miss Isobel. Me'll fix the mistress. After that, they goin' set fire to Montpelier great house while the field negroes burn the fields and kill the slave-drivers. Atlas and Hyperion goin' deal with the massa.

—But them two is man, Lilith say.

—Doing the only thing them good for. They won't know till the time anyway.

—You chère amie lucky. He supposed to leave the estate two day before, Homer say.—Just make sure you not in the carriage with him.

—What me must do? Look like you have everything plan out, Lilith say.

—You comin' with me, Callisto say.—Sometime you need two hand to kill one, 'specially that Miss Isobel.

—Me sure you can kill her all by you lonesome.

—Not me, baba, you.

—Give her one of you knife, Callisto.

Callisto pull up her dress. Her pussy so bush up that it look like black undergarb. Both thigh have strap and both strap have sheath for knife. Callisto pull a strap and hand everything to Lilith.—Me want it back, she say.

Robert Quinn mumble again and Lilith watch him chest rise and fall. Maybe if she put the pillow over him head, he wouldn't know. But he bound to wake up and Robert Quinn is a mighty strong man. He goin' leave two day before, she think to herself, repeating till she settle her spirit. After Coulibre, Lilith tell herself that she not goin' shed the blood of no more white man. Homer make things seem that if anybody deserve to have they blood shed, is backra. Plenty evil come from they hands, but Homer never kill one yet.

As the clock strike two, we kill whoever in the house. Then we go to the gun closet. Wilkins forget that he keep a key stuck under one of the drawers. Feel for the wax.

Is a hell of thing killing a man, any man, not just a white one. People think that having power over a life make you feel like God and them right. But God have the backbone to deal with how terrible he be, little nigger girl don't. Perhaps white man have it also, considering how much nigger they kill. Lilith wish the rage would come back so that she would stop with the thinking. She stay up, waiting for the tall dark woman to appear in a corner, the woman who might be a warning or a promise. A warning that Lilith making the same mistake again. Lilith thinking of a white man who goin' treat her like a white woman and take her out of nigger fate. Robert Quinn turn again. She not no fool, Lilith tell herself. She not a sleeping princess and Robert Quinn is not no king or prince. He just a man with broad shoulders and black hair who call her lovey and she like that more than her own name. She don't want the man to deliver her, she just want to climb in the bed and feel he wrap himself around her. She whisper something that difficult to say in the daylight. *Robert*, she say. *Robert*.

Judas nigger at Worthy Park get press clean through by the cane juice mill. Nobody did present to chop off him arm when it get stuck in the roller. Athena and Chiron, we have to deal with them.

Athena and Chiron. Athena most time deal with the cleaning and Chiron be one of the footmen. They take to pleasing the massa all the time, doing more than they have to and calling the massa to show him that they do it. Chiron report other footmen who lazy or who gather herb from in the swamp land and smoke it. When time a nigger get a nine lash for burnin' some of the mistress' silk, is Athena did tell Miss Isobel. Lilith come to know that even though Miss Isobel ask for her over and over, is Athena who by her side of late. Athena clean out her commode and bathe her and wash her hair and tell ever'body in the kitchen how the mistress so beauteous. Athena usually go downstairs to tell Massa Humphrey that Miss Isobel want to see him and stand guard at the door until Miss Isobel ready to receive gentleman company. Lately Athena been watching Homer when she go anywhere or talk to anybody and one time Homer see a little piece of Athena dress behind the door when she was talking to Callisto. *Them two be the niggers who love slavery more than free and if they get a free hand, wouldn't know what to do with it.* Lilith think if they don't act soon, Athena goin' tell Miss Isobel that the niggers up to something, if she don't tell her already. *Gorgon, tell it to Atlas. Fix Athena. Me will deal with Chiron.*

Fix Athena. Lilith close her eyes and see Athena on the floor convulsing and trying to scream but only blood coming out of her mouth, so she coughing and choking. Blood running down her nose and bursting from her head. Lilith mind going backways from end to beginning, from moonrise going back down in the sea to blood sucking and gurgling back into Athena mouth and the right leg unbreaking behind her back and her cracked skull coming back together and her whole body lifting off the rock and her scream push back in her mouth and her fall upwards past the cliff rock that crack her back, right back into the hands of Atlas, who gag her and throw her over the cliff again. Lilith look at her own body and imagine blood bursting from her belly. She look down at her black breasts and her belly and feel the night warmth telling her nothing. *What happen when the militia finally arrive, what we goin' do?*

—What they goin' do with near thousand nigger in revolt? Every able man must head east and make for the Cockpit Country. We goin' set up we own Maroon town. Watch how the place goin' be so big and so wide and so full of nigger that they can't do a thing to stop we. You think infantryman goin' head into wild bush just to hunt nigger? And even if they do, them not cut out for bush life. We goin' be ready, Homer say.

—We goin' starve, Lilith say under her breath, but Callisto look at her like she hear.

—You plan to drive cow, chicken and goat up there with you? Lilith say.

The room look at her.

—We make do with plantin', huntin' and thiefin' if we have to, Homer say.—You don't come from the Africa, you don't know. But we goin' back.

—Now me know you head take you.

—Not in body, you fool. That thickness must come from you white half. We goin' set things up like in the Africa. Six village in a circle, one to one to one.

—And what about the Maroons? Them niggers in league with backra ever since the treaty. They always turning in runaway nigger, Lilith say.—You know that yourself.

Lilith know that be the one thing that make Homer slip and she do. She pause, not too long for the others to notice but long enough that Lilith do.

—Maroons can go to hell. Them brutal when is one or two but coward like little girl when is many. You think is just three or four nigger running 'way? This be two hundred from here, three hundred from there and three hundred more from five or six estate. How them fi stop we? And if they try me will kill them meself! Pshaw! Saint-Domingue nigger can do it and they be the same nigger we be, that even you be. All it take is some smart thinking. That be why womens do the thinking and plotting, just like woman do in the Africa, Homer say.—You did know say is the woman pick the king in the Africa? The king be always the oldest sister's boy pickaninny. A woman who give birth to Ashanti man bigger than the man himself.

—Me didn't grow up in no Africa.

—That be the pity. Mean you still don't know what freedom be, even if me tell you plain. But you soon know, or God help all o' we.

Robert Quinn roll over on him back. She like to wait until he sleeping deep and climb in bed and lay down on him chest, with him hair feeling like a cushion. Quinn sleep heavy but he reach for cuddling whenever she touch him. That be the only time when Lilith let go of her being negro and he being backra. Is the only time when he touch her back and don't flinch. He caress the memory out of her. Sleeping on him back, he is new territory to discover. She can put her hand above him nose and feel him breath or rub her hand on him chest or run circles round him navel. She can even kiss Quinn on the neck or sometimes the lip but 'fraid to wake him up. But now Lilith can't go in the bed. Now she only watching. Now every time he turn she thinking 'bout something he do or say. Lilith don't know if she thankful or love-full. Or maybe she do know but niggerwoman must never say them things. What kinda nigger rather be slave to free? Why her mind getting heavy with them kinda question?

Make sure you don't give the backra no reason to stay.

On the way back from the cave Lilith walking with Homer. That time in Quinn kitchen feel like a long time ago and the womens now walk wide apart. Lilith in front trying to put all the Homers together. But maybe the time too late. There was a time when Homer was some-where between mother and sister, with the funny nasty talking that friend share with friend, like Dulcimena. But this new Homer nearly make Callisto slit her throat. This new Homer have no lightness 'bout her no more, not even when she make joke. This new Homer counting and planning all the time and talking too much in Africa tongue. This new Homer ask if Robert Quinn like dasheen and she should come in the morning and get some. Lilith want to ask if she plan on fattening him up before she kill him but hold her tongue.—Be wicked if you wish and good if you plan, but stop trying to be both, Lilith say but not to Homer. This strike her as something that Homer would say. A certain Homer anyway.

—And when you kill off the backra and burn down him estate, what next? Lilith say.

—Then we free, Homer say.

—Free? So it easy?

—We have the torch. All we need now is the spark.

—Surely.

—Nigger time now. Time to make we own life.

—And what happen after the militia come? What 'bout tomorrow? The day after that?

Homer stop.—Me done answer question, she say.

—You, who always have answer for everything? What going happen when the guns run out and the militia keep coming? What 'bout the Maroons?

Homer stop.

—We deal with that when we come to that. One thing at a time.

—Tell that to them nigger who don't know 'bout you. You sending all of them right into Maroon and militia hand. You who know better than anybody how they stay. What 'bout that?

Homer don't look at her.

—You really don't know. Jesus, you don't know.

—Lilith.

—Everybody so hot for blood nobody seeing true. You think you pickneys goin' come back?

—Quiet you mouth!

—You don't give damn 'bout no freedom or no black man land, you just want somebody to bleed for you pickney.

—Me say shut up! Or me'll make you every hole spit up blood before sunrise, you hear me?

—Sick and tired of hearing you.

—Me sure is not me you talking to.

—That make two of we, 'cause me sure is not you me talking to either.

Lilith and Homer still walking, Lilith in front. Both walking through a trail right in the middle of the cane piece.

—You think me is a idiot? Homer say.

Lilith stop and turn around.—Me think you is not you, she say.

—Me don't know why everybody in this plan but me know why you in it and is not no freedom business. And everybody goin' get capture or kill.

—You think this is just 'bout me? Mayhaps if you wasn't living on top of Irishman you'd ask somebody. Why you don't ask Iphigenia, eh? Why you don't ask why she always cover up like the time cold? Ask her what happen when them drivers see her by the fence and say she running away. How them tie her up, mash up some burning coal and sprinkle her body with it. Gal so scarred up that the only thing she show now be her finger. Why you think she chat so nasty 'bout fucking all the time? 'Cause she know that not even blind nigger goin' want her. You ask Callisto 'bout her one eye yet? You ask Hippolyta? She'd love to tell you. She'd love to tell a nigger anything.

—Then why she don't—

—You say you smart, so use you head. What kind of nigger you be, eh? One man hot up you bush and you change. He did nice when he leave all the mark on you back?

—He didn't whip me.

—Chile, if that is what you have to think to make the ruttin' sweeter, carry on.

—This not 'bout me, Homer, no matter what you say.

—It not 'bout me either! Damn fool. You must be the only nigger who not nigger. Besides, too late now. Every estate in the east goin' rise up. Freedom comin' whether you ready or not.

—Freedom, or death.

—One and the same in the colonies sometimes. Anything better than this. Negro blood cryin' out. You of all people, you supposed to hear when blood cry out.

—You know, it take me a long time to see that all you have is goddamn mouth and two Obeah trick.

—Myal.

—Me couldn't give two shake of a rat's arse.

—What a way you talk white these days, whiter than alabas—

—Oh, quit you mouth, Homer. 'Bout blood cry out. What you know 'bout blood? Blood don't nothing but red. Me, me smell them. You ever kill anybody? Me smell them.

—Is you mind.

—You is a right one to talk 'bout mind. Me smell them. Whatever me did want get from the white man, me get it and more. You can't understand that. You still want you blood. Me get my blood and see me here. Nothing different. Nothing better. Revenge don't leave me nothing but them burning skin smell that me can't blow out of me nose nor wash out.

—When we take over the estate, flesh goin' cook like goose.

—You listening to me?

—When you make sense me will listen to you.

—Of course, Homer. 'Cause everybody listen to you. All of them want to get free so bad them don't even see that you not making no sense. Not one thing 'bout this rebellion make sense—

—What don't make sense 'bout it, you damn Judas nigger? If you love slavery so bad then stay.

—Them dead, Homer. Too late now to try be a mother.

Homer try to slap Lilith but Lilith catch her hand. They look at each other for a long time before Lilith let go.

—You think you is woman? Homer say.

—Me think me is Lilith, Lilith say.

—Make sure you know which side you on.

—Is not me, me worried 'bout.

Homer head for the great house and Lilith head for Robert Quinn.

Lilith leave Robert Quinn sleeping and go to her room. The next morning coffee wake her up. She pull on her dress and go in the kitchen to see Robert Quinn pouring himself a mug.

—Morning, luv, he say.

Lilith nod and curtsy little bit, but then feel fool for doing so as soon as she do. Quinn dress himself in a blue shirt and black breeches. Him boots sleeping on the floor with yesterday mud all over. He place a straw hat on the table.—Feeling a wee bit like a peacock, he say. Quinn sit down. Lilith go over to the counter to commence making breakfast.

—I thought we had an understanding, lovey.

—Massa?

—I thought we understood that ye should make my bed yours from now on.

—No, massa, me didn't understand that.

—Well, I'm sure ye comprehend now.

—Yes, massa.

—Oh, do appear more pleased about it, lass, I'd think ye get no pleasure from lying with me.

—Oh no, massa. Me get plenty pleasing.

—Then condemn me to an empty bed no longer.

Lilith liking how he sounding. He sounding like verse man or singing man by what he saying and how he saying it. She 'bout to smile but a-frown.

—But you soon leave, Massa Robert.

—Aye, that's a truth that depresses me greatly, lovey. Depresses me greatly. There was at first only one here I held any great affection fer, now there's two. Two that I'll leave behind. Unless... unless. The devil I'll be. I shall be back before breakfast, he say, kiss her on the cheek and run though the door. Lilith wait on him and tap her toes. In a blink he come back through the door, cussing in Irish. He sit down on the table, pull on him boots, flash a smile at Lilith and go through the door again.

Breakfast didn't done cook before he come back. Robert Quinn swing open and slam the door into the wall. He stomp inside with him face redder than ever.

—The feckin' sniveling son of a jackal bitch! Consumed with spite he is, that feckin' bastard. Nothing but goddamn spite!

—Vindictive son of a bitch. Never in all me life seen a man with such malcontent as that whoreson, he say.

Robert Quinn sit down at the table and shuck off one boot, then the other.

—I'm sorry, luv, I'm far too cross to eat.

Lilith set down the plate anyway. He stare at it for a while, then look at her. He pick up a johnnycake, dip it in gravy and eat.

—I tried to buy ye, Robert Quinn say. Lilith nearly drop her plate. —I tried to buy ye, but the bastard said no. No, he says. Just no! Oh, he's wicked now, him and his whoring wife to be!

—Massa Robert!

—I shall not hold me feckin' tongue in me own goddamn house! I worked good and hard fer it indeed. He thinks this is the end of it, he's sadly mistaken. When word gets out about what his future wife does in Kingston, he'll be sorry he crossed the likes of Robert Quinn, ye can bet on that, lassie, aye! Ye can wager good!

MISS ISOBEL RIDE TO KINGSTON LIKE A DEMON CHASING HER. Robert Quinn, for all him riding, was no expert horseman like she. Galloping down the Half Way Tree Road, he didn't have nothing to guide him but the dust she leave and him own memory of where he go for whorin' when he and Massa Humphrey set foot in the city. He ride down Orange Street, empty at night, and go to turn back 'cause he think he miss her. But few people up and about at this hour and fewer still on horseback. He sees her. Her horse trottin' now and she in Massa Humphrey black coat and breeches and her boots shiny. Orange Street is where all the markets be for fruits and liquor and hogs and fowl, but by the three o'clock hour the only thing on the street be rubbish and rats. And the beggars. A white one stagger up to Quinn begging for a quid or a pence, matey, and Quinn slip him foot out of he saddle and kick him away. The man land flat on him arse and just hiss and ask the road for a farthing then, matey.

Miss Isobel turn down a lane. Quinn never got the name but it head west. Save for one or two lantern that hang above an inn or a tavern, the lane did darker than hell. There be nothing but more rubbish and more rats squeaking and scurrying that too dark to see. Quinn think to dismount, but there was no way he was goin' leave him horse in that place. He ride slow while Miss Isobel trot, mayhaps eighty or a hundred yards ahead of him. Miss Isobel stop at a crossroad and tie off her horse at a building on the corner. As she slip inside, Quinn gallop.

Hog's Breath Inn and Tavern the sign say, the words under a real boar head. Quinn at the corner of the lane and Oxford Street, the beginning of the west end. Greenwich, the contraband port, not far. Hog's Breath tower over all of the lane like it be a lighthouse. Quinn go to knock on the door but it push open, and smell rush him like four whore going at him at once. He grab him nose with him left hand and pull out him kerchief with him right. Lantern all over the wall but the room still feel dark and smell of liquor and lustiness and shit. And sawdust and old food and mildew. Four or five mens sprawled by the bar, two of them sleeping on the counter. The barmaid sitting and looking into the dark like she seeing everything and nothing. A big fat man in old infantry clothes stumble away with a whore who was pulling him along by the crotch. They go upstairs and Quinn follow them with him eye. He look around. A negro fiddler off to the side playing like for dead people. He one of the few who not a-snoring or a-groping or a-fuckin' in the dark. Lantern on the table and lantern on the floor that glow on men's teeth and hand and ears but hide they eyes. Light glow on women's legs that man caressing, and petticoats that man lifting, and bosoms that man squeezing but hide they head. Quinn know this bar. A whore, a white woman with dark teeth and cheeks speckle from the pox, come to Quinn and grope him before he could stop her. He push her away and she barrel into two mens, who get up to fight but fall down from drunkenness. Quinn look around but don't see Miss Isobel. Gone upstairs, she must be.

So much stink fight for space in the inn that a nose would think there be no smell at all. But upstair be more smells, human funk, not liquor like downstairs. There be rumours of a opium den in Kingston but Quinn never would have guess that this is where it be. He push open a room and see white mens, some old, some not so old, and one of them—a short fat man, naked save for him stockings—asking where him wig be, even though it still atop him head. Four or five men in cots, three or four on the floor, Quinn couldn't say for sure, but they all, save for the man looking for him wig, smoking opium. He hear a sound, a giggle, a titter, he not sure but not a sound that a man make, not even the sorta men that sometime flock these parts.

The voice coming from behind him. Quinn try to walk slow, but him boot thick and heavy and each step is a boom. He push open the door and step right into the blade of a sword.

—When she said she was being followed, I thought it was her knack for storytellin' actin' up agin. Seems the bitch was right.

Quinn couldn't say nothing. The room was blue from a oil lamp in the corner with a blue shade, the wick almost gone. The man scrape the sword right across Quinn's throat.

—Who are you?

—Robert Quinn. Robert Quinn, sir. A gentleman.

—A gentleman, you say?

—Aye, and what have ye done with her?

—An Irish gentleman? Quite like a virtuous whore, is it not? The man laugh but the blade was still firm at Quinn throat.—Sir, I'm a liar, killer, thief and whoremonger. I have no qualms about slicing your head off.

—So yer also a coward, then, are you? I should—

—You shall do no such thing! Or I—

—So louddddd. Why sooooo loud?

Is then Quinn look at the bed. Is there Miss Isobel be, her yellow hair spread right across the bed like wine spill. Her legs spread too, like scissors one second, then close up. Her hands stretch across the bed and her breasts free. She looking in they direction but don't notice Quinn. Quinn think she look at him like a blind man would, turning where she hear a sound, but the eyes wet and blank, like she seeing nothing. Her legs scissors open again and stay open. Her pussy bush redder than the wick. She raise one hand to wrap her forehead, then flap back down on the bed like the hand faint from tiredness. Quinn couldn't say nothing. He think to say a million things but he couldn't say nothing.

—You have a guest. A friend.

—Fooli-foolishness dat. Only friend me 'ave down the . . . down the . . . bottom of that bottl—Where the bottle? Where the bottle . . . bombo-claat sum'bitch?

—Ye lousy piece of Greenwich pond scum! Defiled her, ye have!

—Defiled, you say? The man move him sword away from Quinn. Quinn go to grab him musket, then remember that when he rush to follow Miss Isobel he didn't pack it. The man laugh.

—Can I help it if milady hankers for the sweet stuff? Nobody in the room who has no cause to be 'cept you, of course.

Is then Quinn realise that he know the man. He still hard to see in the dark but even in the indoor he still have on the top hat tilt to one side of him head. Him coat on the floor. Quinn thought it was blue but soon see that it purple. The top hat be all he wearing and he stiff.

—Fer Godsakes, man. She's a grieving woman.

—She's not grieving tonight. Tonight she's mad with happiness and tomorrow more so.

—I shall take her. Now!

—Came by her own free will, she did, the man say and lift up his sword.—And by her own free will shall she leave. Now you can either join the play—she hankers for that as well—or get lost.

Miss Isobel start to bellow that she want more. Quinn don't know what to do. Even though for her him have a monstrous hate, he couldn't leave her be. Mayhaps she done with crying and take to doing this, but something stop him from going over to her. She be a lady after all. Or no. He don't know. The man laugh again and climb onto the bed. He wave a mug over her and she grab at it like a greedy pickney. She cuss for him to give it to her. At once. Quinn never hear her speak like a negro before. She and the man who might be white or octoroon.

—Your Irish boy is seeing the ways of the colonies, he say and laugh again.—Is dis you want, raasclaat whore?

Isobel still grabbing for the mug. The man straddle her. He pour some on him fingers and she grab him hand and lap it up so hard he have to yank him hand away. He cup him palm and pour some again and she grab him hand and drink out of it. Then the man look at Quinn. He grab him balls and cock an' pour the mixture all over it. Quinn stagger backways and dash out of the room. But he didn't leave the inn. He don't know why. He don't know what make him stay. What make him take a chair in the corner by a table where two man was snoring and over by the window a woman was hopping up and down a man lap. He there a long time and almost doze off but one of the snoring mens fall off him stool and crash on the floor. Quinn look around and wish he had at least a knife. He wonder if Miss Isobel still up in the room. He wonder how she know the man with the top hat who he remember now from the Roget funeral. Then she run down the stairs. She try to shove her hair back in her hat and stuff her blouson in her man breeches. She about to stumble and grab on to the banister. She look around and shriek. Then she run and almost drop two time. She push through the tavern doors and out she gone.

When Robert Quinn tell Lilith all of this he look like he expecting her to cuss or laugh or wish more evil 'pon the woman. But Lilith didn't do nothing. Nothing at all. That make Robert Quinn hang down him face and she feel queer-like that it matter to him what she think. They was in the kitchen, Quinn at the table where he usually be, watching her cook. Lilith feel he smiling behind her when he tell her.

—I'd near think ye pity the bitch, he say.

—Yes, yes, massa. It sad, though.

—What cause for melancholy does she give ye? Bitch does what she wants, as women do in the colonies. That Humphrey is engaged to her, that's what sad. Feckin' grievous.

—If you say so, massa.

—Do ye have any idea how I've grown to despise that word? Reminds me of Humphrey.

—Is not plenty word that slave had to call white people, massa. That be the one word you give we.

—Lilith, lovey, there's no other man, not a living soul, in this kitchen but yerself and I.

Robert Quinn get up and move over to her. He wrap him arms around her waist and pull her in tight.—My given name is Robert. Some have even been known to call me Robby.

Lilith feel like she can't breathe. White people and black people have a understanding. A code and neither side must break it or there will soon be hell to pay. A white man don't break it if he sexing a nigger, but he break it if mouth and mouth or mind and mind come together.

—Robert, he whisper. Robert.

Lilith start to tremble. She close her eyes and feel him hands traveling up and down her belly, like he looking for an entrance to push through and touch her heart. He kiss her neck and ears and Lilith stiffen. Her hand grip the knife hard. She can't cut no turnip or carrot. She slip 'way from him and go into her room. In the room she hear him coming.

—Luv, I'm distressed that I'm leaving as well. He open him mouth to say something more but he don't. He look like he about to enter the room but he don't. Robert turn and go away. Lilith feeling shudders come over her like wave. She think of Robert Quinn trying to get her to call him like a man instead of a massa. Like she and he be combolo. She keep feeling that some spirit somewhere, perhaps the skinny dark woman, goin' call it wrong and tap her chest seven time. She know the spirit would be right and that white man can come in close to her all he wish, for he is white man. But it not so easy anymore calling him white and she black and that be that. And her mind going tired at saying the same thing over and over. It supposed to mean something that he white and she black, he massa and she slave, and she can't just think that he be man and she be woman and leave that be. But Quinn be the only living soul to look at her as just that, a woman. Not the niggers, not even Homer, who look 'pon her like she be the angel that kilt all them pickney in Bible chapter Exodus. Her mind weary from thinking about Robert Quinn, so Lilith switch to what Miss Isobel doing in Kingston. Now Lilith remembering the smell of Miss Isobel man clothes whenever she come back from riding at night. Between tobacco and rum there was still another smell that perplex her and now she know what. Something that only the mad or the debauched man who haunted with devil supposed to take.

Lilith think that Miss Isobel trying to get back what Lilith take 'way. But people make they own bed and is they fault when they lie in it. Do she mean she or Miss Isobel? Lilith don't know. Maybe both, maybe neither. Lilith want to believe what white people say 'bout black people, that black people thinking be so simple and fool that they don't really think. But her thinking not be simple. Right there, she want white man to be right. She want white man to be right so bad. Lilith hear boots stomp into the house.

—Robby? she hear.

—Robert?

She know the voice. Lilith wipe her face and compose herself. She go to move and stop, wondering if she should just make him call and call until he leave. She go out to the kitchen.

—He not here, massa, she say.

Massa Humphrey nod but don't say nothing. He dress in new dark blue coat with tails and him cravat tie tight. She never see him in cream breeches before and him boots well shine. He put the hat on and turn to leave. But then he turn round sudden and Lilith jump. She think she shriek but don't know. A look flash in him eye for a second, the thing, the spirit, the what-she-don't-know that Lilith see before when he strike her and was ready to do more. He by the door, she by the room, fifteen to eighteen feet between them, but Lilith feel Massa Humphrey hands round her neck. She touch her neck and look away.

—So you're the one who's bedeviled my overseer, he say. Lilith don't say nothing.

—Be sure to inform Mr. Quinn that I seek him, he say and leave. Lilith feel the boots stomping on the floor. She still rubbing her neck when the horse whinny and gallop away.

Crop-time sun beating down negro and white man too. Robert Quinn be the man that keep things in order but he not there and order fall 'pon the other white drivers, most of whom don't know nothing 'bout overseeing and would usually be occupied with sighting out which nigger girl they taking to bed that night. One slave put down her bundle to go tie the next and the white driver ask if she skylarking. She say, No, massa, no, that is where the bundle to go and he say she drop it 'cause she lazy. The driver put down him rum flask and go over to her and whip her with the cowskin till her screaming stop the whole coffle in that part of the cane piece. Three other driver who was off by a tree see the whipping and start laugh, saying if he use too much of that whip on her she'll be no use tonight when he using him other whip. But then they see that the other negroes stop work and start watch. When nigger gang working they is one, but when them stop they is sixty. Sixty tall mens and womens. Thirty-seven mens who shoulder wide like tree trunk, twenty-three womens who strong leg can kick down cow. Sixty negro eye times two. Sixty hoe, sixty pickaxe, sixty cutlass, sixty ways to shed blood and just four backra. Two of four by the tree run into the deep field and start whipping nigger to get back to work, and shouting for the lazy Johnny-jumpers. A driver shout to the one whipping the girl to quit. They strike four nigger and move quick through the field, from one to the other, whipping careless and missing most of the time. The Johnny-jumpers join in. Some of the slaves stay still. The white mens start to shout out for other white mens to come over to this section. They whip again and some of the niggermen turn back to work, but some still stand straight. The white mens start to back away. The womens go to the mens and whisper and they finally go back to work. Callisto and Iphigenia work in the field.

—I just tell one woman to whisper to one man and send it down the field, Callisto tell Homer when she recalling what happen. Homer outside the kitchen getting water from the well. Lilith by the well too with her bucket. Both watching the afternoon. Homer cuss.

—That's why me can't abide by niggerman, you know, that why they have no damn use, the lot o' them, she say.

—How we fi rebel without the mens? No them have the strength? Lilith say.

—Yes, they strong in arm and strong in leg, but they head weak. They don't have the bearing for planning and thinking and waiting, 'specially waiting. That be woman work. If you did—

—If me did come from the Africa me would know. Me hear that the last ten time you tell me. Well, this not be the Africa, Homer.

—Don't me know it. No, this be nigger hell, but we soon turn it into nigger heaven. Just like Saint-Domingue. Me have word from the massa himself. He get letter from Barbados hearing that the Saint-Domingue nigger trying to unite the island. You hear that? They going call it a republic. Me hear that, me almost want cry.

—You? You so dry you can't even spit.

—Watch you mouth. But you right. Me all cry out, me no have no crying left in me. What a way you have sass when you deh with nigger. Round white man you can barely talk, unless him singing Irish shanty.

Callisto laugh.

—Massa Humphrey estate getting restless 'cause he dismiss Robert Quinn, Homer say.

—Nigger 'fraid they not goin' be no Christmas this year, Callisto say.

—Nigger have bigger thing to worry 'bout than no damn backra day. The fruit ripe and in three day we pluck it.

Callisto laugh again and say she have to sneak back to the field. —The way them whitey stupid and careless, me all catch forty wink yesterday, she say and run.

—And the mens? Lilith say.

—Set a dog loose only when you need he to run.

—Massa Humphrey was looking for Robert.

—Looking for him?

—Yes. Me don't know why.

—Maybe he checking if he pack and ready. Quinn wasn't there?

—Robert did gone.

—Oh.

Homer pause for a long, long bit.—Don't make a white man work you again, Lilith. You is not them and them is not you, no matter how soft he touch you these days.

—No man working me.

—Stop the lying, chile. The man work himself right through you bed and now he working right through you head.

—Me say me not—

—You just call the damn man Robert! Two time, fool! Two time! Me just hear you.

—Me...me...

—From me was ten year, me be slave. Me never ask for it and no man have the right to give it to me. If white man want to fuck you, there nothin' you can do 'bout that, but don't make him fool you, that be your business.

—He not like the other mens.

—True indeed, your man special. He so special he goin' married you quick. That must be it, he goin' married a nigger gal—pardon me, mulatto gal—and breed up plenty quadroon pickney. Then you goin' have pretty house and you goin' even get you own slave to whip. Just like he still be whipping and killing nigger.

—Stop it.

—You stop it. Look down the well, gal, look in this bucket, you know what you seeing? A nigger who not going be a woman till she take womanhood for herself. And you goin' have to shed blood to do it. There be four nigger on this estate that we can't trust. Four nigger who getting them business fix tonight. Don't make it be five.

—Me not 'fraid of you. And me not 'fraid of death either.

—You think so?

—You is the one who say me have the darkness in me.

Homer silent.—Look, you and me not got no cause to disagree, she say. Lilith grab her bucket and turn to walk away.

—You ever hear them talk 'bout Venice?

Lilith stop.

—One, two time, she say.

—Right. And they talk 'bout it like they not supposed to talk 'bout it.

—Yeah.

—Come with me.

Homer take Lilith inside the great house, through the kitchen, turning right down the hallway. They pass the sitting room first, then the conservatory. Further down near the end be the library, where Massa Humphrey is most of the time when he not sleeping. Lilith don't remember it. She go inside and see a dim, dusty room with shelf and shelf of book that pile so high that they near touch the roof. The shelves swing right round the room and stop at the wide windowsill that look out to the Blue Mountain. That be where Massa Humphrey put him desk. Homer look outside through the window. Then she go back to the door and look left, then right.

—Miss Isobel upstairs, Homer say.—She and the dressmaker trying to figure how to make the wedding dress hide the belly.

Homer go behind the desk and start look through books on the shelf to the right. She run over the books with her finger and stop. Then she run over again. She pull one out and cuss, then pull out the one right beside it.

—Ah! Homer say and put her lips to the top like she goin' kiss it. She blow and dust scatter like smoke. She open couple page and run across the page with her finger.

—This be the book, the very one here, she say and put the book down on the desk. Lilith move over.

—Me can't read write-up word, she say. Homer hiss and pick up the book.

Entry the____

I've lost track of days and dates and time is a monster to me. Venice! Quinn impressed on me that pantaloons were quite common and knee breeches the mark of a true gentleman. I asked him how would he have known and this remark seemed to have wounded him greatly. I apologised and such was his good, cheery nature that he let bygones be. He makes me think of the West Indies and what it would be like. Maybe the Irish do have more fire in their chests. Ah, Venice, the Madonna of whores, the whore of Madonnas. The Piazzetta is enough to make Virgils or Blakes out of the most common of men. Alas, it is Carnevale and I venture forth to meet my destiny. Let her be pleasing in bosom and bawdy in speech, for this is Sodom. Onward!

Entry the____

Two days in Venice. Sodom AND Gomorrah.

Entry the____

Encountered a few of the fairer sex last night. Fairer than our Prince Regent's own mistress, I daresay. But do I call them fair? They seemed ripe for the plucking, for the man with a fat purse, of course. One in particular strikes me, but alas I am not as bold as Quinn.

—Enough of this shit, Homer say and turn five more page, then backwards two.—See it deh! This one, she say, and poke the book twice.

Entry the____

The most despicable of villains is better than I. Oh, the malcontent that resides in this poor, poor flesh. I regret that grief brings me to verse and makes a mockery of it. But how was I led? Oh God, but that this poor flesh.... None of this was my intention, but one day God will lord his judgement over me. The night was young and already filled with young men with the devil in their hearts and blackness in their souls. I will try to be curt. We came upon ladies of the night, women of the oldest profession, who spoke a smattering of English. One I took fancy to and I daresay it was mutual. She carried her fan in the right hand, across her face when she looked at me and I know the ways of Venice. I knew an arrangement was to be had. Then she placed the fan in her left hand and opened it. That confirmed her intentions, surely that must have been so! She led me to her boudoir. Quinn, out of magnanimity, took her friend, who was rather unfed and not as fair. She reached for my sword, so daring was she! and I, I will not repeat such things here, for they are best left out. But she was a thief and she played me for a fool. Thinking I was asleep she rummaged through my things until I made a noise and startled her. She ran for the door but I was swift and I caught her. She had a little knife. It felt like but a little prick but the little knife was deep in my shoulder. Maybe it was the sight of my own blood that made the devil possess me. I forgot all that was intelligent, decent and manly. She grabbed my face and scratched me. This made me even more furious and less sensible. My hands were the devil's and they worked her. Quinn rushed in and used all of that Irish strength to pull me away. I would not be denied. I started to fight him as well, but he overpowered me. The woman cursed and cursed, saying that she will go for a magistrate for she knows we are British. Then go, you filthy whore, Quinn says and brushed her away. I'm no whore says she in English, sputtering, I remember. And right there both myself and Quinn realised that this lady, if she can be called that, knew or was perhaps accustomed to far beyond her station. A woman seeking her own pleasure was she, perhaps no different from us young men who come to Venice Carnevale with too much blood in our constitutions. There was no question that against two Britons this woman would be listened to. Oh, she went on about how she would tell how she was dragged from her lodgings and ravished, she a poor young lady of the city. And how these men were from the British Isles who were at war with their cousins the French. Quinn grabbed her by the hand and dragged her out the door. I was not listening for it, so the first clubbing sound shocked me to the very bone. Two more came hence. I looked towards the doorway and there was Quinn, wiping his cane and telling me that we must leave Venice that very night. He would arrange it. I try not to think of it. This demon within me. I had not been so furious, so bereft of good sense since I divested Thomas Thistlewood of his front teeth and punched his eye shut at that tavern in the East End. Quinn stopped me there as well. I remember that is how we met. Now he comes along, I daresay to save me from my own madness. Now resides inside me the hope that this will never be known and the fear that one day it will.

—That be how them two work. Massa Humphrey make the mess and Massa Quinn clean it up. You was him last mess, if me memory right. You still think he be angel? Well, angel soon bawl for him tea, so take you bucket and go, Homer say.

—Is what Massa Robert do to that woman?

—What wrong with you? First you can't read, now you can't hear?

—What he do to that woman?

—What you think, girl chile? You born fool? He quiet her.

—What that mean?

—Don't try me patience, gal. She cussing-cussing one minute, then Robert Quinn take her out, then three blow and all the cussing stop. He quiet her the same way them nearly quiet you. Them same two.

—That don't—

—Don't what? You must be horse, 'cause them blinkers 'pon you tight. Whatever story you want to make up so you can still make him tea and get sweet fuckin' is your business. But don't say you didn't see for yourself.

Lilith leave her.

—*Where've ye been? he say.* Lilith jump. Robert Quinn in the kitchen waiting for her. Him eyes heavy. Lilith wonder if him still keep that cane in a safe place. Lilith step inside so slow that one foot knock the other foot. She know he looking at her and she can't look at him. Between what she hear 'bout Quinn and what she see is what she know, and Lilith don't know what that is. Then he jump up from him seat and knock it over. He jump at her and Lilith shriek. He didn't hear. He grab her by the waist and wrap him arm round her. He squeeze tight and lift her up, then he bury him face in her bosom and wiggle him head around and laugh out loud.

—By God, I think Humphrey has come to his senses, lovey! He's asked me to stay!

· 28 ·

So it come to pass that nobody could find Athena. Lilith know what happen. Or at least she know what Homer know. Lilith wondering if Athena actually guilty, for Homer looking lately like she who would do something terrible just over what somebody might do. Sometimes Homer talk to her dead pickneys, telling them that they going back to the baba-pla as soon as they can rest in peace. The rest she say in Africa-speak and Lilith stop trying to figure out what she mean. Most time, Homer do this early in the morning when she alone in the kitchen and Lilith by the door outside, listening for what Homer saying to herself. Sometimes Homer chant, sometimes she very silent save for sniffling and moaning. Whenever she do that Lilith try to imagine what her children used to look like, if they was skinny and grey like Homer.

Lilith up early in the morning because her mind heavy again. Homer and Miss Isobel. Seem death pull and pull away at woman until all she have left is her common sense. But then death pull that away too. One woman drinking laudanum and the other want to drink blood. Lilith don't want to go inside the kitchen to talk to Homer, so she go back to

Robert Quinn quarters. On the way back she pass by the greenhouse. That early in the morning Lilith don't expect nobody but as she pass by she hear a voice. Gorgon, she think, either talking in her sleep or getting rut by some dirty little niggerman. Lilith think about this and can't picture any man rutting that midget. This make Lilith curiouser. Lilith hear the voice again, rough and gruff, like a little man, like Gorgon, but she hear another voice too, a sharp whisper that both loud and quiet. Callisto. The third voice she can't reckon. But she know that she know it. She know well enough to not like that voice at all. Lilith push herself up to the window and look inside. There beyond row and row and shelf and pot of hibiscus and rose and tulip and bougainvillea, they whispering and talking: Gorgon, Callisto and Iphigenia. Gorgon excitable as usual, swinging her hands up and down and jabbing as if she stabbing cow. Callisto shake her head and touch Gorgon shoulder. Gorgon push her off. Callisto slap Gorgon shoulder and Gorgon yelp. She go to rush Callisto but Iphigenia jump in the way and hold her back, saying something that Lilith can't hear. Then Iphigenia say something, looking first at Gorgon and then at Callisto. Both hold they head down low until Iphigenia done talk. Then they quiet. Then Callisto say something and Gorgon nod. Iphigenia smile and go to say something but she look up suddenly. Lilith stoop down quick and wonder if she get catch. Gorgon she could outrun and Iphigenia, but not Callisto. She hear they voices again and look up slow. Iphigenia again doing the talking. Callisto finger on her mouth as she nod yes. Gorgon mouth say something that look like *now*. Lilith sure. Then they set to leave and Lilith jump. She look left and right and have nowhere to go. The doorway in her direction. Lilith rush to the side of the greenhouse, moving round the side as they coming, almost step for step. She hide by the side as they leave.

—Bitch have it coming, Gorgon say.

Lilith wait until they out of earshot. There be only one nigger on this estate that Gorgon, Callisto and Iphigenia all hate.

She run back to Robert Quinn quarters. Lilith all sweaty and trembling and she touch her chest trying to calm herself. Gorgon, Iphigenia and Callisto all plotting 'gainst her. But how she to know? As much as they can't stand Lilith, she don't give none of them niggers reason to fix her business. Lilith can't imagine what she do. She start to think that she reading two meaning out of one word, that she becoming Homer. Then she remember that most of them did angry that Homer did break the six and add on a seven again, 'specially since the last number seven was that bitch Circe. But Circe not a turncoat at all, just not the monster nigger that Homer want. Lilith look round for the biggest, sharpest knife in the kitchen. A hand grab her by the waist and she scream. Robert Quinn laugh as he lift her up.

—Lord, lassie, 'tis only me. Wasn't going to trouble ye, but since yer up, fix us some breakfast, luv, he say.

Robert Quinn gone off to the field and Lilith figuring that since Callisto and Iphigenia work outdoors, she don't have need to fear them two. That leave Gorgon. Lilith think about Callisto and Gorgon and hate them more, especially Gorgon because she just add one more thing to make her mind heavy. Maybe is heaviness that driving Homer to talk to her dead pickney, cooing like they be baby one minute and chanting like they be African spirit the other. But Gorgon is a coward, Lilith come to see, and she not goin' act alone. At least so she hope. Lilith start to wonder if there be anywhere that she goin' have a little peace. And the only person that make her smile is a white devil that used to whip her. She want to hate him for taking her into the room of white woman feelings because a nigger know that sooner or later something or someone goin' remind her that she black. Maybe Callisto. Maybe Quinn. Now that he staying, one more weight get put on her back and she can't stand it. Sometimes she wish the great God would come and flood out everybody again. The field, the estate and the county. The country and the world. Maybe everybody start again and slave is free and free is slave. She chuckle.

Lilith in the kitchen trying to get Homer alone. No sign of Athena. Miss Isobel come down and ask where she be and Homer say that she sickly bad and confine to her hut. Miss Isobel ask to see her and Homer say that she too sickly ma'am, with the flux, a lady like you the flux will kill for sure. At first Miss Isobel screw up her face. Lilith remember that Miss Isobel know nigger ways and nobody fool her about bloody flux the last time. Lilith feel her heart beating but Homer still like a tree. Then Miss Isobel turn to go back upstairs, the flask sticking through her dress like a third titty.

—Pigskin bitch. You can smell it 'pon her a mile away, Homer whisper to Lilith.

—Pig smell?

—Paregoric. What, you is the only nigger that don't smell it too?

—Not paregoric, laudanum, Lilith say, but not to Homer.

Homer mixing batter in a bowl for cake.

—Soon come the mistress birthday, Homer say.—Cake coming today, present coming tomorrow.

Lilith wonder if that was Homer talking like Homer.

—We need to have words, Lilith whisper.

—We need to have words, eh? Me don't think you have nothing me need.

—Eehi? You think so, how about you needing me to keep quiet?

Homer mixing the batter but she look up a Lilith. Her eyes red but pale. Lilith look at Homer brows and her hair getting whiter.

—What evil deh 'pon you now? Homer say.

—Me'd tell you but wall have ears and floor love chat, Lilith say, looking at Pallas.

—Didi.

—Dido they call me. Get the name right one time, the little girl say.

—Dido, dodo, doo-doo, go on mix this till you can't see no more grain, Homer say as she hand over the batter to a girl that Lilith not sure she see before. Outside they commence to walking but not so far that a driver would ask what business they have outside of the house.

—What happen to the old girl?

Homer laugh.—You in Massa Quinn bed too long, she say.

—And you too . . . You know what? I can't bother.

—The old girl is a no-girl now. Some uncanniness happen where Miss Isobel clothes all cover in mud and stink with liquor and whatever and the mistress say is the girl thief out her clothes to parade around and do nastiness and then try to put it back in her room when the mistress catch her.

—What?

—What is right. Thieving is serious business on this estate. Johnny-jumpers deal with her quick.

—All this happen and me never know?

—That be the way with you of late. Anyway, me have cake to bake so talk you talk.

—Where Athena be?

—Athena be where she can best help the struggle. This is what you call me out for, woman?

—What you do to her?

—Look around you, chile. How you think this goin' end? Anyway, you don't seem to have no reason for taking up me time so me gone—

—Callisto and Gorgon plotting something.

—Eehi.

—Callisto, Gorgon and Iphigenia.

—Surely.

—Me see for meself. This morning in the planthouse.

—You see them plotting.

—That is what me say.

Homer pause for a long while. Then she turn and go. Lilith go after her.

—That is it? That is all you have to say? Me say they plotting.

—And me hear you.

—How you know they not plotting they own thing? Against you?

—Well, Homer say and pause.—We all soon know what we know.

Homer go to leave but Lilith grab her hand.—Put a end to it, Homer. This getting out of hand.

—For why? All you care 'bout is Mr. Irish.

—And all you care 'bout is dead pickney. As soon as you hear them dead, you dead too.

—Leggo me bloodcloth hand if you know what good for you.

Lilith let go and Homer continue to walk. Then she stop.—Besides, that ship sail off already. Nothing we can do 'bout it now, she say. You goin' tell the estates and tell the niggers to forget free? You think any nigger want to spend they days under white man but you? Lilith watch her go back to the kitchen. She remember a Homer who use to walk so fast that she almost fly and had a back so straight that she seem like her own wall. Not this Homer now.

Lilith go back to her house. She go the door and hear somebody rummaging through the cupboard. She smile.

—If massa not hungry for one thing, he hungry for anoth—

Gorgon jump. She drop a knife. Homer say it before but she didn't notice it, how Gorgon 'fraid of her since she come back.

—What you want?

—Me no want nothing from you. Me gone to Worthy Park Estate since dem don't know how fi grow flower. Homer say to tell you—

—Me just see Homer.

—Homer say—

—You deaf, midget? Me say me just see her. Anything she need to tell me she can tell me her damn self.

—You goin' want to know when next we meet.

—Two day hence.

—No. Tonight.

. . .

Night promising to come and Lilith dreading. Not even Robert Quinn latest mission, to teach her how to read this John Donne, can take her mind off the dread. Perhaps Quinn sense something or not, but he don't say. He go to sleep with Lilith resting on him chest. She wait until he start to snore.

In the kitchen, Lilith grab a knife. She swing and dash and jab and cut in the dark. Then she imagine jumping a woman, grabbing her hair and slashing her throat. But Lilith know there is nothing she can do about six womens. And who knows, maybe they after somebody else. Maybe they after Homer. And even if is Lilith, she kill plenty people already so they better watch out. Lilith make the badness push her out the door, but fear was making her slower. She step one foot then the next in the grass. A owl fly past with a big rat in her claws. Lilith put the knife in her apron and set out for the cave.

By Lilith own reckoning, seven people dead because of her. Eight when she count the poor nigger girl who get lynched for what she do. Maybe she sick with murderer madness, she think. Lilith curse her mind that give her the madness to kill, then leave her with nothing to live with being a killer. The number stop her as she walk. She look at her hand and don't see no monster. Don't every niggerwoman have blood on they hands? Mayhaps that be the nigger way. This colony always one step away from bloodshed anyway and mayhaps she not different, no better, no worse than any other soul. Then another Lilith raise her voice, a Lilith that silent for the most part, to say that it is evil whitey who dead, a son of a bitch like Massa Roget and a plain bitch like Mistress Roget, and a dead whitey can't hurt nobody. And them two boys would have just grow up to become monsters raping and killing negroes, as be the desire of every white man in the colony.

But the other Lilith say, You stupid nigger, memory tricking you. Is not seven or eight, is nine. Lilith remember the eye first, then the nose and the mouth and even her pussy and arse spitting blood on her little daughter. Andromeda, who dead over nothing but a dress that Lilith get whip and rape by white man for. Maybe she be not the child of Jack Wilkins but Satan himself. Seven souls, she thinking. Nine souls. What kind of woman can walk right after killing seven souls? Nine souls. And what about Bessy, the old nigger woman from Coulibre? Was she nine or ten? And what about that jumper nigger the first time? The sound of numbers run around her head and Lilith in the darkness and can't remember if she set the fire because McClusky dingus go up in her pussy or the Massa Roget finger, or if the mistress whip her or Miss Isobel. Homer said this 'bout the girl who they think burn down the house: you can't kill so many people and don't kill a part of yourself too. Homer said that once, but not to Lilith.

At the mouth of the cave Lilith feel for the knife in her apron. A weak light flickering inside, light from one candle. Lilith don't hear no voice. Perhaps an ambush waiting in the cave. She feel for the knife again, thinking that she should take the thing out or at least grab the handle.

—Move, a voice say.

—If you know wha' good fi you, say another.

Gorgon. Gorgon behind Callisto so her mouth free. Lilith grip the handle of the knife tighter as she step into the cave and move towards the light. She feel other people behind her and wish she could run. She think to draw the knife but the blade might glint even in the weak light and give her away too quick. Lilith wonder if this is justice, if God finally decide to deal with her. If dead niggerwoman and broke-neck white woman and drowning white man and burnin' pickneys all laughing and waiting for her to come knocking at hell gateway. Lilith stop and somebody push her down.

—Well, look who decide to finally join we, Homer say.

Lilith move over to the side and make sure her back to the rock.

—Worthy Park nigger let loose that plot afoot in Montego Bay. Most of the militia heading west, Callisto say.

—Good.

—Not so good. Word also spreading 'bout Montpelier, that we might frig things up.

—Who the raas say that?

—Nobody have to say nothing. Me not sure me hear one straight plan from you yet, other than to do what everybody doin', Callisto say. Nothing but silence follow her.—Who we killing first, massa or mistress? Where we setting fire to, east or west? Cane field or ratoon? What we goin do 'bout the other Montpelier turncoat niggers? Where everybody heading when they flee, through the river or over the Blue Mountain? You do anything but tell we nigger verse?

Homer look 'pon Callisto for a long time. Lilith trying to read her face but it lost in the dark. Pallas looking on the ground and Gorgon look up and down and sideway.

—Tell Worthy Park—

—Mayhaps you tell them youself.

—Oh. Is so it go. Everybody bright and uppity nowadays. Is you plan this whole bloodclaat thing or is me? Is you bring everybody here or is me? Is you make you hungry for free or is me?

—Cool yourself, Homer. We don't—

—Don't tell me to cool meself! Me be the head nigger here! Me!

Everybody quiet and looking round at each other. Lilith watching from the side, trying to pick Homer out in the dim light. Homer stop pace.

—Worthy Park nigger got no call to talk 'bout me, no damn call! Them same damn fool go tell white man the plan last year. White man! Take two nigger to fix that backra business and one more to make it look like mishap.

Homer start to laugh.

—Backra won't know what clock a-strike when we cut him throat, Homer say.

—Eehi? Callisto say.—Maybe backra laughing already.

—Enough with you, Homer say.

—Pallas, some people here so chummy with white people dat dey tongue loose. Loose like dey mouth turn whore, Callisto say, but Pallas don't say nothing.

Lilith feel for the knife in her apron and grab the handle. She push herself further back into the rock. Pallas fidget, Iphigenia start chuckle and Hippolyta stand off by the light. Lilith feel her heart about to burst through her bosom.

—Somebody here done love slave life so much that nobody can come between her and backra loving.

—Callisto, chat you chat and stop trying to be Homer, Pallas say.

—Eehi. Seem Homer perfect picking not so perfect. A Judas nigger in here. Right in here wid we.

Homer not saying nothing.

—Who? Pallas say.

—She, Gorgon say and point.

Lilith jump. She scream and Callisto appear from the dark behind Iphigenia, grab her by the hair and pull back, then slice right cross her throat. Blood splash on Pallas. Callisto let go and Iphigenia clutch her throat, stagger right into the rock and drop to the ground.

Homer jump too.—Jesus Christ! What the bloodcloth you doing? What the bloodcloth unu doing!

—The woman was a turncoat, fool, Callisto say.

—What you just call me? Homer say.

—Fool me just call you, you fool, Callisto say.—You same one don't know when clock a-strike. You know how long this bitch betraying we? From you bring her in. Every week she send word to Judas nigger in Jackson Lands to pass on to the massa. She thinking massa goin' give her reward for all that she know. Only that Judas nigger wasn't no

Judas. She play one that so we can see who the betrayers be. See her there. Iphigenia. Damn fool. Last night we tell her say is Hippolyta we coming for.

Hippolyta jump.

—'Cause of that she think she safe. Then the bitch run to the fence to tell Jackson Lands nigger everything. Gorgon go that estate today and the nigger tell her everything Iphigenia tell she.

Iphigenia still shaking on the ground, garbling blood and trying to clutch her throat, but blood flow past her fingers like flood. Her blood black in the dim light. Her head strike the ground. Homer stiff like a wall. She walk straight over to Gorgon and slap her. Gorgon dash after her like a wild dog but Pallas get in the way. Gorgon push her off and go after Homer, who stand still.

—Cool you bloodcloth foot! Callisto say. Gorgon stop. Lilith gripping the knife hard.

—The river. The river down by the end of that trail. Put a rock in her petticoat and tie up the ends. Then throw her in the water, Homer say. She trying to be calm but her voice seesaw. Homer sit down on the chair and say nothing else. She stare off in the dark and look at Lilith once.

—Me don't take orders from you, Callisto say. Gorgon bark like dog but leave the biting to Callisto. Lilith thinking this make sense. If there was somebody to be killed, then Callisto would do the killing. She look at the one-eye woman in the dimness and wonder if Callisto is the one she is most of a sister to. Lilith remember the fear she feel when she kill Massa Roget. And something else. Something that higher than when Robert Quinn love her. Something higher than the breeze that rush across the back of her neck when she think of the Ogun that she not to say. Something higher than feeling white. Something that she can't name or call.

Homer still not saying nothing.

—You think anybody waitin' on word from you? Niggers on five estate know you mind dead. And you don't have no use. Better for we if you go live with you dead pickney now. Cho! If people didn't still 'fraid o' you me'd arrange that meself. Come, Gorgon.

Callisto and Gorgon grab Iphigenia, Callisto the foots and Gorgon the hands. They drag the body down the passage Homer point to.

—Make sure, Homer say weakly.—Make sure you put rock in her dress so that...six tell six tell six...

Homer words get cut short by a splash. Hippolyta hiss and run. She hold her head down and look at her hands. Lilith still by the wall and still holding her knife. Lilith don't know if Homer whispering, whimpering or counting. She just then seeing that Pallas crying. Pallas get up and leave, walking first, then running away. Lilith and Homer alone in the cave with the candlelight and shadow dancing round them.

—Me son never lie to me once, Homer say.

Gehenna

ROBERT QUINN JUMP FIRST. HIM RISE FAST AND STARTLE Lilith. As soon as she hear footsteps in the kitchen, Quinn already grab the musket. The footsteps march to the bedroom door and not trying to be quiet.

—Robert.

—Shhh, luv, he say.

The footsteps sound like heavy boots.—Quinn, the man say.

—Quinn.

The man push the door open as Quinn cock him musket and aim.

—Good heavens, man, I could have killed ye! Quinn say. Massa Humphrey in breeches and boots but still wearing him nightshirt, which tuck in halfway.

—Quinn, come with me. Now, he say.

—Well, I can hardly come naked, can I? Quinn smile but Massa Humphrey dead serious.

—Join us outside. We have no time to lose, Quinn, Massa Humphrey say, but he look at Lilith. Lilith jump out of the bed and fetch him new breeches and a white blouson. Quinn boots was in the kitchen.

He pull them on and go outside. Massa Humphrey didn't wait. As soon as he see Quinn he ride off, followed by a slave-driver. They leave a horse for Quinn. Lilith watch him mount the horse and ride off, shouting to Massa Humphrey, Have some patience, will ye. Lilith run to the great house.

Homer at the kitchen window watching the sun rise over the Blue Mountain. She alone. Lilith out of breath and think her loud panting would draw Homer attention but Homer still at the window and the kitchen quiet.

—Mass—Massa Humphrey. He just come for Robert, he just knock down the door and come for him and they ride off.

—Don't call any white man by they Christian name round me, Homer say.

—Where they ride off to?

—God he knows.

—Something happen for sure. Massa Humphrey did serious, serious, serious.

—You know, white man God is stupid thing, but he have—

—Homer, you listening to what me say?

—But he have one thing that me like. One thing. You know what that be?

—How me to know that?

Homer touch the window, moving closer like she see something that Lilith don't.

—The one thing me love 'bout white man God is that with him, things that happen, thing that goin' on now and things that don't yet come to pass be one and the same thing. He no got no yesterday or no tomorrow. Everything is now. Me don't expect ordinary nigger to understand—

—Me understand plenty, Homer.

—Me was just thinking that if me could ever be like God, then past and present and what to come don't mean nothing. That even though me pickneys dead, me still holding him and holding she and me still watching they grow. Me can touch they chest and feel it rise and f—

Homer step away from the window and wipe her eyes.

—What a terrible thing 'pon this world the white man must be. What a wicked, terrible, brutal creature, nothing no wicked like he so. That is the only thing they can teach we. Watch today when they see how much we learn.

—But they ride out for some reason, Homer. I don't like it.

—You don't care for nothing that have to do with you own people free.

—You don't care neither. Me know what moving you and you not out to build nothing.

—They kill the motherness out of me.

—They kill more than that.

—Me ever tell you 'bout you mother?

—No, no, no, no. Don't bother try me this morning, woman. Nothing you can—

—Thirteen year old when Massa Jack fuck her out o' spite, sake of her brother Bacchus. Rape her, really. Pretty girl, that one. Pretty, pretty girl. You know what she name?

—Me goin' back to me kitchen.

—Demeter. Demeter she name. Most beautifullest thing ever live on this estate, backra or nigger.

—Me know what you trying to do, you bitch. Me know what you trying to do.

—After Jack Wilkins kill Bacchus, the first thing he do is make sure Demeter pretty face no pretty no more. That was a spirited chile, spirited, spirited. Just like you, but not even she deserve that. You know how bad Jack Wilkins do her? So bad that even he feel pity afterwards.

—Stop it, Homer.

—You don't want to know 'bout you mother?

—Me no got no mother.

Homer quiet. She go back to the window again.—And me ain't got no pickney. When we nigger goin' get something, eh?

Lilith think to leave but then Pallas run inside.—They have gun today! They all have gun, the slave-drivers, she say.

—What?

—You hear me, Homer. They have gun. Somebody must did tell them something. Somebody do something. Me no know. The massa upstairs?

—No. A driver wake him up and he and Robert Quinn ride out from early morning.

—Goddamn. Goddamn, Homer. What they up to?

—Me look like Humphrey Wilson keeper? How me to know?

—But...

Pallas make the sentence die. She look at Lilith, but no answer come from Lilith either.

—They coming, Homer say.

The three men galloping hard. The driver first, then Massa Humphrey, then Robert Quinn. When they reach the great house Massa Humphrey tell the two groundsmens to tie off the horses to a tree and don't take them back to the stable. Lilith can't read nothing on nobody face. Lilith, Homer and Pallas go outside as if they get summon, running down to the last step. Lilith cover her eyes from the sun as the mens come towards them. Robert Quinn not looking at her. Massa Humphrey step past them, him nightshirt still hanging out of him breeches.

—Have that girl fix us some tea, Homer, considering these days Lilith's tea-making skills are reserved for Mr. Quinn only. The slave Miss Isobel is particularly fond of. Athena? Atalanta, Minerva, whatever Jack Wilkins named the wench.

—Athena? Athena sickly, sir, with the flux.

—Good lord, the flux? The flux, did you say?

—Yes, massa, me don't know what them nasty girls doing so. Me have her lock 'way in the quarters, sir. She not no use to nobody the way she smelling.

Massa Humphrey nod.

—The flux, you say?

—Yes, massa.

—Has anybody else come down with this malady?

—Not yet, sah.

—Nevertheless, I'll have her moved today.

—Massa?

—Today, Homer. I will not have her infect another soul on this estate.

—She not goin' infect nobody, sir, me check on her already and she keeping to her own.

—Really? Homer, you really are a remarkable creature, aren't you? Truly remarkable. But tell me, how could you have managed to look in on the girl—just now, I take it—when she lies dead at the foot of a cliff not too far from where we stand?

Homer step back and gasp. Pallas step away from her. Lilith can't move. All of a sudden, Massa Humphrey pounce 'pon Homer and Robert Quinn not stopping him.

—A murderess in our midst, is it? A murderess? Massa Humphrey say and push her. Homer yelp. She raise her hand to protect her face but too late and Massa Humphrey punch her straight on the nose. Homer stagger back but Massa Humphrey grab her dress by the bosom and slap her across her left check, then her right, then her left again. Pallas jerk toward her, but both Quinn and the driver raise their rifle. Massa Humphrey grab Homer by the throat. Her eye open wide and blood running from the corner of her lip.

—I would never have thought this of you, Homer. Never in an age or more. Would you mind terribly telling me what a slave of mine is doing dead and broken at the foot of a cliff? And why would you be here lying about it? A girl that Richardson said was Athena. And I thought to myself, that's the girl that Homer said had the flux. The very same. Only four days ago you told Miss Isobel that she was very ill, do you deny it?

Homer don't say nothing.

—*Do you deny it?*

—Mass . . . Mass . . .

—Oh, get her out of my sight! Massa Humphrey say and push her to the ground. Massa Humphrey walk to the doorway, then stop.

—Richardson, I will have an answer from her. Today. Do whatever it takes. And Richardson, find whose name matches the number on that shirt and hang him.

Richardson is a big man. So big, is a wonder that even a horse can support him. With him bulky leg and large swell calf, broad shoulder and thick neck and bald head and red eye and missing teeth, he be perhaps the only white man that scare nigger on appearance alone. He scratch the three-day growth 'pon him face and smile. Word was that whenever a slave gal try to fight him off, he would grab her neck and let her know that he got no problem with fucking a dead nigger. Richardson step over to Homer, grab him rifle and butt her in the face. Homer out. Richardson grab her left foot and drag her down the steps. Pallas and Lilith watch as Homer head bang one, two, three, four down the steps, her left ankle in him hand, and her dress lifting up and exposing her. Quinn grab Lilith by the hand and drag her away. Pallas crying.

The cliff was actually a bend in the road that take one to Kingston. A small trail wrap round a hill with nothing below but rock and sea. Somebody must did try to kill Athena at night. She fight him back and grab and tear off him shirt. A bloody rock at the side of the road speak to what kill her. She dead before he throw her over, for there was a trail of her blood from the middle of the road straight to the cliff and the print of a big man foot stepping back into the same blood as he run away.

All this Robert Quinn say to Lilith back in him quarters but he don't look at her.

—Me can't believe it to be true, massa.

—Nor I. Certainly not Homer, but who can ye trust these days. Who can ye...

—Massa...

Lilith feel the silence on her back. Before she even turn, Robert Quinn grab her arm and twist it behind her back. Lilith bawl.

—Yer in her company all the time! All the time! Are ye in league with her? Are you in league with her, damn you?

—No, massa! Me not in league with nobody. Me...

Lilith bawling as he twist her hand harder. She buckle and fall hard on her knee.

—I don't think I believe ye. You two were especially close. Are ye planning something, the two of ye? So help me, I'll break this hand off!

—Lawd God, Massa Robert! Lawd! Lilith bawling getting louder.—Me don't know—Me don't know nothing 'bout Homer, swear to God-Jesus!

—Me memory's not as bad as ye wish it, Lilith. I recall several times you going to meet the woman. At night too. Late night. I swear, you niggers are planning something, after all the kindness I've shown you.

He twist harder. Lilith bawling loud now.

—Nobody not close to me, sah!

—Ye expect me to believe that these niggers and ye don't have each in the other's confidence? Ye expect me to believe that Homer and at least one more is involved in a murder plot, and ye have no knowledge of it? None at all?

—Me never know, sah! Oh, lawd!

—How could you not know?

—Nobody talk to me, sah! Nobody talk to me!

—Since when! Since fecking when? Don't make me any more cross with ye, Lilith. Don't fecki—

—Since me start share bed with white man, massa! Since me sleeping with you.

He stop and let go of her. He pace for a while, then stop and look at her.

—What am I, a fecking plague? Am I some sort of leper? he say, but Lilith don't answer. She clutch her hand, still crying.

—Nobody have nothing to do with me. Not since me come back from Coulibre, not since me living here with you, she say.

Quinn go over to the table and sit down in a chair. He sigh loud and scratch him head.

—Goddamn. Were ye lying I'd feel bad, but yer probably telling the truth and that makes me feel a lot, lot worse.

Hundred sixty-four was the number on the shirt. The piece of shirt that Athena tear off when she was fighting the murdering nigger for her life. Who know where her spirit be now, but she do one last thing to make sure her death get avenge. Hundred sixty-four. Robert Quinn bring numbers to the estate to make things simpler. So number hundred sixty-four slave have number hundred sixty-four shirt and number hundred sixty-four pantaloons. Hundred sixty-four mark when he get feed two times a day, hundred sixty-four mark when he spend the allotted hours in the field working. Hundred sixty-four belong to Atlas.

Richardson go in the field after Atlas. Atlas see him and McClusky coming and run. Atlas run clear down a trail in the cane piece when another driver chase him down on horseback and strike him with a club. Richardson ask who him in league with and why he kill Athena. Or if he tickled pink by killing young women. Atlas say he no know what dem a-talk 'bout and Richardson shoot off two of him left toe. Atlas scream clear across the field. Every driver lift up the rifle and aim, shouting to the slaves to go back to work, and the Johnny-jumpers strike who they please. Atlas bawl again that he no know and he didn't have nothing to do with no poor murdered girl and he love all girl and would never kill such a pretty girl like Athena, who never would hurt even flea. Richardson have two driver hold him down. He step on Atlas wrist with him boot and shoot off a thumb. Atlas scream and holler and bawl and yell and whimper. He still saying that he no know nothing 'bout no young girl. Richardson say he was the one who find the body himself coming back from Red Horse Tavern in Kingston. Blood smear the road leading straight over the cliff. He climb all the way down himself and find Athena stinking up the rocks, half her body almost gone in the sea. Athena still have most of him shirt in her hand. Richardson ask Atlas what anybody could have over him that he gone lose a thumb and two toe already. Atlas bawling. Richardson tell the drivers to turn him over. A driver further off fire in the air and say, Git back to work, the lot o' ye! And the niggers watching go back to work. Atlas still screaming and bawling when Richardson rip down him pantaloons and shove the rifle hard and rough until it gone full up Atlas arse.—I'll send your shit all the way up to yer eyeballs, Atlas, so help me God I will, he say and Atlas finally scream out, She does bewitch me! She does work Obeah on me! She Obeah me, lord massa! She make me do it!

—Who? Richardson say.

—Homer. Homer! Atlas say.

Callisto tell all this to Pallas. By the noon hour, everybody ordered to the cotton tree. Lilith remember that tree well. She walk three pace behind Robert Quinn and they don't say nothing from the morning. Noon gone white. Most of the niggers assemble round the tree with the slave-drivers at the back, all with rifle cock and loaded and extra musket on they shoulder. Massa Humphrey watching from the terrace. Lilith look around and see Callisto in front but across from her, and Hippolyta in the back, tiptoeing to get a better look. She don't see Gorgon.

They string up Atlas first. Him screaming into a gag. They put the nigger to stand on a small barrel with him hand tie behind him back. The noose already round him neck. A driver shouting to the niggers 'bout the perverted Atlas and Homer who killing little girls for their amusement. Atlas murder the girl and Homer hide the dastard deed. —May God have mercy on you and let you out of hell one day, the driver say and kick away the barrel. The noose grip round the nigger neck. He swing and kick and spin but that only make the noose squeeze tighter. Is years since anybody get hang at Montpelier. The body jerk and sway and piss burst from him cocky and wet the dirt.

Then they bring out Homer. Richardson push her and she stumble. Homer naked, with her skin stretch over bone and her hips sticking out and her ribs poking through her side. Few on the estate would know what Homer body look like, so plenty gasp and few look away when they see how she look like animal. Her back, arse and thigh cover in scar big like animal stripe, her titties chop up and scar up so that is only nipple left to tell you that she born to suckle. But all over her from arm to leg to foot tight with muscle. Homer try to walk straight but Richardson butt her with the rifle for showing uppityness. They tie her wrists and pull her up till she on level with dead Atlas. Homer gasp and wince but say nothing. Her head drop down like she falling asleep. Homer pussy hair white like her head. The driver talking 'bout how she of all people, the one nigger who was expected to be an example for all other nigger to follow, turn out to be such a decadent pervert and murderess. How a slave under her supervision came to such an untimely death and neither she nor Atlas will tell why. How there is no way to comprehend such evil, one can only drive it out with the smart of a good, severe whipping. Homer head nodding and rolling up and down like she agree.

Richardson dealing with this one himself. Homer spinning a little so the whip land anywhere it choose. The first lash strike her back and Homer grunt. The second lash hit her back and coil round her belly.

Homer start to jerk like she having fit. She not screaming, only grunt-ing. Homer body tough from much scar and her skin strong and not even a welt mark on her yet. Richardson notice and the fourth and fifth lash come harder. Homer spinning worse and the fifth lash strike her breasts. Homer scream. The whip cut through her black skin leaving a white gash that turn red with blood, then pink when the blood start to flow down her skin. Her wet body change the way the whip sound on her skin and every lash sound like a burst of flame. Robert Quinn turn away and leave. Lilith wipe her eyes and see Callisto. Callisto look at her and nod. Lilith, who can't wipe away tears faster than they fall, shake her head no. Callisto nod again, closing her eye and pressing her lip together like that be the final word. Yes, she nod.

Lilith go back to Quinn quarters to see him go to the bedroom. Lil-ith pull down some banana and cut a large sweet potato in half.

—Oh, I'm not in any sort of mood for lunch today, Lilith. I'll have tea, please, thank you, he say.

Outside, Homer still getting whip. Lilith wonder what break her first, the nakedness in front of everybody who hate her or the whip-ping. Outside sounding like Richardson take a break, for Homer no longer screaming. Lilith listen hard and finally hear the crack of the whip cutting through the quiet again.

—Is it ready, Lilith?

—Yes'm....yes, she say.—I put little molasses in it.

—Then I best be about drinking it, then. Goddamn, luv, this is feckin' bitter.

—Everything that good for you bitter, Lilith say.

—Is that so? Quinn say.—Well, thank goodness fer all that's sweet in the world.

He go over to the dining table and sit down.

—Awful business with Homer. Truly awful business, he say and get up and go to him room. He don't come back for a while and when he do he yawning and stretching.

—Bejesus me, I'm tired. Have you seen my hat, Lilith, the brown leather one? Haven't been able to...

—I know where it is, Lilith say and go into the room. In the closet behind old breeches him navy coat buttons shine back at her.

—Found it, luv? Quinn say.

—Yes, massa, Lilith say.

—So we're back at massa, eh? Well, bring it here then. Bring it—

Lilith hear a crash. She run out but stop at the entry to the kitchen. Quinn look down at the cup that just slip from him hand. He bend over to pick up the pieces and nearly collapse. He grab on to the kitchen counter and him knees buckle. Quinn try to walk to the table and almost fall. He grab a chair back in time and balance himself. Quinn try to pull himself up. Lilith look at him eye and see him frighten, not just frighten, but frighten like nigger fear. He look at the shattered teacup and the tea steaming on the stove.—Ohh my G...Oh my Go...he say. He pull himself up, but slip and grab the tablecloth and pull everything off on the floor. The plate shatter and the pot of beef turn over and throw the beef out. The beef slide all the way up to Lilith foot. She follow it back to him on the floor. Quinn gasping, he eyes red. He look at Lilith, red with fury, then white with sadness. He trying to catch breath as he pull himself up again. Ye, ye, Lilith?... Ye...yhh..., he say. Quinn pulling himself over to Lilith. Lilith wipe away the first tear but let the rest run down her face. Quinn eye red like he crying too. He stagger over to where Lilith be and leap at her like a wild boar that get shot. He grab her by the neck. Him weight slam her against the wall and Lilith shriek. Robert Quinn breathing heavy. L...L...Lilith? he say. He squeeze her neck harder and Lilith start to gag. He slam her head against the wall until him hand slip. Quinn knees buckle again and he falling. He grab on to her bosom and rip the dress and he fall on the floor. Lilith wail out loud. She look at Robert Quinn lying on the floor and wail again, then she compose herself and grab him by the boots and drag him into the bedroom. She sweep the broke cup into a sack and hope he did drink enough.

Homer gone fifty-six lash and she still screaming. Most nigger would pretend to be out by now, just so the whipper would have pity and stop. Richardson look like he just starting. Blood dripping on the ground. Massa Humphrey watching from the terrace with no feeling on him face. Miss Isobel come out for a little but go back inside. Then a huge flock of noisy bird fly frantic over the great house, making a ruckus and Massa Humphrey look up.

—Richardson. Richardson, quit! Stop, will ya? A slave-driver say.

—Fookin' hell, I'm just getting into the thick of it, Richardson say.

—Master Wilson's calling you.

The drivers disperse the niggers back to the field, leaving Homer swinging. Richardson run up to the terrace but Massa Humphrey running down the step. Massa Humphrey run to him horse and Richardson look up in the sky and gasp until Massa Humphrey shout to get his arse on a horse. Richardson look up in the sky again. High up and flying over was black smoke, thick like a cloud. Black smoke coming from the east. From Worthy Park plantation.

Lilith watching Robert Quinn in the bed. Usually when he sleeping he breathe heavy but now he peaceful. Lilith know that he not going call her lovey again. She not goin' see him again unless is in front of a gun barrel. Lilith think 'bout what she not to think. About a different Montpelier where Robert Quinn live with her and she wear white to a wedding and they have three pickney all different colour. Or a different one where she is just the woman of the cottage and she accept that life even though she be him wife in every way but name. Dreaming is for fool nigger, she say to herself. This time next year he would be hunting new pussy in Spanish Town and forget all about the green-eye niggerwoman who betray him. Lilith tell that to herself so that she can hate him a little. It don't work, so she tell herself more.

Homer close her eyes.

Two o'clock.

From six estate, house negro women find a secret place that open to the sky, reach for the abeng and blow. They blow a sound long and strong. White mens and black mens hear it but the womens in the field act first. As soon as the abeng blow, they stand still to they side with the cutlass, hoe and rake. The mens confuse at first and keep on reaping.

—What sort of lark is this? say one of the white driver.

—Git back to work before I flogs the days work of ye! Go on now, git goin'.

The womens stand still. The mens watching. They look at the womens as they shake they heads. One woman, then two, then five, then ten. And still more. The mens nod and understand. One by one, each man rest him hand with the cutlass to him side. Three white mens up but one was still sleeping.

—Git yer arse up, McClusky! We've got trouble, ye bastard! say one as he kick McClusky in the foot.

—Fuckin' hell! McClusky say and rub his eye. He sit up from under the tree he was sleeping.—Wot's it now, Jerry, wanna go over for a hit again, d'you?

—Look, ye son of a bitch.

—Wot the devil? McClusky jump up and uncoil him whip.—All right, all right, everybody's had their spot o' fun, now git back to work, the lot of you! Come on.

The womens and the mens still.

—Oh? Is that wot it's gonna be like, yeah? You think you can do as you well please, is that it? We'll see about that, yes we will.

McClusky swing and lash a woman clear 'cross her belly. She scream but don't move. He lash her again.

—Git back to work, says I! he say. The other drivers looking around at the niggermens and womens all standing still and staring. McClusky getting redder.

—I'll lash the fuckin' soul out o' you niggers when I'm done, goddamn black bitch. McClusky swing the whip again, but a man jump in the way.

—Oh, so you want some of my discipline as well, Poseidon? Well, come and git it, you half-plucked blunderbuss.

McClusky pulling away the whip, but Poseidon grab it. McClusky try to pull, but Poseidon hold on. Poseidon yank the whip and nearly pull McClusky to the ground. McClusky gulp. He look left, then right, then left, and only see blackness.

—I says, I ... git, git back to work, the lot o' you! Right now says I, I say right now! Poseidon yank the whip out of McClusky hand and wrap it round he own arm. The mens and womens turn to McClusky and the three white mens behind him.

—McClusky, one of them whisper.

—Shut up, Charters! There shall be no uppity niggers on my watch, not as long as I have this to say about it. McClusky grab he musket and aim. The other two men aim they rifle too. The mens and womens still.

—Not so uppity now, eh? Git back to work, you black bastards! McClusky say. But then a voice raise up from round the back.

—You all have only one shot each, so take you four, Callisto say.

—Why, you! McClusky say and fire after Callisto. He miss and the mens and womens scatter. Charters fire him rifle and one of the womens yelp and fall. The third driver fire and hit a man in the head, who spin and shower the ground with blood. The fourth driver fire but him rifle jam. McClusky turn to run but Callisto too close. She jump at him and swing the cutlass. It slice into him neck and blood burst forth. McClusky eyes nearly pop out of him face. He clutch him neck and blood pour through him finger. Callisto and two womens chop and chop and chop until all three womens cover in blood. The three drivers try to run. They shout for the Johnny-jumpers but them niggers was running already. The negroes in that section circle the mens like a flood and swallow them up. They stop screaming. The negroes still stomping and chopping.

Pallas enter the library. She go behind Massa Humphrey desk and pull out the bottom drawer. She move her foot just in time before the drawer smash her toe. Pallas push her hand deep into the space and cuss. She pull her hand back and push again. Nine other womens come in, including Gorgon. Pallas cuss again. She push her hand in the space again and smile this time. She pull out a key and run over to the big wooden cabinet that have two angel carve on each door. The women line up and she give each two rifle and a box of bullet. Pallas pull one and show them how to load bullet.

—Once you get to the river head east, she say.—And watch for them Maroon niggers, they still get one pound for a dead nigger. Kill anybody you see.

—What if the massa come back? a woman say.

—They goin' to come back, Pallas say. By then it goin' be too late. Some of you stay here until me give you the signal. The rest of you run to the field to give the mens the gun. You need to take some fire to the field too. Remember, any nigger that start to fuss, shoot them.

A man take a shovel and jam McClusky neck to shuck the head off. They kick the bodies and pull off they clothes. The mens take the clothes for themself even though they too cut up and bloody to wear. Then they hear a cart coming. They 'bout to rush it and see that is Gorgon.

—House nigger! They worse than whitey! one of them say.

—Worse, eh? If me so bad, how come me bring you dis? she say and throw a shotgun to Poseidon.

—Twenty more in the cart. House nigger worse? See de real Judas nigger dere, catch him! Two new Johnny-jumper name Nestor and

Pollux try to disappear in the bush. The field go after them. Seven man grab Nestor and chop off every limb.

—Me is nigger just like you! Pollux say.

—They force me just like you! Pollux say.

—They never beat me belly with riding whip! Only you, a woman shout back. The flood of nigger consume him. He scream four time, then no more. When they pull back, in the dirt be a chop-up nigger with him cocky stuff in the mouth.

Hippolyta run to the cart and take a pail from Gorgon. She dip dry cane leaf in the coal until fire catch. The other womens and mens follow suit. They throw the flame at the foot of the cane stalks. Fire rise and roar and sweep the field section like a great plague in the Bible. The smell of sugar cane burnin' bitter and sweet. The slave have to run fast to not get burn. Two womens run too slow and the fire close them in. They scream but nobody going back to save nobody.

Callisto leave Gorgon in the field and run to the cotton tree. She push the barrel under Homer and climb. Callisto saw and saw with a knife until the rope pop and Homer drop into her arms. They both nearly fall off the barrel. Callisto put her arm round Homer waist and help her back to the great house.

—Me can walk, goddamn! Me can walk, Homer say. But she make three step and nearly fall. Callisto catch her and help her back to the great house. All around they hear the sound of crackling and burnin' and the sky start to rain with cane ash. Callisto leave Homer in the kitchen and go fetch her a dress. Callisto have to put the dress on and as soon as the dress cover Homer, blood seep through the cloth and the whole dress look it make with a pattern of red stripe goin' all the way down.

Only one slave-driver on horseback and he get away. In another section they kill the Johnny-jumpers first, chop off they head and stick it on a cane stalk. Then they run through the cane piece rooting out more turncoat nigger. A niggerman who didn't like a niggerwoman 'cause she wouldn't fuck him and call him stink, shout out say she is turncoat nigger and they jump her and stomp her and beat her to death before she could scream out that he not telling true. They sweep in the field for driver and Johnny-jumper and leave the field burnin'.

Plenty mens, when they see woman giving command, don't like that at all. They do as they please and break into the stable and try to grab horse. But niggerman can't ride. Plenty horse get 'way. One horse near kick a nigger head clean off. He still upright with him head swinging down like loose branch. Outside, other man push the womens away and try to get the negroes to go where they say. Some heading for the hills already while some setting more fire to the ratoon field, the produce field, the coconut field and the pasture, which cause the cows and goats to run. Soon black smoke rising from Montpelier like a tower, just like the smoke that rise from Worthy Park in the east and Ascot Pen in the south. Soon the sky so black with smoke that afternoon look like night.

Callisto getting word that the negroes, the mens in particular, out of control. She cuss loud. She still in the kitchen with a rifle in her lap with Homer.

—Nigger setting they own house afire, Homer say.

—Goddamn man! They can't do nothing right! Callisto say. Homer slam her hand on the kitchen counter. Callisto look at her. Homer head still swinging and swaying.

—Come, we leaving now, Callisto say.

—You go. Me have unfinished business, Homer say.

From behind Miss Isobel room door come the sound of bolting and key locking. Then the *bang bang bang* of things she shoving up to the door to bar anybody from coming in.

Massa Humphrey and Richardson reach the gate. He riding up the narrow hill road that lead to the great house but get caught up watching the cloud of black smoke and him fields burnin'. Some negroes see and run to him with hoe and pickaxe and shovel. Massa Humphrey ride through them, firing him musket and shooting one in the neck and trampling a woman who was waving a stick. Then Massa Humphrey hear a crack to the west and an echo in the east. Him horse buckle and crash to the ground. The throw send him flying and he fall down the hill side of the road and roll until a rock slam into him head and stop the fall. Richardson look over for a little, then go on riding.

Lilith in the bedroom watching Robert Quinn sleep. She run to the window and see some negroes walking up to the cottage. Some carrying stick and some carrying fire. Lilith run outside with two of Robert Quinn musket.

—We come for de overseer, a man say.

—You go all over the field and miss him? Lilith say.

—He deh yah wid you, he say.

—No man keeping my company. Why you don't find some Johnny-jumper to kill?

—Them all kilt. Fi him time now.

—No damn nigger coming in this house.

—Black cow, you cain't kill all o' we.

—But me can kill one. Who want to dead first, step up and get you judgement.

They look at her. She look at them. Nobody move.

—We coming back, the man say and the group run off.

Lilith run back in the room. Robert Quinn still sleeping. Lilith look at the great house and think of Miss Isobel. She look to the west and the east and see fire dancing underneath a cloud of black smoke. She hear cheering and yelling and shouting and screaming. A herd of cows run past, knocking down every post and barrel in the way. More nigger run past the house and she clutch the musket and feel for the pellets in her apron. She run to the next window and see a group of mens run up the stairs and into the great house. The mistress and Miss Isobel.

The burnin' cane wake Massa Humphrey mother. She remember that today is the day she go riding.

—Patrick! Patrick, what is that smell? Do not even think to enter my room with such a fetor, the mistress say. The room door swing open and Homer step in. She still wobbling and her eye shut more than open.

—Who is it? Who is it, I said? And what is that goddamned smell? Where's Patrick? I said where's Patr—

—Patrick d…Patrick dead two year, two year now, you stupid, shrivel-up cunt.

—Oh, my God—

—Hell he be, and you soon pay a visit.

—Homer? What is the meaning of this? What is the meaning of all this?

Homer cock her rifle.

—You know what this mean?

—Oh, dear lord. Oh, dear lord. What do you want from me? I've always treated you niggers well. I have always treated you well!

—You, you is the one who tell old Jack Wilkins to whip me, then sell me pickneys.

Homer out of breath.

—Pickneys? What would you want with pickneys? You're brutish animals, brutish! What need have you for children? I did you a favour. That I de—

—They's dead. All of them. The pickneys Jack Wilkins make nigger rape out o' me. The pick…pickneys that you, you, you sell just 'cause you don't want me to have or love nothing but you.

Homer swaying like she drunk. She swing round the gun and hold the nozzle.

—For that, me goin' deal with you special, she say.

Callisto running across the path. Lilith seeing her from her window. Bullet fly through the sky and explode in Callisto head. Gorgon scream and run to the body. Whole heap of negro run away but some stay to watch the plantation burn. The great house still standing and Wilkins' house and the cottage where Lilith be with Robert Quinn. Lilith watching out from the window, she looking at the field as they burn and the negroes as they run past the house. Sooner or later some goin' stop and try to burn the house down again. Sooner or later they coming.

—God feckin' damn, I had the strangest dream. I'm sorry, luv, I thought you had...

Lilith turn around. She see Robert Quinn up and looking at her. He get up quick and go to the kitchen, seeing the stove and the teapot. Then her. He over to her so quick that before Lilith could move, him hand on her throat.

—Talk, him say.

But Lilith choking. She grab him arm but he squeeze tighter.

—I said talk, him say. She choking.

—C...c...can't...tal...she say, pointing to her throat. He let go.

—They goin' kill you! They goin' kill you if you go outside. Don't go outside! Don't go, Robert.

He look at her with so much anger that Lilith step back. Him eyebrow raise high and him face getting red. Not taking him eye off her, Robert Quinn grab the musket from the table. He go into him room and come out a minute later with another musket and a rifle and bullets that he stuffing in him military jacket with the shiny button. She grab after him but he push her. He go to hit her again, but eye and eye meet and he stop.

—Goddamn you, Lilith, goddamn you, he say and leave. Lilith look out and see him ride off in the direction of the great house. Far off, the fields burnin'.

Negroes from four estate taking to the hills. Hundreds. Some the Maroons most likely goin' catch, but the number too big to catch them all. Plenty negroes on the estate. Plenty in the great house. Pallas run upstairs and see Miss Isobel room open. She go in to see a light-skin nigger fuckin' Miss Isobel hard while the chocolate-skin nigger hold her up and cussing that he taking till Judgement Day fi cum. Miss Isobel don't look like she living. They holding her up by the arm while the chocolate nigger have her two leg on him shoulder and him breeches at him knees. Pallas fire a shot and they drop Miss Isobel.

—Stinking nasty nigger, she say while she reach for her other rifle. We fighting for freedom and all you want to free is you breeches. Get out before I shoot the two of you.

—You have mouth. What say we have fun with you too?

—Can't fuck me when I shoot you balls off.

The mens quiet.

—Now get out, she say. The mens walk past her, looking at the barrel of the rifle. She point her gun at Miss Isobel. Miss Isobel sputter.

—Oi, Miss Isobel, me know you name. You know mine? Miss Isobel nod and sputter. Pallas stoop down.

—You know me? Me name Pallas, the nigger who soup you love spit in.

Pallas pull off her head wrap and red hair tumble down.—Me same one who hair you can't stand 'cause it remind you that your kind fuck nigger to get me. Me was goin' kill you. Just right now, but guess what, Miss Isobel? Me goin' make you live. Me goin' make you remember for the rest of you life how two niggerman take what is not them to take, just like how you love take what is not yours. Hope you pussy stay tear out and you breed nigger twin too.

Pallas get up and leave Miss Isobel sputtering. She pass the mistress room and see it open slight.

—Homer? What you doing? We have to go, Pallas say.

—Me ready when me ready. Right now, me and the mistress having correspondence, Homer say. Pallas look at Homer barely standing up, her dress stripe with blood. Pallas look down and see the old mistress knees on the floor but Homer holding her up by the neck of her nightgown. The mistress face punch up and bloody. Homer swinging wild and for a instant the two women looking like they holding each other up.

—Next meeting in the hill? Pallas say.

—Next meeting in the hill, Homer say as Pallas close the door.

Lilith by the window as Montpelier go down. Then the window on the other side of the door explode and she scream. The rock land on the floor, followed by a burnin' stick. The carpet catch afire and spread so fast Lilith think the flame chasing her. The floor crackle. Lilith run to the back door but it locked. She turn back and see the fires already attacking the chair and table and the curtains that Quinn just buy. Smoke blacking the space and she can't see. Lilith coughing. There be nowhere but behind her. The door won't budge, but the window open. She climb through, but the drop from the window too high. Lilith thinking about what very stupid and very necessary. She thinking that it can't be more than two yard or so between window and ground. She out on the window ledge now and smoke rushing out from behind her. Lilith stunned that fire could move so fast. She wonder what Robert Quinn doing. And Homer. She jump.

Lilith wonder how safe she be if some of the negroes have her off as Robert Quinn woman. She don't know where to run. What not full with smoke and fire full with niggers running like flock of fowl with they head chop off. Behind her be the niggers that set fire to the cottage, niggers who mark her for killing. Ahead she see something that stun her, but there it be standing still like a dead house. Like everybody forget who live there. Unless nobody is there. And even so, by now even turncoat nigger would burn down the place out of spite.

Jack Wilkins' house.

Wilkins' house have a staircase round the back. Lilith run up to the glass and wood door but it lock. She run back down for a rock and hear some niggers coming. She drop flat on the ground and don't breathe. Soon as she couldn't hear them no more she run back up to the door and break a hole in the glass.

She down the hallway and see a half-open door. Prop up on the bed be Jack Wilkins, him hair wild and white and him chin resting on him chest like he dead. A big explosion shake the room and wake him up. Jack Wilkins stare at Lilith for a long time, then hiss.

—Haven't I done enough for you? What more do you want? he say.

Lilith look at Jack Wilkins and try to think of him as anything but a devil. She think to leave him to either the fire or the negroes, but then he look at her again and she see a weak old man in the bed. Just a weak old man who can't hurt or promise. She look at him eyes and try to see herself.

—You can walk? she say.

Jack Wilkins lighter than feather. She have her hand round him waist and him arm on her shoulder, but she could have easily just carry him, she reckon. She wonder if the smell on him is the father smell. He not weak, just drunk, and even him arm stink with liquor. Lilith seek connection with him once, but now she wondering what connection mean, and snap herself back to the present when she smell the smoke coming through the window. She think of her own burnin' home, the home that she make with Robert Quinn. Jack Wilkins can barely step. As they reach the last step Lilith walk into the mouth of a shotgun.

—And where d'ye think you're going with my husband?

—Fire outside. Smoke was coming through the window.

—But of course. You niggers just want ta burn everything now, is that it? Nothing's too good for you.

At the end of the gun be a short woman who still in her nightdress and her hair as white as Jack Wilkins'.

—Me say smoke was coming in him room. Look 'pon him, he would be dead before him even got good cause.

—All hell could come before I believe the word of a nigger, Missus Wilkins say.

—Hell all around you, you damn fool, Lilith say. The woman shock. Lilith step past her with Jack Wilkins and help him into an armchair. The only armchair in the hall. Everything else, from chair to table to clock to books, pile up by the door. On the floor by the armchair be more rifles and shotguns and muskets than Lilith ever see in her life, twenty, fifty, one hundred.

—He always knew a day such as this would come, the bastard, she say.

—Day like this he damn well cause, Lilith say.

—Loaded they all are, each and every one of 'em. Did it meself. He was never much use for nothing but breedin' niggers. Damn that—

—This all right for the door, but what about the windo—

A rock burst through the window and glass explode. Missus Wilkins scream. Lilith move behind Jack Wilkins' armchair. The man slump over like he sleeping, but jerk every time he hear a sound. She expecting a stick or bottle with fire next, but sounds come through the window of mens and womens with blood on the tongue. The first man climb through. He so tall, he almost touch the ceiling. He look in Jack Wilkins' direction and yell. Him cutlass cover in blood and didn't shine. He charge with him cutlass and Missus Wilkins raise her rifle and pull the trigger. The woman fall back but the man chest burst as the shot lift him off the ground. He fall on the floor and the room shake. Another climb up to the window, a woman this time. Missus Wilkins fire again and miss her. The first woman rush to Missus Wilkins screaming and run right into the bayonet. As the woman yelp and fall off, Lilith grab a rifle for herself. Another woman did come in, unbeknownst to Lilith or Missus Wilkins. Missus Wilkins turn to Lilith, cussing all them confounded niggers, when again bang, and blood explode from her mouth. She cough and cackle and shocked when she see her own blood running down her bosom. Missus Wilkins look up straight at Lilith. As she fall out of the way, there be Hippolyta pointing right at Lilith. Hippolyta hiss, then fire.

A click, then nothing. She pull the trigger again but still nothing. The rifle jam and Hippolyta hiss. She not wearing her long black dress but a tear-up white one, and her legs and chest bony. A thick scar run up from her neck to her left ear. Hippolyta hiss but her green eyes screaming. She throw 'way the rifle, pick up the first man cutlass and charge, making sound like a yellow snake. Lilith fire and Hippolyta face blow to pieces. One more nigger push him head up and Lilith fire again without thinking or even looking. The man scream and fall.

Lilith look down in the armchair and don't know if Jack Wilkins asleep or awake. Him hair long but at the top don't have much. From where she lookin', he could be a old preacher. Gunshot burst from nigger nearby and both she and Wilkins jump. She look over to him wife and Hippolyta, both shot in the head, and the other dead people in the room and think nobody should be living. Nobody at all, not she nor Jack Wilkins. She aim the gun at him balding head. But she couldn't shoot. She didn't even want to and don't know why. Surely of all the white mens to get kilt, he be the one who deserve it the most. The man who rape her mammy. But she don't know her mammy. She never touch her nor smell her nor know if the mammy ever want her. *I'm a wicked son of a bitch*, Jack Wilkins say one time. *Not even the devil ever met the likes of me.* But he save her from the field and he stop them from whipping her—even Quinn didn't do that. And he be her pappy. She don't know what that mean. Mayhaps it mean nothing, especially today. But she shed enough blood already, including Hippolyta, who be her own kin. She not shedding no more. She stoop down in front of him and aim for the window and stay that way till whoever come.

The ground shake with the best of horses. Redcoats. His Majesty's regiment coming in from Spanish Town. There be fifty or sixty but they all on horseback, making a noise like thunder and whipping up dust. With they red jacket and shiny sword and brown musket and big black horses, they look like an infantry just rise up from hell. The sun going down and blast a purple in the sky. At the great house a fire blazing.

Pallas set fire to the kitchen when she leaving. Montpelier is a house with plenty book, oil, wood and paper. Fire catch and spread like rumour. Massa Humphrey yell as the redcoats pass by and one stop to pull him up on the horse. The redcoats ride right up to the stairs and watch a third of the house on fire. Massa Humphrey jump off the horse, followed by the redcoat, and set to go inside when they hear a bump. Massa Humphrey look up to the window to him mother room to hear an explosion of glass as a body burst through the window and land from two floor up to the ground. Massa Humphrey rush to the body. Homer step to the window and raise her hand. The sunset hit her body and she change to black. She wave the rifle in the air. The redcoats fire and riddle her body with bullet. She dance from the rifle fire and her whole body shoot blood. She make a yell, then fall, with half her body hanging off the balcony. Massa Humphrey bawling like a baby. Like a little girl. He on him knees and he pull him mother body to him and wrap her up in him arm. He bawling and can't stop. Some of the redcoats rush inside while some ride off to secure the estate. By now, hundreds of the negroes gone. Evening turning into night, but the flames blaze the county alight like it be day. Fire on the ground, black cloud in the sky, burnin' sugar and flesh in the air.

In Jack Wilkins' house, Lilith believe what the evening tell her 'bout Robert Quinn. She know from the minute the tall dark woman appear in the room, unawares to Jack. The skinny dark woman take leave of her and go through the front door. Lilith stay by the armchair and watch her father.

· 30 ·

No woman can afford to feel anything for a man in 1801. That be the source of eternal misery. Lilith pondering them things when they catch her on the road to the gate, beat her till she pass out and throw her in the back of the cart with other runaway nigger. The redcoats find Miss Isobel still knock out and dishevel with her dress up her neck and her pussy out a door. The commotion wake her up and she scream. She grab her dress and pull it down and bawl that she is lady of good means and superior birth.

Commander Forster of His Majesty's regiment is no stranger to war. So he begin each time he talk. Forster say that if everybody did take heed of the Barbadian code of 1688, this would never happen. If everybody did remember that niggerman so barbarous and savage that good ol' England law was unfit, then no white man would have get catch off-guard. He say that to other redcoats as they watch Montpelier cane field burn to the ground. Four days later when he talking, the fields still smoking and the sky still grey and smelling of burned sugar and flesh.

One of the redcoats say that is only 'cause so many slaves run away, and not so much was around to stand and fight, why they didn't overrun the whites and take over the county. The redcoats scratching them head 'cause they can't explain how so much nigger manage to plan something so big and still keep it quiet. By the time they chop off a slave woman fourth toe, she tell how they plan to exterminate all backra and set up village states all over the county like what be in the Africa. Like what Tacky was goin' start in 1760. They think she mad. Rumour start to spread that is woman who plan the whole thing, which make white man and niggerman, slave man and free man perplex, cause such devious and nefarious thinking was beyond the capabilities of the fairer sex, much less a bunch of goat-rutting savage womens.

The fifth white man they find was Richardson, breeches gone, cocky stuff in mouth and bullwhip stuff up arse. The sixth white man they find was Robert Quinn. He dead beside him horse, also dead. Him shirt soak through with red. Massa Humphrey in between weeping, say that Quinn died trying to save the estate, an estate that was not even his, and he was a man he loved more than him own blood. Ninety and four whites dead in the revolt all over the county and seventeen unaccounted for. Some of the white mens get shot and some of the white womens get rape but plenty white people get kill in all sort of wicked way. Massa and Missus Newforth from Worthy Park get find in bed, they head chop off and switch to each other body. Some slave must did remember that twenty year before, Massa Newforth draw and quarter a runaway negro and hang a section at each end of him slave provision ground to warn uppity nigger not to take step. There be no white body that was leave alone. Even the ones who get shot also get chop, burn, hang, and some even get throw into a boiler alive. Even white pickney. Nobody know how much nigger dead.

Plenty negro try to escape to the mountain on foot, but most didn't get that far. The redcoats catch dozen and dozen including Gorgon, who was dragging Callisto body. Other negro use night darkness to escape, only to get catch by Maroon nigger who set down on them like they was waiting all along. With they musket and rifle and spear and cutlass, they round up over one hundred slave who too tired to fight back or run anymore. Maroon nigger deliver the runaway slaves by they lonesome, though some of the womens they keep.

The slaves that get catch know them fate. By the night, all of Middlesex County smell of flesh. Bleeding flesh, burnin' flesh, starving flesh and rotting flesh. At Worthy Park, most negro get shot in the head, then hang until they rot to the bone. At Ascot Pen, most get whipped, then hang up to burn, most times over a fire that set slow so that the slaves will burn for two days straight but can't faint or die quick. But Montpelier nigger get a different fate. Montpelier master lose the two people he love the most in one day, and after crying for three day straight like a mother who lose her pickney, nothing leave in Massa Humphrey heart but blackness.

They leave the capture niggers in a cage, all stack tight. Some whimper that they never do nothing and is error. Some shout that they glad for the first taste of white kill. Lilith quiet. Day and night, living and dead don't make no difference to she no longer. She find a corner and crouch down and stay there, burying her face. Morning, noon and night pass and she try not to think of Robert Quinn. She will hear Lovey, or Luv or just Lilith said in the Irish way and just shake and shake and scream till her throat sore. On account of that, no nigger stay too close to her. She see the great house, half burn down with just the frame of that part of the house standing, and she think of Coulibre. Days pass and the cage take up with sweat, shit and dead nigger. Lilith look out and see a white man walking through the ashes, with smoke blowing across and hiding him one blink, showing him the next. Her heart jump when she see the black hair, but then she realise that is red hair blackened by ash. Massa Humphrey stepping through damage like a ghost. She see him and he look at her.

The next day, Massa Humphrey wave him hand and one of the redcoats open the back door of the cage.

—Lilith? Who answers to the name Lilith?

Lilith don't answer.

—Come now, you stupid niggers, I've very little time for skylarkin'. Who answers to the name Lilith?

Lilith don't answer, but all the nigger step away from her.

—I reckon that's you. Well, come on!

Lilith don't budge. The redcoat grab her by the foot and yank her out of the cage so that she fall on the ground, her back and head hitting the dirt.

—Report to your master at once, the redcoat say. Before he could shut back the cage, a niggerwoman run out screaming down the road. She get as far as fifty or so pace when a redcoat lift up him rifle, aim like he be on a hunt and shoot off the back of her head. The redcoat look at Lilith and point to the great house.

Lilith inside the great house looking at the hallway. On the left, the red carpet still on the floor and the paintings still on the wall, and the looking glass and the vase and pretty things. But when she follow the carpet and the wall, suddenly they break and there be nothing beyond but ash. Nothing but ash and wood and burned cloth and the sunlight coming in 'cause there be no roof. She find Massa Humphrey by the piano in the middle of the sitting room, where every other piece of furniture, chair, table, cabinet and bookshelf turn over. The chandelier pull down from the ceiling and pieces of glass scatter all over the floor. Lilith watch her step.

—Jack Wilkins says that you were protecting him, he say.

Lilith don't say nothing.

—See to Miss Isobel, Massa Humphrey say. He staring at the piano. He still in the blue shirt and grey breeches he was wearing the day of the rebellion, but both smudge up with blood that dry to look like wine stain. He hair mess up and wild and he right cheek have a long cut.

—Go! he say and Lilith run upstairs.

Part of the banister break away and all sort of rubbish on the steps. Rifles and bullets too. And clothes and shoes and food and painting that get cut up and rip up to pieces. Lilith smelling flesh and piss and old dust that wake up. Miss Isobel door not lock, but Lilith can't push it open. She push and push and it only budge a little. She push again and make enough space to scrape through. On the other side of the door is a chest push against it with two chairs and the commode. Lilith didn't look good enough yet before she hear a crash. She turn around only to see a big broomstick coming after her with a screaming pile of hair behind. Lilith jump out of the way and the broom ram into the wall. Miss Isobel get hit hard in the chest and fall back flat on the floor. Lilith help her up and take her to bed. Miss Isobel smell of mildew and negro. Lilith leave her sitting up but hunch over on the bed. Miss Isobel start to tremble. Lilith go downstairs to what left of the kitchen. Most of the walls gone and the cupboards burn down but the stove still there and working. Lilith draw some water from the well and try not to hear the screaming and shouting niggers. When she go back upstairs, Miss Isobel still hunch over on the bed looking at her trembling hands.

—Come, Miss Isobel, Lilith say and touch her hand. Miss Isobel jump back.

—Don't come any closer! Don't come any closer! Miss Isobel say and jump off the bed. But then her head go light and she almost faint. Lilith catch her and help her to the bath.

Lilith undress Miss Isobel and she lean against the dresser. Her left eye swell up and purple. Lilith pull Miss Isobel dress over her head and see her breasts beat up and bite up. The dress fall to the ground. Between her legs and her pussy so beat up that it purple too. Lilith help her into the tub and pour warm water over her. Miss Isobel jump, screaming that she is a lady, she is a lady, she is a lady. Lilith hold her down and remember a white man she push under the water. Lilith pour water over Miss Isobel head and Miss Isobel weep. Lilith trying to not think 'bout him.

That evening, everything clear on Sister Jack Hill, the highest point on the Montpelier Estate. Massa Humphrey and Robert Quinn used to smoke up there under a tree and argue 'bout book stuff or share whore story. Now Massa Humphrey there burying him greatest mate and him beloved mother. The preacher be the same one who come by in Christmas to tell slave to be grateful for slavery and the massa. Now he saying ashes to ashes and dust to dust and Massa Humphrey just stare at the two boxes like is he they holding in there. Miss Isobel hang back and Lilith hang back farther. The two womens dress in black. Lilith find dress in the mother room. She remember looking out from the shatter window and wondering where Homer body be. Massa Humphrey start cry again until he get so loud he echo on the hill. Miss Isobel touch him on the shoulder but he push her away so hard that she nearly fall. The preacher shout out that he should unhand her and remember that he's a gentleman and Massa Humphrey grab a stone and fling it after the preacher. The stone clap him right between the crack of him arse and the preacher yelp. He demand money right there and then and Massa Humphrey pick up some more stone. The preacher run down the hill so fast that he trip and fall and roll halfway down. Massa Humphrey leave the two womens on the hill.

By the fourth day the grounds work up a great stink. But it was niggers working up the most stench. Pack tight in the cage for four days, some fall sick, some fall dead or lose they minds and beg skipper not to throw them off the ship. Nigger funk fly with the wind and menace the whole county. Miss Isobel finally shout out to Massa Humphrey that he need to hire help in Spanish Town to deal with the matter. Massa Humphrey hire several white man, but is a different matter they come to deal with. Two day before, he go into town with something he did sketch with ink on parchment paper.

Now, on the way up the great house be trees that line both side of the road all the way up. The branches hang so far over that even at noon the road dim as if in moonshadow. Plenty branches, thirty, forty or fifty. The time did come for counting sturdy branches. Branches that could hold a good weight. On the seventh day, when the smell and the tightness of the cage start to drive the negroes mad, up from Spanish Town come the blacksmith and him cart. The blacksmith tell Massa Humphrey that he lose two cousin in this, the Great Atlas Revolt. They name it the Atlas Revolt because he was the first man name that anybody remember. When Massa Humphrey see the blacksmith he neither smile nor frown, but put on the blank face that hide a black heart.

—Are they quite according to my instructions? Massa Humphrey say.

—Down the last nail, Your Grace, the blacksmith say, smiling with him two brown teeth.

—Do not presume to mock me, sir.

—I don't presume to anything, Your Grace, only to tell you that your instructions were carried out, the blacksmith say.

Massa Humphrey round up some new white mens from Spanish Town, Ferry and Portsmouth. The judgement that come next come to Achilles first. Four white mens drag him out of the cage and beat him up first so that Achilles could barely stand up. Then they tear off him clothes, kick him down in the ground until him look like ash. The blacksmith pull the cloth off the cart to show something that no white man or negro see for nearly ten years on the estate. Gibbets.

Them was no ordinary gibbet. They forge out of Massa Humphrey own rage. Achilles see the gibbet when they place one on the ground and scream and try to run, but he drop on one knee. Him left foot did break from before. The four men yank the nigger up. The gibbet build like a cage with a iron loop at the top for rope to hang through, two slat of iron that run down the side and one down the front that make the metal cage look like the shape of a man. They then weld bars going right around, four to hold a nigger in tight. The mens throw down Achilles in the open gibbet. On the inside of the gibbet nails stick out and as they close it they stab right into Achilles' flesh. He go to scream again, but they shove an iron gag in him mouth too and he mutter like monster. Achilles can barely fit in the gibbet. That be how they make it. They close it shut on him and pull him up. Achilles bound tight in the gibbet from head to crotch. The harness hold him in, leaving only him foot free and dangling. They pull him up on a branch on the first tree. Achilles swing and blood run down. Him mouth gag and he scream through him eye until him eye all scream out. They open the second gibbet for a woman.

Two day later, them done. Massa Humphrey watchin' from him window and he neither happy nor angry nor melancholy. Miss Isobel see a big nigger and run back to her room. Lilith lock in Jack Wilkins' house, and wrap herself in Robert Quinn blue shirt, trying to smell him back to life. She don't look outside at hell. Thirty-seven negroes, man and woman, hanging from thirty-seven gibbets one or two to a tree. They screaming in the gag so the whole stretch sound like bawling coming up from hell. And dripping blood to wake up fly and mosquito. All the way up the road niggers be hanging like uncanny fruit. In a week most of the negroes stop living and the wind roll through, carrying the sound of death rattle. Who don't dead live on in torment as the crows get tired of waiting. Rumour spread in Spanish Town that anybody who set out for the Montpelier Estate better be prepared for a sight that no gentleman can unsee. Educated man call it the Jamaican Appian Way.

Gorgon last longest in the gibbet.

Pallas never get her day in court. The white mens in Spanish Town did hungry for blood so they ransack the gaol and pull she and ninety other negro and tie them up to stalks and burn them by slow fire. The niggers take three days to burn and nobody could pass out or die quick. After that, five hundred negro get ship to Honduras while some get ship back to a place that rumour to be in the Africa. Before Pallas dead, she speak a curse on the Wilson family and then make a song 'bout how Miss Isobel ruin 'cause two nigger rape her. The song reach other negro tongue and they sing it so loud that it fly all the way back to

Montpelier. Miss Isobel demand that Massa Humphrey go to Spanish Town to defend her honour and Massa Humphrey say as soon as she develop some honour he would gladly go to town to defend it. Miss Isobel lock herself in her room with her laudanum and didn't come out.

Day turn to week and week turn to month. Miss Isobel soon realise Massa Humphrey forget everything 'bout marriage and not bothering to remember. She clutch her belly and give herself such a conniption that Lilith have to give her tea to sleep. Massa Humphrey take to riding at evening to Sister Jack Hill, where people say him talk to Robert Quinn. From there, Lilith watch him as he watch the estate. The one field of cane that untouch. The seven field of ash. The half of the great house that still standing. Nobody hear if he goin' rebuild or no. He just ride up to the hill and kneel between the two grave and be as unmanly in him grieving as he wish.

Then it come to pass one night that Lilith gathering Robert Quinn stuff that didn't burn when the moonlight cut a shape in the doorway. A man shape. She run into Robert Quinn bedroom but Massa Humphrey jump her and they crash on the bed. He on top of her and Lilith screaming and crying and Massa Humphrey ripping her dress off, one hand pressing her head down in the bed and the other tearing away the cloth. He growl and yell and Lilith don't know what he saying but she crying. He punch her back and tell her to shut up, shut up, godforsaken wicked black bitch, but she not still. He hold down her head and pull down him breeches. He hump and hump and hump and breathe heavy until he stop. Lilith try to turn round but he hold her and cuss. He cuss louder and louder but let go. Lilith turn over again but he grab her breasts and hump and hump but then stop and collapse on her. Lilith don't know if he whimpering or crying. He don't look at her. With all him humping he didn't enter her at all. He breathing heavy and him breath foul. Lilith lie still under him, not daring to move but not wanting to move either. They stay there and she feel tears running down the side of her cheek and don't know if is from him or her. He try to ram her again. She look past him red hair into the ceiling and listen to the bed creaking. She wrap her arms round him back and know he not entering her but act like he be. She close her eye tight and thinking that him hair long and black, that him eyes cheery and light and that he calling her lovey. Then they both lay still and leave it to the cricket to make noise in the night.

· 31 ·

EVERY NEGRO WALK IN A CIRCLE. TAKE THAT AND MAKE OF IT what you will. But sometimes when a negro die and another negro take him place, even if that negro not be blood, they still fall in step with the same circle. The same circle of living that no nigger can choose and dying that come at any time. Perhaps nigger take things as they be for what used to be will always be what is. Maybe it better for backra and nigger that things go back to what people think is the best way until the fire next time. White man sleep with one eye open, but black man can never sleep.

Time now to give account of the league of women. The blind niggerwoman in the bush, she tell me everything. This was not the story me did plan to tell. Massa Humphrey realise that he can't stop cry if he remain at Montpelier, so he sail back to England. Maybe he recapture him manhood back there, Miss Isobel say when she know he can't hear. He didn't take Miss Isobel. Massa Humphrey leave all estate matters to an attorney and allow Miss Isobel to live at the house after it rebuild. He never take Lilith to bed after that first time and by the time he gone the two womens in the house both big in belly. Miss Isobel try to go back with him the day he set sail and demand that he be a man and a father. Massa Humphrey say that whether or not he be a man is his own affair, and as for her and her child, perhaps she should petition Kingston, since any man could claim the bastard. But he leave her at the estate, which some take to mean that him admit that the pickney could have been him own. Miss Isobel swear that she goin' pour all her hatred and ill will into the little boy for his father and Massa Humphrey reply that he'll burn down the whole county then. Who knows, perhaps it will be a nigger baby, he say also. Miss Isobel slap him, but he slap her back. She swear to him that she will never leave Montpelier, to which he say that was quite fine since he'll never come back.

Lilith don't even think of Massa Humphrey. The attorney let her continue living in the overseer house with Jack Wilkins until he pass away. The attorney hire a new overseer but he live in a house build since the rebellion. The attorney let slip once that this was Massa Humphrey specific wish, as he himself didn't take too much to the society of negroes. The first thing the new overseer set about was to buy new negroes, but seasoned negroes or those born in the colony, no nigger from the Africa and that take quite some doing. Word was that this was folly, since the interest in the West Indies was fading and slavery might soon over. Lilith didn't get any free paper, but she act like a free negro. She work in the kitchen and cook and clean for Jack Wilkins and do her own thing as be to her mood. She still be the only negro that could go near Miss Isobel. When Lilith by her own company, she rub her big belly and say luv.

Time to give account of the league of women.

Hippolyta didn't have no face left after it get blast off with a shotgun. She dead in Jack Wilkins' house and a song rise up 'bout the papa who kill him daughter. Nobody did know her much when she was living and they know her even less when she dead, for her spirit still yelp in the dark and hide in the corner wearing a black dress with a high neck to hide where slave-driver cut her throat when she did but a pickney and take 'way her speakin'. Hippolyta song quick and harsh. A song rise up against Hippolyta, a chant to keep her spirit away from the living and grant her peace.

Callisto take four white man herself, was the account that Gorgon give while she was swinging in the gibbet. Gorgon say that Callisto was a woman who laugh all her life but never smile once. From the day Jack Wilkins shoot out her eye for kicking a white overseer in him balls, her mind never set right and in the storm of gunshot was the best way she could dead. Gorgon spend the rest of her short life haunted that she didn't get to hear the last thing Callisto say. But she take four white man herself, and in the fields and the bush a new song rise up under the quiet, about *Callisto, Callisto, who bring backra down to so-so.*

Gorgon die by the gibbet but she do things before that. Gorgon loud and rude and act like she bad before the rebellion, but as the rebellion got worse, she hide behind Callisto like a monkey. She slow Callisto down and Callisto get shot for the trouble. Short almost like midget, Gorgon get out of hard work because Jack Wilkins be her daddy and he know she be no use in the field. She love him for taking her out of field hardship, but she hate him for making her owe him. But she the only one that Jack Wilkins ever call him blood. She call him Papa Jack and he never strike her. Something in that drive her mad 'cause she know she could never be the Coromantee that she want to be in her spirit. That make her wilder than wild and badder than bad, but she hide behind Callisto when she frighten. Gorgon was the only nigger who didn't scream in the gibbet, but she talk. She make song out of the names of the women, but not Lilith. Gorgon sing her song high, she sing her song low, she sing it until she run out of voice. She dead after eight days. The song about Gorgon was short and had no word, since all that need to sing she sing already.

Pallas make for the mountains but lose her way. In all the running Pallas didn't see that she on the wrong path, on the wrong side of a wrong hill. That be what the song of Pallas say but nobody remember if is true or lie no more. Night was coming down and Pallas hiding under leaf until she hear rumble in the bush. She run deeper into the forest and see the first Maroon before he see her. He naked and have a rifle on him back. She behind bush and see him coming in her direction. She stop and cock her rifle. The second Maroon run right up behind her and don't make a sound. He swing back him hand to blackjack her but she swing round swift and shoot him in the face. Pallas running on the ground but the first Maroon running through the trees. He hop to one branch and jump to the other and grab a branch and swing, then disappear in deep bush. Pallas running on the ground and didn't look up to see him flying above her. But when he jump down to land on top of her head, she swing round with the shotgun and shoot him balls off. Then she take the gun and bludgeon him head until she can't tell the difference between head and dirt. The third Maroon nigger fire on her. Bullet fly through the bush with a *zip-zip-zip*. They *zip-zip-zip* so quick and so quiet that much time pass before Pallas notice that her left shoulder was bleeding. She curl herself like a snail and roll down a bare hill until she near land in the river. Pallas hide behind a rock. She reload. She wait for him to come down. She looking up and the river below make noise over the rocks. She didn't see the Maroon until he jump her from behind. They roll and tumble and end up in the river. He on top and he push her head under the water. The Maroon hand pushing down tight on Pallas neck and Pallas flailing about. But she grab a rock and clap him in the temple with it. The Maroon fall back in the water and Pallas jump on top of him. She grab another rock and hit him in the head. Then she hit him again and again and again and again until a streak of blood wash down the river. She put on him clothes and head back into the bush. A couple Maroon pass by her and she wave, signaling that the runaway might be deeper in the bush. Nanny Town Maroon make they woman bear arms. Accompong Maroon don't. This was Accompong. Before she could even notice, they swarm her and use a rifle butt to knock her out. The Maroons hand her over to the redcoats and the magistrate charge her and others with insurrection and mass murder and throw her in the gaol. White man fury bigger than white man justice. They break in the gaol and drag her out. They beat her hard, then tie her up to a stake and burn her slow so she wouldn't pass out but feel herself burnin' to death. Her song long and mournful but when the song reach the end, it dance and the spirits jump.

Homer didn't die by gunfire at the mistress window. Homer die the day she get word 'bout her pickneys. Pickneys that nasty nigger rape out of her, but pickneys she love nonetheless. Homer was the mistress' personal slave and many of the evil things that happen to her was because the mistress was so miserable that she make it her mission to make everybody round her miserable as well. Especially a negrowoman with nothing in this world but the mercy of her mistress. There be something in the negro smile that confound the mistress because she know they didn't got no reason to smile. Her husband, the mistress grow to hate, but Homer she hate from the day they assign her. Then she grow to need Homer and hate her even more. There was a quilt of scar on Homer back too and some of that the mistress leave herself. But Homer bide her time. Homer watch, Homer wait and Homer plot. And Homer find the right group of woman with just enough cause to join her. Woman who have a right to be free 'cause of birth but get robbed of it. Woman who carry Jack Wilkins' malice in they very being. Woman who could see the moon and know when be the time to shed blood. Homer kill Homer and reborn herself as the struggle. They never find Homer body. Homer song get sing in a whisper like a night spirit leaping from a tree. Her song be in the dark of the eye where secrets be.

Turncoat nigger Iphigenia cover all over in coal burn. But that wasn't the worsest. Every burn leave a scar that grow big and bumpy so that the woman cover from neck down to toe. No man was ever goin' want her so Iphigenia start to think 'bout what she want for herself. She forget black, she forget nigger, she forget everybody who couldn't help her when they was raining burnin' coal all over her skin. That leave only she to take care of she. Iphigenia thinking that if she tell massa 'bout the plot she would get British pound and freedom for sure. Turncoat nigger Iphigenia ain't got no song.

The blind niggerwoman in the bush, she tell me everything.

What can a niggerwoman do but endure? What can me do but tell the story? Who is there when we recall great womens? My name write in blood and me don't answer to it much.

Me was but nine year in age when me mother start to teach me how to read. The book she teach me to read was *Joseph Andrews*, which she find under a pile of osnaburg cloth that used to cover Homer bed. As soon as me read that, me move on to other book, for nobody care who or what go into the library no more. Me read John Donne and *Lives of the Poets* and Edward Long's *History of Jamaica* and *Sense and Sensibility*, a new book leave behind by the attorney. And she teach me how to write. That was the most forbidden of thing and it still be so, but there be no man, black or white, that can stop her now. But she didn't teach me for me but for her, for when the time come to write her song she have somebody true to be her witness. Somebody who know that one cannot judge the action of a niggerwoman who only wanted to be everything and nothing. Mayhaps she 'fraid of how the time was goin' judge her. Mayhaps she don't care, for she tell me everything as if me was a stranger and not blood.

Atlas the slave get him name from somebody me read about in Thomas Bulfinch book. He be the man or man-god who get punish to carry the burden of the earth on him back. Me not no Heracles but me know why she telling me everything. Me know what Atlas trying to do to me, to shift onto my back. For somebody must give account of the night women of Montpelier. Of slavery, the black woman misery and black man too. And me goin' sing the song and me mother goin' sing it and even the blind niggerwoman who live in the bush, who thin like stick, who hair white like cloud and who smell of mint and lemongrass, going sing it too. We goin' sing once, then no more.

The womens. That woman. Me look at that woman. Me mother call me Lovey Quinn from birth. Me used to hate that name. Me did hate that name when me start writing but me come to peace with it now. Any niggerwoman can become a black woman in secret. This is why we dark, cause in the night we disappear and become spirit. Skin gone and we become whatever we wish. We become who we be. In the dark with no skin I can write. And what write in darkness is free as free can be, even if it never come to light and go free for real. The first time me write, me wanted to tell a different story, a story 'bout me, not a story 'bout her, but such is she that every nigger story soon become a tale 'bout they mother, even the parts that she didn't tell herself. The first time me ever write 'bout me mother was December 27, in the year of our Lord 1819. This was the first thing me write.

You can call her what they call her. I goin' call her Lilith.

Thank You

To the great, kind and gifted Bob Mooney, who first read this book and knew where it was going long before I did. To the wonderful, generous and sharp Ellen Levine and the brilliant, inspiring and maddening Sean McDonald.

Thanks also to everyone at Hallin Bank, where I have now written two novels; Bill Landauer; Kaylie Jones; Bonnie Culver; Mike Lennon; Rashidah Ismaili AbuBakr, who in one conversation changed the very core of this story; my favourite living Irish writer, Colum McCann; Robert McLean, who I should have thanked in my first book; Johnny Temple and Akashic Books; my James and Dillon families; and Ingrid Riley.

Thanks to the history I learned and the history I had to unlearn.

And yes, my mother is now permitted to read this book.

MARLON JAMES was born in Jamaica. He is the author of *A Brief History of Seven Killings* (Oneworld, 2014), which won the Man Booker Prize, the American Book Award, the Anisfield-Wolf Fiction Prize and was a finalist for the National Book Critics Circle Award. His debut novel, *John Crow's Devil* (Oneworld, 2015), was a finalist for the *Los Angeles Times* Book Prize, shortlisted for the Commonwealth Writers' Prize, and was a *New York Times* Editors' Choice.

The Book of Night Women is his second novel, and won the Dayton Literary Peace Prize and the Minnesota Book Award, and was a finalist for the National Book Critics Circle Award. He teaches at Macalester College in Minnesota and divides his time between Kingston and the United States.

Also by Marlon James

A Brief History of Seven Killings

Winner of the Man Booker Prize 2015

JAMAICA, 1976

Seven gunmen storm Bob Marley's house, machine guns blazing. The reggae superstar survives, but the gunmen are never caught.

From the acclaimed author of *John Crow's Devil* and *The Book of Night Women* comes a dazzling display of masterful storytelling exploring this near-mythic event. Spanning three decades and crossing continents, *A Brief History of Seven Killings* chronicles the lives of a host of unforgettable characters – slum kids, one-night stands, drug lords, girlfriends, gunmen, journalists, and even the CIA. Gripping and inventive, ambitious and mesmerising, *A Brief History of Seven Killings* is one of the most remarkable and extraordinary novels of the twenty-first century.

'This seething, hot, violent, action-packed novel is enormous in every sense... Extraordinary.' *The Times*

'The most original novel I've read in years. A haunting, incendiary work.' Irvine Welsh

'A vivid novel that deserves all the praise it has received.' *Sunday Telegraph*

Hardback ISBN 978-1-78074-587-9
Paperback ISBN 978-1-78074-635-7
eBook ISBN 978-1-78074-588-6